W9-BTA-173

Praise for *New York Times* bestselling author Sharon Sala

"Drama *literally* invades the life of an A-list Hollywood star, and the race is on to catch a killer."
—*RT Book Reviews* on *Life of Lies*

"A wonderful romance, thriller, and delightful book. [I] recommend this book as highly as I can.... Exciting... and will keep you glued to the pages until you reach the end."
—*USATODAY.com*'s *Happy Ever After* blog on *Life of Lies*

"In Sala's latest page-turner, staying alive is the biggest challenge of all. There are appealing characters to root for, and one slimy villain who needs to be stopped."
—*RT Book Reviews* on *Race Against Time*

Praise for *USA TODAY* bestselling author Delores Fossen

"Clear off space on your keeper shelf, Fossen has arrived."
—*New York Times* bestselling author Lori Wilde

"[*Savior in the Saddle*] takes off at full speed from the first page and doesn't surrender an iota of the chills until the end."
—*RT Book Reviews*

KING'S RANSOM

NEW YORK TIMES BESTSELLING AUTHOR
SHARON SALA

ISBN-13: 978-1-335-40658-3

King's Ransom
First published in 2001. This edition published in 2022.
Copyright © 2001 by Sharon Sala

Nate
First published in 2012. This edition published in 2022.
Copyright © 2012 by Delores Fossen

This edition published by arrangement with Harlequin Books S.A.

For questions and comments about the quality of this book, please contact us at CustomerService@Harlequin.com.

Harlequin Enterprises ULC
22 Adelaide St. West, 41st Floor
Toronto, Ontario M5H 4E3, Canada
www.Harlequin.com

Printed in U.S.A.

CONTENTS

Sharon Sala is a *New York Times* bestselling author. She has 123 books published in romance, young adult, Western and women's fiction and in nonfiction. First published in 1991, she's an eight-time RITA® Award finalist. Industry awards include the following: the Janet Dailey Award; five Career Achievement Awards from *RT Book Reviews*; five National Readers' Choice Awards; five Colorado Romance Writers Awards of Excellence; the Heart of Excellence Award; the Booksellers' Best Award; the Nora Roberts Lifetime Achievement Award presented by RWA; and the Centennial Award from RWA for recognition of her 100th published novel.

Visit the Author Profile page at Harlequin.com for more titles.

KING'S RANSOM

Sharon Sala

For Kathryn, who suffered,
endured and prevailed

Chapter 1

A fetid smell, an odor of liquor, rough ugly words, and promises of what he was going to do filtered through Jesse's exhausted sleep. She heard a deep, rasping breath and knew it was not her own. Her heart stopped.

He knew the moment she awoke, because he clamped his hand loosely over her face, pinching her mouth and cheeks, pushed the knife point against her throat, and told her not to scream.

It was the wrong thing to say to Jesse LeBeau. She had never liked being told what to do. Her terrified scream erupted into the menacing silence of the room and later Jesse would remember thinking, *tonight I'm going to die!*

His anger was evident as he growled an ugly threat and began to face what he had unwittingly unleashed. This wasn't the way it was meant to happen.

Jesse fought like a woman possessed as her constant screams and fierce struggle for possession of the knife threw the intruder into a frenzy.

He felt the girl's fingernails catch deep into the flesh of his cheekbone and rake the entire length of his jaw. He lost control of his emotions and the situation entirely, forgetting, in his fury, why he'd ever entered her house.

"Bitch!" he yelled, and thrust downward over and over with the knife, only to connect with air or bedclothes. He struggled, trying to gain control of her flailing fists, and blanched as her knee connected with a tender part of his anatomy. That was all she was going to do to him. He would have no more of this cat-woman. He raised the knife upward once again and suddenly his hand come away empty.

There was no time for surprise as he felt the first thrust of the knife right above his shoulder blade. His wild shriek of pain only added to the confusion going on in his head. This wasn't the way he'd planned any of this. Now he was on the defensive and fear overrode all his other emotions. He struck out wildly with doubled fists, trying to connect with the source of those damnable screams, but the ear-splitting sound of the woman's fear and rage, and the constant pain in his chest and back were more than he could bear. He moaned softly and slumped forward heavily.

Unaware of his near unconscious condition, Jesse continued to stab blindly at his dead weight as it forced her deeper and deeper into her mattress.

Suddenly she was free! Somehow she'd managed to roll his still body aside. She crawled from the bed on hands and knees, still clutching the knife, still screaming. She ran on fear, unaware her attacker was not moving, imagining she could feel his hand on her shoulder as she dashed from her home in St. Louis and into the street. Her screams had alerted the entire block of her neighborhood, and she was vaguely aware of lights coming on in one house and then another. But no one came out to help her.

It was the scream of the siren from the police car flying around the street corner that silenced Jesse. The psychedelic whirl of red and blue lights momentarily disoriented her and she staggered as it came to a screeching halt only inches from where she stood.

"Lady, drop the knife," the policeman ordered, as he stood with gun drawn behind the open door of his cruiser, uncertain about what kind of situation he was facing. All he could see was a very bloody woman with an oversized butcher knife.

"Please," Jesse begged, and started forward, unaware of the picture she presented with blood-covered night clothes and a knife in her hand.

The policeman took a deep breath and ordered again, in a much louder voice.

"I said, drop the knife!"

Jesse looked stunned. What had happened to her world? She looked at the policeman's face, the gun in his hand, and slumped to her knees on the pavement.

"Here," she whispered, and laid the knife on the ground in front of her. "Now will you help me?"

"Jesus, Captain!" the officer said, as they carefully walked through the house where the attack had taken place. "Look at all this blood. Looks like someone was butcherin' a hog. And here," he continued, as he pointed toward Jesse's bedroom window, careful not to touch anything as the crime lab crew continued their sweep of the premises. "The bastard crawled out of the bedroom window, probably when the girl ran for help." The streaks and smeared blood on the wall and windowsill made the man's exit point easy to read.

Captain Shockey was four years shy of retirement, short and overweight, a nondescript individual with a mind like a NASA computer. He could read a crime scene like a trucker reads a map. And it had been a long time since he'd seen anything like this disaster. This was a decent, family-oriented neighborhood, a comfortable, but unpretentious house. The victim was an elementary school teacher, and obviously meticulously neat. The bedroom looked like what he'd seen in Vietnam. Blood was on the walls near the window in an obvious spray pattern. He was guessing the girl had nicked one of the attacker's veins. The bedclothes were torn from the bed, slash marks and pools of blood had seeped into the mattress. Bloody footprints went in two directions. The larger ones, wearing shoes, had staggered toward the window, the smaller, bare footprints were widely spaced, and led toward the hallway the girl had used to get out of the house.

Shockey could tell by the distance between the little bare prints that the girl had been moving very fast. Hell, he would have been, too. How she had survived anything like this was beyond his comprehension. He knew his next stop would have to be the hospital to question the victim. He hated that part of the job because all it did was make them relive the terror. But it was necessary if he was going to catch the nut who'd done this.

"Is she in any shape to talk?" he asked the officer.

"Yes, sir," he answered, as he stepped aside to let the photographer get a better shot of the bed and window. "I never saw anything like her. She's not very big, can't be more than three or four inches over five feet, but she's all fire, and until we catch this guy, I don't think her fire's goin' out. When I was talkin' to her earlier, I felt like I was the one being questioned." He grinned slightly at the captain's raised eyebrows and sardonic expression. "Also, I didn't see too many deep cuts on her, except for her hands. They looked bad. I think most of the blood on her belonged to the perpetrator. Hell," he said, then swallowed hard as he looked away from the sharp gaze of Captain Shockey. "She took that knife away with her bare hands. I don't know if I'd have had the guts to do something like that."

Shockey patted the young officer on the back—a rough, locker room pat—and answered.

"You never know what you're capable of, boy, until you face the wall. Check and see if there're any family or next-of-kin to notify. She's going to need all the moral support she can get. Come on, get cracking," he urged. "We've got us a real bad one to catch this time. Maybe we'll get lucky and find him dead. From the looks of this place, it's possible."

"Yes, sir," the officer answered, and watched Shockey rumble between the lab crew, side-stepping them like he was dodging fresh cow patties. If anyone could find the perpetrator, Shockey was the man for the job.

The sharp, persistent ring finally penetrated King McCandless's deep sleep, and he rolled over in bed, taking a wad of bedclothes with him, as he fumbled for the clock. Then he realized it wasn't the alarm after all; it was the phone. A deep, pulling sensation in the pit of his stomach brought him fully awake as he turned on the lamp and saw the green digital numbers on his clock. Nearly four in the morning. Not the time for good news. Rolling over to a sitting position, he let his long, pajama-clad legs brace him as he grabbed the phone in the middle of another ring. Taking a long, slow breath, he let his deep, raspy voice break the silence.

"Hello?" As he heard the male voice and the authority behind it, he shuddered unconsciously. It reminded him of the call he'd received when his father, Andrew McCandless, had died. "Yes, this is King McCandless."

He didn't see his bedroom door open, or see the worried expression on the face of his housekeeper, Maggie West, as she shakily tied her robe around her plump stomach. Her long, gray braid hung over her shoulder and she pulled at it nervously as she watched King take the call.

Maggie's heart caught in her throat. She saw the blood drain from King's face. It *was* bad news! She knew it. No good ever came of a phone ringing this time of the morning. She watched him nod, and repeat an address back to the person at the other end of the call.

King slowly laid the phone in its cradle and buried his head in his hands, unaware of Maggie's presence.

"What?" she asked, assured of her right to know by her almost twenty years of service to the McCandless family. Her frantic tone of voice startled King.

He turned, saw Maggie's worried face, and had to swallow twice before he could speak aloud the horror he'd just absorbed.

"It's Jesse," he whispered, and then had to clear his throat before he could continue. "Someone tried to kill her."

"Merciful God in heaven. Is she…is she hurt bad?"

Maggie couldn't stop the free flow of tears that sprang to her eyes. She'd put in ten years raising that child, too, even if she wasn't a McCandless.

Mike LeBeau and Andrew McCandless had been partners in the early 1960s and 1970s during an Oklahoma oil boom. When Mike had been killed on a drilling rig during an ice storm, Andrew had become Jesse's guardian. She had only been twelve. Jesse was absorbed into the McCandless clan like she'd been born into it and she'd stayed happily, until two years after Andrew McCandless's death. Then, for reasons known only to Jesse, she had quietly taken a job in St. Louis, Missouri, and never come back. They still kept in touch, but she'd gently refused all their invitations to visit.

In answer to Maggie's question regarding Jesse's condition, King had to consider his words before he spoke. She couldn't be in the hospital and be okay, but he didn't know any details.

"I just don't know, Maggie," King said, as he yanked the bedclothes away from his long legs with a jerk. "But I'm damn sure going to find out. Help me pack, will you? Don't skimp on clothes. I don't know how long I'll stay. I just know I won't be back without her."

Maggie's nod of approval went unnoticed as King grabbed the nearest pair of jeans from his closet and headed for the dressing area of his bathroom.

Relieved that there was something positive she could do, Maggie began emptying drawers of freshly laundered underwear, shirts, and socks into an oversized suitcase that King pulled from a hall closet. Between the two of them, King was dressed, packed, and on his way to Tulsa and the airport within the hour. If he was lucky, he should just about make the next flight.

Steam was rising from the pavement as he pulled his car into a parking garage at the airport. It was already above 85 degrees and no relief from the mid-July temperatures in Oklahoma was expected.

"Gonna be another hot one," the parking attendant said, as he would to everyone he waited on that day. "Gonna park her long?" he asked, eyeing the opulence of the shiny black Lincoln.

"I have no idea." King fixed a hard, dark stare on the attendant. "But I expect it to be here when I get back."

"No problem. No problem with that at all, just so's you have the parkin' stub. Know what I mean? Can't be givin' these babies away to just anybody. No sirree!"

King was distracted. He could have cared less about the car and allowed the attendant's spiel to flow over him unheard.

A trickle of perspiration ran slowly down his back as he raced to the ticket counter just in time to get his boarding pass. He wondered if the sweat was from the heat or from fear. Damn it all to hell and back, he hated to fly. He grimaced, took his assigned seat, and knew that only Jesse's predicament could have persuaded him to use this method of travel. All he was concerned with was getting to her as quickly as possible.

An anonymous blue van was parked under the overhanging branches of a huge sugar maple. The motor was quiet, but no one would have noticed it anyway. Nearly every house in the area was shut tightly against the heat, with air conditioners going full blast. It was always hot this time of year, even at night, and no one was ready to lose sleep for a few dollars' worth of electricity. Maybe later when they received their costly utility bills, but not yet. This was the reason no one saw a man staggering through the shrubbery, trying to make his way toward the van. And the houses were far enough away from Jesse's that they wouldn't have heard her screams for help.

The man in the bushes was following the sound of the van's running motor. He was so blinded by the pain in his chest and back he could barely focus. The clumsy duffle bag he was dragging behind him kept getting hung in the thick bushes.

The driver fidgeted, glanced several times at the luminous dial on his watch, and knew it was taking far too long. How much time could it possibly take to subdue one very small woman, tie and blindfold her, and carry her less than a block through the alley?

Just as he had started to exit the van to investigate, a police siren broke the silence of the night, and he nearly fell from the van door. When he caught himself, he also thought he could hear a woman screaming for help. Jesus Christ! he thought. *I should have known that fool couldn't pull this off.* Instinct told him to leave, but he knew if the idiot was caught, he would be implicated in an instant.

His meandering panic was interrupted. His heart thudded to an abrupt halt as he saw the stooped figure stumbling about in the hedge bordering the alleyway. He dashed toward him, thinking he would help carry the girl.

"Oh hell! Oh hell!" the man moaned, as he fell into the driver's outstretched arms. "Get me out of here."

"Where's the girl?" the driver snarled, and grabbed hard at the man's arm.

"Aieee," he shrieked, and then staggered backwards in pain. "I didn't get her. But she hurt me. She hurt me bad. You've got to get me out of here and get me some help. I'm bleeding to death."

A long string of curses erupted from the driver's mouth as he saw the blood. It was everywhere. The fool was covered in it, and even worse, had gotten it on him, too. Enraged, he shoved the wounded man toward the van, slid the side door open and shoved him and the duffle bag roughly toward the gaping hole. He slammed the door shut, not caring whether the man was completely clear of the door's force. Hurrying to the driver's side, he quickly concealed himself from any curious eyes. For two cents he'd finish the job the girl started and leave the fool for the street sweepers. But he didn't. He was a careful man and decided to dispose of this garbage in his own way.

"What in hell happened?" the driver snarled, as he turned up the opposite alley, driving as quickly as possible without alerting the neighborhood. It was only after he'd gone several blocks and turned onto a main thoroughfare that he'd turned on his headlights. "Can't you do anything right, Lynch? You owed me, and this botched episode does not cancel anything. Do you hear me?"

"Jesus, I'm hurt bad. You got to get me to a doctor. And it ain't my fault things didn't go right. You didn't tell me what she was like. Dammit, man, I could have stuffed a tiger in a gunny sack easier than this. Hell," he groaned, slumping lower into the seat he'd pulled himself into, "she shouldn't have fought me. She made me mad."

"What do you mean?" the driver asked in a menacing whisper. "You didn't hurt her did you? This blood all better be yours. You weren't supposed to kill her, just kidnap her. Answer me! Is she hurt?"

"To hell with her," he whined. "Just look at me. I'll have scars for life, if I don't bleed to death."

"You tell me now," the driver snarled, and slammed the van to a screeching halt in the middle of a deserted street, "or I swear to God, I'll finish what she started."

It was obvious to the injured man that his condition was less than important. He should have known not to get mixed up in something like this anyway.

"She ain't hurt hardly at all. Just a few scratches. I wasn't trying to kill her," he whined, and felt himself losing a grip on reality. "She just made me mad, that's all. Now please, get me some help!"

For a few moments, the van remained motionless. Then it accelerated slowly, as if the driver couldn't quite decide what he was going to do. Finally it picked up speed and disappeared into the darkness.

Jesse had adamantly refused any kind of anesthetic that would render her unconscious. She wasn't about to be put to sleep. The last time she slept, someone tried to kill her. She wasn't going through that again.

She welcomed the roughness of the warm, wet washcloth on her face. She knew the nurse was being as gentle as she could as she washed away the ugly traces of her ordeal.

As the bloodstains disappeared, the fragile beauty of the young woman appeared—a heart-shaped face, thick, dark wavy hair just below shoulder length, and wide, sky-blue eyes above a near perfect nose with just the tiniest inclination to tilt. But there was no happiness to pull her soft, generous mouth into its usual smile. Jesse LeBeau was trying hard not to lose her mind and the only way she knew for certain she could do that was to avoid being put back to sleep.

"Okay, little lady," the doctor said, acquiescing to Jesse's demands for only local pain-killers. "There isn't that much to put back together. I think you can take it. After all, you're a real toughie, aren't you?" He kept up his banter, trying to take Jesse's mind off the actual act of minor surgery that he was going to perform on her hands. "And, I do understand…okay?"

"Okay," Jesse whispered on a shaky sigh of relief, and allowed herself to relax momentarily. "Just remember you promised." Her chin wobbled a bit as she struggled with the urge to scream and scream and never stop. "My students at Lee Elementary wouldn't break a promise to me, so you can't either."

Jesse managed a slight smile and then took a deep breath as the first needle full of the pain-killing solution entered the shredded area of her hand.

It took longer than expected, but she managed to stay alert as they worked. It was only after she was in her assigned room, groggy from all the drugs they'd shot into her system, that she'd let down her defenses and dozed off. Then the medicine kept her lethargic enough that she couldn't pull herself from the somnambulant state. She hung, suspended in a world of nightmares, where, as she had feared, she relived her attack over… and over…and over.

The elevator door opened as one lone passenger emerged. He stood unmoving, silently assessing the lay of Garrison Memorial Hospital's second floor. He was just recovering from the tension of the flight. He'd had to find a hotel and deposit his luggage, when all he wanted to do was get to Jesse. He'd let his imagination run to all sorts of horror but felt that the sooner he saw Jesse for himself, the better he was going to feel.

Loud talking, telephones ringing, and carts being shuffled about alerted King to the location of the nurses' station. He started down the long corridor, his nostrils twitching as he recognized the familiar smells of hospital disinfectant, the faint but unmistakable scents of flowers in the various rooms, and always, in spite of the constant antiseptic cleaning, the smell of sickness and dying. His muscular legs covered the distance quickly.

Several of the nurses watched his approach with more than usual interest.

"Look at that!" one of them whispered. "Don't you love it? Boots, jeans, sexy walk, and all."

"Yes," the other nurse answered. "I'm sort of partial to those slim hips, broad shoulders, and that big old cowboy hat. Makes me wish I'd been born about a hundred years ago."

"What do you need with a hundred years ago, dummy? Right there comes the civilized version of your dream."

"Well," she drawled, as King came closer, "I don't want them too civilized, if you know what I mean." And then she whispered, as King came closer, anxious that her words not be overheard, "Ooh, is there no justice? He's got that lean, hungry look, too."

She was referring to the chiseled planes of King's face. They were distinctive features inherited from his Scottish ancestors. The high cheekbones, shapely nose, once broken and nearly mended as good as new, a strong, stubborn chin and full, yet firm lips that were capable of a sardonic or sensual twist, depending on his quicksilver mood. Dark hair and dark eyes were the only features he had inherited from his mother's side of the family. His sport coat was draped casually across his arm in deference to the heat and humidity beyond the air-conditioned corridors of the hospital. The heat King was generating at the nurses' station had nothing to do with the outside temperatures. His appearance was stunning, but he really got their attention when he asked for their latest patient.

King spoke even before he came to a complete stop. His voice was deep and raspy, a voice women always found incredibly sexy. It was actually the result of riding into a low-hanging clothesline on a horse—in the dark.

He had been celebrating his eighteenth birthday in a most unsatisfactory manner, as his father often reminded him over the ensuing weeks. He'd been a bit drunk. He knew never to drink and drive, but no one told him not to drink and ride. They didn't have to tell him again after his accident. He hadn't been able to talk for a month, and when he finally could, the husky rasp was all that was left of his voice. That was the last time he ever rode a horse full tilt in the dark, and the last time he ever got drunk. King McCandless was not a fool twice.

"Jesse LeBeau," he asked, "what room please?"

The RN on duty stepped out of her cubicle as she heard the name of their incognito patient. They had been instructed by the police to check every visitor asking about the young attack victim.

King's dark eyes followed the woman who stepped up to the desk to answer his question.

"What business do you have with her?" she asked crisply.

"Listen, lady," King answered, "I got a phone call about four o'clock this morning that probably took ten years off my life and I've been on a damn plane ever since, trying to get here to Jesse. Now can you tell me where she is, or do I have to go find her myself?"

The nurse knew rope when she saw it, and this man was just about at the end of his. She came around the desk and motioned for him to follow.

"She's down at the end of the hall. Room 202. It's a single, makes it easier to maintain security, and there's an officer at the door. You have to get past him. And your name had better be on his list or threats won't make a whistle-stop worth of difference."

Her sardonic tone was not lost on King, and he turned his head sharply, eyeing the nurse with new-found respect and a silent look of apology. He smiled slightly as he saw her accept. Sure enough, it took several pieces of identification proving he was actually who he claimed to be before the guard would allow him inside.

He hesitated, suddenly afraid of what he might see when he opened the door. But his hesitation disappeared when he heard the soft, agonizing moans and mumbled cries for help. King took one frantic look at the guard. He answered with a grimace and a shrug. He was helpless to stop what was going on behind the closed doors, too.

"She's just dreaming, Mr. McCandless. It's been going on for hours."

King muttered under his breath as he shoved his way past the guard and entered the room. It was obvious Jesse's agitation had been going on for some time. The bedclothes were in a wadded mess. The high, chrome guard rails were in place to keep Jesse from rolling out of the bed, but she had bunched herself completely against the back of one, trying in sleepy desperation to escape her attacker.

King couldn't describe the emotion that overwhelmed him as he witnessed the terror she was living. His first instinct was to awaken her, get her to see she was no longer in danger; but something made him hesitate. He didn't want to frighten her more. A cold rage filled his mind, and he knew, if he ever had the chance to do anything about it, the man responsible for her injuries and terror would know far worse before King was through with him.

He took his sport coat off his arm and laid it across the foot of her bed. Walking quietly for so big a man, he came around to stand beside her and began to speak softly, hoping to penetrate her semiconscious state enough that she would know who was present when she awoke.

Her hair was fanned out across the pillow, and dark, tiny wisps had plastered her heart-shaped face in damp disarray. He resisted the urge to touch her and had to satisfy himself with a vocal approach instead. All the while he was talking, he was thinking of the joy he'd felt, when he realized there were no tubes or machines hooked to her fragile body, beeping her life signs for all who entered to hear. That had to mean she was not in any serious danger. All he could see in the way of obvious injuries were the bandages on her hands. They were hard to miss since she kept waving first one and then the other weakly in the air, continuing to fight the man who'd attacked her. The sight was finally more than King could bear. He spoke a bit louder, trying to penetrate her dream world.

It was the first time in nearly three years that he'd seen Jesse. They'd spoken off and on, but always by phone. Jesse kept him at a distance emotionally, and King was still at a loss as to why. One day everything had been normal, and the next thing he knew, she had taken a job and left the Double M Ranch. He hadn't been able to decipher his feelings then, and he was still unable to put his feelings for Jesse into words. She was just his Jesse, the kid who'd followed him all over the ranch and then turned to him in desolation when Andrew McCandless died. The friendship he'd felt for the young girl had deepened into a close relationship with the woman. But he hadn't had time to absorb the difference before Jesse left. There was still a big hole in his life that no one had been able to fill.

He started to touch her, anything to stop the horrible nightmare that was stuck on instant replay in her mind. But the decision was taken from his hands. She thrashed out wildly, bumping one of her bandaged hands on the guard rail. The pain penetrated her semiconscious state with a rude awakening.

Jesse moaned and blinked, trying to assimilate her surroundings and the unfamiliar smells that assaulted her senses. Her heart accelerated. She couldn't stifle the small scream that slipped from her lips as she saw the silhouette of a tall man standing beside her bed. It was only after she heard the familiar, husky voice that she allowed her heart to slow down to a sprint instead of the race in which it had been indulging.

Oh God! she thought. *He looks so big and gorgeous and worried.* And for the first time since her ordeal had begun, Jesse felt safe.

"King?" she whispered, afraid to believe her own eyes.

"Jess," he said softly, holding out his hand to let her make the initial contact. "Oh, Jesse Rose, what did he do to you, honey?"

It was the old, familiar term of endearment that did it. Jesse hadn't been able to cry, but now she felt it coming from so deeply inside her, she was afraid she couldn't stop. No one ever called her Jesse Rose but King. No one else would dare.

King reached down and lowered the guard rail on one side of her bed.

"Will you let me hold you, Jess? I just need to feel for myself that you're all in one piece. You've scared Maggie and me out of years we couldn't spare, sweetheart."

The husky plea was unnecessary, because the moment the rail went down, Jesse was in his arms.

He gathered Jesse, bedclothes and all, in a gentle but fierce embrace, breathing a sigh of relief in the dark cloud of hair on her neck. He felt her tremble and heard her trying to swallow the misery that wanted out of her heart.

"Just let it go, Jesse Rose. I've got you now, honey. And, I swear to God, no one will ever hurt you like this again. Do you hear me? No one!"

King swung her up in his arms, cradling her like he would a child, and carried her to a big, stiff-backed chair by the window. He lowered himself carefully and swaddled Jesse in his lap like a baby.

She let herself absorb the essence of this man…her King. Once he'd been her world. And then… She stifled the thoughts and buried her head against his shirt front instead. She couldn't deal with old hurts. The new ones were too overwhelming. Sobs flowed into deep, racking gulps of misery, and the strong arms that cradled her kept her from flying apart.

"I was scared, so scared, King. I thought I was going to die!"

"I know, honey. I know. It's okay now, Jesse," he muttered as he rocked her gently in his arms. "Cry all you want. I won't let you go."

Jesse cupped her bandaged hands carefully against her chest and let the tears flow, relishing the utter and complete feeling of security that crept inside her heart. For the first time since her attack, Jesse believed she would survive. She wasn't alone now. King wouldn't let anyone hurt her again. She believed that as surely as she knew the sun would rise each day.

The guard outside the door heard Jesse's sobs and carefully peeked inside to assure himself that all was well. The big man seemed to have everything under control. It was obvious that the girl was glad to see him. He nodded once at King's sharp look of distrust toward the opening door, and then quietly pulled it closed.

Chapter 2

Several hours later, Captain Shockey and another officer who doubled as a police artist came down the hall to Jesse's room. The guard saw them approaching and stood at attention.

"Anything new?" Shockey asked, as he started into Jesse LeBeau's room.

"That McCandless fellow you called got here just before noon. He's still inside."

Shockey grunted in surprise. He looked down at his watch and noted it was almost four in the afternoon. Almost twelve hours had elapsed since the girl's attack, and they still had no strong leads. Just a blood type, the knife the girl had taken away from the intruder, and a trail of blood that ended in the middle of a street. No fingerprints, no witnesses other than the girl, and she hadn't been able to give much of a description. Shockey was hoping the police artist could get more since she'd had a chance to calm down. Shockey was beginning to believe this wasn't just a random, spur-of-the-moment attack. It had been thought out to the degree that the perpetrator was wearing some kind of surgical gloves and had an accomplice waiting. But waiting for what? If they had been planning to steal her belongings, the accomplice had waited. It was too far to carry televisions, stereos, silver, and the like. And, in Shockey's experience, someone intent on rape or murder didn't usually work with an accomplice. Something just didn't ring true on this one. *Well,* he thought, as he stepped around the guard at the door, *maybe we'll get lucky and come up with a pretty good sketch.*

King was dozing between trying to balance himself in the stiff-backed chair and stretching his long legs against the corner wall while still cradling Jesse safely in his arms. She looked so tiny and so hurt, yet there was something different about her. He supposed it was just that he hadn't seen her in so long. He gazed hard at the delicate shape and plane of her face while he held her against his heartbeat. While he was trying to absorb this new and different person he held so intimately within his arms he fell asleep.

The sound of the door hitting against the back wall woke him instantly. He straightened up from his slumped position, knew he was going to have a crick in his neck, and glared silently at the intruders, indicating with a look at Jesse that they keep quiet. It did little good. Evidently the older of the two men who entered wasn't the patient type.

"You'd be King McCandless," he said, making no effort to lower his voice.

Jesse jumped at the sudden, loud voice and uttered a small cry of fright as she awakened to two men looming over her.

"Dammit!" King muttered. "It's okay, Jesse," he said roughly, and began to pull himself from his slumped position while not losing his hold on Jesse.

"What? What's wrong?" Jesse asked, trying to absorb the presence of the other men in her room. She sensed King's antagonism. Had something happened while she was asleep that she'd missed?

"Nothing's wrong, honey," King muttered. He laid Jesse back in bed, quickly pulling the covers around and over her to shield her bare legs and thighs from the two men. "They were just leaving."

Jesse recognized the ominous tone of voice and knew that, if she didn't intervene, King would find himself in trouble for assaulting a police officer.

"Wait, King," Jesse urged, placing a bandaged hand carefully on King's arm. It wasn't much of a restraint, but her voice was all that was necessary. King focused on the intensity of her eyes, imploring him to listen. "They're police. They told me earlier, before you arrived, that they would be back. I just forgot. Captain Shockey," Jesse said. "This is King McCandless. He's the son of the man who finished raising me after Daddy died. He's just about all the family I have."

A funny pain shot through King's chest as Jesse spoke the words "all the family." He hadn't realized how true that was, and felt guilty that he'd let so much time pass without forcing her to come home, or at least talk about what made her leave. Unfortunately, now was not the time. Jesse's imploring look slowed his anger and he gently brushed the hair away from her face. He sighed, then turned back to the men.

"Shockey," he acknowledged, as the older of the two men shook hands with him.

"Sorry for the intrusion," he said, for all who cared to listen. It was all the apology they would get. He had a job to do. "This is Officer Ramirez, Miss LeBeau. He's going to try and help you remember all you can about the man who attacked you and then try to draw his likeness. But he'll need your help. You've got to think of the intruder, what he looked like, what he felt like, what he smelled like." He saw the look of horror on the woman's face and wondered if she had enough spunk in her to do the job. She'd been through a lot already. "I know you don't want to, little lady. But I need you to close your eyes and pull this man out from wherever you've buried him. Okay?"

His blunt, matter-of-fact manner was just what Jesse needed to fortify herself for the ugly job ahead of her.

Jesse's lips trembled and the tears that pooled in her eyes slipped down her cheeks, past the dark, purple bruise on her face. King shook with fury. She wasn't up to this. He started to intervene when Jesse's voice stopped him.

"I'll do whatever it takes, Captain. I want him caught more than you do. If he's not, I'll never feel safe again."

"Good girl," he said, and motioned for Ramirez to come forward.

The police artist had been through this many times and did all he could to put the victim at ease. His low, soothing voice and casual manner soon had Jesse absorbed in trying to remember every minute detail.

As Jesse worked with the police artist, losing herself

in the task of remembering what she'd been so desperately trying to forget, King stepped away from her bed and motioned Shockey aside.

"When they let Jesse go," King said, "I'm taking her back home with me." His words were almost a dare for the older man to disagree. To King's surprise, he did not.

"Probably a good idea. She doesn't need to be alone at this point." He squinted his eyes a bit as he leaned back and looked up at the big man who'd backed him into a corner of the room. Damned if he couldn't use someone like McCandless on the force.

"Where's home anyway?" Shockey asked, and pulled a notebook from his jacket pocket. "Might need more information from Miss LeBeau and you'll want to know when the man is apprehended. We'll need her to come back and identify him then, you know."

King nodded in agreement and the look of peace and pleasure that suffused his face was noticeable when Shockey mentioned home.

"Home is the Double M Ranch southeast of Tulsa and Broken Arrow, Oklahoma. We raise a few cows, enough feed for them to get by, and once in a while, drill an oil well or two. But most of that was my father's love. Mine are the horses."

Shockey didn't raise an eyebrow, but he made a silent note to himself to do some more checking on this big man. *Drill an oil well or two,* he thought to himself with a grin. *Oilmen were a breed alone.* They were big gamblers, used to taking chances, but so were the horsebreeders.

"You race 'em?" he asked nonchalantly.

"No," King answered, and the light in his dark eyes

gave away his deep love for the land and the horses that ran on it. "I raise them and sell them. And they're Arabians, not racehorses."

Arabians! That *was* a costly enterprise. Shockey knew he would certainly check into this man's background. He didn't know much about the business, but he suspected this man could probably buy or sell just about whatever he chose. There was an air about him. And that name… King. Hell of a name to stick on a man. He seemed to be doing okay with it, though. Didn't let it intimidate him at all. Shockey interrupted his own rambling thoughts and said, "Yeah, well, that's just about all I need here. When Ramirez is through, you're pretty much free to go."

"I'll need to go to Jesse's home before we leave to get some of her things. Is there a problem with that?" King asked, uncertain about disturbing a crime scene.

Shockey shook his head. "Just let me know when you want to go and I'll meet you there. It's not pretty. You'll need to be prepared. I guess she'll want to clean it up before she moves. Not many people will stay in a home where something like that has happened to them. Not many can."

King was taken aback. He hadn't even thought that far ahead. Shockey's words gave him something more to digest.

Shockey spoke briefly to Ramirez and frowned at the picture emerging on the flat white surface of artist's paper.

King watched Shockey leave and felt like he'd just been sized up and found lacking. He didn't think he would ever like him personally, but suspected Shockey was very good at his job.

Ramirez finally finished with a promise to let King have several copies of the sketch to take back home with him.

"I didn't remember much more," Jesse said morosely, fidgeting with the sheet covering her legs. "It all happened so fast, I just didn't concentrate on what he looked like as much as getting the knife and getting away from him."

"You did all you could, Jess," King said, watching her face for signs of stress. "More than most."

The ordeal had been very trying for her. She'd had to go over and over every phase of the attack while helping the artist, and more than once had broken down in tears at a particularly traumatic point. His heart ached for her.

She shrugged and sighed, slumping down into the muddled pile of bedcovers, and tried with little success to brush the hair away from her face and neck. There wasn't a lot one could do with both hands bandaged. Someone had to help her bathe, go to the bathroom, brush her teeth, eat. There was virtually nothing Jesse could do for herself at this point, and she was frustrated beyond belief.

King watched her for a moment and then offered a suggestion.

"Jesse, would you like me to brush your hair? I know the nurses help you all they can, but most of their grooming is hit and miss. I guess they're just too busy for more."

The offer was a welcome one. And, with a bit of twisting and rearranging, King was soon giving her tousled hair a new look.

The brush bit through her hair, digging through the tangles all the way to her scalp. It felt wonderful. King's husky voice and the long, soothing strokes relaxed Jesse as nothing else possibly could. She groaned aloud in pleasure and closed her eyes at the almost sensual feel of the deep, repetitive strokes.

"That feels absolutely wonderful," Jesse whispered, and opened her eyes to see King watching her in the small mirror opposite her bed. She couldn't tell what he was thinking, but he had a most interesting expression on his face. She smiled to herself as she thought, *He looks like he's just seen a ghost.* Then she decided, *Maybe he didn't see a ghost. Maybe he just saw a stranger.*

Jesse knew King was used to seeing her as the gangly twelve-year-old child, desolate in the face of her father's death, and then as a late-blooming teenager, self-conscious of a maturing figure, and with no one to explain life's mysteries except a very kindly housekeeper thrust in the role of mother. He had never seen her as Jesse LeBeau, the woman. It was about time.

King was dumbstruck. He'd accidentally caught a glimpse of Jesse's face in the mirror as he worked, and the sight of her eyes closed, her lips slightly parted in sensual delight as the brush bit into her scalp, her head tilted back, resting against his chest as he brushed, had made another, more intimate thought pop into his head. It startled him that he'd ever considered it. It made King realize he didn't even know this woman. He knew who she'd been. He just didn't know who she'd become. King couldn't get the idea out of his head that she would look exactly like that as someone made love to her. That thought followed with an instant flash that he didn't want anyone putting that look on her face but him. Guilt, shock, and a bit of intrigue flowed through him and his hands stilled, forgetting why he held the hairbrush, or why Jesse was propped up against him. He just stood and stared at her image in the mirror, unaware that Jesse was staring back.

Her slow, teasing drawl broke the silent staring match, and King's face flushed a dark red as she spoke.

"You're very good with your hands," she said, knowing that he was going to take it the wrong way. She'd seen the way he was looking at her. She also knew it was going to embarrass him and she delighted in the flush it produced.

"Uh, yeah. I guess so," he mumbled, trying to get off on a different subject. "I should be," he said. "I do most of the brood mares' grooming myself."

Jesse's eyebrows shot up, tickled beyond words that he'd just claimed his expertise with a brush lay entirely in his skill of horse grooming. Not the most recommending thing he could have said in reference to Jesse's hair. Her delight echoed in the room while King's face got redder and redder, as he realized what he'd just said.

"You little witch," he growled, knowing Jesse had been teasing him. He wasn't sure just how much he'd revealed of his thoughts, but she'd been sharp enough to pick up on some of them. He didn't care that she was laughing at his expense. The pleasure he got from hearing her laugh at all was worth it.

"Sorry," Jesse said, as she finally caught her breath between giggles. "But you were asking for it. Horses indeed!"

King smiled back, allowing her to enjoy that much of his faux pas. Thank God she hadn't picked up on the rest of it.

Little did he realize, but Jesse knew exactly, or so

nearly that it didn't matter, what he'd been thinking. She wasn't dreading going back to Oklahoma with him. Maybe it was finally time.

The blue van turned off the street into a narrow, tree-lined driveway leading to Lynch's place. The driver silently cursed the day he'd decided to let Lynch handle the kidnapping. It had been so simple. No one was to get hurt, everyone was going to get rich, and Jesse LeBeau would be turned safely loose later. King McCandless would be a less wealthy man, but that would have been okay with the driver. It wasn't fair how some people had so much money and others, like him, never had enough. To make matters worse, it had cost the driver a pretty penny to get Lynch patched up and not have it reported to the police.

The driver stopped in front of a small, run-down duplex partially hidden behind a row of oversized lilac bushes. The leaves on the bushes were limp and dusty, suffering in the July temperatures from lack of water and care, just like the whole area. The shabby surroundings fit the driver's idea of where Lynch would live. He looked in disgust at the house, and then back at the pitiful excuse for a man dozing in his passenger seat, slamming his fists against the steering wheel in frustration and shouting.

"Wake up, Sleeping Beauty! Get out of my sight and stay indoors until you're healed. Your stupid face, vague though the rendering may be, was plastered all over the news this evening. Even I recognized you. All you need to telegraph your part in this disaster is to venture outside plastered with bandages and stitches."

Lynch stared, his doze disturbed by the driver's vehemence. He looked around in surprise, noted the familiar house, and for the first time in longer than he could remember, thought that he was glad to be here.

"I'll be in touch," the driver snarled. "So don't get any ideas about leaving town. We're not through with each other just yet."

Lynch nodded, opened the door, and very carefully lowered himself and his duffle bag from the van. He hurt in so many places, he couldn't have argued to save his soul. Besides, he knew he'd bungled enough already. The least he could do was keep his mouth shut. He knew this man well enough to know that his looks belied his true nature. He was very dangerous.

He watched the driver try to maneuver the van out of the narrow drive without the aid of a rearview mirror. He had to back out the same way he'd come in and wasn't doing a very good job. A small, wilting bunch of marigolds went under the wheels of the van and a piece of an overgrown hedge with it. He saw the driver's mouth moving at a very fast pace and knew he was probably cursing him and everything in sight. Therefore, he decided to remove himself from sight and lessen the number of things upon which the driver could vent his fury.

He entered the duplex, shutting himself away from the eyes of the world.

Maggie was putting the finishing touches to Jesse's old room, anxious to have her last chick back in the nest, if only for a while. She frowned as she heard the sounds of a car coming down the graveled driveway. She knew without looking that it was Duncan. He always drove too fast. He did everything fast. Even life was lived at fast-forward. Maggie personally thought that he missed the best life had to offer because he never took time to look for the little things. Maggie did her best to hide her disapproval of Andrew McCandless's younger brother. However, she suspected Duncan was all too aware of her opinions.

Duncan had only been ten when his beloved older brother, Andrew, became a father. From the first, he'd resented the child. King! The very name had burned a brand of hate in his heart. And then when Shirley, Andrew's wife, died less than a year later from a fall off a horse, King drew even more attention. Orphan indeed! What did they think he was? His parents had been dead so long he could barely remember what they looked like. Andrew was the only parent he acknowledged. Duncan fostered the antagonism and hate with a subversive skill. None, save possibly Maggie, knew just how deeply he resented being the McCandless that didn't count.

Maggie sighed loudly as she heard him enter the house with his usual lack of manners. He didn't live here anymore and as far as she was concerned, family or not, he should knock.

"Maggie? Anybody?" Duncan called, turning around in the hallway, trying to locate some member of the family. He saw himself in the hall mirror as he turned, and lifted his hand to pat a lock of hair back into place. The act was unconscious. He was good-looking and knew it. Except for the ten years separating them, he and King could have passed for twins.

Maggie came down the hallway in time to see Duncan's act of vanity. *That figures,* she thought, and then answered Duncan before he could call out again.

"Here," she said, and found herself swinging about the room, lifted off her feet in his exuberance.

"Where is everybody?" he said, as he twirled Maggie around and then planted a kiss on her cheek. He put her back on firm ground with a tweek of her face.

"Stop it, you fool," Maggie spluttered, trying to pull her dress and apron back into place. She didn't even want to think how her hair must look. Its usually neat bun was probably coming apart at the seams.

"Maggie, love, you like it and you know it," he teased, and then repeated his question. "Where's King? I need to talk to him."

Duncan watched an odd expression come and go in the elderly housekeeper's eyes and knew something was wrong.

"What?" he coaxed.

"King's not here," she said, and started toward the back of the house to the kitchen, confident that he would follow. He wouldn't leave until he got what he came for and that was usually money. Also, Maggie was more at home there, and she wanted to be on familiar territory when she broke the news about Jesse. Duncan wasn't going to take this well.

She suspected Duncan had always been attracted to Jesse, especially after she'd turned twenty-one. That's when she'd inherited the bulk of her father's estate that had been held in trust. There were shares in producing oil wells, a refinery, a goodly portion of the land of one of the newer Tulsa suburbs; the list went on and on. Michael LeBeau had not believed in banks. He'd invested nearly everything he made and, when he died, had been richer on paper than in the bank. Nevertheless, it had made Jesse a well-to-do woman. It just hadn't seemed to matter. She had continued her college studies and graduated from Tulsa University with a degree in education. It had delighted Andrew, but he didn't think for a minute that she would ever put it to use. He'd died believing Jesse's world would always be in order.

Maggie lifted a large bowl down from one of the cabinets and began to assemble the ingredients necessary for double fudge chocolate cake. It was Jesse's favorite.

"Maggie," Duncan persisted, "where *is* King, if he's not here?" He sighed to himself and resisted the urge to shout. She was so infuriating. She knew what he wanted. Why didn't she just come out and tell him? Everybody treated him like a fool. If they only knew, he was nobody's fool.

"We got a call. Jesse's been hurt. She's…" but she wasn't allowed to finish her sentence.

"Hurt?" he shouted. "Why wasn't I notified? What happened? Was it a car accident? What? Dammit, woman, talk. Don't I count for anything around here?" He grabbed Maggie roughly by the shoulders and shook her.

"You weren't notified because, as usual, you weren't home," Maggie said, and shrugged out of his tight grasp. "And…it wasn't an accident. Someone tried to kill her."

The look on Duncan's face surprised Maggie. Tears came to his eyes and his mouth worked, trying to speak past the emotion that threatened to choke him. He finally pulled himself together and wiped a hand roughly across his face. He reached blindly behind him and, when he felt the wooden back of the kitchen chair, lowered himself carefully into the seat as if his legs would no longer hold him.

"Kill her?" he mumbled. "No...no, not kill her. How bad is she hurt? Is she...disfigured in any way?"

Maggie gasped aloud at his lack of sensitivity and then frowned. That *would* matter most to someone of his caliber. She refused to answer him until he looked up with a pitiful expression on his face. She reluctantly relented.

"King called about two hours ago," she said, continuing to measure ingredients into the mixing bowl. She had to keep herself busy, too. She was too horrified by what had happened to her girl to let herself stop and think of the implications until she actually held Jesse in her hands. "I don't think she's hurt too badly. She had some severe lacerations on her hands and some bruising on her face, but other than that, I believe she's okay."

"Thank God!" he whispered aloud, and buried his face in his hands. "If her injuries are minimal, then we must be thankful that she is alive. I'm just so glad she's still the same."

"I doubt she'll ever be the same," Maggie snapped, and began stirring vigorously. She had to do something to keep her hands off this man. He made her so mad.

Duncan got slowly to his feet and shoved his hands in his pockets. He began backing out of the kitchen, bidding Maggie goodbye as he continued his crawfish exit.

"I'll call you later to check on Jesse. Maybe I'll go see her as soon as she's able to go home."

"She's not going home. King is bringing her here," Maggie said.

"Here? Wonderful," Duncan said, his attitude of dejection changing by the minute. "I'll just give them time to settle in, and then I'll be over. Cheer her up and all. It'll be great to see her again."

"You better call first," Maggie warned, but her words bounced off the front door. Duncan McCandless was gone. He'd disappeared as quickly as he'd appeared.

She shook her head, dismissing the futility of trying to make him into something he was not. His brother Andrew had been the only one with any sense. King was following in his father's footsteps, but for some reason, Duncan McCandless just hadn't figured out how to grow up.

Chapter 3

King spent his nights with Jesse on a cot furnished by the nursing staff, going back to the hotel every day just to shower and change. He wanted to be at the hospital for her, as much for her protection as for her peace of mind. The intruder who'd attacked Jesse was still unapprehended. He'd simply vanished. The few leads the police received went nowhere. No hospital, no medical facility of any kind in the entire state, had reported a man with the kind of injuries Jesse had inflicted. The police had begun to talk of the possibility of the perpetrator lying dead and still undetected. However, neither King nor Captain Shockey agreed with that theory. They believed he was out there somewhere, hiding, biding his time.

King had been reluctant to leave Jesse for even a short time until one of her friends from school heard of her attack. She started coming by every day after her summer classes were dismissed. Her name was Sheila. King liked her and could see why Jesse liked her, too. She was short and blond, funny and forthright, and best of all, she made Jesse smile. Everyone else skirted around Jesse's attack. They were afraid to say the wrong thing—afraid that what they said would hurt her feelings or bring back bad memories. But not Sheila. She was the best thing that could have happened at this point in Jesse's life. It did King good to hear Sheila's anecdotes and her suppositions of the probable nightmares Jesse's intruder was having, too. Sheila's nonsense was closer to the truth than they could have imagined. Lynch's days and nights were pure hell.

Lynch was going crazy. He'd been shut inside his house for days. The shades were drawn, and he had no way to cool himself in the sweltering heat. The utilities had been cut because of non-payment. He was running out of food. He needed to get some more peroxide to treat his slowly healing cuts and, most of all, he needed a drink. He'd made up his mind that, when it got dark, he was going out. There was an all-night convenience store less than four blocks from his duplex, and after midnight hardly anyone frequented the location. The only problem was that he didn't have any money. But he'd worry about that later. Right now, he needed a drink and he needed food. He settled back to wait for sundown. He had a plan.

King's phone call to Maggie had been just what she needed. He smiled as he replaced the receiver, patting his pockets to make certain he had all the papers and

keys necessary to go back to the hospital. His assurance that Jesse was healing and that they would be home
day after tomorrow was good news indeed. Her stitches
were to come out in the morning. Then, after going
over minor exercises in physical therapy, Jesse would
be released.

But King still had to get inside Jesse's house and
pack enough of her belongings for a long stay. He had
made up his mind she wasn't coming back to St. Louis
until it was safe. Now, he had to convince Jesse.

She wasn't going to be as easy to persuade as she'd
been when he first arrived. Then, she'd been so frightened and in so much pain she'd pretty much let him
make the rules. But as she grew stronger, so did her will.
Jesse was obviously still very relieved to see King come
back into her room each day, but she had reerected that
secret wall of silence between them. A couple of times
King had tried to draw her out; get her to talk about
her decision to leave the ranch. Each time, Jesse would
change the subject. He knew in no uncertain terms that
now was not the time. She wasn't ready to deal with it,
so he let it drop. But time was running out, and so was
King's patience. She *had* to come with him. She didn't
have a choice until the intruder was caught.

The hospital room was dark and quiet. The only light
came from the hallway outside the partially opened
door. King watched the play of emotions on Jesse's
face. She hadn't said no. She hadn't said yes. In fact,
she hadn't said anything at all. That was what was bothering him.

"Jesse, for the love of…" then he caught himself.
Anger would get him nowhere. He took a deep breath and

started over. "Honey, I just don't understand. The ranch is your home. You'll be safe there with your family."

But Jesse's soft interruption startled him. He didn't know what to make of it.

"I know that you'll take care of me, King. You always have. But you're not *really* my family. I don't have any family." The harshness of her words was softened with a smile. "Just very dear friends."

Her denial hurt in a way he could never have imagined, yet he refused to be deterred.

"Okay," he agreed, letting his breath out in slow, measured puffs of frustration. "I'm not your brother, but by God, I feel like one, and I want you safe. Is that so bad?"

He knew the instant he said he felt like her brother that he was lying to himself and to Jesse. But the thought behind it was sincere, and he let his statement stand.

Jesse read the hurt in his face and knew he'd never understand. That's partly why she'd left. She hadn't wanted a brother. She'd wanted more from King than he could give.

"I'm not your sister," she said more harshly than she intended, and took a deep breath before she continued. "Most of the time I don't feel like I belong to anyone. I teach other people's children, not my own. I go home to an empty house and grade papers until I get tired and, usually, I just go to bed. I know I made my choices, and though they aren't what I particularly desired, they're mine. But I appreciate, more than you can ever know, that you were here for me. I couldn't have survived this nightmare without you. And…"

King held his breath.

"And," she continued, "I'll come home with you. But

just until the man is apprehended. Then I have to come back to this life and my job. This is my world now, King. It's the only one I belong to."

King breathed a huge sigh of relief and pulled Jesse into a big hug. He felt her momentary resistance and then smiled to himself as he felt her relax, allowing him the familiarity. Just as soon as he got her back to the ranch, he was going to get to the bottom of her silence.

Jesse knew every word she spoke and every denial she put in his way would only make King more determined to crack the shell of secrecy she'd erected around herself. She didn't know what was going to happen when she went back to the Double M with King. The only thing she did know was that pretending he was her brother was not going to work again.

Jesse was in therapy, being briefed on the types of exercises she must do to regain full mobility in her hands. Her stitches had been removed earlier in the day, and while she was horrified at the maze of tiny red lines crisscrossing her palms, she counted herself lucky to be alive still. Scars were something with which she could deal.

King had made arrangements with Sheila and Captain Shockey to meet at Jesse's house and pack the needed cloths for their trip. Sheila willingly agreed. She had been at Jesse's home often enough to be able to find anything they would need. Shockey had agreed earlier to accompany King. While it was still the scene of a crime, King had free access with Jesse's permission.

It was pure curiosity on Shockey's part to see how McCandless would react. He had a gut feeling there was more to Jesse LeBeau's attack than just a pervert crawling through a window. Until a case was solved, he trusted no one.

King's cab pulled into Jesse's driveway as Sheila and Shockey arrived. He was glad. He wanted to get this over with as soon as possible.

"It's not a pretty sight," Shockey warned as they entered the stuffy confines of the darkened interior.

Sheila shuddered and looked about nervously, half expecting someone to jump from behind a sofa or out of a closet.

"It wasn't a pretty thing to do to anyone. I don't imagine it is," King growled, his voice even deeper and rougher than usual. He raked his hand through his hair, ruffling the ends out of order. He just wanted this job over with. This was the first time he'd been to Jesse's home. He felt curious and a little guilty. He should have come sooner. He looked around, searching for signs of the Jesse he knew. There were none. It may as well have been a hotel room. Nothing looked lived in. There were no pictures, no mess, no personal items...nothing. Her life here was a puzzle. It looked like she'd just been eating and sleeping here, not really living. It almost looked like she'd been waiting. But waiting for what?

"Well, come on," King said. "Let's get this over with. Lead the way, Captain."

Shockey made a mental note. A plus for McCandless. He didn't know where the rooms were located. Funny, if they're so close, he hadn't been inside this house. Something didn't add up.

Sheila's gasp was nothing to the rage King felt as they walked into Jesse's bedroom. Nothing had been cleaned, nothing had been moved. For the first time he realized just how valiantly Jesse had struggled and how desperately she'd fought to survive. His voice came out in a dark, ugly threat and his entire body shook as he turned to Shockey and growled a warning.

"You better find him before I do."

Shockey nodded with a silent promise as well as a silent warning to King, and then left them to their task.

It was completed in haste and silence. No one spoke much until they were outside.

"Sheila," King said, watching the little blond get into her car. "I'm sorry you had to go through this. But Jesse and I really appreciate your help. I probably wouldn't have packed any of the right stuff."

"I didn't go through anything," she answered. "Jesse is the one who's suffered. And as far as help, I didn't do so much. She would have done the same, and more, for me." She started her car and began to back from the short drive, then stopped and lowered her window. "Take good care of Jesse," she called. "She's a good friend. Please don't hurt her!"

King frowned as he watched her hesitant wave and then she disappeared around the curve. *Why would she think I'd hurt Jesse?* None of this made any sense at all.

Physical therapy was a nightmare. Jesse was extremely nervous. Everyone was a stranger. She could hardly concentrate on the therapist's instructions, for her furtive observation of the people that kept coming and going through the therapy room. The guard hadn't come with her to therapy; at least she hadn't seen him. She desperately wished King would hurry and get back. This was the first time she'd been alone since the attack. The staff went about daily duties and Jesse wished she was back in her room. Every time she saw someone that fit the general description of the intruder, her heart would skip a beat. Twice she'd forced herself not to demand the unsuspecting men remove their shirts so she could see for herself if there were wounds on their upper bodies. She was driving herself into a state of paranoia she knew wasn't healthy. But someone she didn't know had tried to kill her. Until he was apprehended, Jesse was going to be afraid.

"Dear Lord," Jesse whispered to herself. "What if they never find him? How do I learn to cope with this?"

Finally the therapist was through. She left with a promise to tell a nurse that Jesse could go back to her room. Jesse sighed impatiently as she watched her exit between the tall, swinging doors that led back into the hall. It had been a matter of some argument whether she should walk down one floor to have her therapy. Finally, they had insisted she be brought down in a wheelchair. It was hospital policy. So she waited for someone to come and take her back to relative safety.

Jesse alternated between anticipation and joy when she thought about going back to the ranch with King—seeing Maggie again, all her old friends, and, she'd have to admit to herself, even Duncan.

Duncan! How could someone who looked so like King be the absolute and total opposite in personality? Duncan was the dark. King was the light. As a child, that was how Jesse had pictured them. But Duncan was a McCandless and she was not. Any problems she had with him were to be kept to herself. She was the outsider, not he. So she held her silence.

Her daydreams were interrupted as the swinging double doors opened. A man wearing hospital whites entered, pushing a wheel chair. Jesse's heart gave a sharp thud and she began to shake. He looked like...

he was the same age and build. Jesse looked around wildly. He couldn't be coming for her. It had to be for someone else. It was then she realized she was all alone in the room. The man kept coming toward her with a smile on his face. She stood, frantically searching for an exit, a door into another room. Somewhere to run. A place to escape? There was nothing!

"Miss LeBeau?" the male nurse questioned, as he saw her agitation escalate. Something was wrong. Maybe they'd sent him to the wrong place. Or maybe this wasn't the right patient. "I came to get you and…" but he never got to finish his sentence.

"Nooo!" Jesse moaned softly, and started backing slowly away. Her fear was so great she didn't think she was going to be able to breathe. She couldn't go through this again. He said he came to get her. She was too frightened and hurt to fight again. "Please," she begged, holding her hands out in front of her with a motion for him to come no closer. *Oh God! Not again!*

Suddenly it dawned on the man. He knew who this was and he wanted to wring his supervisor's neck. This was the young woman who had been attacked several days ago. They should have known to send a female nurse. They'd made such a point of having no men enter her room, and this mistake, innocent though it may be, could do her irreparable harm. It was obvious to him that he was a vivid reminder of her recent ordeal.

"Miss LeBeau, please." He spoke in a calm, author-itative manner. "I'm not going to hurt you. I'm just a nurse. But I understand, okay? You wait there and I'll call someone else to take you back to your room."

Jesse knew he was talking. She could see his lips moving. But the blood was roaring in her ears so loudly, she couldn't hear what he was saying. Then he stopped. He was backing slowly toward the door. She saw him call out to someone in the hall. She stood helplessly, waiting in terror.

"I need some help down here," he called urgently, motioning toward the nurses' station. "Some of you get down here quick, and you better be female."

King and one of the staff doctors were on their way to physical therapy to see how Jesse was progressing. He wanted to talk to the therapist himself and see if there was anything specific he might do to help her regain mobility in her fingers and hands after they went back to the ranch.

He saw a male nurse standing at the end of the long hallway, half in and half out of the swinging doors, saw a flurry of activity at the station as several of the nurses started hurrying toward the man in the doorway, and felt a twinge of apprehension. When he got close enough to read the sign over the doorway where they were headed, he started to run. It was the physical therapy room. Something was wrong and instinct told him it was with Jesse.

King heard the male nurse's low voice explaining the situation as the others arrived. His suspicion was confirmed. He looked past the group standing bunched in the doorway as they discussed the best possible way to handle the situation without further endangering the patient. King started to push past them.

"You can't go in there, mister," a nurse said. "There's a patient in there who needs special help. The staff psychiatrist is on his way."

"She doesn't need anything but me," King growled, and started to force his way through the group. "What in hell did you people do to cause this?" he muttered. "She was fine when I left."

"Let him pass," the doctor said as he arrived, quickly assessing the situation.

King stepped inside the door and looked around, trying to determine what had triggered this reaction. He could see nothing obvious but Jesse's intense fear. How was he going to get through to her without causing her harm? He waited, hoping she would come to him. But she didn't move, and the expression of horror on her face didn't change.

Jesse had backed herself as far into the room as she could go. When she felt the corner of the wall cradle her back, she slid down weakly into a crouched position, unable to run any farther. She hadn't taken her eyes from the man standing in the doorway.

The man was talking to people on the other side of the door, but she couldn't see their faces. Maybe he called for help. If there were too many, she couldn't fight them all. She moaned softly and beat her fists weakly against her knees. Jesse's rationale was gone. She had flashbacked to the original attack, and was living it all over again.

Her breath came in sobs as she frantically searched the room's sparse furnishings for some kind of weapon. She'd had one before, but she couldn't seem to find it now when she needed it. The man was going to kill her. She just knew it! Her eyes followed the baseboard as it ran the length of the room, still searching. There! Under the window! A piece of pipe! That would work! Jesse fixed on the pipe's location and began crawling on her hands and knees, oblivious to the pain in her palms as she pulled herself across the floor. Someone was coming through the doorway. She had to hurry. Jesse was breathing in harsh, choking gasps, her mind fixed on gaining control of the weapon. She still wasn't ready to die. Her fingers closed around the piece of metal as she clutched it tightly with both hands. She pulled herself upright and stood silhouetted against the backdrop of the bright midday sun streaming through the windows.

"Oh, dear Lord!" one of the nurses whispered to herself, as the group stood in shock, witnessing the terror and strength of heart that Jesse LeBeau possessed. Tears burned and blurred the nurse's vision as she turned away, unwilling to witness the suffering caused by the rape of Jesse LeBeau's mind.

"Be careful," the doctor urged as King entered, standing ready to assist if physical restraints became necessary. He was surprised that this had happened. The patient had seemed in control. He supposed that alone should have alerted him. No one could experience this type of trauma and not suffer some kind of emotional stress.

"Jesse," King called. He stood unmoving in the center of the room. "Jesse, it's me, King. Honey, put the pipe down. You know I won't hurt you, don't you, baby?" He kept repeating the plea, over and over, hoping to reach some part of Jesse that was still rational.

The deep, husky rasp was so familiar. Jesse blinked furiously, trying to clear away the veil of tears that kept blurring her vision. She heard him calling, over and over, repeating her name in the same, safe, familiar voice. The man who'd hurt her hadn't said her name. He'd only screamed ugly, foul things. This man was different. He wasn't trying to hurt her. He wasn't screaming at her. Maybe… She began to lower the pipe.

King cursed softly under his breath and resisted the urge to wipe the sweat from his eyes. Any sudden movement could startle her and send her back into the nightmare.

"Jesse Rose," he called softly, and saw her begin to tremble. He breathed a harsh sigh of relief as he watched the pipe slip from her shaky fingers and bounce once before it rolled back against the wall.

"King?" Jesse whispered, suddenly aware of her surroundings. It was the strangest sensation. She didn't know how she came to be standing so far away from the door, nor why everyone was looking at her so curiously. Her hands hurt. They hadn't hurt like this in days. She gasped as she looked down at the rawness. A few tiny drops of blood were seeping from one of the deeper scars.

"What happened?" she moaned, and stumbled, but didn't fall. King's strong, familiar arms gathered her close, pulling her safely against the comforting beat of his heart. She buried her face in the soft linen shirt, recognizing the aftershave and the low growl in his voice, and relaxed.

King caught her just as her legs gave way. He swung her up into his arms, softly murmuring over and over against her cheek.

Jesse clung to his strength. She felt as if she'd just run five miles uphill. She was limp and shaking, and more and more aware of the small group of people whispering among themselves as they witnessed the drama that had unfolded before their eyes.

"I'm sorry," she mumbled, slowly realizing what must have happened, and embarrassed at the turmoil she'd caused. She turned her tear-stained face up to

King, searching his face for approval. All she saw was a hard, tight-lipped expression and flat, angry fury in his eyes. She thought it was directed at her. "I got scared," she began. "And I couldn't find the guard, and you weren't here…"

"No!" King said, brushing a gentle kiss against her brow. "Don't you apologize for anything, Jess." His dark eyes flashed as he continued. "We're the ones who should be sorry. I shouldn't have left you, and—" his voice held a definite promise of menace "—I don't know where in hell your guard is, but I'll bet I find out."

Jesse knew that tone of voice and the expression on his face. She'd never been the recipient of his anger, but she'd been a witness. It wasn't pretty.

"King," she cautioned, trying to pull herself together enough to think. "You can't do this." Her tone was that of a mother to a child, and oddly enough, King paused to listen. "You can't take the guard out behind Tilley's Bar and Grill. We're not back home in Tulsa. You can't hurt the officer."

"No," he muttered, "but I can damn sure hurt his feelings. And when I find him, I will."

Jesse sighed and leaned her head under his chin. She'd give him the right to that much. She wondered where the damn guard was, too.

Suddenly she was overwhelmed with the need to be through with all this. She was so ready to leave the hospital, St. Louis, and the whole terrible nightmare behind. She wanted to go home.

Sundown came, and with nightfall also came relief from the sweltering heat. Up went the shades and windows, and whatever breeze was strong enough to penetrate the dense shrubbery around the shabby duplex was welcomed. Lynch sat in the darkness by an open window and listened to the sounds of the neighborhood, as one by one, voices quieted and lights went out in the surrounding houses. Finally, all that disturbed the night was the occasional frenzied barking of a dog that was quickly silenced by its owner's angry shout.

It was time. Lynch wasn't waiting any longer. He needed out and he needed a drink. He had searched the unkempt closets all afternoon for something to wear that would cover his wounds and still not look out of place in the extreme heat. He'd come up with some old jean shorts and a T-shirt with a high neck and three-quarter length sleeves. It was the best he could do. His rummaging had solved another problem. He didn't have any money, but he'd found a partially used pad of blank checks from his lucrative days as a working man.

He felt a burning anger inside at the unexpected turn his life had taken. He wouldn't be in this miserable shape if it weren't for that woman. She'd messed up everything. He would have been fixed for life if she'd just cooperated. Instead, here he was, broke and injured, and it was all her fault. Then his anger turned toward the man who'd drawn him into this ill-fated scheme. Some big wheel he'd turned out to be. He hadn't even paid him for his trouble, and he hadn't come back like he'd promised.

Lynch patted his pocket, assuring himself that the checks were in place. He had no remorse about writing a check on a closed account. He planned to be long gone before the check had a chance to bounce.

Damn, but it feels good to be outside, Lynch thought as he pulled the front door shut behind him. He stood in the shadows, glancing furtively around to make certain he was unseen. Satisfied that he was unobserved, he started down the narrow drive with an almost jaunty air.

He stood underneath the eaves behind the convenience store and waited for the lone customer to pay for his gas and leave. The fewer people who saw him, the better off he would be. Finally the customer left. Lynch hesitated no longer.

"How ya' doin'?" he asked the clerk, as he sauntered in and pulled a scrap of paper from his pocket. "Just need a few things," he volunteered unnecessarily, and started searching the aisles.

Carefully noting the customer was alone and on foot, the clerk nodded and continued to refill a cigarette rack over the cash register. It didn't pay to be careless in a job like his and he didn't like working this shift anyway.

"This'll do it," Lynch said, as he carried the last of the items—two six-packs of beer—to the counter.

The clerk nodded and began ringing up the items. He rang up the total, told Lynch the amount owed, and began to sack the small pile of foodstuffs.

Lynch casually wrote out the check for the amount of purchase only, just as the sign at the cash register requested. Then he slid the check and his I.D. to the clerk.

The clerk was tired, distracted by the fact that he was having to work this graveyard shift, and anxious to get the lone man from his store. He took the check without even asking for a second identification and stuffed it into the cash drawer.

His "thank you, come again," was muttered as an afterthought.

Lynch was jubilant. He'd done it. He grabbed the sacks, one in each hand, and used his chest and stomach as props for the cumbersome load. But he couldn't mask his pain as one of the heavier sacks pressed sharply against his healing cuts.

"Hey, buddy," the clerk asked, as he saw the grimace on the man's face. "You all right? Need any help?"

"Naw," Lynch mumbled, biting his lip to keep from swearing as beads of sweat popped out on his forehead. "No problem. I'm just a little sore. Had an accident a while back and I ain't quite healed."

The clerk nodded, continuing to watch as Lynch juggled the sacks to a better, less painful position. Finally, satisfied that he could manage the load, he backed away from the counter and started out the door.

"Hey, mister," the clerk yelled sharply, "you're bleeding."

Lynch cursed under his breath and continued walking out the door. The heavy sacks had re-injured a slow-healing cut. Hurrying more with each step he took, he refused to acknowledge the clerk's observation. He didn't look back.

The clerk watched the man disappear into the darkness. Then something made him go to the door, just to see which way the man went. But he'd hesitated a bit too long. No matter how hard he looked, he saw nothing beyond the ring of light shining down on the store parking lot. He had started back inside when a police notice taped at eye level by the door caught his attention.

It was a sketch of a man wanted in connection with the attack on a woman in St. Louis. As he read, he remembered seeing something about it on the news, but he'd heard no more and had forgotten all about it until he began to read the notice. He chuckled to himself, remembering as he read that the woman had turned the tables quite nicely on this creep. He looked at the picture again. Something…something about the shape of the nose and mouth looked familiar. He remembered reading that the man would have suffered multiple stab wounds on his upper body. His heart jumped, and then raced. *What if…?* He cursed, absorbing what he'd just read and then looked back out into the night.

"Hell," he muttered, "let it go. Who wants to get involved with the cops?" But he couldn't get the woman out of his mind.

He went back to stocking the shelves along the narrow aisles, trying to put the incident and growing suspicions out of his mind. But his conscience wouldn't allow it, and with a snort of disgust, he went to the phone and dialed the number printed on the police sketch. It probably wouldn't amount to anything, but he'd never be satisfied until he made the call.

The call from the convenience store clerk was the first solid lead the St. Louis police department had received. Shockey took the follow-up interview himself.

He listened intently to the clerk's recitation of events leading up to the blood appearing on the man's shirt, took note of the type of clothing he'd worn and the odd, almost furtive manner in which he'd left the store.

"Was he in here long?" Shockey asked.

"No, he didn't have over half a dozen items. If it hadn't been for the six-packs of beer, it'd all have fit into one sack, easy."

"Do you happen to remember what he bought?" Shockey asked, and turned the end of his Eversharp, adjusting the new lead to just the right length.

"Oh, I dunno," the clerk muttered. "You know, the usual junk food. This stuff ain't exactly supermarket quality. Uh…let me see. There was bread, a stick of that summer sausage, some cans of vienna sausage, the beer of course…and, oh yeah!" he added. "A package of Oreo cookies. I think that's about all." Then he remembered. "No, wait! I forgot about the other stuff. But it wasn't nothing to eat. He got a bottle of peroxide and some of them big patch adhesive bandages." He looked pleased with himself as he recalled the events. This was just like on TV.

Shockey made note of the last two items and suppressed a surge of elation. It was too soon to assume this was his man. But, so far, so good. Shockey was not one to jump to conclusions.

"So," Shockey repeated. "He paid you, took his stuff and left. Is that about it? He didn't happen to mention where he lived, or worked…anything like that?"

"Naw. It was just like I said. I took his check. He took his food and walked out the door."

Shockey absorbed what the clerk had said.

"He paid by check?" He couldn't disguise the surprise and elation in his voice. This guy couldn't be the one. Surely he wasn't that stupid. "Did he have identification?"

"Yeah, a driver's license," the clerk mumbled. "I didn't ask for more. Here's the check, though. Thought you might want to take a look at it. I almost forgot to tell you."

Shockey took the check, made a note of the information he needed, and handed a copy of the info to one of his detectives. "Here, check this out right away. I want to know if this guy's on the up and up, and if his is a current address. And," he added, "I don't have to tell you to hurry, do I?"

"No, sir," came the answer, as the detective immediately disappeared.

Shockey turned his attention back to the clerk, who was obviously growing weary of the repetitive questions.

"You sure this is all you remember?"

"Yeah," the clerk sighed. "That's just about it. Like I said, I almost didn't call. He didn't look exactly like the sketch, but I didn't think I needed to remember what he looked like. He was just another customer."

But Shockey knew there was one vital piece of evidence still left to recover. "I'll need to confiscate your surveillance tapes," he said.

The clerk looked blank and then understanding dawned as he looked up at the cameras above the cash register.

"The tapes!" the clerk cried, excited that there was still more he could contribute. "He'll be on the tapes."

This couldn't be the man, Shockey thought to himself, as he carried the tapes to his car. Surely no one was so stupid that they would commit a crime like attempted murder, then pay for something by check and get videoed all at the same time. Shockey almost laughed aloud. He couldn't be this lucky.

Chapter 4

King muttered an odd litany of gentle oaths as he heard the pilot's announcement that they would be landing at Tulsa airport in less than five minutes.

"Thank God!" Jesse heard him say, and couldn't resist a smile. She knew how King hated to fly and how valiantly he'd tried to mask his fear just to be strong for her. He was always in control of every situation; so dependable and reliable. This one weakness he tried to ignore was really quite endearing.

King's solution to things over which he had no control was to ignore them. Unfortunately, it was very hard to ignore the fact that he was thousands of feet above the ground.

Jesse's stomach did a flip-flop of its own as the plane touched down on Oklahoma soil. In spite of all her protests and hesitation, she was very glad she'd decided to come with King. She knew that if she was ever to get over the intense terror she felt when she was alone, and the paranoia she had experienced in the hospital therapy room, it would be here, with those who loved her best.

King's fingers cupped her hand as the plane touched down, and she heard him sigh loudly in relief. Suddenly she was as anxious as King to get off the plane. She couldn't wait to set foot on McCandless territory. She hustled King from the plane, and aided in locating their luggage. It was only after they'd loaded the bags into the black Lincoln King retrieved from the parking garage that she felt she was finally on her way home.

"Thank you," Jesse whispered to King, then leaned over and softly pressed the firm cut of his cheek with her lips.

Her actions startled him. He was so intent on negotiating the ever-present detours on the downtown expressway that he nearly swerved into a large, orange barrel with a single flashing light.

"Hellfire," he muttered, as he quickly righted his course and looked about to see how many drivers behind and beside him were cursing his existence. "What was that for, girl?"

His heart had skipped at least two beats and was now doing overtime, trying to compensate. He didn't know why the simple act had so upset him. Jesse had kissed him plenty of times during her years at the Double M. But somehow this felt different. He angrily squashed the thoughts that swiftly entered his mind. This was no time to let his fancy wander. This was Jesse. He didn't think of her like that…did he?

"Oh," Jesse sighed, her eyes dancing with delight.

"It was for coming to get me. For bringing me home. For just being you."

King smiled. He, too, was glad she was home. She'd talked all during the flight about seeing Maggie, her old friends on the ranch, and schoolmates. She'd delicately *not* asked much about his confrontation with the negligent hospital guard. Jesse had talked about every thing and everybody except Duncan. King wondered why he was so conspicuously omitted. But before he had a chance to ask, Jesse's excitement distracted his line of thought and it was forgotten in the delight he felt as she turned in the seat beside him.

"We're here," she announced, pointing to the two giant oak trees that stood sentinel at the gate of the Double M Ranch.

Jesse's eyes were shining, a mirror reflection of the clear, blue brightness of the Oklahoma sky. She let herself absorb the healing power of home—the soft, rolling hills that flattened out into wide valleys, fenced off from the long, graveled road snaking between the scattered stands of native trees—home! Everything was so dry, wilted, and dust-coated. And Jesse thought she'd never seen anything as beautiful. Although they rode in air-conditioned comfort, it was obvious by looking out of the window, that this was just a stop-gap from the sweltering heat. They needed rain. Oklahoma always needed rain this time of year. And, one day soon it would rain, and rain too much. Then they would have to cope with floods. That was Oklahoma. That was home.

The ranch and outbuildings came into view as they rounded the last sharp curve and the stand of post oaks. The many barns, sheds, granaries, and corrals where King's horses reigned supreme were in tip-top condition. The newly painted stalls housing the Arabian brood mares gleamed painfully bright against the landscape of quickly dehydrating vegetation. Jesse absently noted the height of prairie grass behind the horse barns and knew the early spring rains had sparked quick growth that was now close to being ready for harvest. Soon they would cut and bale the natural prairie grasses for highly prized horse fodder.

The main house came into view as they passed the first of the sheds where some of the farm machinery was stored. Jesse couldn't suppress the quickening tears. It was so dear and familiar. She'd spent the better part of her life growing up inside those walls. Nothing looked different. It was still a long, rambling structure that had been added to only once, when Maggie came to live.

Andrew McCandless had been in dire need of someone to oversee King's teenage years and then later, just when Maggie thought raising children was behind her, Jesse had arrived.

The house was cedar and brick with a verandah that ran the entire length of its front. It had not been landscaped professionally, but the shrubbery around the house was varied and healthy. Someone had been watering vigorously to keep it all looking so green. The lawns had not suffered, and the trees and shrubs looked well cared for. Jesse suspected Maggie had left all that to Wil Turner, the foreman. He had a real affinity for growing things and made no bones about his expertise.

"There's Maggie!" Jesse cried, and then choked back a sob. It was obvious she had been expected. Several more people had gathered on the verandah, waiting to see for themselves that their little Jesse was truly okay.

"And I see Charlie…and Turner…and Harvey and…oh, King," she whispered thickly, trying not to cry.

He'd barely stopped the car before Jesse was excavated from the Lincoln's cool depths and swallowed by the crowd of well-wishers. She was quickly hustled into the house away from the heat, leaving King to deal with the luggage alone. He didn't care. He would have carried suitcases for a month just to have her back.

King placed the last of Jesse's bags on her bed so she would be able to unpack. Her hands were still quite tender and she wouldn't have been able to lift them. He hoped Sheila hadn't left out anything important. From the weight of the bags, he doubted it.

King smiled as he looked around the room. There were flowers on the dresser, on the bedside table, even on the window seat. Maggie had possibly overdone it a bit. Yet he knew how dear Jesse was to them all and suspected Maggie had sorely missed her presence over the last three years.

Jesse LeBeau had been the only female, other than Maggie, on the McCandless's domain for as long as King could remember. She reigned supreme and it was obvious from the welcome she'd just received that she still held the crown.

King looked around, satisfied that all was in order, then closed the door to her room. He followed the sound of voices coming from the kitchen and hurried to join the crowd.

Everyone was talking at once. King could hear the melee from the hallway and hoped it wasn't too much for Jesse. He needn't have worried. Wil Turner, long-time foreman of the Double M, had Jesse in a seat of honor. She'd always been a small child, and to keep her

safe and out from under foot, whoever had been looking after her would usually seat her on a corral rail or
the back of a pickup truck. Today it was the corner of
the kitchen cabinet. Jesse was smiling, enjoying their
banter, and allowing their high praise of her actions to
heal her wounded spirit. Their praise would probably
have angered severe feminists. But as far as they were
concerned, it was the highest honor they could bestow.
They vowed their Jesse had "fought like a man." She
was a true heroine.

King remained unseen in the shadows of the kitchen
doorway and allowed himself the luxury of watching
Jesse. Her hair was dark and windblown, caressing her
bare shoulders with a careless touch. The pink thing she
wore was something between a dress and pants. King
didn't know the name for the culotte-skirted dress, but
he knew he liked it. It was soft and clung in all the right
places to very feminine curves. Her long, bare legs dan-
gled with carefree abandon. And, somewhere between
the front door and the kitchen, Jesse had stepped out of
her sandals. King smiled. She was truly home.

"Just look at that," Turner urged. The men gathered
closer as he held Jesse's injured hands palm side up.
"You got sand, little girl," he said gruffly, and patted
her knee. "We're real proud of you, Jesse. And your
daddy would have been, too. You've got real fightin'
spirit. If I could just get my hands on…"

Jesse threw her arms around Turner's neck and
kissed him soundly, stopping the threat from being
spoken. Then she jumped down from the cabinet and
gave each of her old friends the same blessing as they
began to leave.

King wondered if he'd looked as dazed and silly when Jesse had kissed him.

"Come on, boys," Turner called, catching a glimpse of King's shadow in the doorway. "Time to get back to work." He turned and waved as they filed out the door. "Welcome home, girl. Don't you worry none. We'll take good care of you here."

Jesse felt like she'd been pulled through a "dust devil," one of Oklahoma's famous little whirlwinds that skips across the prairies, sucking loose bits of sand and grass up into its tiny vortex. She was hot, breathless, and as satisfied as she'd been in ages.

Jesse turned and faced the elderly housekeeper who'd remained oddly silent through most of the boisterous welcome. Tears rose, filling her eyes and blurring Maggie's image. But Jesse couldn't stop the flow. She didn't have to pretend with Maggie. She knew it all.

"Come here, love," Maggie crooned, and gathered Jesse into her arms. "It'll be all right. Time will heal everything he did to you. It will heal these," she gently patted Jesse's hands, "as well as what's inside." She pointed to Jesse's breast. "Now, if you think you can stand it, I just happened to have a big, double chocolate fudge cake that's going begging. Don't suppose you want to ruin your dinner?"

Laughter bubbled from deep within Jesse's heart and pushed the fear and misery back where it belonged. It did her good to hear the threat Maggie had thrown in their faces over the years. Maggie had a tendency to bake the most mouth-watering treats in the county and then tell all who entered her kitchen that they couldn't have any for fear of spoiling their meal.

"How about my dinner?" King teased, as he entered the room.

"Nothing ruins your appetite," Maggie growled in a teasing fashion. "You may as well sit down, too. But don't think I'm always going to be this easy. This is a special occasion. We've got our girl back home, safe and sound."

Jesse smiled lovingly at Maggie's attempt to lighten the emotionally charged atmosphere and then flashed a conspiratorial look at King. It was all the prompting he needed.

Maggie rarely broke a rule and, adults or not, King and Jesse delighted in being recipients of the exception.

Jesse sighed, replete from the ice cold milk and rich chocolate treat. It was good to be home.

"Duncan called," Maggie told Jesse, as she and King helped clear away the dinner dishes.

King had been furtively watching Jesse's progress as she carefully scraped and stacked, doing everything except actually carrying dishes to the sink. He knew she needed to feel useful, but didn't want her to overdo things on her first day.

The look that passed through Jesse's eyes, clouding their brightness, when Duncan's name was mentioned surprised him. It was something between revulsion and fear. Jesse's silence spoke loudly to his instincts. He wondered, as he continued to carry plates and bowls to the sink, what else was going on with Jesse that he knew nothing about.

Maggie's prattle fell into the silence, using up the emptiness in the kitchen. She seemed to be the only one unaware of her announcement's impact.

"He stopped by a couple of days after King left for St. Louis," she continued. "Seemed real upset at your news, Jesse." Then Maggie looked up. Her words ended abruptly. She sensed something was out of the ordinary, but didn't know what it was. She shrugged and finished her message.

"Anyway, he said he'd stop by tomorrow. I think he's a bit partial to you, Jesse," Maggie announced, and then couldn't resist rolling her eyes a bit at the unlikely thought. "About the only person besides himself he cares for." Realizing what she'd just said in King's presence, she blushed, but refused to refute the truth of her words.

King grinned wryly at Maggie, excusing her blunt statement as he'd always done. Maggie was as much family as anybody on the Double M and she had a right to her opinions. Unfortunately, this one was definitely on the mark. Duncan was a hard one to know.

The odd thing was that King had always been aware of Duncan's almost flirtatious manner around Jesse. It had never bothered him before. Duncan flirted with every woman within seeing distance…even Maggie. But this time Maggie's words hit King in a different way. He didn't think he liked the idea of Duncan and Jesse at all. From the expression on Jesse's face, neither did she.

"I told him not to come early," Maggie added, "but you know Duncan."

"That's fine," Jesse finally managed to say, aware King had noticed her hesitance. "I knew I'd see him sooner or later."

King frowned. It was such an odd acknowledgment

of the impending visit. It seemed to him that she viewed it as something to get over with.

"If you two will excuse me," Jesse said, looking everywhere but at King. "I think I'll turn in early. It's been a long day."

"Sure," Maggie urged, bustling about the kitchen. "Go on to your room, honey. I'll be there shortly and help you get ready for bed."

"I think I'll be fine," Jesse said, and then caught herself before she refused all offers of help. There was one thing her hands still weren't strong enough to tackle. The faucets on the bathtub in her room were old and stiff. She knew she'd never get the water on.

"There's just one thing I may need help with and King can do that, dear," she said. Maggie looked worn to a frazzle. It had been a long day for someone her age as well. "You know how stiff the faucets are on my bathtub. I'll need someone to run my bath. Maybe in a day or two, when my hands get stronger, I won't have to ask."

"Sure I can, Jesse." King had also noticed how exhausted Maggie seemed to be. They were all so used to her coping with every aspect of ranch life that they hadn't noticed she was growing older. It was good that Jesse was back. Maggie needed company. "You go on to bed, too, Maggie. I'll lock up and see to Jesse's needs. After all, I haven't done such a bad job for the last few days, have I, Jess?"

Jesse smiled shyly and turned away, suddenly afraid he would see more in her expression than she wanted him to.

Maggie didn't argue. She just gave Jesse a weary hug before heading toward her own rooms off the kitchen area. "Sleep tight," she called back, and then closed her door.

"Come on, Jesse Rose," King teased. "You're next. By the time I get all my women put to bed, it'll be time to get up."

All his women indeed! Jesse glared at his back as they walked down the hallway leading to the bedroom wing and wrinkled her nose at him in teasing fashion, knowing full well he couldn't see her actions.

"Just because you have no middle name," she muttered, "doesn't mean you need to wear mine out."

"Well," King answered, stating his point with unequivocal assurance. "After naming a baby King, what in hell else could follow?"

Jesse grinned and followed him into her room. She watched him disappear into her bathroom, and heard the sounds of water splashing full force into the depths of the old-fashioned claw-foot tub. She loved it, and had refused offers of having a new model installed years ago. It was long and deep, and was ideal for soaking. But the fixtures were old and stiff and resisted all but the firmest of grips.

"It's running," King announced, as he entered the bedroom area. "Need any help unpacking? I don't know what Sheila included, but if you don't have something you need, just make a list. I'll take you to Tulsa anytime you want to go."

"I'm sure I can manage," Jesse said, and continued to search through the open bags while King waited for the tub to fill. Her hands felt the familiar, well-worn softness. She smiled, pulling a faded, black, oversized T-shirt from beneath the neatly folded lingerie. Thank goodness for Sheila! She remembered.

"It's my favorite," Jesse said gleefully, holding it up under her chin and spinning around to the mirror over her dresser.

King watched the look of glee on Jesse's face and then saw what had made it appear. He didn't know whether to laugh or taste the smile on her face. The feeling that pulled at him was unfamiliar and probably marked the beginning of a sleepless night. He couldn't get past the image that flashed in his mind of taking that damn "Bo Knows" T-shirt off her body and making sure he was the only one who "knew" Jesse LeBeau.

"The tub's running over," Jesse cried, and dashed toward the bathroom, right behind King.

"Sorry," he mumbled, mopping at the floor with the fluffy white towels Maggie had provided. She was going to kill him for using them on the floor, but he'd grabbed them before he thought. "I'll get you fresh towels," he offered, then grinned sheepishly at the look of merriment on Jesse's face. "If you don't tell Maggie."

They both burst out laughing and the tenseness he'd felt moments earlier disappeared. He didn't know what was getting into him. Jesse didn't deserve his betrayal at this crucial time in her life, and he had no intention of frightening her with any sort of out-of-character behavior. She'd suffered all the surprises she needed for the time being.

"I'll be fine now," she said, pushing him out of the door of her room. "And, King," she called as he entered the door of his room across the hall, "thanks for everything."

She closed the door without waiting for an answer and King felt oddly alone.

Jesse had dawdled long enough. She'd unpacked,

admired the flowers, taken a long, soaking bath, done the prescribed exercises on her hands, brushed haphazardly at her hair, and knew it was time. She was going to have to get in bed, turn out the lamp, and try to sleep. Just the thought of closing her eyes made her sick. She rubbed sweaty palms down the sides of her "Bo Knows" T-shirt and silently cursed the helpless feeling that was threatening to overwhelm her. Logically she knew she was safe. King was just across the hall. No one could hurt her here. But logic was lost in the terror that took over her senses when the lights went out and she was in bed...alone.

"Damn him," Jesse muttered aloud. "I won't let what that creep did—or tried to do to me—ruin the rest of my life. I won't."

She walked around the familiar old four-poster bed, pulled back the lightweight coverlet and crawled on her knees up into the middle of the mattress. The central air-conditioning made sleeping under a sheet quite comfortable, but Jesse couldn't bring herself to lie down or turn out the lights. Finally, she allowed herself the luxury of just leaning against the nest of pillows at her back. She was so tired. She'd only close her eyes for a moment. She wouldn't turn out the light, not just yet...not until she accustomed herself to her old room again...and the shadows...and the night sounds in the country. She fell asleep within minutes, curled into a tight little ball. And, in spite of all her determination, she began to dream.

It was always the same—the instant knowledge that she wasn't alone, the awful smell of an unwashed body, the odor of alcohol, the rough ugly words...and the knife. Jesse moaned softly, tossing about as she lay uncovered in the middle of the bed, kicking weakly in her sleep. The moans became a plea for mercy, the plea became a cry, the cry a scream.

King was on his feet and inside her room before he fully realized he'd gotten out of bed. But he knew what was wrong with Jesse the instant her terrorized screams had pierced his sleep.

Hesitating no longer than the time it took him to reach her bed, he scooped Jesse up into his arms with a single motion and spoke her name aloud in a calm, soothing tone of voice. She was awake almost instantly. It took another moment before the tears came, but when they did, they were cleansing; washing away the nightmare King had put to an abrupt end.

"Is she all right?" Maggie asked, trying to mask the panic she'd felt as she heard Jesse's pitiful cry. She'd reached the room only seconds behind King and had seen the natural way he'd handled the tense situation. Instinctively, he'd done the right thing. She took in the sight of the scantily clad girl, the big, half-dressed man holding her tightly, and squashed the thought that crept into her heart.

"She will be now," King said, lowering Jesse to the floor, refusing to relinquish his hold on her. "We've been through this before, haven't we, Jess?"

Tilting her chin back with the tip of his finger, he wiped away the last of her tears and sighed. "It's okay, Maggie. Go back to bed. I'll stay with her for a while. I should have anyway. She hasn't been alone since the attack and this was just to be expected."

"I'm sorry," Jesse whispered, as she leaned weakly against King's strength. She felt his heartbeat against the back of her head, and knew by the race of the rhythm that she'd frightened him as much as she'd frightened herself. "I seem to be saying that a lot lately, Maggie. You didn't know what you were letting yourself in for when you wanted me here, did you?"

The quiver in Jesse's voice and the vulnerability in her brimming eyes was enough for Maggie. Whatever it took to make her girl whole again was going to have to be all right.

"Don't be silly," she answered. "You're not a bother. You're family. Now, King, you go on and do whatever you've been doing to help our girl get through this."

She wiped at her eyes and pulled nervously at her long, gray braid, then bustled out of Jesse's bedroom, talking to herself as she disappeared down the hall. "Whatever it takes…that's what we're going to do. Whatever it takes."

King took in her tear-strained face, the rumpled T-shirt, the bare legs beneath, and knew he was asking for trouble. But for Jesse's sake, he didn't have a choice.

"Come here to me," King beckoned in a husky voice, and took her with him across the hall. Turning back the covers on his king-sized bed, he pointed to the unused side and gruffly announced, "I'm not sleeping in your room. That bed's too damn short." He softened his words by the gentleness of his touch as he crawled between the sheets and pulled Jesse down beside him. "Now go to sleep, Jesse," he whispered, and gathered her stiff little body against him.

He felt a slight hesitance from her before fear overrode propriety. She backed into the curve of his body, relaxing with a shaky sigh as she felt the cool firmness of his long, muscular arms pull her against him.

"Thank you, King," she whispered, and drifted off to sleep.

Don't thank me yet, he thought with a silent groan, as the soft curves of her hips settled against his lower stomach. *I've got to get through this night a sane man.*

Turner's old rooster crowed twice before Jesse forced herself to open her eyes. It had been so long since she'd been awakened by anything other than alarm clocks that it took her a moment to re-orient herself. Last night came crashing rudely back. All the fear and terror of the night had ended simultaneously with being wrapped securely in King's tender grasp. She allowed herself the luxury of watching the first early rays of the sun catch in the gold-tipped hair on King's arms and reveled in the quiet strength emanating from him, even as he slept.

The weight of his arm across the flat of her stomach was only a little heavy and Jesse knew she would have gladly welcomed all of him in a way King would never imagine. She turned her head slightly and tried not to let the catch in her breath alert him as she watched him sleep. He was so beautiful. She smiled to herself. Men weren't supposed to be beautiful, but…tell that to her heart. She couldn't quit watching his mouth as he slept peacefully, unaware of her. It was slightly parted, and the thought of tasting the firm, full-cut lips was intoxicating. Her gaze wandered upwards toward the thick, dark lashes that lay fanned over his upper cheekbones and knew that they covered dark eyes that rarely missed anything. Hair lay in mussed abandon on his wide, sun-tanned forehead. She resisted the urge to gently comb it away from his face. Instead, she allowed herself to see King as few saw him; quiet and vulnerable.

But this was getting her nowhere and making her

more than a bit miserable. Jesse sighed softly and
stretched, trying to get enough incentive to move. Yet
she didn't want to move, ever. This was exactly where
she'd yearned to be for as long as she cared to remember. The only thing wrong with the picture was that
she was here for all the wrong reasons. King was doing
this out of love all right, just not the kind of love Jesse
wanted from him.

She felt the strong, solid length of him, and his even,
steady breathing. Carefully, so as not to alert him, she
began to scoot from under his grasp. Even asleep, King
sensed her movement and pulled her back against him.
Jesse felt his hand splay over her stomach, then slide upward until he seemed to find a more comfortable spot.
She held her breath as his hand wandered, then let her
breath out slowly as his hand come to rest just under
the soft, generous curves of her breasts. His sigh of satisfaction made quick tears come and go in Jesse's eyes
and she blinked furiously, anxious that he not awaken
to see her in this state.

She'd successfully hidden her true feelings for King
for years, never allowing herself to dream that something such as this would ever come to pass. But now to
be thrust in such close quarters for the wrong reasons
was the epitome of irony.

Jesse closed her eyes, let imagination turn her in
his arms, taste the sun-browned flavor of his muscular
chest and work her way upwards with tiny kisses and
nips until she reached the chiseled perfection of his
mouth and welcomed King and the day together. The
thought was intoxicating. She knew she had to move
before the thought became deed.

Carefully, she lifted away the lightweight sheet covering them and slid her fingers gently over King's hand, reluctantly removing herself from his grasp. Allowing herself just one small luxury, she very gently brushed her lips across the hand that had held her safely through the night. Then she quietly scooted to the side of the huge bed and slipped from King's room without looking back.

He'd been awake since the moment her fingers touched his hand. He'd started to speak, and then something made him remain silent. An instinct...or curiosity...he didn't know which. But he hadn't moved. Nothing could have prepared him for the jolt that shot through him as Jesse's lips brushed across his fingers. Reflex made him clutch a handful of the bedsheet. He gritted his teeth to keep from calling her name—calling her back to his bed as she walked out the door.

"What in hell is happening to me?" King muttered aloud as he watched his body betray him.

Rolling over with a painful groan, he pressed his aching body into the unyielding mattress and knew it wasn't what he wanted under him. He also knew nothing was going to make the ache go away. He suspected it was only going to get worse.

Unwilling to face, or even investigate, his new feelings for Jesse, he chose his usual way of dealing with an out-of-control situation. He was going to ignore it. He crawled out of bed and headed for the shower.

"Just coffee," King growled in his husky rasp. "Not hungry."

Maggie's eyebrows shot skyward as she heard King speaking what she called "McCandless shorthand." It was a strange family trait that surfaced in times of stress or anger. Andrew... King...even Duncan had all exhibited varying degrees of the family trait. Maggie suspected all was not well in King's world. She also suspected Jesse had something to do with his cranky behavior.

"Good morning to you, too," Maggie said wryly. "Did someone get up on the wrong side of the bed?"

"Been a lot better off if I'd never gotten in the damn thing," King muttered into his coffee cup. Then he quickly swallowed a curse with the fiery gulp of the steamy brew.

"It's hot," Maggie warned too late, and turned away so King would not see her smile.

"I'll be out most of the day," King said, and added as he started out the door, "Keep an eye on Jesse. I think she'll be fine…but…" he cautioned, remembering her flashback episode at the hospital. "If you need me, just find Turner. He'll know where I am."

"You'll miss Duncan," Maggie reminded him. "He said he'd be over today."

"Hell!" King muttered, and then mentally rearranged his earlier plans. He had every intention of being present when his uncle arrived. Something was going on between him and Jesse and he wanted to see for himself.

"I'll be in at noon," he said, leaning over to kiss Maggie's cheek, "in a better mood."

"Humpf," she replied, and watched him walk toward the horse barns, his long legs quickly covering the distance. Then he disappeared into the dark, cool depths of the airy building.

Chapter 5

Jesse mentioned virtually nothing of the preceding night's events, nor did she mention anything of the aftermath. She had been hiding her feelings for King for so long that it was second nature to be noncommittal.

She and Maggie worked side by side as they went about the daily chore of putting the huge, rambling ranch house to rights. They chattered idly, visiting about nothing in particular, yet it was obvious that the daily routine was becoming almost more than Maggie could handle alone. Jesse was certain King didn't realize the increasing difficulties Maggie faced daily. Each passing year added problems, none of which she could control. There were aching joints, a slower stride, and small moments of weariness that she could not hide, even from herself.

Jesse knew that she probably wouldn't have noticed

the differences in Maggie if she hadn't been gone for such a long time. Coming back home now was like seeing everything and everyone for the first time.

"I might have known," Maggie said with a sigh, as she looked out the living room window she had just dusted. "Here comes Duncan just in time for lunch. I'll set another place."

Jesse looked about wildly, uncertain whether to follow Maggie to the kitchen and prolong the moment when she'd have to face Duncan, or stay and get it over with. She opted for the latter.

There was no time to change into something less revealing than the blue, terrycloth shorts and shirt she was wearing. It had been too hot to wear much else after the struggle she'd had with Maggie's vacuum cleaner. Jesse had insisted she was perfectly capable of using it. But the constant pull and push of the handle and the weight of the machine itself had almost been too much for her still tender hands.

Oh, well, she sighed, *I could be wearing a nun's habit and Duncan would still undress me with a single look. And I don't remember where I left my shoes.*

So, Jesse waited, defenseless to postpone the inevitable confrontation. She gritted her teeth as she heard him bounding up the front steps of the verandah, whistling some unrecognizable tune a bit off-key.

"Something smells wonderful," he shouted as he entered the house, paused in front of the mirror on the hall tree and smoothed his hand over his perfectly groomed hair.

"Duncan," Jesse said, as she came into the hallway holding out her hand in greeting. "It's been a while, hasn't it?"

The forced gaiety and exuberance fell from his demeanor like a deflated balloon. He'd known Jesse was here. He just hadn't expected her to initiate the meeting. He couldn't put into words what he was feeling. But it was something between anger and shame.

He kept remembering the last time he'd seen her. And after what had happened recently, he wasn't certain how to behave. Her outstretched hand couldn't be ignored. He slipped back into his bravado and sandwiched her offering of greeting between his hands in a none too gentle grasp. Instantly he remembered her injuries, but not soon enough to prevent her gasp of pain.

"Jesse, dear," he mumbled. "I'm so sorry. I didn't think. Here, let me look."

"No," Jesse argued. "It's all right," and tried to pull her hand away.

She struggled unsuccessfully as Duncan grasped one hand and then the other and turned them palm sides up. He couldn't hide the shudder that ran through his big frame as he gazed fully at the healing evidence of her ordeal.

"Your hands!" he whispered, and pulled them upwards to his lips. "Dear God! Your hands," he muttered again. "Said you weren't hurt. Lied…" he said brokenly, "lied."

"Duncan! Please!" Jesse struggled, and finally succeeded in pulling her hands away from his mouth. He was acting strangely. And his words made no sense.

"Lunch is about ready," she announced, and tried not to run toward Maggie and the kitchen area where she heard her working out obvious aggression on the pots and pans. "And," she added, unnecessarily, "King will be here soon."

It seemed that speaking his name would give her some measure of insurance against Duncan saying something that she didn't want to deal with, especially now.

Duncan was in shock. His feet were moving. He must be saying all the right things. But he couldn't for the life of him remember what he'd said. Seeing Jesse had brought back all too vividly the last time they'd been together. It was not a memory he liked to recall.

Jesse was experiencing a similar jolt of memory and wished, all too fervently, that this day would soon be over.

"So, Jesse's moving to St. Louis?" Duncan asked, barely controlling his glee at the news. Maybe, if he got her away from this damn ranch and his perfect nephew, he'd have a chance with her.

Duncan had seen, all too clearly, the way Jesse looked at King. He'd also been aware, long before the others at the ranch, that Jesse LeBeau was a very beautiful, desirable woman. And, since turning twenty-one, she was also a very well-to-do woman. All of the above were attributes Duncan McCandless felt absolutely necessary in a wife. He scoffed at working a nine-to-five job. He shouldn't have to. After all, he *was* a McCandless.

His periodic appearances at the oil company that Jesse's father, Michael, and his brother, Andrew, had founded, were none too well received. He was tolerated solely because he was a McCandless. He'd inherited a goodly portion of the company stock at Andrew's death. But the dividends were not enough to keep Duncan in the manner to which he'd accustomed himself. He was growing weary of trying to devise ways in which to make a quick buck. As far as he was concerned, Jesse was the answer to his prayers. All he had to do was court her and marry the rest of the money he felt was, by all rights, his anyway. Duncan also planned to capitalize on the likeness that existed between him and his nephew. After all, if she liked one man's looks, another so much alike should suffice. And King had his head in the clouds as far as Jesse LeBeau was concerned. His mind was on everything but romance. Duncan considered Jesse an easy mark.

Unfortunately for Duncan, Jesse saw way beyond the surface of both McCandless men. He would have never wasted his time and money had he known how repulsed Jesse actually was by all his posturing.

She'd only been in St. Louis a month when Duncan made his first move. His plans had been carefully orchestrated and the "chance" meeting between him and Jesse was a success.

Leaving the Double M had been difficult for Jesse. Then, when King had not called or written other than to satisfy himself that she'd arrived and settled in safely, she'd been devastated. She didn't realize King was simply giving her the space he thought she desired. Her decision to leave had been a shock. King and Maggie had finally come to the conclusion that she just wanted to be on her own for a while, and had made every effort not to intrude. Their lack of communication fell right in with Duncan's plans. His casual offer of dinner in had been eagerly accepted. It began his forays into the life of Jesse LeBeau.

The "chance" meeting escalated into a weekly visit that he purposely let seem entirely her decision. Jesse was lonely, and for a short while, was swayed by Duncan's charm and likeness to the man she loved.

But the weeks grew into months and King did not come. Jesse grew tired of pretending to herself that anything was going to change. All the while, Duncan maintained a manner with Jesse that could only be called gentlemanly. He was certain that it would only be a matter of months before she'd capitulate and all his plans would come to fruition.

But instead of falling in with Duncan's ideas, Jesse began to withdraw more and more. Finally even Duncan sensed his looming failure. That was when he made his mistake. Although she never returned the casual hug and kiss he gave her at the end of each visit, she didn't refuse them either. Duncan saw only dollar signs, not the signs of annoyance that Jesse struggled to disguise.

But Duncan's pressing financial problems and Jesse's obvious withdrawal escalated his carefully laid scheme. He'd refused her attempt to cancel their dinner engagement at one of St. Louis's finest restaurants after severe weather warnings. Instead, they'd arrived at the proposed time while the pouring rain slowly turned into icy pellets. Duncan had studiously ignored Jesse's worried glances outside the restaurant window until even he began to see the stupidity of staying longer. However, he had taken the bad turn in the weather as an opportunity he wasn't going to pass up.

"If you don't care for dessert, Jesse, dear," he said, slipping his hands over hers as she placed her napkin at the side of her plate, "I believe I'd better get you home. It seems the roads *are* getting worse, and I don't want to take any chances with your safety."

He leaned over in the circular booth they were sharing and slipped his hand under the collar of her sweater as he spoke, refusing to acknowledge the flash of distaste that clouded her eyes.

Jesse had been trying for several weeks to find a way to lessen the attention Duncan kept showing her. But she was at a loss. At first he'd been a welcome visitor—someone from home. Yet he always made Jesse slightly uncomfortable by the way he looked at her, and the practiced casualness of his touch. She'd tried to get out of this dinner all day. The weather was uncertain and she needed to average the grades of her students and have them ready to post on report cards when Christmas break was over. It *had* been a long, lonely holiday. Finally she'd weakened at Duncan's persistence.

"Yes," she eagerly agreed, as he suggested they leave. "I'm finished. And the roads look worse."

She was anxious to get home and away from Duncan. For some reason, she sensed something different about him. His behavior was making her uneasy. There was an almost desperate quality that she didn't like. She didn't like it at all.

The drive home took forever. The roads had worsened. They made it home safely due only to the fact that nearly everyone else had the good sense to stay indoors and off the roads.

Duncan saw Jesse to her door, bestowed his usual farewell, and quite off-handedly remarked he'd probably break his neck before he got back to his hotel.

Jesse felt a twinge of guilt, but remained stubbornly silent as she watched him get in his car and begin the hazardous job of backing down the slope of her icy driveway. Suddenly, before her eyes, Duncan's car spun in a complete circle and came to rest on the neighbor's yard. She opened the front door and stepped out, calling anxiously as she saw Duncan groggily shake his head.

"Duncan," she called, "are you hurt?"

He looked up at the sound of her voice, opened the door and stepped out with a huge smile on his face. He shrugged his shoulders as if to indicate his innocence in the whole proceedings and started walking carefully back toward Jesse's house.

"No, I'm not hurt," Duncan answered. "But it looks like you're stuck with me until morning. Hope you don't mind. I'll just stretch out on your sofa. You'll never know I'm here."

There was absolutely nothing Jesse could say to deny him entrance. She also didn't know that one of the few things Duncan could do well was handle a car. He'd been "shooting doughnuts" on the ice since he was a kid.

The next two hours went smoother than Jesse could have hoped. He was considerate and unobtrusive as she finished averaging and posting the student grades in her book. She heard Duncan moving quietly about in the kitchen, but the only obtrusion he made was to bring a pot of her favorite apple-scented tea and set it and a cup and saucer within reach. She looked up to thank him, but he was already gone.

Maybe I'm making more of this than I should, Jesse thought. *He's actually being true to his word.*

Finally her work was finished. Jesse slammed the pages of her grade book shut with a satisfied plop. She pushed her chair back and stretched her legs out before her, stood and wearily tilted her head from side to side, trying to work the kinks out of her neck and tired shoulder muscles.

"Need a back rub?" Duncan asked softly.

His voice startled her. She turned to see him watching her from the doorway of the den. Jesse shuddered. She hadn't been aware of his presence and it made her uneasy.

"No, no. It's fine. A good night's sleep will take care of it," Jesse answered anxiously, hoping he would move away from the doorway so she could escape to relative safety in her bedroom. But Duncan was too big and compelling, and kept looking at her in a very unsettling way.

"Well," she said brightly, "if there's anything you need during the night, Duncan, please feel free to help yourself. Food, extra blankets, anything..."

"There is something I need, Jesse, dear." He began walking slowly toward her. "No. Something I want."

Jesse's heart stopped and then raced. All speech left her as she began backing away from Duncan. But there was nowhere to go.

"Don't be afraid, my dear," he crooned. He slipped his hands on either side of her neck and cupped her face, tilting it toward his dark, fathomless gaze. "You know how I feel about you. You must! Please, let me show you how precious you are to me. Let me stay with you tonight. Let me take care of you, always."

"No...no," Jesse whispered, feeling revulsion at his touch. She struggled uselessly within his grip, and fought down the rising black tide of fear that threatened to overwhelm her. This couldn't be happening! She had to be dreaming, because this *was* a nightmare.

"You've misunderstood, Duncan. I don't think of you that way. You're Andrew's brother—King's uncle. I've always thought of you as family. Please!" And the last came out with a sob as she struggled wildly to get away from his lips on her neck…on her face…on her mouth. "Don't touch me!" she screamed, and pushed with both hands, pressing and hitting against his chest with all the strength she could muster. It wasn't much, but her struggles broke his grip and Jesse fell back with a choked cry.

She wrapped her arms around herself, trying to keep the nausea that was boiling in her stomach at bay. She no longer hid the repulsion she felt in his presence.

Duncan's eyes narrowed, and an ugly smile came and went on his handsome face.

"What's the matter, princess?" he sneered. "Aren't I good enough for you? Or am I not what you wanted after all? Let me guess…the princess wants the King, not the jester. Am I right?"

Jesse gasped, suddenly aware of how defenseless and alone she was…and just how angry Duncan was.

"Get out!" she ordered, drawing strength from deep within. She pointed her finger in his face and began advancing toward him. She wouldn't be afraid…not in her own home. "Go home, Duncan."

Unconsciously Duncan backed away, surprised by her vehemence, but the ugly smile and threat in his demeanor remained. He wasn't prepared to give up on this woman and her money this easily. He was too desperate.

"You forgot about the weather," he reminded her with a gleam in his eyes. "I can't leave yet. It's too dangerous."

"No, Duncan," Jesse said ominously. "Not as dangerous as it will be if you stay here. Get out! Get out now…or I'll tell King."

She couldn't have made more of an impact if she'd

slapped him. His easy way of life depended on staying within his nephew's graces.

"Damn you," he whispered, as he grabbed his coat and gloves from the table in her living room. "One day you'll be sorry, princess. One day you'll be very sorry!"

Jesse held her breath as he slammed the door suddenly behind him. She quickly locked the door and then sank limply onto the living room sofa. Her eyelids teared and she blinked furiously. Duncan was gone. She had nothing to cry about. Then she lowered her head to her knees and cried herself to sleep.

"Lunch is ready," Maggie announced to Jesse, as she practically ran into the kitchen. She raised her eyebrows, but judiciously said nothing, as Duncan entered right behind Jesse with an odd expression on his face. Maggie knew there was old trouble between them but kept her thoughts to herself.

"I'll go get King," Jesse offered breathlessly, and gave neither Maggie nor Duncan a chance to object. She exited the kitchen on the run.

"You better put on some shoes," Maggie called, but it was too late. Jesse was gone. "Here," she said, as she placed a stack of plates in Duncan's hands. "You can set the table." She ignored his look of outrage and surprise and turned back to her pots and pans. It wouldn't hurt him to earn his meal for a change.

The hot, loose dust in the driveway made tiny poofs between Jesse's bare toes as she hurried toward the horse barns. The thick, sweet scent of honeysuckle along the backyard fence wafted through the air, and Jesse inhaled deeply, satisfied, in spite of the heat, to be away from the cloying atmosphere inside the ranch house. A daring little sweet bee lit on the back curve of Jesse's thigh and then quickly lifted off just before her hand reached him.

Jesse squinted her eyes against the glare of the noonday sun and stopped for a moment in the shade of one of the red oaks lining the long driveway of the Double M. She held her breath and listened, then turned with a smile toward the gleaming white stalls where King's brood mares were kept. She could hear him, even from here, issuing a short, decisive order to one of the hands. A horse's neigh pierced the air in objection as men's voices continued to call back and forth to one another. Jesse rounded the corner and slipped silently into the welcome depths of the cool, airy barns that opened at both ends to capture the maximum flow of air.

A shiny, red king cab pickup truck pulling a matching air-conditioned horse trailer was backed into the barn area. It was obvious that King had just sold some of his stock.

She watched as a young filly and two colts, part of his herd of two-year olds, were carefully loaded into the comfortable depths of the long trailer. She couldn't hide her admiration at the way they responded to King's handling. The beauty and clean lines of their distinctive build, their long, delicate legs, the magnificent width of their chests and long, flowing manes and tails belied the spirit and endurance for which the true Arabians were bred. She knew King suffered mixed feelings each time he had to part with his stock. Although that was why he raised him, selling them was always a difficult hurdle to pass.

King carefully led the last of the young horses into the trailer and then stepped back, allowing the men to remove the loading ramp and fasten the end gate of the trailer securely. It was only after he watched to assure himself that the truck and trailer had successfully cleared the barn opening that he spied Jesse standing in the shadows. He began walking toward her.

Jesse saw him wave and smile, then saw a frown appear on his face and knew why before he got within shouting distance.

"Lunch is ready," she said, hoping she could sidetrack his train of thought. It didn't work.

"Where the hell are your shoes?" he growled, and glared fiercely at the wide, blue eyes staring back at him with feigned innocence.

This was an old battle they'd fought for years. Jesse knew it was only for her own safety that he continually cautioned her, but she loved the feel of going barefoot. And at the age of twenty-five, she was unlikely to change.

"Come on," Jesse chided, ignoring his bluffed anger. She hurried toward the ranch house, assuming he would follow. "Maggie's waiting."

King narrowed his eyes and tried to ignore the gentle movement of her breasts under the skimpy little blue top she was wearing, but didn't succeed. Then he realized she had nothing on under it. That made things even worse. The sexy sway of her hips in the matching shorts did nothing to help the increasing pressure behind the zipper of his Levi's, and he cursed roundly under his breath as he hurried to catch up. Maybe if he walked beside her and not behind it would turn his mind to a safer channel.

"You didn't answer me, Jesse," he said, as his husky voice broke the silence between them. "You know not to come barefoot around the barns." Then his voice grew gentle, and he slid his hand along her arm, tightening on her wrist as he pulled her to a stop and made her face him. Her quiet statement blew everything else from his mind.

"Duncan is here," she said.

King felt her pulse jump beneath his fingers, and he sighed in frustration. He'd wanted to be present at the first meeting between them. He didn't know exactly why, but he suspected there was an old, unsettled problem he should know about. Yet he was uncertain about how to get the information from Jesse. She could be so damn hardheaded.

"And," she continued, gently pulling her wrist from his grasp, "I'll try to be more careful. I promise."

King didn't know whether she meant she'd be more careful about where she went barefoot, or more careful around Duncan. But it was too late to ask as Maggie's impatient voice hurried them both inside.

King quickly washed and changed into a fresh shirt, brushed most of the dust and grass from his pant legs, and hurried to the table. He'd kept them waiting too long. It didn't pay to pull this stunt with Maggie many times. She'd fed leftovers to the barn cats more than once rather than put up with tardiness at the table. He'd eaten dozens of baloney sandwiches because of it.

The food was good, the cool comfort of the house a welcome relief, and the conversation was casual and very ordinary. Yet King had never sat through a more uncomfortable meal in his life. Maggie talked on and on about the weatherman's repeated daily warnings of fire danger due to the extreme drought. Duncan alternated between charming Maggie and looking at Jesse with an expression King felt almost obliged to punch off his face. He reluctantly decided that would not be wise, and sat silently, fuming over a situation he didn't understand.

Jesse blithely refused to look at either Duncan or King. Instead, she talked too much about absolutely nothing. King didn't know whether to shout or leave in disgust. The decision was shelved as the shrill peal of the telephone startled the quartet around the table.

"I'll get it," Jesse offered, anxious to get away from the antagonistic atmosphere hanging over the table. She scooted her chair back so quickly, King didn't even have time to blink as she grabbed the wall phone by the kitchen cabinets.

King watched the expression on her face change to one of disbelief and then terror. He debated with himself for about half a second until he saw her chin quiver. That was all it took. He rose from his chair with a violent move and grabbed the phone from her hand.

"Who the hell is this?" he asked. But the voice that answered him was not what he'd expected.

He sighed as he pulled Jesse gently into his arms, and absently rubbed his thumb against a tiny mole behind her ear. The ill-concealed elation of Captain Shockey's voice and the message he had for them were what they'd all been waiting for, yet at the same time, fearing would come.

"Do you have him in custody?" King asked, and then turned and frowned at Duncan as he abruptly stood upright, knocking his chair over backward with a loud bang. He turned away too soon and missed the look of pure panic that accompanied his uncle's odd behavior.

"Okay," King said, after listening to Captain Shockey's

request. "I want to propose an alternate solution to this new turn of events. Since all you have at this time are pictures, couldn't you send copies to the Tulsa police department so Jesse can view them there? I don't think she's up to a trip back to St. Louis just yet."

King felt the breath leave Jesse's body as she stood stiffly beneath his hands, waiting anxiously for an answer to King's request.

"Great!" King said. "That's even better. And, Shockey," he said after a pause, "thanks."

He hung up the phone and turned to face his waiting audience.

"The St. Louis police, acting on a tip from a store clerk, think there's a good possibility that their suspect was caught on videotape as he entered and exited their store. They are sending a copy of the tape here for Jesse to see. You don't have to go back to St. Louis, sweetheart. You don't even have to go to Tulsa." He felt her relaxing against him. "It's going to be okay."

"Well, that's wonderful news, isn't it, Maggie." Duncan said loudly, and reached down to set his chair upright. "I've got to be running along now. Thanks for the meal. And, Jesse…it was good to see you again. Take care." He disappeared.

"Well," Maggie muttered. "Easy come, easy go." Then she turned and pointed at Jesse's drawn countenance. "And you, my dear, are due a rest. I don't want any argument. King…" she pointed again, including him in her orders. "See that she minds for a change."

Jesse stifled a sob, threw her arms around Maggie's neck, and kissed the mass of tiny wrinkles on her cheek.

"I love you," Jesse whispered in her ear. "And I almost always mind you." Then, ignoring Maggie's snort, she let King lead her from the kitchen.

"Are you all right?" he asked softly, as he watched carefully for any signs of undue stress. He didn't want another flashback episode.

"Yes," she answered. "Thanks for helping me. I don't know what made me freeze up. Hearing Captain Shockey's voice made everything come crashing back. For a few hours today, I almost let myself believe that everything was more or less back to normal. The phone call was just a bitter reminder of how I'd been fooling myself."

King struggled with the urge to kiss every tiny frown that lined her forehead and made the usual tilt of her mouth droop with despair. The more he was around her, the more he had to struggle to keep his hands off. He didn't know what was happening to him, but he knew whatever he was feeling for Jesse had nothing to do with pity.

"Would you mind running me a bath, King? I'm too sticky and dusty to sleep on anything but the back porch unless I clean up."

King made himself ignore the touch of her hand on his arm and refused to meet her eyes. He shoved his hands deep in the front pockets of his Levi's and muttered, more harshly than he meant to, "Just use my shower. I've got to get back to the stables. There's another buyer due soon and I don't want to be late."

He backed out of her doorway and had to force himself not to run away from the stunned look on her face. He knew he'd sounded harsh and impatient, but showing his true feelings at a time like this didn't seem prudent. *Hell!* he thought as he walked aimlessly toward the barns. *I don't even know what my true feelings are.*

Jesse felt quick tears fill her eyes at the harshness of his voice and his hasty exit. She'd known this "coming home" thing wouldn't work from the beginning. Unfortunately, for her own safety, she had no choice. No one saw her leaden steps, or the droop of her shoulders, as she pushed the door to his room open and quietly closed it behind her.

It was late afternoon when King looked up from the rail he'd been nailing firmly back on the corral fence by the barn. He saw a cloud of dust coming closer and closer down the long driveway and frowned. He pulled an already damp handkerchief from his hip pocket and halted the salty beads of moisture on his forehead just before they slipped into his eyes. Then his heart quickened, and his feet began to move toward the ranch house before his brain told him why they should. It was the familiar shape of the white, four-door sedan and the long antenna whip on the back of the vehicle identifying it as a police car that made the hair on the back of his neck stand on end. He realized it would be another sleepless night.

"Hell of a deal," the sheriff said, as he solemnly greeted King. He'd known the McCandless family for years, and held them in high regard. He had a daughter near Jesse LeBeau's age, and knew how he would feel in similar circumstances. He hadn't known of the attack on Jesse until he'd received the phone call and instructions from St. Louis. Later the same day, the special express package he now carried firmly in his grasp had arrived, and he knew what he had to do.

"How's she doing, King?" he asked.

"It's been rough on her, Sheriff. But she's a survivor. She had to be or she wouldn't be here today. I just hope to hell this is the man. I want the bastard behind bars."

The sheriff nodded in understanding and followed King into the house.

"Have a seat," King indicated with a sweep of his hand, as he ushered the sheriff into the den where a television and VCR rested on the shelf of the entertainment center. "Maggie will bring you something cool to drink. I've got to go find Jesse."

A quick word to Maggie produced the answer to Jesse's whereabouts, and he went toward the bedroom wing while Maggie fixed the promised refreshments.

King knocked softly on Jesse's door. Nothing and no one seemed to be stirring. He knocked again a bit sharper. After receiving no response again, he pushed the door open, expecting to see Jesse sound asleep on her bed.

The room was dark, the shades pulled against the glare of the hot July sun, and he blinked a moment, giving his eyes time to adjust to the change of light. When he was finally able to see, he frowned. The room was empty. King wiped a weary hand across his face and decided to freshen up before he went looking elsewhere. He didn't have far to go.

Jesse was curled up in the middle of his bed. Even in the deepest of sleeps, she hugged his pillow against her chest and face as King had held her against him the night before. The loose cotton shift she was wearing was twisted and bunched high above her knees and gave King much too much leg to try and ignore.

"God give me strength," he muttered softly, and walked over to the side of his bed. He felt his breath

catch in his throat and had to swallow twice before
he could say her name. Finally it came out in a husky
growl.

"Jesse, you better wake up, girl, or you'll never sleep
tonight."

His teasing voice penetrated her dreamless slumber, and she smiled into her pillow before rolling over
on her back, stretching lazily against the teak-colored
comforter on his bed.

"Hi," she said slowly, and a soft, gentle smile creased
her lips as she stretched her hands above her head, pulling her shift a tiny bit higher.

King didn't even know he'd moved. But he suddenly
found himself on his hands and knees, straddling her
bare legs as he braced his hands on the mattress on either side of her shoulders.

"You lost?" he whispered, and gently pushed a dark,
wavy lock of hair from her eyes.

Jesse forgot to breathe. Her eyes widened and she
knew her heartbeat could probably be heard in Tulsa.
Please don't let this be a dream, she thought, and refused to move a muscle for fear the dream would vanish.

"No, I'm not lost," she finally answered, and looked
long and hard, trying to read the expression in King's
eyes. "I'm never lost when I'm with you."

Her words hit him in the stomach with fist force.
"Oh, honey," he whispered, and leaned forward, gently
tasting the sleep-softened expression on her mouth.

The touch was fleeting. The taste just a hint of what
lay beneath him if he only dared take it. He raised up,
leaning back until he was sitting on the back of his
bootheels and felt as if he were being sucked up into
the vortex of a storm. He doubled his hands into fists

and pressed them fiercely into his knees to keep from touching her again. If he moved, he was afraid the next time he wouldn't stop with a taste of Jesse LeBeau.

Jesse closed her eyes as she saw him coming closer and was finally convinced she wasn't dreaming as King's lips met hers. It may as well have been a branding iron. The sensation was no less a mark of possession in her heart. Every inch of her skin felt alive, every beat of her heart in tune with his own. Just as she started to lock her hands behind his head and pull him closer, he moved away. Jesse had to force herself not to cry aloud at the pain she experienced, or at the distance once again between them.

She watched in wide-eyed silence while he seemed to struggle with some overwhelming emotion, and wondered as she watched, why he had so suddenly stopped. Finally she could no longer wait, and gently ventured a touch on his leg and hand.

"King?" she began, but was never allowed to finish.

Jesse's voice startled King. It brought him back to reality with a painful jolt.

"Hellfire," he muttered. "I completely forgot why I was looking for you."

He rolled off the bed with one motion, and stood silently, holding out his hand for her to join him.

Jesse blinked in confusion, and then reached upward. King gently pulled her from his bed.

"What?" she asked, trying to make sense of the mixed signals she was receiving from King. Then she couldn't mask the shudder as he spoke.

"The sheriff is here with the tape, Jesse. He needs for you to take a look at the suspect. Come on, honey. They're waiting for us in the den."

"Just give me a minute," she mumbled, and started toward her room. "Oh," she added, trying to blink away the tears in her eyes. "You didn't have to break the news to me so gently, King." Jesse had deciphered his actions as nothing more than gentle consideration. "I'm not going to fall apart again. I promise."

King stood in stunned silence and let Jesse walk away. He felt unable to move or speak. He didn't know whether to be glad or sorry that she'd misinterpreted what had just happened on his bed. Finally, all he could do was curse himself roundly and hurry to the waiting group in the den.

Chapter 6

Night sounds kept teasing at Jesse's concentration as she fought the sheet twisted around her legs. She'd spent every moment since her head touched the pillow trying uselessly to block out the image of the man on the videotape. Her mental state upon entering the den had not been the best, thanks to what had—or had not—transpired between her and King. She watched the first few frames of the video without actually seeing anything.

Suddenly the man in question had turned and the camera caught him full face. Jesse gasped loudly and took a few steps backward in shocked recognition.

"It's him," she cried, and turned around wildly in the partially darkened room, half expecting him to materialize.

King had been carefully watching her face for signs of recognition. He knew the moment Jesse connected with the image before her. He saw her panic and caught her backward progress before hysteria had time to set in.

Jesse was frantic. Her frightened blue eyes brimmed with unshed tears as she grabbed King by the forearms, trying to shake him into believing her.

"King! It's him. I know it! That's the man who tried to kill me!"

"Are you certain, Jesse?" the sheriff asked. "You couldn't possibly be mistaken?"

"No!" she shouted, and shrugged out of King's protective grasp. "I saw that man as 'up close and personal' as I've ever seen anyone in my life." Then her voice lost it's sarcasm and the adrenaline in her system began to subside. "You don't quickly forget the man who tries to kill you, Sheriff. You've got to tell Captain Shockey. They've got to find him! Find him quick! Then I'll be safe. Then he won't hurt me…or anyone else again."

She sank limply onto the arm of an easy chair and buried her face in her hands. "Turn off the tape. I can't look anymore."

"I'll make the call from here," the sheriff said, gesturing toward the phone on King's desk.

In a matter of minutes, after passing on Jesse's confirmation to the St. Louis police department, the sheriff also discovered they already had a name and address for the man in the video. They had simply been waiting for Jesse's verification before getting a search and arrest warrant. The phone call was short, the news something of a relief. Finally a name and a face had been added to the case.

"Wiley Lynch," Jesse muttered. "A man named Wiley Lynch tried to kill me." She turned away from her stance by the window and asked poignantly of no one in particular, "Why?"

Maggie looked away, unable to find words to help Jesse.

King started toward her but was stopped by a look from Jesse as she quickly turned away, unwilling to see the pity on their faces. She stumbled from the den.

Jesse heard the sheriff leave and heard Maggie's and King's hushed voices. She knew they were talking about her, and quietly slipped out the back door. She'd had enough turmoil for one day. She had let herself believe that King actually felt something for her. Then, after discovering he was only trying to break the news of the sheriff's arrival as gently as possible, her world had fallen the rest of the way in on top of her. The sight of the man who'd tried to kill her was the final touch to an otherwise horrendous day.

She sought solace in Turner's company and actually found herself enjoying the evening chores that she helped him finish. He didn't know what had just transpired, and treated her as if everything in her life was back to normal. It was just what she needed. King and Maggie hovered too much, although she knew it was done out of love. There was only so much sheltering possible. Part of this nightmare was for Jesse alone.

Getting through the awkward silences during dinner wore her out. Jesse quickly excused herself and left King and Maggie to themselves. She didn't want any help and she didn't want to talk to King. Finally she'd given up trying to outwait the sunrise and gone to bed. But sleep wouldn't come.

Jesse kicked the sheet from her legs in frustration and sat straight up in bed. She leaned over, turned on the table lamp, and ran her fingers roughly through her hair. She couldn't sleep and she wasn't seeking solace in King's arms, or in his bed, again. There was only so much she could endure, and the limit was imminent.

In a matter of seconds, she'd slipped out of her night shirt, into a pair of old gym shorts, and a tattered midriff-length T-shirt. She had to get some air. Maybe then her mind would slow down and let her get some rest. Jesse started toward the door and then stopped. She walked back to her closet and pulled out a pair of canvas deck shoes.

"Not at night, Jesse girl," she said to herself, unwilling to chance stepping on a scorpion or a snake, both common Oklahoma nightcrawlers.

She walked quickly and quietly through the house, sure of her direction and destination because of years and years of past residence, and because Maggie never rearranged furniture.

The screen door squeaked just a bit as Jesse slipped outside the back door. She stood on the porch, inspecting the moonlit yard and shadows for things that didn't belong there. Satisfied that all was as it should be, she stepped off the porch and sighed in satisfaction as a faint, but steady breeze lifted the hair from her neck.

King awoke, sudden and swift, and lay silently for several seconds, trying to determine what, if anything, had called him from his tangled dreams. He listened, half expecting to hear sounds coming from Jesse's room. And then, when another faint but familiar sound filtered into his room, he hit the floor running, grabbing pants and boots in succession.

Jesse's room was empty. He pulled on his jeans and boots, stopping only long enough to stomp first one boot and then the other on sockless feet. He recognized the sound he'd heard. It was the squeaky hinge on the back door. Where in hell was she going?

Jesse had been so withdrawn since the sheriff's arrival it was beginning to worry him. He feared that the stress she kept suffering would cause another flashback, or some other kind of set-back. He didn't know how to help her. She wouldn't talk and she wouldn't let him touch her.

But he feared it wasn't all due to the arrival of the tape. King also feared that his waking her and then actually crawling into bed with her had either frightened or repulsed her. He didn't know whether to say anything or just let it pass. If he made too much of the incident, it might embarrass Jesse further. The trouble was, King didn't quite know what to make of his actions either. He'd been more surprised than Jesse when he'd found himself on top of her. No wonder she wouldn't look him in the eye. He didn't know what she was thinking or feeling, but in some vague way he felt he'd let her down.

He hurried out the door and just caught a glimpse of her shirt before she disappeared around the curve in the driveway leading to the barns. He sighed with relief as he saw the direction she'd taken and knew where she was going. *Now,* he thought as he followed closely behind, *what in hell am I going to say to her when I get there?*

The barn was dark, light coming only from the doorways and the huge open window in the loft where hay was loaded and stored. The smells were comforting and familiar to Jesse. She leaned her head back against the wall and let old memories assail her. The faint but unmistakable scent of dry manure was nearly undetectable because of the fresher, aromatic bales of prairie hay, sacks of sweet feed for the horses, and the tang of well-oiled leather. Jesse knew exactly where she was, even with her eyes closed. She's spent the better portion of her life on the Double M with Andrew, then with King and the horses. A horse nickered softly, and Jesse smiled, knowing it probably sensed her presence. But it wasn't the stalls she was concerned with tonight. Tonight she wanted back a better, happier time in her life, and she knew where to find it. Up, above the earthen floor of the barn was a place—her place—and she needed desperately to find it—for the peace of mind it might still offer.

Jesse walked slowly but surely in the dim shadows towards the steps fastened firmly up the back wall of the barn leading to the loft. She knew that if there was a good breeze, it would come through that big opening above the ground floor where the bales of hay lay stacked like a grass castle. She grasped the steps firmly, wincing slightly as her hands closed over the rough wooden planks. Hand over hand she climbed, carefully placing her feet in firm positions as she advanced upward until her head poked through the opening in the loft floor. She paused, looked around in satisfaction, and pulled herself the rest of the way through the opening.

It was just as she remembered, a private world of hay, moonlight, and dreams that danced across the hand-hewn planks on the floor. Jesse took several tentative steps forward and then turned in delight in the center of a moonbeam as if it was a spotlight and she a soloist on a stage. She'd done it as a child and become lost in the fantasy, but tonight the fantasy wouldn't come. Jesse sighed and felt a deepening sadness as she watched the motes of dust she'd disturbed with her little dance settle back in place on the loft floor. Maybe it didn't work after you grew up. Maybe it didn't because you had to believe in dreams. It hurt too much when dreams die, and today Jesse had felt the last of her dreams of a life with King helplessly disappear. The pain was more than she could bear. She sank limply to the floor.

"What am I going to do?" Jesse whispered aloud, and then let the pain engulf her.

King heard her moving around on the floor above and stepped aside just as a tiny shower of dust and bits of hay filtered down through the cracks of the floor. He knew what a special place the old hayloft had been to Jesse in the past, and suspected she had run to it now as a place of refuge. He debated about the wiseness of disturbing her and started to leave, allowing her the much needed time for solace. It was the muffled sobs spilling into the silence of the night that stopped his exit. He couldn't make himself leave her like this. Quietly he climbed up the steps and was standing in the shadows of the loft before Jesse knew he was present.

Sobs shook her fragile shoulders as she sat curled in upon herself. A cloud passed over the face of the moon, then cleared, bathing Jesse in a translucent glow so bright she seemed to be carved from marble. King watched, worried and confused. This sadness was not fear. It was despair.

A sudden thought struck him dumb and kept his feet stationary as he admitted to himself that he was the only other thing that could have possibly upset her today. At last, he knew he was going to have to face Jesse and make her talk to him as they should have talked long ago. He spoke her name.

The sound of his voice above and behind her made Jesse jump to her feet in shock.

"What are you doing here?" she asked angrily.

"Please, Jesse," he pleaded, and started toward her with outstretched hands. "Don't cry, honey. Talk to me. Whatever it is, you know I'll help. Is it something I've done? If it is, just tell me now! I can't stand to hear you cry."

"Stop right there!" she ordered, quickly wiping away tear tracks with the palms of her hands. "I don't want you here." Her voice shook. She could barely speak above a whisper as she continued. "You can't take away all my problems, King. You can't change what has happened to me, and you can't solve everything that goes wrong in my life. Besides," she accused, "where were you for the last three years? I took care of myself, by myself. Where were you King? Where were you?"

Her accusation hit him full force, and left him standing speechless and oddly ashamed. Then, he took a deep breath and threw the accusation back in her face.

"Where was I, Jesse? Right where you left me, girl. And you tell me this…and you tell me now," he said with a husky growl. "Why did you leave the Double M, Jesse Rose? Why did *you* leave me?"

His question staggered her, and she turned quickly away, unwilling for him to see her shock, afraid he would read the truth in her eyes. She stumbled toward the stacked bales of hay and started to climb…upward… anywhere…just as long as she didn't have to face King with answers she wasn't prepared to give.

"No, you don't, girl," he growled, grabbing both her ankles before she could climb another bale. "Get down before you fall and hurt yourself."

Jesse stopped and turned slowly, knowing full well that King wouldn't loosen the firm grip he had on her legs. And so they stood, silently assessing each other's mood and determination.

"You're hurting my leg," Jesse finally said, and watched the pupils in his eyes darken and dilate with emotion. She knew he was angry at her. It wasn't often that he was met with the kind of resistance that Jesse kept throwing at him.

But it wasn't anger that Jesse saw in King's eyes. It was passion, the likes of which he'd never experienced. The feel of her skin beneath his hands was skyrocketing through his brain. He knew that her skin would be even softer in secret places.

He looked up at her tear-streaked face, and then down at his hands wrapped securely around her delicate ankles and shuddered, struggling with the urge to let both hands roam up the long, delicate curves of her calves, feel the little indentations he knew were behind her knees, and test the softness of the skin on her thighs. He couldn't get his mind off the thought of what lay above and beyond, and only steel-rimmed determination kept him from following his dreams. The sound of Jesse's voice drew him back, and he frowned at the disgruntled tone of her voice.

"Are you going to keep me here all night?" Jesse muttered, and struggled futilely with the iron grip he had on her legs.

I'd like to keep you here forever. King blinked, and wondered if he'd just said the thought aloud. He decided he had not, because Jesse seemed still to be waiting for an answer.

"Come here," he growled, and narrowed his eyes,

daring her to move farther away. He slowly released his hold on her legs and held up his hands. She still had to descend from the stacked hay and King grasped her firmly under her arms and lifted her down.

Jesse leaned forward, knowing that he would catch her, and let him take the full brunt of her weight. She felt the sides of her breasts brush against his outstretched hands, watched his jaw clinch and the planes of his face harden as the muscles tightened beneath his skin. Jesse felt breath leave her body as he pulled her down against his bare chest. Every angle, every bulge, every heartbeat was magnified, as her body slid slowly down his entire length. His feet were planted firmly, using the strength of his heavily muscled legs to brace them both. Jesse slid right down to the space between.

She couldn't resist the urge to test the feel of the muscles encasing the heart she heard beating against her cheek, and let her hand lightly caress the breadth of his chest before she drew her hand away, letting her sense of smell and sight continue to touch King in a way she dared not.

She saw a line of moisture beginning to form in the cleft in the middle of his chest before it gained in strength and became droplets that would slide toward his flat muscled stomach, past the brass buttons on the waist of his Levi's and beyond to...

She shuddered, then inhaled, trying to regain her composure, and was inundated by the scents of soap, a woodsy, pine fresh scent from his shampoo, the ever-present smell of good leather, and the other, more undefinable scent of King, the man. She felt his heartbeat, the pulse racing beneath her fingertips, and knew he was feeling something, if only anger. She wanted to

look at him…hoping…praying that she would see more
in his eyes than she felt under his skin. But she resisted
the urge and didn't move.

King forgot to breathe. When he did, it came out
in a low groan as she slid slowly, slowly against every
yearning, aching muscle in his body. When she put out
her hand and touched the heartbeat beneath his chest,
every muscle in his body tightened at once. He felt like
a piece of coiled steel and knew it would take only the
slightest touch from Jesse before he came unwound. She
looked so soft and fragile, but King knew the strength
and power in her. She would be a match for any man.
He felt her hesitate and begin to pull away. The sensation was actually painful.

"No," he whispered before he thought, and slid his
hands around her waist.

"What?" Jesse asked, her heart beginning to pound
louder and louder in her ears. She knew if she said more
it would be too much. Then he would know what she'd
spent years trying to hide. She couldn't endure his re-
buff. She wanted to love him—not this…and not in
anger. "No what?" she insisted.

"Don't go." It came out somewhere between an order
and a plea.

"Why?" she persisted, her heart racing with every
breath she took, her body trembling beneath the posses-
sive touch of his hands. "What *brotherly* advice could
you possibly have for me at this time of night, King
McCandless?"

Her voice taunted, the words teased, and King felt
himself losing the fragile grip he had on reality as their
sibling-like relationship was thrown back in his face.

"I'm not your damn brother," he growled, and pulled

her up against the aching fullness of his body. "And, what I want to give you, Jesse, has nothing to do with advice."

"Dear God," Jesse whispered, and felt her legs beginning to give way at the picture his words drew in her mind.

Jesse knew the power between them was growing, and she knew that if she didn't stop this, he'd take her here and now, on the dusty floor of the loft, and never forgive her for letting it happen.

"King," she whispered, allowing his hands to venture farther and farther upward beneath the worn softness of her shirt, to the warmth and fullness of the soft, bare skin on her breasts.

"What?" he muttered, barely able to focus and answer her. The sensation of holding Jesse in such an intimate way was driving everything but need farther and farther away.

"I asked you first," she said, and felt his attention catch at the strangeness of her words.

"Asked me what?" he repeated, lost at the turn of conversation.

"Where were you the last three years of my life? Why didn't you come to St. Louis, King? Duncan came… why didn't you?"

Her voice broke, and the sadness of her words overwhelmed him. It was only after he found himself standing alone in the pale beam of moonlight by the window, watching from above as Jesse slowly made her way back to the ranch house alone, that her last words soaked into his consciousness. And when they did, it was too late. Too late to call her back. Too late to stop the jealousy and rage that sent him to his knees.

* * *

A light gray, nondescript sedan pulled into the narrow tree-lined driveway, and then stopped suddenly as a young boy darted across the driveway on a bicycle.

The man behind the wheel of the car and the boy on the bicycle looked at each other in stunned silence, each thanking their own luck for the near miss. Then the man rolled the car window down and frowned as a fly darted in through the opening.

"Damn!" he muttered, knowing he'd ride with that fly the rest of the day. "Hey, kid!" he called. "You better be more careful. You could get hurt pulling a stunt like that." He took the wide-brimmed Stetson off his head and wiped at the sweaty place along his forehead where it fit too snugly. He needed a haircut. Then his hat wouldn't fit so tight.

The boy watched wide-eyed, and then remembered where he'd been going in all his excitement.

"Thanks, mister," he yelled. "I'll be careful." He pointed up the driveway in an excited tone of voice. "You going up there with the other cops?" he asked, deciding that this man was a sheriff because of his cowboy hat.

"What cops?" the man asked suddenly, looking around with extreme interest.

"The ones up at the drunk's place. They been there since daylight. But Petey, who lives in the house by me, says no one was inside when the cops busted down the door. I'm going to see. I want to be a cop when I grow up." He puffed out his skinny little chest with importance.

"Say, kid," the cowboy called, but got nowhere since

the boy began riding off on his bicycle, yelling over his shoulder as he pedaled away.

"I got to go. And I'm not supposed to talk to strangers."

Curses filled the car as the man slammed the hat back on his head and shut himself in with the fly. He backed carefully out of the drive and quickly drove away.

"At least he was gone," he muttered, and wondered what to do next. He knew he had to find Lynch before the police. Wiley Lynch would sell his mother for a drink. There was no way he'd keep his mouth shut about the LeBeau episode. He headed back to his motel to make some phone calls.

"This *was* the right place," one of the officers said to Captain Shockey. "We couldn't be more than six hours behind him." They were judging the time of Lynch's departure by the state of food scraps left on the kitchen table.

Shockey nodded his head, while his sharp little eyes scanned the place for something…anything…to confirm his growing suspicion that Lynch had not acted alone. He was a meticulous investigator, thorough in details that were not always popular with his staff, but invariably paid off in uncovering vital clues to his cases. Right now he had the men going through every piece of clothing, every piece of garbage inside and outside the house. Lynch had obviously not paid his city bills for several weeks and services, including garbage pickup, had been disconnected. There was quite an accumulation of the stuff, and it was hot as blazes in the house. It stunk to high heaven.

The search had been in progress for nearly an hour

when one of the officers outside the back door shouted. There was something…a tone of voice Shockey recognized, and his adrenaline began to flow. He'd known this would pay off. Lynch was obviously not a smart criminal. He'd already made two serious mistakes. He was bound to make others. The second mistake he'd made was getting caught on videotape after passing a hot check. The first was ever breaking into Jesse LeBeau's house.

"Captain," the officer said, barely suppressing the excitement in his voice as he carefully opened an old, stained duffle bag and pulled a crumpled piece of paper from inside the torn lining. He held the paper with something that looked like long tweezers to keep from damaging the evidence, and carefully handed it to Shockey.

"Look at what I found inside this bag. I wouldn't have even seen it, but I thought the stains on the bag might possibly be blood stains. I checked closer, and this was caught in the lining."

"I knew it," Shockey muttered, as he turned the paper for a better look. The carefully clipped letters from newspaper print spelled certain guilt for Wiley Lynch. "I knew there was more to this than a random break-in! This is a ransom note! He was trying to kidnap her. If she hadn't resisted…if she hadn't fought…" Then his train of thought sharpened and he focused again. "Good work!" he said. "Get this to the lab immediately, along with that bag. Now I know he must have had an accomplice. This note was constructed with precision and neatness. There's not a crooked cut on one of the pasted letters. Lynch couldn't cut his own throat right. Someone else put this together. Let's find out who."

Shockey hurried toward the front of the house, intent on getting back to headquarters. He had to notify McCandless about this new twist. The LeBeau woman could still be in danger. The kidnappers might try again.

A small boy on a bicycle was riding in and out among the parked police cars, obviously lost in a game of make-believe, imitating the sound of a siren, pedaling furiously in a fantasy chase.

"Hey, kid," Shockey called. "You better get on home. This is not a safe place for you to play."

"I'm gonna be a cop when I grow up," he announced, as Shockey started to get in his car.

"That's right?" Shockey asked, and looked again at the serious expression on the skinny little kid who was watching his every move.

"Yeah!" he cried. "You got a badge? Can I see it?"

"Yeah, sure, kid," Shockey agreed, and pulled the folded piece of well-worn leather from his pocket. It wasn't often he ran across a kid who liked cops. Usually it was just the opposite. He couldn't resist doing a little public relations work.

"Boy!" the kid whispered, as he ran a dirty little finger over the shiny metal shield with Shockey's identification number on it. "I told the sheriff down the driveway I was going to be a cop, but he didn't have no badge. Not like this he didn't."

"What sheriff, son? Why did you think he was a sheriff?" Something made Shockey pursue this odd little kid's rambling story further.

"Well, he was coming up here before he nearly ran me over…" He looked up cautiously, suddenly afraid that it would come out that he hadn't looked before he darted through the thick undergrowth. But nothing was said to correct him, and so he continued his story, tracing every curve and ridge in the silver badge as he talked. "And, I knew he was a sheriff cause he had a big hat like the ones on television."

Shockey's eyes narrowed. *Nothing odd in that,* he cautioned himself. "Go on," he urged the kid.

"Well, I told him you guys was already up here, and I guess he decided to leave, cause he rolled his car window up and drove away. That's all."

"What did he look like?" Shockey persisted. Something told him if he'd arrived thirty minutes later this morning, they might all have been saved further investigation.

"I don't know. Just a cowboy. I got to go now," he said, and reluctantly handed back the badge.

Shockey watched the kid leave, pedaling furiously as he darted between two of the parked black and whites. *Cowboy? What would Wiley Lynch be doing hanging out with a cowboy?*

He set the thought aside for the time being and hurried to his car. He had to make that phone call to Tulsa.

Chapter 7

"Where's Maggie?" Jesse asked breathlessly as she dashed through the kitchen door into the house.

King looked up and tried not to glare at Jesse's exuberance. Her hair was windblown, the black and white polka-dot tank top she was wearing was half in and half out of the tightest pair of blue jeans he'd ever seen anybody wear and breathe in at the same time. And, to make matters worse, she was barefoot.

"Where are your shoes?" he shouted, and then took a deep breath along with a calming gulp of lukewarm coffee.

He'd been dawdling over breakfast for half an hour, waiting for Jesse to appear, and then she came through the door like a Texas twister. It was obvious she'd been up and about far longer than he had.

"My shoes are on the porch," she answered calmly.

"They're dirty. I didn't want to track up the floor. Where's Maggie?" she repeated, refusing to let King's bad mood spoil the most perfect morning she'd had in years.

"In her room," King answered reluctantly, and felt his gut kick at the backside view of Jesse in those jeans, as she dashed through the kitchen toward Maggie's private rooms.

Jesse knocked once and then let herself in as she called out, "It's me."

"Come in, sweetheart," Maggie answered, as she came from the bathroom where she'd obviously been putting the finishing touches on hair and make-up. Her short, ample figure was corseted and bound with determination. Her long, gray braid was set higher on her head than usual, and her little round face was lightly decorated with blush and lipstick. She looked like an aging cherub. She also looked adorable.

Today was Friday. It was double coupon day at her favorite supermarket and she had a grocery list a mile long.

"Would you mind picking up my birth control pills?" Jesse asked, as she pulled a piece of paper from the pocket of her shirt. She'd been using them for years to correct a very painful and irregular period. "I called my doctor in St. Louis yesterday. He said he'd call in a prescription at this pharmacy." She handed the paper to Maggie.

"You still have to take these?" Maggie asked, and looked sharply at the expression on Jesse's face. She'd always known about Jesse's problem. She'd hoped time would correct it. Obviously it had not.

"Yep," Jesse grinned, leaned over and kissed Maggie's frown. "But don't worry. They haven't made a scarlet woman of me yet."

Jesse laughed at the horrified expression on Maggie's face, and then suddenly they were both chuckling loudly.

King heard the laughter and felt an awful tinge of jealousy. He couldn't make Jesse laugh. He hadn't even been able to make her smile since they'd come home. If anything, he'd only made matters worse. He was tired, miserable, and worried, and knew he couldn't take many more nights like last night. He hadn't slept a wink, knowing Jesse was across the hall. He'd thought all night long of Jesse and her statement that Duncan had come to visit her in St. Louis. He just couldn't get past the thoughts that jeered at his conscience during the long hours until dawn. Why did he care who went to see Jesse? He had made no effort to be one of the visitors. He had simply let time and Jesse slip through his fingers. He heard the women coming from Maggie's room, and yanked a piece of newspaper up in front of him.

Maggie rummaged through her purse, checking for all the necessary lists and coupons, then waved a casual goodbye in Jesse's direction before hurrying out the door. It was obvious Maggie was going to make a day of her trip to Tulsa.

Silence filled the kitchen, and Jesse debated with herself about trying to talk to an obviously disgruntled man. She wisely decided to keep her own counsel, and started back outside to retrieve her boots and get on with her plans for the day when something odd about King's newspaper caught her eye. Without saying a word, she walked over to King, gently peeking over the wall of newsprint he'd erected between them. Ignoring the furious glare he shot her way, she carefully took the paper, turned it over until it was right side up, handed it back, and watched with glee as a dark red flush crept up past the neck of his brown, plaid workshirt.

"Do you mind if I ride Tariq?" she asked.

King slammed the useless paper down on the kitchen table and stood with a jerk. He leaned over until they were practically nose to nose and growled.

"Looks to me like you already did."

Jesse shrugged self-consciously, knowing Tariq was King's favorite, and the one he usually chose to ride when out on the range. He was a large, white, spirited Arabian with an easy gait and Jesse preferred him to several of the smaller, more highly strung horses.

"Do you care?" she persisted, and tried to forget how angry King could get if pushed too far.

"Obviously what I think matters damn little to you, Jesse Rose. Do what you want...you always do." Then before she disappeared completely, he couldn't stop himself from grabbing her hands and turning the palms up for a careful inspection.

They looked healed. He knew they were getting stronger and stronger each day, by the amount of use she gave them, but his Arabian stallion was a big, high-spirited mount. He wasn't sure her grip was strong enough to handle him. He sighed, reluctantly dropped her hands, and looked up, unable to decipher the odd, almost expectant expression on her face.

"Be careful," he warned, and was saved from making a complete fool of himself by the phone's ring.

Jesse bolted out the door, grabbing her boots on the run.

By the time King hung up the phone and hurried toward the corrals, Jesse was long gone toward the big, shady pond more than half a mile away.

"Turner," King shouted, as he neared the corrals, new fear mixing with the old at what he'd just learned.

The phone call had been from St. Louis. King still had trouble assimilating Shockey's news. Kidnap Jesse? What in the world would someone hope to gain? She wasn't *that* wealthy. Almost everything she'd inherited was invested in a way that would take months, even years, to liquidate. She didn't *have* half a million dollars. And she had no family. Who would a kidnapper think was going to pay the ransom?

Then King stopped. He turned slowly as a terrible possibility entered his mind. He looked around at the land with new vision—McCandless land that went for miles and miles, the more than comfortable ranch house, the millions of dollars invested in the Arabians, the cattle, oil interests—and he knew who the kidnappers had targeted. It was King that would have come up with the money, and easily enough at that. The kidnappers had to know he would give everything he owned if it meant Jesse's well-being.

King shuddered, wiped a shaky hand across his eyes, and swallowed hard, pushing back the nausea that boiled inside him. Jesse was to have been the victim, but it was King's ransom they were after.

"Turner!" he called again, and breathed a sigh of relief as the older man came hobbling through the doorway of the hay barn. Turner waved at King, indicating his whereabouts.

"In here," he called, and waited as King came running.

"Jesse," he asked quickly. "Where?"

"Didn't say," Turner replied, and then frowned at the worried expression on his boss's face. "What's wrong?" he asked. "She'll be okay. That horse loves her...always did. He ain't gonna hurt Jesse."

"The police," King muttered, pointing toward the house.

He was back in McCandless shorthand, but Wil Turner was more than used to it. This was the second generation of McCandless he'd worked for.

"What about the police?" he asked, and led the way back inside, out of the hot sun and wind.

"Just called. Wasn't attempted murder. Jesse stopped a kidnap attempt. They also didn't get the sonofabitch. He's still out there."

"Well, I'll be," Turner muttered. "This does put a different light on things, don't it, boy? Well, now. I'm sure she can go for a horse ride here on the ranch and come to no outside harm."

King started to argue, but Turner's slow drawl and common sense were beginning to calm the fear and rage boiling inside.

"King," Turner continued. "Jesse went that direction." He pointed toward the hills, away from the roads and ranch house. "And the only way to get to Jesse there is to come through here. That is unless they come by helicopter, and it don't sound to me like them kidnappers is that smart. Just look what one little girl did to their plans. What do you say?" He waited for King's reply, and then added with a rueful pat on King's back, "I'll send one of the boys after her right now, if you think best. I know what she means to you...to all of us. But I also know how bad this has been on her. First time

I seen her really smile since she's been here was this morning when she got on that horse."

King paced between Turner and the barn door several times before jamming his hands in his pockets in frustration.

"Let her ride," he finally agreed. "But if she's not back by noon, we're going after her."

"You got it, Boss," Turner agreed, and wisely went back to work.

The sun was bright, almost white in the faded blue sky. Not one puny cloud dared to show face in the building heat. The dry, brown grass broke and scattered like dust as King's big stallion ran at an easy gallop. His nostrils flared, and his ears twitched at the sounds coming from his rider. He didn't know what laughter was, but he responded to Jesse's joy and pleasure. He tossed his head and nickered at a herd of Black Angus cattle trying to graze on the brittle pasture land.

Jesse felt the stallion's power beneath her, but knew no fear. He was nothing she couldn't handle. She trusted Tariq completely. King had trained him well.

"We're almost there, boy," Jesse said to the horse, and watched his ears twitch at the sound of her voice.

She knew when the horse smelled the water. His stride lengthened and he strained at the resistance of Jesse's grip on the reins. She didn't dare let Tariq have his head. Her hands weren't strong enough to hold on, or even stop him, if he was allowed to run at full gallop.

Finally they topped the gently rolling hill above the pond and stopped. Jesse let Tariq run the short distance to the water's edge where the bits of tender green grass still grew in sparse abandon. She dismounted and let the reins trail the ground without tying Tariq, knowing King trained his horses to stand in this manner. The big horse blew softly through his velvety nostrils, tossed his head, and then began to graze slowly along the edge of the pond and down the gentle slope of the dam.

Jesse didn't hesitate any longer. Looking around carefully just to assure herself that she was truly alone, she kicked off her boots and began to peel away her sweaty clothes, layer by layer.

The water was cooler than expected. She grimaced as a wave lapped at the calves of her legs, then slipped up past her thighs as she waded deeper. Finally she leaned forward and slipped silently into the inviting depths.

It was heaven. Jesse knew from past experience that absolutely nothing was as exhilarating as a skinny dip on a hot, summer day. She swam. She floated. She waded at waist deep level until the skin on her back began to draw and tingle. Jesse knew she'd probably stayed too long and would have a good sunburn, but it had been worth it.

She reluctantly waded from the water and dabbed at the quickly drying moisture on her bare body with the tail of her shirt. Once out of the water, Jesse felt compelled to hurry. She'd just pulled on her last boot and was trying in vain to run a comb through the wet tangles in her hair when she heard a loud commotion begin over the next hill.

She whistled for the horse, and breathed a sigh of relief as he quickly answered her call. He came at a trot, also disturbed by the noise coming from over the hill. He pranced sideways as Jesse tried to mount. She spoke sharply and yanked on the reins, bringing Tariq back into position, then swiftly mounted. The closer she rode toward the sounds, the more certain she knew what she would see when topping the hill.

Sure enough, something was after King's two-year-olds, and Jesse quickly spotted the trouble as the herd separated, running wildly away from a pack of dogs chasing at their heels. Jesse watched in frustration, unsure of what to do first, when one horse went to his knees. She gasped and started forward when the horse recovered as quickly as he'd fallen and continued his flight to safety.

She breathed a sigh of relief and decided to turn Tariq toward the ranch to go for help when a series of events took the decision out of her hands.

One of the young horses was cut off from the others with knife-sharp precision, the same way a pack of wolves would cut off their prey from a herd before closing in for the kill. The horse ran full tilt through some scrub brush, and plunged headlong in wild flight into a small pond used for watering the stock. Jesse saw the floating plastic milk jugs spaced out across one end of the pond just before the horse plunged headfirst among them. She knew instantly that someone's trespassing onto King's property was going to cause great harm.

"Oh, no!" she whispered, and leaned over Tariq's massive neck, clutching at his long, wiry mane. She saw the horse below begin to thrash wildly about in the water, unable to run any farther, unable to move. He'd been caught in a trot-line—a long fishing line that Turner called a lazy man's way to fish.

The line usually ran the length of a pond, or across the neck, and had large, barbed hooks set at spaced intervals and at certain depths, angling for the big ones that rested along the pond bottoms when weather was hot and dry. The jugs were used as floats and markers, so that the fisherman could pole a boat along and check each jug to see if the hook dangling below had catch waiting to be harvested.

Jesse knew that if she went back to the ranch, it would be too late to help the horse. The dogs would have killed it before any help could possibly arrive. Without thought for her own dangers, she urged Tariq down the hill. Her screams and shouts and the stallion's wild race toward them halted the dogs. They scattered, tails between their legs.

"Now what?" she asked herself, as she quickly dismounted and looked about, hoping the dogs had headed for easier game. "Okay," she said, talking aloud in an effort to calm the trapped and frightened horse. "It's just you and me, boy."

She took the rifle from the scabbard behind the saddle, wrapped the reins firmly around the saddle horn, knowing Tariq would run as long as they stayed in place, and slapped him sharply on the rump. She watched the big horse disappear over the hill, racing back toward the ranch, and hoped she'd done the right thing. She knew the quickest way to get help was to send Tariq home alone. She also knew it would probably scare King to death, but she felt she had no choice.

She checked the rifle, making certain that it was loaded, pumped a shell into the chamber and then took it off safety. She'd be ready if the dogs came back. She just hoped to God they didn't. She was a terrible shot.

"Okay, pretty boy," Jesse said in a low, calm voice and stepped slowly into the water. The water came over the tops of her boots, slowly seeping down inside as she waded toward the trapped horse. But she soon had to stop as her progress agitated the horse further. She had no choice but to stand knee-deep in the muddy water, waiting between the frightened animal and whatever came into her gun sights. Help had to come soon.

"Sweet Jesus!" Turner said under his breath, as he saw Tariq come racing down the hill toward the ranch. "King!" he shouted at the top of his voice, and ran to open the corral gate.

King had started to the house when he heard his foreman's frantic call. What he saw sent him back to the barns with a prayer in his heart and on his lips.

"She's been at the pond for sure," Turner said, pulling a bit of green grass caught in Tariq's bridle.

King nodded, yelled for two of the men to follow in the ranch truck, and headed for his horse. He grabbed the reins from Turner's hands and swung into the saddle. His feet never touched the stirrups as his long legs scissored the air. Dust boiled and grass flew from beneath the stallion's hooves as King turned him toward the pond and gave him his head.

He squinted his eyes against the blinding glare of the sun and dust flying through the air in the hot summer wind. Tariq's great speed and endurance proved itself worthy. He made it back to the pond in record time.

King pulled back sharply on the reins and felt the big horse sawing the bit back and forth in his mouth as he fought King for domination. King persisted, and the big stallion finally came to a halt under a withering blackjack tree beneath the pond dam.

He searched the entire area frantically, unable to see any sign of Jesse. His heartbeat was as erratic as Tariq's behavior, and his breath came in sharp, choking gasps.

He wanted to scream Jesse's name aloud, but couldn't find the air in his lungs to do so. Just as he caught his breath enough to call out, a gunshot echoed through the meadow. Tariq jumped nervously beneath him. Only the powerful grip of King's legs kept the horse from bucking him off. King spun the horse around in the general direction of the shot and kicked Tariq in the flanks. The great horse needed no further urging as he rapidly climbed the hill's steep incline.

"Somebody better hurry," Jesse muttered aloud, and tried to mask her panic as the dog pack reappeared on the crest of a hill above the small pond.

The dogs saw her and stopped, barked several times, but didn't move from their position.

Jesse knew it would only be a matter of time before they got up the nerve and try another run. Desperation and hunger made vicious animals out of man's best friends. These weren't naturally wild animals. They had once been someone's family pets. But they'd been dumped; abandoned by those they had trusted. Now they only had themselves to depend on. Unfortunately for Jesse, these kinds of animals had less fear of humans than a wolf or coyote would have, and Jesse knew she might not be able to stop their charge.

The young horse snorted wildly, also sensing the dogs' reappearance, and thrashed weakly, still frantically trying to free himself from the heavy nylon line and sharp hooks. But his movement only drove the hooks deeper and wrapped the line tighter. Finally, he stopped, trembling with shock and pain. Jesse's low, easy crooning broke through his panic, and he turned pain-filled brown eyes her way.

"Whoa, boy," Jesse whispered softly, and held out her hand, letting the horse smell her, touch her out-stretched fingers with the soft pelt of his nose. She just wanted to let him know she was still here. "It's gonna be okay, pretty fellow," she said softly, knowing the sound of her voice was somewhat calming to the animal. "King will come and he'll take good care of you… yes, he will." She couldn't stop the tears that came to her eyes as she continued. "He took care of me. He'll take good care of you, too."

Jesse winced as the sun beamed down on her already burning skin. She dipped her hand into the water, cupped it, and carried a handful to her hot, sweaty face, sighing with short-lived relief as she splashed the overheated areas with the muddy water. It dried almost instantly in the intense noon-day sun.

She shifted the gun to a different position. Her hands were cramping and aching, unused to gripping anything as tightly as she was holding the rifle. But she didn't flinch. She kept her gaze on the dog pack lining the hilltop.

Nearly twenty minutes passed with no movement from the dogs, and Jesse looked frantically down at her watch, shaking it to make certain it still worked. The watch was running all right, and so were the dogs as they came down the crest of the hill.

Jesse's heart stopped. Then she took a breath, glad the other horses were completely over on the other side of the meadow. She took aim. She knew if the horses had been anywhere close, she'd just as likely hit one of them as a dog. Suddenly she wished she'd paid more attention to Andrew McCandless's instructions, but it was too late now. The dogs were closer, running with an ominous silence, intent on one goal. Food! Woe be to anything, or anyone, who got in their way.

Jesse could hear the horse behind her begin to thrash around in the water. He, too, sensed impending doom, but she couldn't worry about that now.

She took a deep breath, shaky aim, and fired at the big shepherd dog in front of the pack, then pumped another shell into the chamber.

King took one swift look at the scene before him, reached behind his saddle for the rifle that was usually within hand's reach and then groaned. Jesse had it. With little urging, Tariq retraced his steps, and flew into the confusion below with wild abandon.

Jesse heard the hammer of horse hooves coming down the hill behind her, and prayed it was help arriving, because she'd missed her shot. She watched in fright as the dogs regrouped for another run. She heard King call her name, and turned with relief as he dismounted on the run and jumped into the water with both feet. His only goal was to reach Jesse before the dogs did.

King snatched the rifle from her hands, shooting three times in quick succession. A sharp yelp of pain sent the dogs running back up the hill, and King managed to hit two more and wound another before they disappeared.

He watched them run out of rifle range and knew how closely he'd come to arriving too late. He turned silently, took one long look at Jesse standing wet and bedraggled, threw the rifle onto the edge of the grass, and pulled her into his arms without saying a word.

She felt him shudder, and heard him swallow several times before he pulled back and tried to speak.

Jesse knew he was angry with her because his dark eyes literally took her apart at the seams. He kept running his hands carefully over her body, up and down her arms several times, as if assuring himself she was still in one piece.

He wasn't going to be able to stop the quick tears of relief that gathered in the corners of his eyes, but didn't care if Jesse saw them or not. He'd been too frightened to have time to get mad. Then when Jesse hugged him he couldn't have worked up a good mad if he'd tried.

Jesse sighed wearily and leaned into him, too tired and worn out to worry about him getting the wrong notion.

"What took you so long?" she asked, trying to lighten the situation between them.

King cupped her face in his hands. His thumbs lightly traced the sensual fullness of her lower lip, as he let himself absorb the fact that Jesse was truly safe. He felt the intensity of heat radiating from the skin beneath his fingers and sighed. What he was about to do would probably set their relationship back even further, but he couldn't help himself. He leaned closer, felt Jesse stiffen beneath his touch, and saw her lips opening. She never got the opportunity to voice her thoughts. King took her breath and thoughts away as he pulled her out of the water, off her feet, and into his arms.

He felt hot and cold at the same time, as the taste of Jesse's lips sent his sanity begging. He'd known, somewhere in the back of his mind, that this would happen—that touching her would be all fire, demanding and consuming, as she answered the pressure of his kiss with a claim of her own. He couldn't think past the softness of her mouth and the tiny, almost undetectable moans that he heard every time he started to let her go. King held her against his body and felt every muscle in him swell with wanting more. He needed to lay her down on the hard, dry grassland and lose himself in Jesse's sweet warmth. But this wasn't the time, or the place, to see how far Jesse would let him venture into uncharted territory. He drew back reluctantly and stroked her lips with his fingertip, needing the reassurance that she was still within reach and touch.

"Honey, you scared me to death," he said huskily.

Jesse blinked, trying to regain a measure of her equilibrium, but the sight of that beautiful, demanding mouth, just inches away, that had nearly driven her mad, and the touch of his fingers on her lips, made the world go around and around. Finally, the soft whinny of the injured horse brought them both back to their senses.

"The horse, King! It's caught in a trot-line. I couldn't get close enough to help him."

"Horse?" he muttered, slowly coming to his senses. Then realizing what she was trying to say, he turned toward the trapped animal. A string of muffled curses fell from his lips as he saw the young horse's plight. King whistled for Tariq, got a lariat from the saddle, and quickly made a makeshift bridle for the trapped animal. Walking slowly through the water, until he reached the horse's side, he carefully placed the bridle over the horse's head and ran his hands slowly down it's neck and mane.

"Let me see what you've done to yourself, fella," King said as he worked. He handed the other end of the rope to Jesse, then carefully began to trace the course of the nylon under the water.

The horse nickered, recognizing a familiar smell and voice, and stood quietly as King's husky growl and gentle hands quickly freed him from the trap of hooks and nylon cord. Several hooks were imbedded too deeply, and King refused to touch them. Instead he cut away the cord and left them for the vet to remove. He waded the length of the pond neck, angrily pulling at the remaining rope and floats and nearly had it cleared when the ranch pickup truck topped the hill above the pond and started down the steep incline.

As soon as the driver came near enough, King called out, sending them back to the ranch to get a horse trailer for the injured animal. He wasn't about to walk the young horse back in this heat after such a trauma.

He threw the trot-line to one side of the grass to be picked up by his ranch hands, and eyed the dead animals on the opposite hillside. The men could dispose of them, too. He wasn't leaving Jesse or the horse.

She sat on the grassy edge of the pond, pulling first one boot off and then the other, pouring a stream of muddy water from each. She watched King lead the horse from the water and tie the end of rope to a piece of deadwood. This horse was too young and frightened to trust it not to run.

"Couldn't wait to take off those boots, could you?" King teased softly, trying to ease the tension growing between them. And then he frowned, becoming aware of the increasing redness on Jesse's face and neck and down her bare arms. "Looks like you took off more than shoes today, didn't you, Jesse Rose? You're gonna be sick."

Jesse looked up and smiled shyly before passing off an answer with a shrug of her shoulders, then wincing at the movement.

King muttered under his breath. He unbuckled his belt and pulled his shirt tail out of his Levi's.

Jesse's eyes widened. She managed not to stare as she sneaked delighted peaks at King's impromptu strip-tease. Then she couldn't resist adding, "If we only had a little music while you took it all off."

King's eyes narrowed. He glared as he handed her his shirt and jammed his wide-brimmed Stetson on her head. "Shut up and put this on," he ordered.

Jesse needed no further urging. She sighed with relief as she covered her burning skin.

"We have to talk," King said, "but now's not the time. I've got to get you, and the horse, back to the ranch." Then his voice deepened and the ominous tone scared Jesse to death. "There's something you need to know."

Chapter 8

King watched the veterinarian drive away from the ranch and started into the house, only to be stopped by Maggie's arrival with a carload of groceries. By the time pleasantries had been exchanged and all the groceries carried inside, half an hour had elapsed. King was worried about how to tell Jesse that the attack had been more than attempted murder. He didn't know how to tell her about the kidnap attempt without frightening her more. Maggie's advice gave him no easy way out.

"Just tell her, King," Maggie ordered, as she moved about the kitchen, putting away the day's purchases. "She's tougher than you give her credit for. And, when you go," she added, pulling a small, white stack from her purse, "give her this."

King took the sack and started toward Jesse's bedroom. He was more than halfway there before it dawned on him that he was delivering a prescription. His first thought was that Jesse was sick and hadn't told him. But the flat, round shape inside the sack could only mean one thing. Feelings went off inside him like a four-alarm fire. He'd seen those packets inside more than one woman's purse. Birth control pills! *Why is the thought so upsetting to me?* he wondered. He knew it was modern, wise, accepted. But he didn't like the idea of Jesse needing to be protected. That meant being exposed to the possibilities of pregnancy, and that meant a man involved with Jesse in a manner that made his blood pressure rise. By the time he got to her room and walked through the open door, he'd worked himself into a silent rage.

Jesse heard footsteps, knew they were King's, and sighed miserably, as she lay face down on her bed, as near naked as possible yet still retaining a measure of decency. There wasn't an inch of skin anywhere on her body that had escaped sunburn, and she was in no mood for a lecture about her methods of saving horses.

"Maggie said to give this to you," he growled, and slammed the sack on the pillow beside her face.

Jesse took one look at the sack and smiled to herself in spite of her misery.

"Thank you very much," she said in an off-hand manner.

"I don't even know you, do I, Jess?" King muttered, trying to ignore all the bare skin in plain view. There wasn't much to the bath towel, nor much left to the imagination. Keeping Jesse covered was proving to be vital to King's sanity.

"You never paid any attention to me before, or you'd know I've taken these since I was seventeen. They cor-

rect a very miserable medical problem that's none of
your business," Jesse said sharply. She groped toward
the nightstand for her sunburn lotion. "If you want to
know about my current medical history, smart ass, try
rubbing some of this aloe vera gel on my back. My sunburn is killing me."

King turned as red as Jesse's back and was glad she
couldn't see his face. He yanked the tube of lotion from
her hands and sat down on the side of the bed, trying
to ignore Jesse's body. He was more disturbed by what
was not visible than by all the bare skin he *could* see,
and hesitated momentarily before he unscrewed the cap
on the tube of lotion. The gel was a cool, clear green
as King squeezed it into the palm of his hand. But it
quickly liquified into a clear film on Jesse's hot skin.

"Oooh," Jesse sighed with relief, as the aloe quickly
took away the miserable burning sensation. "That feels
wonderful," she mumbled into her pillow. King smiled
to himself and continued to apply the gel with long,
gentle strokes.

"I should have remembered. You have a great set of
hands," Jesse teased, and grinned into her pillow as she
felt his hands instantly cease movement on her body.

King practically vaulted from the bed, slapping the
plastic tube back on the nightstand within Jesse's reach.

"Damn you, Jesse," he muttered. "One of these days
you'll push me a little too far."

King was furious with himself as well as with Jesse.
He let her bait him and then fell neatly into every pot-
hole of the conversation with his usual lack of grace.

It had been difficult enough having to touch her in
such an intimate manner, knowing full well that he
wasn't going to do a thing about it. It didn't do his

blood pressure any good to know Jesse was as aware of it as he was.

"I need to talk to you," he said, pacing the floor by her bed, nervously trying to sort out his thoughts.

"Look," Jesse began. "I'm sorry I took a chance you didn't approve…"

"No," he interrupted. "It's not about that. It's about the phone call I got when you left to go riding." Then he couldn't stop from adding, "And decided to play Annie Oakley instead."

"What about the phone call?" she questioned, not liking the turn of conversation, or King's tone of voice. She carefully turned to face him. The bath towel slipped and she pulled it quickly back in place as she turned, then winced as the bedclothes collided with her tender skin.

"For God's sake!" King whispered, watching in horror as the towel covered even less of her front. He grabbed a soft, cotton robe from her closet, then practically threw it at her. "You're going to have to suffer for a few minutes. I've had just about all I can take from you today, Jesse Rose."

His words were short and clipped, his voice gruff, and Jesse knew he meant it. She grabbed at the robe and shrugged into the arms, belting it loosely around her while King stood with his back to her bed.

"You can turn around now," she said, and tried not to grin. The look on his face took the laughter out of her voice.

"Shockey called," King blurted out, unable to find any easy way to say this. "They found Lynch's house. But he'd already gone."

"Great," she muttered. Frustration and disappointment overwhelmed her. She combed her hands through her hair in short jerky movements. She'd been counting on his arrest. She was so tired of being afraid.

"That's not all they found," King said, and then squatted down beside Jesse's bed, needing eye contact to finish his message. "Honey…they also found a ransom note."

Her shock was obvious; her reaction extreme. She bounded from her bed as if trying to escape from the implications that went with King's announcement.

"Ransom? Why in God's name would someone try to kidnap me? I don't have any family. I don't have money like that…do I?"

She sounded so little…and so lost. King sighed, wanting to assure her, yet knowing that the rest of what he had to say was only going to make matters worse.

"No, baby," he said. His voice became even huskier as emotion thickened his speech. "I don't think they expected you to come up with the half million."

Jesse's mouth flew open, and she sank back on the edge of the bed with a stunned expression on her face.

"Half a million…dollars?" she asked, her eyes wide with shock. "They *are* crazy. I don't have anything like that."

Jesse watched King pace before the window, jam his hands in his pockets and then turn to face her, an almost defiant expression on his face.

"I don't think you were the target, Jesse. I think I was. You were just the victim."

Jesse heard the pain in his voice and saw the guilt on his face. She realized with startling clarity that he was probably correct. But she wouldn't allow the guilt he stood ready to accept.

"None of this is your fault. No more than it's anyone's fault to be a victim of any crime. Greed is what's at fault, King. Not you. And not me."

King let out a slow, uneasy breath. Gratitude for her understanding made him feel a bit easier, yet he was uncertain if Jesse had grasped the full implication of the news. He walked over to the bed and sat down beside her. He separated her hands from their tight wad in her lap and lifted first one and then the other up to the light. They were very nearly well. All that remained was the tiny network of red lines that faded more with each passing day.

"You know what this means now, don't you?"

Jesse looked up at the expression of concern on his face and something...some other undefinable look that he kept trying to hide. She restrained from touching him, letting her eyes caress him instead.

His dark hair lay in tousled abandon. There was a piece of grass stuck in the collar of his shirt, and Jesse watched his dark eyes follow her every movement.

"Yes," she finally answered, then slowly pulled her hands away. "It means this is not over. That they could try again."

She couldn't disguise the tremble in her voice, nor the tears that sprang to her eyes. She also knew that she might not be as lucky if a next time ever came. She wanted to cry. *It wasn't fair, and it was no one's fault.*

"I think I want to be alone now," she whispered, refusing to look at the hurt and rejection she knew was on his face.

"I'll leave you for now, Jesse Rose," King whispered as he leaned over and brushed the top of her head with his lips. "But you'll never be alone. Not as long as I'm alive. Remember that."

She let the tears spill over and the sadness come as King left her room. Was this nightmare ever going to end?

Lynch was gone all right. The man slammed the phone down with a furious jerk and began to pack. Lynch had disappeared from the house. He was not in the city. He was gone from the state. His sources were good; the information solid. He had a terrible, sinking feeling that he knew where Lynch was headed.

He looked at himself in the dresser mirror, saw the peeling paint and the crack on the wall behind him, but couldn't look at the face staring back in accusation. How had he let this happen? It had gotten out of hand so quickly. All he'd wanted was what was due him. No one was to have gotten hurt. He knew he was on a downhill road, and the only thing waiting for him at the bottom was disaster…unless…unless he could find Wiley Lynch soon.

He grabbed his suitcase and headed for the door. Now there was only one place left for him to go. He had to go back, to the beginning.

"Thanks for coming," Duncan said, as he greeted King. "Come in, please. I've just returned from a short trip. The place is messy."

King frowned as he followed his uncle into the room. He hated these visits. He was always ill at ease around Duncan. And the only time he received an invitation to visit was when Duncan was short of money.

He watched with a forced lack of expression as Duncan sauntered over to a wet bar opposite the living room window and poured himself a drink. He shook his head, refusing Duncan's offer to pour him a glass.

Duncan shrugged and downed the shot of whiskey neat, fortifying himself for what lay ahead. He walked toward the window of his Tulsa high-rise apartment and looked over the skyline of the metropolis.

The apartment was the epitome of good living and as usual, way beyond Duncan's means. But he liked to live fast and high, and this was the best way to go.

"How much do you want?" King drawled, anxious to get the meeting over with.

Duncan turned his head sharply and swallowed the angry retort that bubbled into his mouth. He supposed he deserved that.

"I don't want any money. I want to know how Jesse's doing."

Duncan's refusal of money left King speechless. That was a first! He narrowed his eyes and a muscle in his jaw clinched and jerked before he answered.

"She's fine. Recovering from a sunburn. Maggie said she told you about the ransom note." King watched a strange, dark look come and go on Duncan's face.

"Yes, she told me," Duncan answered, and then turned his back to King as he continued. "You've got to be careful. He may try again."

King watched Duncan's strange, evasive behavior, and felt a sense of confusion at everything going on around him. He'd had just about all of the odd little answers and hints he was going to take. He took a deep breath and threw his suspicions out into the room between them.

"Duncan, why is Jesse afraid of you? What's between

you? She told me you visited her in St. Louis," King accused. "What the hell did you do to her?"

"Do? I didn't *do* anything. And of course I visited her. Just because she moved didn't mean she died."

Duncan was smooth. His manner was cool. He didn't know what Jesse had told King, but he doubted she'd said much. Knowing his nephew as he did, if she'd told the whole story, he would have been greeted with a punch in the nose. King was so single-minded about everything.

Duncan had learned long ago to persuade, not provoke. Still, he'd never been able to achieve the measure of success that seemed to fall into King's lap. He failed to see that King worked long and hard to earn the respect and rewards that Duncan felt were his due by virtue of birth alone. They were so alike, and yet so different.

Duncan cast a sly, sideways glance at King's stiff, defensive attitude and couldn't resist a final dig.

"Didn't you ever visit Jesse? She was very lonesome."

King looked long and hard at his uncle's bland expression. He didn't believe anything that came out of his mouth.

"I asked you a question," King whispered. "What happened in St. Louis? Why is Jesse afraid of you?"

Duncan glanced quickly at King, and saw him waiting for an answer with an expression on his face that made Duncan very nervous.

"She has nothing to be afraid of," he said quietly, and walked toward King. "Not from me…not anymore."

"What do you mean…anymore?" King asked with a husky growl, and took a step forward.

Duncan waved him angrily away, his voice rising to a shout.

"The person Jesse needs to fear is still out there. We have to make certain he doesn't get close to her again. What are you doing to protect her?" Duncan's voice was hard. His demeanor startled King. He answered with no reservations.

"She's never alone," he said. "The men have seen the video of Lynch. They have the police sketch posted in the bunk house, but Jesse doesn't know it. And I don't want her to. Please don't say anything. I don't want her to feel like she's under guard."

Duncan nodded and walked toward his front door, carrying the refilled glass of whiskey in his hand.

"Well, King, thanks for coming. I just couldn't help worrying, and I felt uncomfortable talking about it in front of Jesse. If there is anything I can do to help, don't hesitate to ask. I will do anything you need." Then a strange, sad expression filled his eyes and he took a big gulp of whiskey. "I can do anything except come up with the half million."

King tried to hide his surprise. This odd visit was coming to a very unusual end.

Duncan slapped him jovially on the back as he left.

"Catch you on the offer of a loan some other time, nephew. I'm never going to be this noble again."

The two men stared silently at each other for what seemed an eternity, each looking at a mirror image of the other and at…what might have been.

Finally King held out his hand and caught Duncan off guard. Duncan gulped hard, swallowed a big knot of misery he'd been carrying around forever, and muttered as he and King shook hands, "See you around, boy…and take good care of Jesse."

The door shut in King's face and left him standing in the apartment hallway, feeling as if Duncan's farewell had been final.

King couldn't sleep. His conversation with Duncan kept replaying in his mind. He'd suspected something had happened between Jesse and Duncan. Now, he was convinced of it. Why wouldn't Jesse talk to him? She used to talk to him constantly about everything. The niggling truth answered his own questions. She used to talk to him, but he suspected he rarely listened. He hadn't listened. He hadn't noticed Jesse changing and growing. He'd let her grow up and away, and never realized what he'd had until it was gone. Then he hadn't known how to get it…or her…back.

"King?" Jesse's soft voice startled him. He turned over in bed. She was silhouetted in the doorway of his bedroom.

"What is it, honey?" he asked softly, but suspected he already knew the answer.

"I can't sleep," she whispered. "My sunburn hurts and I can't get Lynch's face to go away."

The catch in her voice was his undoing.

"You want to stay here for a while? The bed is big. I won't bump your sunburn, but I can't promise not to snore."

Jesse tried to stifle a sob. King's attempt to lighten her mood only made it worse.

King was out of bed in an instant. Sunburn or not, he needed to hold her, satisfy himself that she was here and safe. Twice today he had realized how close he'd come to losing Jesse. It was only this morning, but it seemed a lifetime ago, that Tariq had come tearing down the hill toward home with an empty saddle. He couldn't forget the complete and sudden sense of loss that had encompassed him. Then, after his visit to Duncan, he'd realized how far away he'd let her slide without even realizing it. He didn't know how he was going to do it, but he wanted Jesse back.

"Come here, honey," he whispered, carefully hugging her against his bare chest.

He felt every curve and pulse point of Jesse against his skin and through the lightweight fabric of his pajama bottoms.

A fierce surge of desire, so intense it made his legs shake, swept over him. He stepped away, aware that if he remained too close, Jesse would also feel his need. He knew he couldn't get back in his bed with Jesse ever again and not make love to her. There was no nobility left in him, no more restraint.

"Lie down, Jess," he growled in a husky whisper. "I'll go get your sunburn stuff. Maybe that will help a little. I can't do anything about Lynch except promise you with my life that he won't get close to you again."

"Okay," Jesse agreed, and reluctantly let him go. Sunburn or not, she'd felt his body harden and knew he felt something for her, if only lust by proximity. Then she felt ashamed. She was actually beginning to consider taking him on any terms that he'd offer.

King sat in an overstuffed arm chair by his bedroom window and watched Jesse sleep. The sunburn was making her restless, but at least she was getting some rest. King knew there was none for him. Not while Jesse lay on his bed alone. He ached with the need to curl around her, hold her against him all through the night, then make love as the first rays of sunshine came through his windows.

He wanted to watch the look of pleasure come in her eyes as he gave her all he had to give. But he didn't move…and he watched alone as the first ray of sunshine appeared, heralding another dry, hot day.

Chapter 9

The hot wind and sun were merciless. The wind teased like a woman, blowing intermittently against King's bare brown back just enough to make him pray for the next gust to hit the rivulets of moisture that ran in a steady stream into the waistband of his Levi's. But the breeze was weak, and the temperature high, and King ended the injured horse's workout much sooner than normal. He walked him to an empty stall and turned him over to one of the ranch hands to cool down and groom.

It had been nearly a week since the incident with the dog pack. The horse was virtually healed. Although Jesse and the horse seemed to have suffered no lasting effects from the episode, King still woke up in a cold sweat from the nightmares.

He took off his Stetson, slapped it sharply against his

thigh to knock off the dust, and walked over to the long, metal horse trough inside the corral. The water that first gushed from the tap was hot and slightly muddy. King stood, letting it run for a moment until it cooled and cleared. Then he leaned down and let his mouth meet the heavy stream of cool well water. He sucked greedily, replacing body fluids that the extreme heat had sapped. When his thirst was quenched, he leaned down farther and let the water run full force over his head and down the back of his neck.

Jesse lay on her stomach on a loose pile of hay and watched King as he worked. She remained unnoticed from her vantage point in the open loft window and ignored a persistent horsefly that kept dive bombing her bare legs. Her sunburn had turned a nut brown. She was nicely camouflaged in the hay and knew she'd remain undetected unless she moved or called aloud. She had no intention of doing either. The view of King from the loft was too splendid to disturb.

Jesse watched the play of muscles ripple across King's bare shoulders as he worked the horse's lead. Sweat ran down his neck and onto the powerful muscles of his chest, making them shine like polished wood. His jeans were dark, splotched by the patches of perspiration that came through the fabric and molded to his long, powerful legs with damp affection. His boots were dust-coated, completely covered by the dry, dusty fog that hovered ankle high on the floor of the corral.

She knew his strength of mind, and strength of character, but it was his sheer physical strength that drew her attention today.

Years and years of long hours and hard work had honed his body to solid bone and muscle. There wasn't a soft, weak spot anywhere. The only thing soft about King McCandless was the spot in his heart reserved for Jesse. She knew it was there, but she wanted more than compassion and affection from the man below her. She wanted pure, unadulterated love and passion.

Jesse shivered, watching as King leaned down to the running water to quench his thirst. She watched his mouth open to drink greedily from the tap, remembering the last time she'd felt that mouth on her own lips, and wished she could trade places with the water. She could quench more than thirst if he'd only let her. The kiss he'd given her at the pond had not been compassionate, nor had it been affectionate. It had been, in Jesse's estimation, devastating. But King had turned off as suddenly as he'd turned on, and Jesse hadn't been able to find the switch to his emotions again.

She sighed with frustration, and watched King turn the water off, jam his hat back on his head, and disappear into the shady depths of the barn. She lay unmoving, trying to follow his path with her ears instead of her eyes. She listened closely to him issuing instructions about ranch business and then laughing aloud at something someone said in return. She couldn't hear what they said, but she could easily hear the joy and pleasure in his voice. She sighed and wondered if she'd ever be able to make him laugh like that. It seemed all he did nowadays was frown at her, or yell when he caught her barefoot.

The horsefly darted one last time at the bare space between her shirt top and the waistband of her shorts. It flew away into the sunshine when her hand swatted at it and came much too close.

King saw the top of Jesse's head just above the pile

of loose hay near the loft window as he leaned down to get a drink. It startled him, and he wondered, as he quenched his thirst, how long she'd been watching him...and why? He carried on, seemingly unaware of her presence, and then walked nonchalantly into the barn. He stood at the foot of the steps leading to the loft and, when he heard no sound or movement, pulled off his boots, hung his hat on a nail by the steps, and quickly and quietly climbed into her hideaway.

It was suddenly too quiet below, and Jesse held her breath, listening...listening.

She jumped when she heard the sound of his voice right behind her, and guiltily rolled over in the hay. King was standing at her feet with a look on his face that stopped her heart. She let her gaze run from the still-damp hair, quickly past those knowing dark eyes, to the droplets of water caught in the hair on his chest. Her look lingered longer than necessary on the tight, damp Levi's that almost lovingly cupped and molded every interesting bulge and muscle, and finally stopped her perusal at his sock-clad feet.

"You cheated," she muttered. "Where are your boots?"

King had intended to tease, but the thought disappeared with the inclination when Jesse rolled over on her back and took him apart at the seams with those secretive, big blue eyes.

Her shirt caught under her and pulled tightly across her breasts, molding them in an invitation he found hard to resist. He closed his eyes for a moment, trying to block out the image before him, and knew that resistance wasn't the only thing getting hard. It was no use. This feeling for Jesse wasn't going to go away.

He knelt down, straddling her bare, tanned legs, and braced himself above her.

Jesse felt an energy between them spark to life, and heard his heartbeat stop and then pick up rhythm with her own. She started to speak, and then forgot what she was going to say as a tiny drop of moisture clinging to his thick, dark lashes finally fell, hurtling downward to land at the corner of Jesse's mouth.

King watched, fascinated, as the droplet paused. Then, as it started to slide down the delicate curve of her chin, he lowered himself to meet it and caught the droplet with his mouth.

Jesse felt his tongue along the edge of her chin. She closed her eyes as his teeth nipped at the pale, blue vein in her neck that pulsed beneath her tan. Her hands slid up the length of his arms, feeling the muscles jumping with strain. He held himself poised above her, and Jesse felt the magic between them begin to expand.

King was watching her closely, anxious for a reaction to what he'd done.

"What are you doing?" Jesse whispered.

King watched the light flare in her eyes, and felt her heartbeat pounding beneath his chest. It was moments before he could speak. He wanted more…much more… than that tiny taste of Jesse.

"I don't know, Jesse Rose," he answered huskily. "But I do know this…"

"What?" she asked, her eyes widening as she saw his head dipping closer and closer.

"I'm going to do it again."

The sun and the heat, the sound of men's voices, and the horses nickering back and forth in the stalls below disappeared in one blinding flash as King took

Jesse in his arms. There was nothing…nothing but the smell, and the taste, and the touch of Jesse filling him. He shook with a need so powerful, so overwhelming, he couldn't think. All he could do was take. Take what he'd thought of, what he'd dreamed of, ever since he'd brought Jesse home.

Her body was soft beneath him, and it made him ache with bone-jarring need. Her arms slid around his waist, pulling him closer and closer into a waiting heat.

King groaned, then reluctantly pulled away. He grabbed her hands and propped himself above her, holding her hands trapped between their bodies.

Emptiness overwhelmed her. He'd done it again. He'd let her go. Tears pooled in her eyes and slipped silently out of the corners as Jesse let desolation overwhelm her. Now, he was either going to feel sorry for her or make excuses for what had just occurred. Either way, she didn't want to hear him shut her out.

"Honey," he whispered, and bent down, quickly kissing each of her hands held trapped against his chest. "I still don't know what's happening between us. But if I don't stop now, I know what will. I don't want ever to do anything to hurt you…you know that."

He watched as Jesse slowly nodded, then pulled her hands away from his grasp. He felt her fingers trace across his lips, and caught them gently with his teeth before they ventured farther.

Jesse gasped as his teeth pressed down just enough to restrain, and felt a quickening in the pit of her stomach answer the pressure of his teeth.

"King?" Jesse asked, her voice thick and heavy with emotion.

"What, baby?"

"If you stop now, will you promise me something?" she asked, and fixed him with an uncompromising stare.

"Anything," he answered, and pressed a kiss of promise on the tilt of her nose.

"Will you promise that if we do this again…the next time…you won't stop?"

"Sweet Jesus, Jesse Rose," King groaned, and rolled over in the hay, taking Jesse with him until she was sprawled full length on top of his chest and down his legs. He wrapped her in a fierce hug, and buried his face in the curve of her neck.

"Do you know what you're doing to my will power?" he asked.

"Robbing you of it, I hope," she answered, and felt the surge of his need beneath her.

A car honked in the distance and King jumped, suddenly remembering the buyer who'd promised to come by today.

"You take more than that, girl," he muttered, as he dumped her unceremoniously in the pile of hay and struggled to his feet. "I lost my memory and good sense, too."

He turned as he started down the steps, and gave Jesse a look that made her hot and cold all over.

"Jesse," he called softly.

She looked up at the banked fire in his eyes and held her breath.

"About that promise I made…"

She waited. The horn blared again, insistently disturbing the silence between them as King whispered.

"I never broke a promise to you yet, Jesse Rose. I'm not about to now. Next time, honey…next time."

King was gone. Jesse fell back into the hay and lay

quietly, staring blindly at a broken spider web high above her head in the rafters. *He said "next time."* She couldn't stop the silly smile that appeared on her face anymore than the heart-wrenching thought that followed. *Now I know he wants me. But will it be love?*

Jesse sat quietly in the living room, staring blindly at the television. If she pretended to be absorbed in the program, maybe Maggie would quit casting those anxious looks her way and King would stop fidgeting.

She'd hardly touched a bite of her evening meal, pleading loss of appetite due to the heat. The excuse hadn't washed with King or Maggie, but they'd allowed it to pass unchallenged.

Jesse was angry and overwhelmed with a feeling of helplessness unlike any she'd ever known. Just when it seemed a portion of her life might be coming together, another piece would begin to unravel.

The principal of her school in St. Louis had called. It had taken him all of three minutes to destroy what was left of Jesse's world. He'd related everyone's good wishes for her safety and health in the same breath he'd told her he'd hired a substitute teacher for her classes. Just, of course, until her "problem" was solved. The police had advised him of a possible kidnap attempt at school should her case not be solved before the semester started. It hadn't taken him long to realize what he had to do for Miss LeBeau's welfare, as well as the welfare of the children. Of course, she wasn't being replaced permanently; this was only until everything was settled.

The worry Jesse had about his statement was that her problem might never be solved. Where did that leave her? Now she had a house she couldn't go back to, a job at which she wasn't welcome, and a man who had tried to kidnap her still at large. And, here she was, hiding in the very place she'd sworn never to come back to.

"Excuse me," she muttered, looking at neither King nor Maggie, as she bolted for the front door.

They watched her go, looking helplessly at each other for guidance. Finally, at Maggie's insistence, King followed her outside into the summer night.

The night sky was unusually dark, although the moon was almost full. But Jesse didn't notice the absence of stars or the accumulation of clouds slowly gathering in the south. She was too full of herself, certain that her life had taken a downward spiral she'd never be able to stop.

A chorus of bullfrogs competed with the cricket string quartet for dominance in the night symphony. Somewhere off to the west, a coyote's single yip preceded an entire choir of howls and calls that sent a shiver down Jesse's spine. They echoed the loneliness and emptiness she felt inside. She shuddered as the coyote chorus ended as abruptly as it had begun. A few fireflies fluttered in the black space above the horizon, flickering like earthbound stars and just as hard to catch.

Jesse walked out into the enveloping darkness and let it close around her, drawing her into its secrets like a moth drawn to the light. Scents assailed her senses from every direction, and Jesse knew she could have pinpointed her location at any given moment.

The honeysuckle, heavy with sweet-smelling blossom, reclined over and along the fence around the front yard and blended its tantalizing odor with the sharper, astringent tang of towering junipers. The air was still, and only the soft, gentle night sounds intruded into Jesse's thoughts. She felt anxiety slowly seeping away. She put her hands out in front of her and when they connected with a rough, grainy textured barrier, she climbed upon the top rail of the wooden fence and took a precarious seat.

The front door slammed loudly, telling her someone had followed her into the darkness. Probably King. Her suspicions were correct and she heard his voice call out to her.

"Here," she answered, then heard him coming her way.

"What, Jesse?" King asked with his usual abbreviated speech.

"Everything is out of control," she finally answered. Her voice was barely above a whisper. She was afraid to say it too loud. What was left of her world might come apart, too.

King didn't respond, but stood silently, allowing her time to collect her thoughts before she continued.

"As of today, I no longer have a job." Then she added, "At least until this is over, which may be never. I have a house I can't go back to. I have nothing."

"Yes, you do," King answered in his deep, husky growl. "You have Maggie…and Turner…and me." Then he grudgingly added, "Hell, you even have Duncan worrying about you, and I've never known him to care about anything but himself."

He heard her sharp, indrawn breath and then nothing. No answer, no response at all to the mention of Duncan's name. King had finally had enough of this silence.

"That does it," he mumbled.

He walked so close to Jesse she could hear him

breathing, yet she could barely distinguish the outline of his shoulders in the darkness.

"Jesse, I want to know…and don't lie to me. I'll know if you do. What's between you and Duncan?"

For the longest time Jesse held her silence and then, finally, she let out a long, defeated sigh, and shifted to a less precarious position on the fence.

"Nothing," she answered quietly, and then added, "at least not now."

King's heart skipped a beat. He wasn't so sure he wanted to hear the rest of her answer, but something made him persist.

"Sometimes you seem to be afraid of him. Has he… has he hurt you, or done something that made you uneasy? If he did…"

"No! No!" Jesse interrupted. "It's just, he wanted more from me than I was willing to give."

"Like what?" King asked harshly, imagining the worst. But Jesse's answer rendered him speechless.

"He wanted to marry me."

"My God!" King finally muttered. "Where the hell was I when all this was going on?" But he knew the answer to his own question before he'd finished asking it. This had all taken place after Jesse went to St. Louis.

"Do you love him?" King finally managed to ask, and felt his stomach begin to draw when she hesitated.

"No. But once, for about five minutes, I considered trying," Jesse answered sadly.

"Were you that lonely, Jess?" King muttered. "Why would you *try* to love?"

It was the longest time before Jesse spoke. She debated with herself about even answering him and then decided it was time he knew.

"I suppose…because he looked like you."

King couldn't think. He couldn't speak. He couldn't have taken a step if his life depended on it. Finally, he managed to speak past the huge, aching knot in his throat.

"Why, if he looked like me, couldn't you love him?"

Her answer nearly broke his heart.

"Because he wasn't you."

King was devastated. Everything about her demeanor told him that he'd just lost something very precious without even knowing it had been there for the taking. It hurt to think. It hurt to talk. But he had to know.

"Jesse, am I the reason you left the Double M three years ago?"

"Yes," she answered sharply. She was angry with herself for being so weak where he was concerned. Angry because King was so blind where she was concerned. "And now, it looks like you're the reason I had to come home, doesn't it? Makes you wonder just how cruel life can be with the little jokes it plays on us from time to time."

She took a deep, shaky breath and then continued.

"Just don't expect me to thank you for making me tell you what you should have known, King McCandless. It's obvious the level of caring between us is not a balanced proposition. Just as soon as this nightmare is over, and I have to believe it soon will be, I'll be out of your life. Everything will be back to normal. So please," she said with a muffled sob, "don't let my presence put any pressure on you. I don't expect anything from you… or Duncan. I've had just about all I can take from McCandless men to last me a lifetime."

She slipped off the fence rail and went past him so quietly he didn't even realize she was gone. Not until he reached out did he discover that there was nothing in his arms but empty darkness.

The clouds belched a long, low, faraway rumble. King looked up at the dark, moonless sky in surprise. Maybe it was finally going to rain. He knew the thunder was far away and moving in the wrong direction to help this dry, dusty land tonight. He also knew it would take more than rain to put his relationship with Jesse back together. He wanted to follow her into the house, finish what they'd started in the hayloft and fill the huge, aching hole she'd just punched in his heart. But now, because he'd been so blind, and made her tell more than she'd obviously intended, she'd resent anything he said or did. She was going to think it was pity, or assuaging the guilt he'd already admitted he felt because of the attempted kidnapping. They hurt her to get to him. Then he'd hurt her by being so damn blind. Jesse was right. The McCandless men had really let her down.

"Dear Lord," King whispered to the starless sky, "help me find a way to make Jesse believe. I can't let her go again. If I do, I'll lose her for sure this time... and I think it would kill me."

He bowed his head and turned, walking back into the house to shut out the night, and to shut himself in with loneliness and pain.

Chapter 10

The wind whipped over the rolling hills, flattening the dry grass and weeds to the ground. It whipped Jesse's hair into her mouth and eyes with stinging gusts. She covered her mouth and nose to keep from inhaling the clouds of red dust that hurtled wildly through the air.

"Hurry!" Maggie urged, as she and Jesse grabbed at the last of the clothes on the clothesline.

Jesse nodded, waved Maggie into the house, and gathered the last of the clothes alone. The dust storm had come up so quickly. One minute the sky had been bright, the sunshine getting ready to do its worst; the next thing they realize, a low hanging pall of rusty sky was hurtling at them in gale force.

"My word!" Maggie gasped, as Jesse staggered into the door with her arms full of dusty clothes that would have to be re-washed. "This reminds me of the Dust

Bowl days. Lord knows we don't want that to happen again. We sure need a rain."

"Here, Maggie," Jesse urged. "Let me start the washing. You've already done this once. This time it's my turn."

"You just talked me into it, honey. Thanks a bunch. I believe I'll go clean up while you start the wash. I feel like I just ate a bowl of sand."

Jesse grinned. "I know what you mean. Oh!" she added, "as soon as I start a load to wash, I'm going to go check on Tariq. He was out in the coral earlier this morning. I may need to put him up if someone didn't already think of it. King took most of the men with him to the stockyards. They're hauling off the herd of cattle that was pastured by the big pond."

"Okay, but be careful," Maggie cautioned, then went through the utility room into the kitchen.

Jesse put on a long-sleeved shirt to use as a shield against the sharp, stinging sand, wrapped a scarf around her head, leaving only her eyes visible, and started toward the horse barn in her makeshift armor.

The wind blew in one long, continuous blast from the Oklahoma corridor, south toward Texas, carrying dust from as far away as the Dakotas, picking up momentum and density as it passed from state to state along the line of the storm front.

Jesse struggled to keep her feet on the ground as she lowered her head and pushed herself forward step by step. She heard King's big white stallion neighing frantically as she neared the barns. The wild winds and swirling dust were driving the horse into a frenzy. There was no place he could go to get away from the storm.

Jesse dashed quickly through the barn and into the

stall area leading into the corrals. She whistled sharply, but the wind blew the sound away from Tariq. He didn't hear her approach. Jesse grabbed a rope, quickly made a noose, and walked out into the corral, letting the long loop drag in the swirling dust. She didn't want to scare the horse anymore than he already was.

"Come here, boy," she called again, and this time Tariq saw her. He answered her call with a frightened nicker, spun about before he oriented himself in the storm, and came toward her at a trot.

Jesse slipped the rope over his head and quickly led him out of the storm into the shelter of the barn.

"Here's an empty stall, fella. I know you don't like to be shut up, but something tells me you won't fuss much today."

Tariq flicked his little ears back and forth, calming at the sound of Jesse's voice and the relief of being away from the stinging dust and wind. He tossed his head as she slipped the rope from his neck, then nudged her arm as she began to rub him down, brushing most of the red dirt from the horse's snowy coat.

She gave him a final pat, walked out of the stall, and shut the half door behind her. The lariat rope lay in a tangle on the barn floor and she picked it up, deftly working it into a proper nest of loops, and hung it on a peg by the stall door. She dusted her hands against her pant legs, and surprised herself when she realized all that she'd just accomplished had been done with no pain or weakness to her hands. She pulled the scarf away from her face and looked down in surprise.

"They don't hurt," Jesse whispered to herself. "My God! They don't hurt at all. Now," she muttered, pulling the scarf back around her face before making a dash for the house, "if only the rest of my life would heal as quickly."

Jesse was heartsick at the growing gap between herself and King. For the last three days he'd purposely absented himself from her presence. When he couldn't avoid her, there was a look of pain and guilt so imbedded in his eyes that Jesse didn't know how to put things right.

She didn't know whether she'd embarrassed him by her declaration, or whether all he felt was guilt at not being able to reciprocate her feelings.

This was what she'd most feared would happen if King realized she loved him. Now he was probably lost to her for good...even as a friend.

Her heart twisted in pain. She stifled the urge to cry and headed for the house.

"Wow!" Jesse gasped, as she blew through the door. "That wind is furious." She shrugged out of her scarf and jacket, tried unsuccessfully to smooth her dark tangles into some semblance of order, and staggered into King's outstretched arms. The wind outside was not as furious as King.

"What do you think you were doing?" he asked slowly, his dark eyes flashing, his mouth grim with anger.

"Putting up *your* horse," Jesse answered, trying to pull away from King's angry grasp before he could finish his urge to shake her.

"Jesse, am I ever going to be able to trust you *not* to get into trouble when I'm gone? You could have been hurt," he muttered, raking her slight figure with a frantic sweep of his eyes.

"You're what's hurting me," Jesse muttered, and

watched in dismay as King's face blanched. She wished she could take back her angry taunt. But it was too late. The damage was done.

King looked blankly down at the fierce grip he had on her arms, and instantly set her free. He turned away, hunched his shoulders and leaned his head against the pane of glass in the kitchen door.

"I'm sorry," he said, clinching his hands into fists of frustration. "I'm sorry, so sorry, Jesse Rose. All I seem to be able to do is hurt you."

He felt a dark, ugly rage building; he felt himself becoming as out of control as the wind outside, and angrily drew back his fist, unconsciously aiming for the window.

Jesse acted on instinct. She caught his fist just before it connected with the glass in the door and hung on to his arm with all her might.

"No!" she cried out. "No, King. Stop it! Stop it now!"

King took a harsh, deep breath and blinked. He looked down at the dust streaks on Jesse's face, the distress filling her wide, blue eyes, and the grip she had on his arm. What the hell was wrong with him? He hadn't lost control of his emotions like this since he was a teenager.

The look on his face was so lost Jesse couldn't help herself. She stepped forward, wrapping her arms around his waist as she laid her head against his chest. His heartbeat was ricocheting against her eardrum, but the longer Jesse held him, the steadier it became. Finally, Jesse felt his arms slip around her shoulders as King relaxed and buried his face in her hair.

"I need you to forgive me, Jesse Rose," he whispered. "I need back in your life...anyway you'll have me. Please..."

Jesse's heart jumped. He finished his plea so softly she had to hold her breath to listen.

"Give me a chance, Jesse. I can't make it without you. I don't even want to try."

Jesse started to answer him, the joy in her heart spreading swiftly to her lips, when Maggie's sharp call of concern brought them both crashing down to reality.

"King, come quick!" Maggie called from the living room where she'd gone to watch television before starting the noon meal.

King and Jesse entered simultaneously, and each saw her concern. There were no words to describe the coming horror.

Easily visible through the floor to ceiling picture window was a massive wall of smoke billowing alone in the aftermath of the subsiding dust storm. A prairie fire! And it looked as if it were heading with great speed toward the ranch adjoining the McCandless property. If they didn't get the fire under control soon, the Double M would be right in its path.

"Call county fire," King ordered. "I'll take most of the men with me. Turner and Charlie will stay here. They'll need to be ready if we don't get the fire stopped in time."

He cast a regretful glance back at Jesse, saw the worry and fear on her face, and couldn't resist. He pulled her into his arms, ignoring the look of pleased surprise on Maggie's face, and kissed her soundly.

"I'm not through with you, girl. I've got to go...and for Pete's sake...and mine," he added, "be careful."

Jesse's spirits soared along with a bright red flush

on her cheeks at the look of surprise and satisfaction on Maggie's face.

"Well now," she chuckled. "I guess grass fires aren't all that's out of control around here. Come on, honey. Let's call the fire department quickly before the whole world goes up in smoke."

Time passed slowly. Jesse watched from the verandah as the county fire trucks went flying down the road in front of the ranch in a cloud of dust, followed by the volunteer fire-fighters in their personal vehicles. From time to time, Maggie would step outside and stand beside Jesse's stiff little figure, waiting sentinel on the porch steps.

"He's going to be just fine, girl," Maggie said, and slipped a comforting arm around Jesse's shoulders. "He's been doing this all of his life. Every year it's the same thing. You know that. Some fool is bound to throw a cigarette from a passing car, or decide to burn trash, even on a day like this. Then all the good men, like King, take time out to help each other. They fight fire. They fight until the fire runs out of something to burn, or they put it out, whichever comes first."

"I know," Jesse said. "But this time it's different."

"No, honey," Maggie offered. "This time you and King are what's different. When did all this happen?"

"For me," Jesse answered, "when I was sixteen, maybe seventeen. One day I looked at him, and he'd changed, or my perception of him had. Whatever. I waited and I waited for him to notice me. I wanted him to see me as an adult, but he didn't."

The break in her voice made Maggie feel guilty. She'd never suspected. Then something else occurred to her.

"Is that why you left us so suddenly?"

Jesse nodded.

"Well, it's obvious King finally noticed something," Maggie teased. "I haven't seen a kiss like that since… since…well, at least since my soap opera yesterday afternoon."

Jesse turned around and burst out laughing at Maggie's words.

The ringing telephone called Maggie indoors and it wasn't long before she stuck her head back outside long enough to reply.

"I have to go to the Winslow place. The fire started on their property and Sue burned her hands trying to put it out. Her baby's not quite two and her husband is gone. I told her I'd help out and spend the night until her husband gets home tomorrow."

"Of course," Jesse agreed, knowing how helpless she'd been when unable to use her hands. And she'd had no one but herself to worry about. "Need a ride?" she added.

"No. One of the neighbors volunteered to come get me. You'll be all right, won't you?" Maggie asked, suddenly realizing the predicament in which she'd be leaving Jesse. They hadn't been leaving her alone. Maggie started to go back in and change her plans when she remembered. "Turner and Charlie are still here, aren't they? And King and the other men should be home before dark."

"I'll be fine," Jesse urged. "Go pack your nightie. I'll watch for your ride."

All too soon Maggie was gone. Jesse watched as the pickup truck disappeared down the driveway in a cloud of blowing dust. She looked behind her at the big, empty house, and back at the ever-present clouds of smoke on the horizon. She couldn't control the shiver of fear that swept over her. *Please God, let King be safe.*

Turner and Charlie waved at her as they came around the driveway from the machine sheds, pulling a wide plow behind one of the tractors. Jesse knew they were going to make a firebreak by cutting through the thick prairie grass with the steel plowshares, turning the fire fodder under, and the clods of dry, Oklahoma soil up to the sky.

The phone rang again, and Jesse dashed to answer. It was King.

"Jesse," he asked in a rush, obviously out of breath. "Are you and Maggie okay?"

"Yes," she answered, then added, "Maggie's not here. Someone came to get her. Sue Winslow hurt herself and needed help with the baby."

"Okay, honey," he said, and then coughed.

Jesse knew he'd just turned his head away from the phone. His voice was so dry and husky she could barely understand him. She feared he'd inhaled a lot of heat and smoke.

"Are you okay?" she asked.

"I'm fine. But I need you to give Turner a message."

Jesse started to tell him Turner wasn't there either, but something made her stop.

"You need to tell him to go get the two-year-olds. You remember, Jess? The ones the dogs chased? If this fire jumps Salt Creek, they'll be in danger. Will you do that, honey?"

"Yes, I'll tend to it, King," she hedged, and knew he'd heard her hesitancy.

"Jesse, are you going to do what I asked you to do?" he growled.

"Turner's not here, King. He and Charlie are plowing a fire break," she said, her words spilling out in a rush. "I can take Tariq and go let the horses out before I can ever get Turner back to the ranch."

"No!" he shouted into the phone. "No, dammit! No, Jesse! Promise me. Don't you dare go after those horses!"

"King, if I don't, they could be trapped. Then you'd lose everything," Jesse argued.

"Jesse Rose," he shouted, and she had to hold the phone away from her ear. "I said don't go!"

But the line went dead in his ear and King threw the phone down in panic. Damn her to hell and back, she would go. He knew it. He ran past the stunned patrons of the corner quick-stop where he'd gone to use the phone, and jumped back into the borrowed Jeep. He would never get back to the Double M in time to stop her. And Jesse was wrong. He wouldn't lose a thing unless something happened to her. *Then* he'd lose everything.

The big stallion was uneasy. He danced sideways when Jesse dismounted to open the wide, wooden gate that separated the meadow above the ranch from the grassland where the horses were pastured.

She could smell smoke in the air, and if she looked closely between the trees in the distance, she could see the first hints of grayish-brown wisps gathering above the treetops.

The wind was blowing against her left cheek as she mounted Tariq and turned him full face into the wind.

She didn't think the fire had crossed the creek yet, and prayed the fire-fighters would be able to stop the blaze before it did. If they could, the Double M would be spared. But Jesse knew time was of the essence, and kicked Tariq in the flanks, urging him at a gallop toward the big pond and the herd of two-year-olds.

She rode Tariq hard, but his seat was easy as he ran. Jesse had no problems staying mounted. Nothing could have prepared her for the panic and terror that lay waiting just over the hill.

The closer she got, the sharper was the tang of acrid smoke filling the air. Jesse's heartbeat accelerated. Smoke was blowing in long, stringy clouds, making her eyes water and her nose burn as she reluctantly inhaled the burning wind. Tariq tossed his head and Jesse knew he, too, was suffering from the effects of the fire. She leaned over in the saddle and urged him on, knowing the horse's instincts were telling him he was going the wrong way.

"Come on, big fellow," Jesse called in his ear. "We're almost there."

It was after they topped the last hill above the pond where Jesse had enjoyed her skinny dip that she saw the extent of danger she and Tariq faced if they tried to rescue the already trapped horses.

"Dear God!" Jesse moaned, her eyes frantically searching the landscape for signs of some fire-fighters or a county fire truck or two. But they were nowhere in sight; there was only a wall of swiftly moving orange flame that was diminishing its distance from the trapped horses in wide, hungry swaths.

A strong, maverick gust of wind blew away the

clouds of smoke that were slowly encompassing Jesse and her mount. And for just a moment, she saw hope.

Below and behind the pond dam lay a narrow corridor of, as yet, unburned pasture. Jesse knew if she could reach it in time and turn the trapped and milling herd in the proper direction, their instinct for survival would take them through. With no further thought, Jesse rode her horse into the thick, burning cloud.

The horses neighed at her arrival. Their panic matched Jesse's own as she quickly circled the young horses, turning them to run blindly into the dense smoke. The wind blew madly down through the draw behind the pond and carried tiny bits of still-burning embers with it, feeding the already bottomless maw of blaze that kept threatening to swallow Jesse and the horses.

Suddenly, the young horses saw the break in the fire. They needed no further urging than Jesse's shout. They erupted as one into the narrowing path and ran in headlong flight, heads up, manes and tails flowing out behind them like the tails of kites caught in the whirlwind.

And then they were through the smoke, the threatening blaze now at their backs, taunting and teasing with imminent disaster as the strong winds kept blowing the fire across the prairie. There was nothing left for Jesse to do but outrun it. She bit back a sob of panic as a strong gust of wind pushed the fire almost beneath her horse's feet. She felt him jump and surge forward, felt the massive muscles bunch beneath her as she wrapped the reins around her wrists and leaned almost full-length across Tariq's powerful neck.

"Okay, boy," Jesse yelled in his ear. She kicked him sharply. "Take us home."

The great stallion leaped forward, his haunches bunched as his hooves dug into the dry, burning earth. And he ran as he'd never run before. He was running for his life, and taking Jesse with him.

King knew the fire had jumped the creek by the direction of the smoke. His stomach roiled and a pull in the depths of his gut told him what his mind refused to accept. He was going to be too late to help Jesse. Whatever happened was happening now, and he was helpless to stop it or aid her in any way. He was too far away. He hit the steering wheel in frustration with his fist, and pressed the gas pedal all the way to the floor.

The fire break was completed. Turner and Charlie had headed back to the ranch when Turner saw the gathering smoke billowing across the grassland west of the ranch.

"Charlie! It's jumped Salt Creek," Turner yelled over the tractor's noisy engine. "We've got to hurry!"

His words were no sooner said then he saw something else that made fingers of fear crawl down the neck of his shirt and grab at his heart. The big wooden gate in the pasture above the barn was wide open, fastened back against the fence to keep it from blowing shut. The only time they ever did that was when moving livestock. Turner knew what had happened without a second thought. Jesse had gone after the horses. He pushed the throttle forward on the big John Deere tractor, and headed for the ranch, bouncing the raised plow behind him in wild abandon. King would kill them all if anything happened to that girl.

Turner had no more than reached the machine shed

when he saw the Jeep hurtling down the long driveway. He knew, somehow, that King was already aware
of Jesse's danger.

The Jeep skidded sideways, sliding precariously
through the loose dirt and gravel, before it finally came
to a halt just in front of the corrals.

King vaulted from the Jeep, and Turner knew by
the look on his face that he was almost out of his mind.

"She's gone, hasn't she?" King yelled, his voice
cracking from smoke and stress.

"Boss, I didn't even know it until minutes ago when
I saw the open gate. Did she go after the horses?" he
asked.

"Hell, yes," King shouted, and turned around wildly,
as if looking for an answer to his fears. "And I as good
as told her to go. If anything happens to her, it'll be
my fault."

His voice broke, and his dark eyes narrowed in frustration and fear as he watched the huge clouds of smoke
the winds were pushing over the crest of the hill. There
was no hesitation in his movements. He started toward
the corral gate with every intention of taking the Jeep
into the fire. But the volunteer fire-fighters' arrival momentarily stopped his progress.

"Looks like your firebreak might stop this, King,"
one of the men yelled as he jumped from the back of a
pickup truck and waved a group of men into position,
just in case the fire jumped the wide strip of plowed
ground. Then he saw King McCandless running toward the gate leading into the fields. "Where are you
going, man?" he yelled. "Don't be foolish. That firebreak will hold."

"Jesse," he yelled hoarsely, pointing toward the now

visible flames behind the blowing smoke. "She's in there…somewhere. I'm going to get her."

Word spread through the crowd of men like the wild fire itself. A woman was trapped in there. They each watched in mounting horror at the wall of smoke that came rolling down the hill toward the barns. There was no way on earth that she'd live through that.

Suddenly, a sound came riding on the wind, stopping each and every man in his tracks. All eyes turned toward the hillside.

"Boss!" Turner called out, and pointed wildly in the direction of the fire. "Open the corral gates. She's bringin' 'em in."

The wild thunder of horses' hooves and the occasional fear-laden whinny could be heard, along with the crackle and roar of the prairie fire. Then they burst through the smoke, running on the hands of the wind, toward the gleaming white walls of the barn and safety.

"There she comes! By God, there she comes!" he heard Turner shout, and King felt the bones in his legs turn to jelly. Fear for Jesse's safety expanded as he watched her tiny figure plastered to the back of his stallion.

The horses were crazed by the fire and the wild race against time. He knew it would take more than a miracle to stop the stampeding herd. He shook off his terror, his eyes fixed on Jesse and his horse. King pushed open the gates to the corral and then began to run.

Jesse didn't even know when they finally cleared the wall cloud of burning prairie and began the descent toward the ranch. Her arms and hands were nearly numb just from trying to stay mounted. So much smoke and ashes had blown into her eyes that they were pouring tears. She could only see through a watery veil, and heard the wild cheers of the men congregated at the edge of the plowed strip of ground before she saw them. When she did, her heart skipped a beat. She bit her lower lip to keep from screaming.

We made it! She could see the wall of white below, and the gate to the corral being pushed open to receive the thundering herd. Then, as quickly as her elation had soared, it now gave way to total terror. She'd made it out of the fire, but she knew she'd never be able to stop Tariq. A tiny moan slipped through her tightly clinched lips. She almost lost her seat as her concentration slipped.

King saw her falter, and terror such as he'd never known gave strength to his arms and legs.

The herd of horses had swerved toward the opening in the corral as surely as they'd run through the opening in the fire. But Tariq ran on, heading for the rails of the fence in wild abandon. He was going to jump…and when he did Jesse would be lost. King stood his ground and met the fear-crazed stallion head on.

King heard the pounding hooves coming nearer and nearer, heard the harsh, panting gasps of Tariq's tortured lungs, saw the horse's wild, red-rimmed eyes roll frantically at the man standing in his flight path. Just as the horse came thundering down upon him, just before he would go under the powerful hooves, King reached out, grabbed the side of Tariq's bridle, curled his fingers around the metal attached to the bit in the horse's mouth and hung on for Jesse…and for dear life.

Jesse only saw the top of his head, and then it looked as if he'd gone under Tariq's hooves. He disappeared from view. Jesse screamed, trying with all her waning strength to pull back on the reins wrapped tightly around her wrists.

The horse tried to rear, pawing wildly at the air with his front legs, but there was an unfamiliar weight tugging at his tender mouth and his struggle was unsuccessful. He fought and jumped, trying to dislodge the weight from his mouth and neck, but it was too much effort. Exhaustion finally took hold as he side-stepped across the plowed stretch of field and ran full tilt into the outstretched hands of the fire-fighters. He stood, head down, foam-flecked and singed, and began to shake, his tired muscles reacting violently to the sudden stop.

Jesse slumped over the saddle horn, and would have fallen onto the plowed ground had strong arms not reached out to catch her. She felt the tight strips of leather being gently unwound from her wrists. Her hands tingled and then began to ache as circulation began to flow.

The men were cheering and laughing, relieved at the happy ending to what had seemed certain disaster. Jesse's wild ride and bravery were nearly overshadowed by the life-threatening sacrifice King had made. They'd all witnessed him catch a stampeding stallion with his bare hands and pull him to a halt with sheer strength.

King couldn't think past the fact that he and Jesse were still alive. He held her cradled in his arms as if she were made of glass, and began to walk through the dry clods toward the barn. The fire would soon be out. The firebreak had stopped it. The horses were safe, milling about in a tight circle inside the corral as they calmed down.

Turner led the big white stallion past King, as he walked on, silently carrying his precious burden. Turner looked quickly away, ignoring the tears running down the big man's face, plowing little clean tracks through the dust and ashes coating his skin.

"Boss," he called back, without turning around to see if King was listening. "I'll tend to clean-up around here. You take her on to the house. See you tomorrow."

King heard, but could not acknowledge, the extent of his old foreman's thoughtfulness. He only knew he was never going to let Jesse out of his sight again.

Jesse felt his heartbeat, wild and erratic beneath her cheek, felt him shudder and then gather her closer. She sighed with relief and weariness, then closed her burning eyes. King was taking her home.

Chapter 11

The house was quiet—a cool, clean haven from the world outside that had nearly gone up in flames. Silence lengthened between King and Jesse until she could stand it no longer.

"King," she began, as he carried her through the living quarters toward the bedrooms. "I can walk, I think. Why don't…"

"No," he muttered, kicking open the door to his bedroom. "I may never put you down, Jesse Rose. I *know* I'm never letting you out of my sight again." His voice broke as he sank down on the bed and propped Jesse against his lap.

"King," she whispered, slowly sliding her arms around his neck. "I'm sorry. I didn't intend for this to happen." She leaned her face into the curve of his neck and kissed a muscle twitching uncontrollably in his jaw. "I thought you were… I thought you fell under…"

Tears of relief kept threatening to erupt, but she couldn't cry. The tears were frozen in the horror of the last few minutes when she'd imagined King dead.

"Hush," he whispered, and pulled her across his lap, dangling her legs on either side until she was facing him.

He cupped her face in his hands, leaned forward, and pulled Jesse toward him. Not an inch of her face escaped the branding touch of his lips as he lay claim to the woman he'd so nearly lost.

Jesse's heart soared. She wanted to laugh. She wanted to cry. Instead, she pulled him closer and captured his next kiss with desperation. Every taste, every pull of his lips against her skin sent pinpoints of heat shooting to the center of her being. She felt King thread his fingers through her hair as he, once more, captured her lips. It wasn't enough and he clasped her roughly under her arms and pulled her closer, moaning in response to her mouth that was opening slowly beneath his touch.

King's breathing was coming in harsh, hurtful gulps as he struggled with the need to breathe and have Jesse all at the same time. Finally, he reluctantly pulled away, and gently ran his thumb across her lips.

"My God, Jesse Rose. I nearly lost you today. I nearly lost you," he whispered huskily, running his hands gently over and over her body, not believing that she was still in one piece. "Nothing would have mattered to me if I'd lost you, baby. Don't you understand that?" He leaned his head forward until their foreheads were gently touching, and gripped her firmly around the waist. "I love you, Jesse. I love you so much it makes my teeth ache. I watch you laugh, and forget what I was going to say. I watch you walk, and forget what I was going to do. I watch you sleep, and know that nothing in my life is worth keeping unless you're beside me."

Then his voice broke, and Jesse felt him shudder and begin to tremble beneath her.

"I need to love you, baby. I've held back too long now. I want you, Jess." His eyes darkened with emotion and he bent down and buried his face in the valley between her breasts. "If you don't want this, you're going to have to stop me, because I don't think I can stop myself."

Jesse slid from his lap and began to walk away.

King numbly watched his world coming to an end. He couldn't think as he watched her leave him.

Dear God, no! he thought. It felt like he'd been kicked in the stomach.

Jesse reached out and turned the lock on his bedroom door. She pivoted around to face him with tears in her eyes, a smile on her lips, and began to unbutton her dust-coated shirt and jeans.

"Bath...or shower?" she whispered, as she walked out of the pile of blue denim at her feet and let her shirt drop beside it.

She was in his arms and off her feet, as King whirled her around the room.

Steam swirled inside the walls of the shower, coating the sliding glass doors until Jesse's vision was nearly obliterated. The water ran in a warm torrent down her body, washing away the remnants of her wild ride through the burning prairie. She reached up to the shelf above her head for the bottle of shampoo. Her hands came away empty. King's deep, husky voice behind her stopped her search.

"Let me, honey," he coaxed, and pulled her away from the water's swift flow.

She smelled the sharp, fresh scent of the lemon shampoo permeate the enclosure, and felt his hands begin to knead through the smoky tangles of her hair, working the shampoo into a rich, cleansing lather. She sighed, and leaned back against his chest, letting those talented hands work their magic on her tired, aching body. Her eyes closed in reflex as his hands continued down the back of her neck, then around, cradling her breasts in each hand as he captured stray bits of lather.

"Feel good?" he whispered against her ear, and was rewarded with a tiny moan of pleasure that fired an answering echo within himself.

He didn't know how *Jesse* felt, but she felt *fine* to him. He stepped forward, placing them both under the pounding force of the spray. Lather ran between their bodies, swirling around their feet, before it disappeared down the drain. King quickly repeated the process on himself, closing his eyes against the treacherous soap, and nearly lost his footing when Jesse's hands began an intimate foray that sent good sense down the drain with the shampoo.

"Wait a minute, sweetheart," he begged, grabbing at a towel as he turned off the water. "You don't know what you're doing." He smiled seductively at the blue-eyed nymph with the curious hands.

Jesse leaned back against the door of the shower and let her eyes continue what her hands began.

"Oh," she drawled, as she watched his body tense and harden with desire, "I think I do."

King's sharply indrawn breath and the fire that kindled in his eyes were Jesse's only warnings. He had her out of the shower and dry before another thought had time to form.

"So," he whispered, as he laid her down in the middle of his bed, then stood back and feasted his eyes on the tantalizing thought of crawling in beside her, "you think you know what you're doing?"

"No," she answered quietly, and her honesty shook his resolve. "But I know what I want *you* to do, King."

Breath constricted in his throat as he knelt beside her and ran his fingers around the instep of her foot, then let them travel the inside of her leg, up...up...until he paused at her threshold, his dark eyes promising passion.

Jesse shuddered, and shifted uneasily on the bed, mesmerized by the touch of his hands and the knowledge that this magnificent man with the magic touch was finally going to make love to her.

"I know what you want, baby," he groaned, stretching full length beside her. "That's what I want, too. I promised, remember?"

His mouth captured a rosy nub, and his hand another, as he began a journey across Jesse that would culminate in a promise kept.

His hands, his mouth, and the weight of his body on hers drove sanity and reason away. Jesse wanted to touch him. She needed to watch him watching her. But she knew if she opened her eyes, or turned loose of the bed beneath her, or moved an inch away from the seeking, pulsing pressure of his body, she'd fly away so far she'd never come down.

Every promise he whispered in her ear would then come true as he stroked and touched, nipped and tasted. Spasm after spasm of building heat waves made an ache so fierce that Jesse begged for release she didn't know how to achieve.

"King, please," she moaned, "tell me what to do."

She moved beneath him, seeking, pushing, yearning for something. Then she felt her lower body lift off the bed as King's hand dipped past a boundary no man had ever passed.

She gasped, let loose her grip on the bed, and dug her fingers into the still-damp tangles of his hair.

King's breath was coming in quick, painful draughts, as he struggled to hold back an overwhelming need to disappear inside the woman beneath him. The softness below would soothe his own aching body, but still he waited as he teased at the throb beneath his fingers.

"Tell you what to do?" he asked, and took the question from her lips with one swoop of his mouth. "You don't need to do anything. I'll tell you what *I'm* going to do, baby," he whispered against her lips. "I'm going to make you forget every man you've ever known, every man who's even crossed your path and wished. I don't want anyone in your life now but me."

He lifted himself over her, nearly blind with a need to dissolve into this woman below him.

Her soft whisper barely penetrated through the blood thundering in his ears, but when it did, it stopped him cold.

"I don't have to forget what never was," Jesse said, and slid her hands down the tightly bunched muscles tensing along his back. Her hands slid around his waist, urging him to finish what they'd started.

King blinked, shook his head slowly, then leaned forward, collapsing his entire weight as he buried his face in the curve of her neck.

"What in hell are you telling me, Jesse Rose?" he pleaded, then lifted himself away, focusing on the clear blue gaze beneath him. He was falling into space, weightless and out of control.

"That I love you, King McCandless. And that I've waited a lifetime to show you how much."

"No...no, Jess," King groaned in disbelief, suddenly afraid to move, yet knowing he had to. It was just that this gift was so much more than he'd expected...so much more than he deserved.

"Please," Jesse begged, and felt his silent answer as he slowly surged forward.

It was only a tiny, fleeting pressure that erupted into one blinding flash of pain, and then the sensation of emptiness Jesse had felt for so long completely disappeared as King swelled within her.

King winced, regretting the need for the tiny gasp he heard, and saw her eyes flutter as she bit against her lower lip to keep from crying aloud.

"I'm sorry. So sorry, baby," he muttered, and bent down, placing kisses of repentance on her eyelids and down the sides of her mouth. "But I can promise you this, it's the last pain I'll ever willingly give you. From now on, Jesse, it's nothing but pleasure."

His body tensed as he took a deep, agonized breath, then began to move slowly in a rhythm as old as time. Just before words became more than he could form, he managed to whisper his promise into the silence of the room before Jesse took him into paradise. "Sweet, sweet, pleasure."

Duncan watched the smoke from his window high above Tulsa, and judged the location to be near, if not actually on, the Double M. He knew it was a grass fire—a big one, judging by the size of the smoke clouds. His eyes narrowed, his lips thinned, and the planes of his face angled and flattened until he was barely recognizable.

"The whole damn place can go up in smoke for all I care," he muttered.

He walked to the bar and poured himself another drink. It seemed these days that that was all he was able to do—drink to avoid what he knew lay in wait. He walked back to the window with his drink in hand and stood silently, debating with himself about the wisdom of going out to the ranch to help. Finally, what was left of his conscience rallied. He spun about, intent on driving to the ranch, when the phone rang and stopped him squarely in the middle of the living room floor.

Now he had to decide whether to answer it or let it ring. It could be a number of people, all of whom he owed money, and he nearly didn't answer. But the persistent, shrill tone won out over his jangled nerves.

"McCandless," he said shortly, then let his drink spill slowly from his glass onto the carpeted floor.

"I know who it is, Boss," the voice whined. "And you know who this is, too. Dammit, you promised to come back. I got hungry, man. I needed to eat, and I needed medicine."

"What the hell do you want?" Duncan asked, his voice low and angry. "And where are you?"

"You know what I want. I need cash. I'm here… in town. And I ain't got no way to disappear. They're lookin' for me all over. You got to help me. After all, this was your idea," he said accusingly.

"It wasn't my idea to hurt her," he said all too softly.

"And it wasn't my damned idea to go passing hot checks and get caught on video at the same time, you stupid son-of-a-bitch. I don't *have* any money, thanks to you. And you better get the hell out of Tulsa, because I'll finish what Jesse started if you don't. Do I make myself clear?"

Lynch shuddered at the still, ominous quality in the man's voice, and knew the moment of truth had arrived. Now not only were the cops after him for attempted murder and kidnapping, but this man, a formidable foe, also had good reason to want him dead. With one last act of bravado, he whined, "Well, if the cops get me, you'll be next."

"No, I won't," Duncan sneered. "I'm not stupid. There's absolutely nothing linking me to you, or the crime, except your word. Who do you think the cops will believe—a concerned member of the family or a murdering crook?"

"You bastard!" Lynch cried. "You got to help me."

"Where are you?" Duncan asked quietly.

Suddenly, Wiley Lynch knew he'd said too much. He had pushed a man he was mortally afraid of too far.

"Never mind," Lynch muttered. "I'll get myself out of town. I'll hitch a ride…something. Just forget I asked, okay, Boss?"

Just then another truckload of livestock pulled into the stockyards by the pay phone Wiley Lynch was using. The constant bellow and lowing of the load of cattle and the truck's shifting gears echoed into the receiver.

"Okay, Boss?" he repeated. But the line went dead as Duncan McCandless gently placed the phone back on the hook.

Lynch stood, staring in horror at the milling crowd of people around him and began to shake. McCandless knew where he was! He dropped the receiver, letting it dangle in the wind and heat, and began to run in a scurrying fashion back to the pile of shipping crates behind the sale barn, unaware of several people's curious, suspicious stares. First chance he got, he would be on a cattle truck heading west.

King lay quietly, absorbing the rise and fall of Jesse's breasts beneath his hand, and watched the first ray of morning lighten the shadows in his room. He raised up on one elbow and propped his head in his hands so he could watch her sleep.

Her lashes lay like thick, curly fans on her windburned cheeks, and King felt a fierce wave of protectfulness sweep over him at the thought of anyone, or anything, ever hurting Jesse again.

She was so small and fragile in appearance, yet King knew what a strong, fierce spirit she possessed. She was more than a match for his physical strength. She'd proven that over and over throughout the night as King would take her to the brink of passion, pushing her right to the edge of reason, and then, just before she felt herself fly into a million pieces beneath his mouth and hands, he'd gather her into his arms, and with one wild thrust send them both falling through mindless space.

He leaned over, gently ran the tip of his finger along the line of her slightly swollen lower lip, humble with the knowledge of what Jesse had saved, then given to him last night. *Please God, may I never make her sorry.*

He inhaled sharply at the quick, intense reaction of his body as Jesse rolled over and buried her face against his chest. He was instantly hard, throbbing with a need he knew only Jesse could fill. Her arms slid around him as she pulled herself against the thrust of his body, and King felt himself lose it as she opened her mouth, nuzzled against his chest, took a hard brown nipple between her teeth and pressed lightly.

"Does that feel as good to you as it does to me?" Jesse whispered.

King's sudden intake of breath told her what he could not. She did it once more for good measure, and found herself on top of his hard, aching body. Jesse had one swift look at the wild flare of passion in his eyes before he groaned and slid into her.

"Does *that* feel as good to you as it does to me?" he asked in return, and pulled her hips down tightly across him.

Jesse gasped and moaned, as he began moving beneath her in a soft, tantalizing thrust.

"Yes, yes, yes," she mumbled. And then she forgot why she'd answered as King took her on a ride she'd never forget.

It was some time later before either of them could move, and even later before they could think. Finally the phone rang, ending their lethargy. King reluctantly released Jesse and rolled over to answer.

It was Maggie and she was on her way home. That message had them both on their feet and hurrying to dress. Maggie would know soon enough about the new turn of events between them, but they wanted to tell her not show her. By the time Maggie arrived, they had coffee brewed and breakfast waiting on the table.

"My stars," she announced as she came through the

front door. "Are you two all right? It looks like the place nearly went up in flames yesterday."

She was referring to the huge, blackened swath covering the hillside. Before either King or Jesse could answer, Maggie took another, closer look at the expressions on their faces. She smiled slyly. "Or maybe it wasn't the Double M that went up in flames last night. Is there something you two want to tell me?"

Guilt painted an embarrassed blush on King's face. He stuttered. Then he started to explain, grinned sheepishly and pulled her into his arms, whirling her around the living room floor, much to her surprise and glee.

"You're not the only love of my life, woman. Put your bag down and come to breakfast. We'll fill you in on what you think you've missed." Then he added, "At least part of it."

The last dish was washed and put away as King came back through the door. He'd been outside, overseeing the damage they'd sustained, and issuing orders for the day.

"Jesse Rose," he called, slamming the door shut behind him. "If you're barefoot, grab your shoes. We're going to Tulsa to pick up the cattle check at the stockyard."

"But I was going to help…" she started to say, when he pulled her off her feet and into his arms, fixing her with an unwavering stare.

"If you think I'm leaving you here alone again, you're crazy, woman. You can't be trusted, and I'm too tired to rescue you again today. Okay?"

Jesse smiled, placed a kiss in the vicinity of his left ear, and whispered softly so that the grinning Maggie couldn't overhear, "How come you're so tired?" she teased. "Was it something I said…or was it something I did?"

"Witch," he growled, and set her down before he embarrassed them both. "Get your damn shoes."

King pulled the Lincoln carefully between stock trailers and semi-trucks that were loading and unloading droves of milling, bawling, cattle. He parked between a Cadillac and a rusted-out pickup truck.

There was less class-consciousness among farmers and ranchers than any other group of working men in America. Whether they ran a big spread or a nickel-and-dime operation on weekends only, they all faced the same frustrations and joys, and at one time or another they all wound up with manure on their boots. Ranching had a way of equalizing men.

"My check will be at the office, Jess," he said, as he parked. "Come with me."

"I know," Jesse chided, as she scooted across the seat. "You don't trust me."

"I love you, baby," he whispered, and dipped his head to steal a kiss from her pouting lips. "Trust *me,* okay?"

The hot breeze whipped the skirt of Jesse's light green sundress around her legs and outlined her slim body in a tantalizing caress. King jammed his hat down on his head and guided Jesse between the parked and moving vehicles.

"Whew," he muttered, as they stepped quickly inside, shutting the wind and heat and the ever-present smell of manure and diesel smoke outside. "You can sit here, Jesse," he said, indicating a row of assorted wood and metal folding chairs outside the cashier's window. "It may take a while. They may not have the check ready. I don't mind telling you, it's just luck that I hauled that herd off to market when I did. The fire would have taken some of them for sure."

Then, realizing what he'd said about the fire, he frowned. Ignoring any curious stares or whispers from anyone present, he cupped her face in his hands and tilted it toward him.

"I wasn't lucky yesterday, Jesse. I was blessed. But not because the stock was saved." His voice was low and husky; his dark eyes filled with promise and regret.

"I know, King," Jesse said, and caressed the hand cupping her cheek. "It's okay. Go on and get in line. I'll just wait here." She took a seat between two grinning women who'd witnessed their interchange.

Lynch couldn't believe his eyes. It was the boss, kissing the same woman he'd hired him to snatch.

"What the hell is goin' on here?" he whined to himself, and slipped behind the pair as they hurried toward the offices.

He'd been trying ever since daybreak to sneak aboard an empty cattle truck, but so far had remained unsuccessful. The drivers were careful to search their empty trailers before taking off. They had no desire to haul hitchhikers. It was dangerous, and it was illegal.

Now Lynch wondered if it wasn't fate that made him miss a ride. Maybe he could still get some money. McCandless wouldn't want to cause a scene in front of the woman. He rubbed his hands together gleefully, and stayed just out of sight as King and Jesse entered the offices. Now all he had to do was wait.

"Hey, boy!" a loud, boisterous voice boomed out behind King and Jesse as they left the sale barn on their way back to the car. "How 'bout a loan?"

King grinned and turned to see one of his dad's old friends.

"*You* need a loan?" King teased. "Not in this lifetime, Booster. You could loan money to the federal government and never miss it."

The grizzled old cowboy's cackle was nearly drowned out by the noise of a truck pulling away from the stockyards.

"Here, honey," King said, as he handed Jesse the car keys. "Go on and get in out of the heat. I'll just say 'hi' to Booster."

"Okay," Jesse said. "Give him my love."

"I'll tell him you said 'hi', too," King growled. "Your love's all mine."

Jesse felt her face flame along with an answering fire in the pit of her stomach. *Lord have mercy,* she thought, as she headed for the car's cool comfort, *I've created a monster.* And then she grinned to herself. *And he's all mine.*

King was momentarily trapped between two long, semi-trailer trucks, one coming, one going. He stepped back against the bumper of a parked truck and ducked his head as the dust boiled up his nostrils and into his eyes. When a man behind him began to speak it startled him. He didn't even know anyone was around. He turned sideways, blinking rapidly as he tried to see past the film of dust coating his vision.

"Hey, Boss," the man whined. "What's the damn deal? I saw you kiss her. If you was on them kinda terms, how come you wanted her snatched?"

King couldn't believe what he was hearing, nor could he believe who he thought he was seeing.

"What in hell?" he muttered as he rubbed his eyes,

anxiously trying to remove the dirt and grit. The man was still there…and he looked just like…

"I need some dough," the man said, and hitched at his pants as they slid down his skinny hips. "Don't tell me again that you're broke. I just saw you go in the office and pick up that big fat check. All I need is a little to get me out of town. I swear you'll never hear from me again. I won't tell no one about our deal. I swear it. I know I screwed up, but you should have told me that LeBeau woman was no sissy."

It was when he mentioned Jesse's name that King was certain who was talking to him. But he couldn't get past the horror building inside his mind. Why did Lynch think he knew him?

"Lynch? Wiley Lynch?" King growled huskily, and started toward him.

"What the…?" Lynch muttered, and felt with certainty that he'd just made a terrible, terrible mistake. He didn't know that deep, unfamiliar voice. He knew the face, but not the voice.

"Who are you?" he asked, and began to stumble backward. "You're not McCandless!"

"Yes, I am, you son-of-a-bitch," King growled. "I'm the one who was going to cough up the half million. And I know who you are too. You're dead."

Wiley Lynch took one last, wild look at the big man, and began to run. He didn't have to look behind to see if McCandless was following him. He could hear him. He knew it would take a miracle to escape the wrath of the big man who was quickly closing the distance between them.

"Miss LeBeau?" a man asked, as he stepped from behind King's Lincoln and flashed his badge.

The sunlight caught and held on the shiny metal as Jesse looked up, startled. Suddenly she was afraid. The man, so out of place in suit and tie, took her firmly by the elbow.

"Oklahoma State Bureau of Investigation," he said, as they walked quickly toward another group of men all dressed in similar fashion. A familiar, short, stocky figure emerged from the men and took Jesse by the hand.

"Miss LeBeau," he greeted her. "It's been a while. You look much better than the last time I saw you. Would you please come with me? The men here have a job to finish, and you and McCandless out of the line of fire, so to speak."

"Captain Shockey?" Jesse said, stunned to see the Missouri policeman here in Oklahoma.

The implications of his presence began to dawn on her, and she spun around, frantically searching the crowded parking lot for King.

"We got a tip last night that Lynch might be here," he said. "Couldn't believe my eyes when I saw you two come out of the offices. Fate plays funny tricks sometimes."

"King," she asked, and clutched his arm in fear. "He was right behind me, and now I don't see him."

Her voice began to shake, and her legs went weak.

One of the OSBI men frowned at her statement. He motioned for some of the men to follow, then one of the trucks blocking their vision finally moved. He stood transfixed for mere seconds before he began to run.

"It's Lynch," he yelled, as they started in fast pursuit, "and McCandless is after him."

The men split up, running in parallel paths, hoping to converge on the fleeing suspect should he try to escape down one of the many narrow paths between the dozens of holding corrals where the livestock were kept until sold at auction.

Jesse started to follow, but was pulled back by Shockey's strong, unyielding grasp.

"Let the men do their job, Miss LeBeau," he urged. "You stay here with me. I'm here by invitation only. This is out of my jurisdiction. But I like to see the end of a case for myself."

She couldn't think past the horrible fear that poured into her brain. All she could remember was that man, and his knife, and the pain. Now King was in danger. She leaned limply against the hot fender of the unmarked police car and began to shake.

Twice King almost had a hand on him, and then Lynch would pivot and dart down another path between the holding pens. A black rage kept him going, unswerving in his determination that this man would not escape again. Not this time. He could feel Lynch's fear. He heard the choking gasps for breath, and knew Lynch was tiring. But he still managed to stay just out of King's reach. Lynch was running for his life.

The wind and heat, the stench of manure, the cattle's uneasy lowing as the race among them heightened brought a growing certainty to Wiley Lynch that he'd reached a point of no return. He wasn't going to escape this big, angry man. His lungs burned. His legs ached. Then he saw it! A slim chance, *but* a chance. He gathered all of his remaining strength, and made one long leap toward a big semi pulling an empty cattle trailer out of the loading chute. If he could just get a handhold on the slat-sided truck, maybe, just maybe…

King realized Lynch's intention and dived for his

feet just as he jumped. He felt the dust on Lynch's shoes come away in his hands, but he missed and fell face down in the dust, inches away from his goal. He looked up in dismay, certain that he was going to see Lynch's escape. Instead, he watched in horror as Lynch misjudged his vault and fell under the rolling eighteen-wheeler.

Suddenly hands were all over King, pulling him to his feet. Dozens of people kept asking him if he was all right.

"What the hell?" he muttered. He was tired, winded and sick at heart at the growing suspicion inside him.

"OSBI, Mr. McCandless," one of them answered. "We have Miss LeBeau. She's fine."

"Well, you can't say the same for that bastard," King said, and pointed to what was left of Wiley Lynch.

He pushed roughly past the gathering group of bystanders, who looked on in horror at what they judged to be a terrible accident. King headed back to his car with a wild, fierce glint in his eyes. This wasn't over yet.

Chapter 12

As word spread of the accident, gathering crowds obscured Jesse's view. She struggled within Shockey's grasp, unwilling to wait quietly while her world might be coming to an end. She could hear the rising volume of voices as more people became aware of the events that had just taken place. Many were not aware that a chase had been in progress, or that the police were already on the scene. Most of the police were in plain clothes and driving unmarked vehicles.

"Please," Jesse pleaded. "I just need to go find him." But she could tell by the determined look on Shockey's face that her plea was useless.

Suddenly King emerged from the pushing crowd of onlookers, and Jesse caught back a sob of relief. She pulled away from Shockey's restraint and began to run. Yet the closer she came to King, the more a different kind of panic set in. King didn't even see her, wasn't aware that she was anywhere close, until Jesse grabbed him by the arm as he started to pass by her.

"King!" she cried. "What happened? Did they catch Lynch? Are you all right?"

King looked blindly down at her hand, then up at the worried expression on her face. A black hole was opening in his mind. He knew he should answer, but he couldn't focus on anything but the growing certainty that he knew who Lynch's "Boss" was.

He shrugged away from Jesse's grasp, and continued toward his car in single-minded determination. Then he remembered, and turned back to Jesse, as she stood watching his actions in stunned silence.

"Give me the keys," he whispered, and swallowed an urge to let his rage take hold.

Jesse began to shake. She clutched the keys tightly in her hands and refused to acknowledge King's command. He wasn't going to shut her out like this. She wouldn't allow it.

"What's wrong with you, King? What happened? Please, sweetheart," she pleaded, as an overwhelming fear began to replace her reason. Something was still very wrong.

"Jesse," he shouted, "give me the damn keys."

Shockey walked up just in time to hear their heated exchange, and knew trouble wasn't over after all. This man was out of control.

"Not until you tell me what happened," Jesse screamed back at him. "This concerns me as much as it does you." Huge tears gathered and began spilling down her cheeks as she clutched the car keys tighter against her breast.

King wouldn't allow himself to think about Jesse. He had a growing horror within him that replaced everything but a need to hear for himself that what he feared was wrong. It had to be.

"Lynch is dead," he finally muttered. Then his voice rose in angry volume as he shouted, "But he recognized me." King spun around wildly, his boots kicking up dust as he pounded his fist on the hood of his car. "He thought he knew me!"

"I don't understand," Jesse whispered, clutching the keys as an anchor against the suspicion that suddenly started the world spinning around her. "He doesn't know you…does he?"

"No…he doesn't know *me*." King muttered, his throat tight and aching as he continued. "But, Jesse… he knows someone who looks like me." He watched comprehension hit Jesse in the face with a resounding slap. "And," he continued, "he called him 'Boss.'"

Jesse staggered, struck dumb by the implication of King's accusation. She let the keys fall from her hands as her knees gave way.

Shockey reached out and caught her as King snagged the car keys just before they hit the dirt.

"Take care of her," King ordered, and started to stalk away.

"You wait a minute," Captain Shockey ordered. "I want to know what's going on here." But his words were useless as King backed the car away from the stunned pair and drove off in a cloud of dust.

"Oh, God!" Jesse moaned, and buried her face in her

hands. She had to do something. She couldn't let King get to Duncan. If he did, one of them would die. Either King would kill Duncan, or he'd die trying. Any way she looked at it, she was going to lose King.

"Miss LeBeau," Shockey ordered, grabbing her shoulders and shaking her gently. "Get hold of yourself and tell me what in hell all that was about."

"Duncan," she mumbled, and started pulling Shockey toward the cars. "We've got to hurry," she began to sob. "King has gone to find Duncan, and if he does, he'll kill him."

"Who the hell is Duncan, and why would King want to kill him?" he asked, allowing Jesse to pull him along as they talked. It was obvious something more was involved. Maybe he was about to find the accomplice.

"Duncan is King's uncle," Jesse muttered. "Please, we've got to hurry!"

"Why would King want to kill his uncle, and what did he mean by Lynch recognizing him?"

"Lynch recognized King, at least he thought he did," Jesse answered, "because King and Duncan could pass for identical twins."

Shockey's hesitance was driving her mad. She screamed aloud as Shockey stopped stubbornly in front of her. "Lynch called King 'Boss.' Don't you see? He got them mixed up. Please, we have to hurry."

The implication was sinking into Shockey's analytical mind as he yanked Jesse into the car seat beside him.

"Yes, girl, I'm beginning to," he answered. "Now give me an address fast. We're going to need help to stop that man."

He wrote down the address Jesse gave him, and

grabbed his radio mike. The Tulsa police were going to have to help. He'd never make it in time to stop King McCandless.

King never knew how he got to Duncan's apartment. He didn't even bother to park properly. He just stopped, left the keys in the ignition, and got out of the car in a trance-like state. He could hear sirens in the distance, warning all who got in the way of their impending progress, but King was past rational thinking. He had to see Duncan face to face; he had to hear him admit what he feared was true, or deny it. King couldn't think past that. He couldn't let himself think about retribution.

His gut twisted in a knot of despair as he punched the twelfth-floor button in the elevator and swallowed the choking rage that rose bitterly in his throat. When the door opened at the twelfth floor, he had to tell himself to move. King knew now that each step he took would be bringing him close to the end of the world as he knew it.

He heard the elevator door open down the hall as he arrived at Duncan's apartment, but he ignored it. All his being was focused on the door in front of him. He took a deep breath, doubled up his fist, and hammered loudly.

"Duncan!" he shouted. "Open the door!" No one responded.

This time, when he pounded loudly on the door, he issued an ultimatum.

"Duncan! Open the damn door, or I'll kick it in."

There was an ominous silence before Duncan spoke sarcastically. "It's not locked, nephew. Do the civilized thing, and use the doorknob, please."

King twisted the knob and slammed the door back against the wall as he entered. His heart jerked to a full stop at the sight before him. He realized then that his worst fears were probably true.

Duncan was half standing, half sitting on a bar stool with a nearly empty bottle of bourbon in one hand, and a pistol in the other. He cocked an eyebrow at the big, angry man before him, the two policemen who followed him through the door, and waved the pistol in their general direction.

"Come in, come in," he called loudly. "I wasn't expecting you." Then he muttered to himself. "Or maybe I was. At any rate, you're here. What can I do for you?"

King looked around in surprise at the men behind him, and then back at Duncan, ignoring the officers' advice to take cover.

The police looked at each other, uncertain how to defuse the situation without someone getting hurt. One of them called out forcefully to Duncan McCandless. "Drop your gun, mister! Whatever's going on here can be settled without violence. Let me have your gun, then we'll talk about this."

Duncan smiled, ignoring their presence, and turned his attention to his nephew.

King spoke in short, clipped sentences, his husky voice so strained it wasn't much more than a whisper.

"Lynch is dead," King said, watching Duncan's face for something…anything…that would tell him he was wrong.

"Well, now," Duncan drawled. "That's good news, isn't it? That calls for a drink." He tipped his head back, tilted the bourbon bottle, and let the fiery liquid run slowly down his throat.

King never blinked. He never moved. But his hands clinched and unclinched at his sides as he watched Duncan deteriorate before his eyes. It was a strange sensation. Almost like watching himself die.

"He called me 'Boss,'" King said softly. "Now why would he do that, Duncan? Why did he think he knew me?"

Duncan sat staring at the men before him. When the policemen started forward, he quietly aimed his pistol at King's chest and muttered, "Because he's a fool."

The police stopped instantly as the armed man took aim at King. But their guns remained pointed at the man by the bar. There was just no way they could disarm him without endangering the unarmed civilian, so they stood by, waiting anxiously for the armed man to make a mistake, or have a change of heart and put down his weapon.

"Why?" King asked, fury and betrayal in his posture and voice.

"Why?" Duncan repeated, and then his entire surface charm vanished. His face and posture changed. Suddenly he didn't look like King at all. He looked old and beaten.

"Because! Because you were born with what I wanted. What I deserved," he snarled. "Andrew was *my* brother before he was *your* father. You were born with *my* face…and they named *you* the 'King.' It wasn't fair. It wasn't fair."

King was stunned. He had to force himself not to shout as he spoke. "You blamed me for being born?"

he growled in disbelief. "You spent…no…wasted your life hating me for an accident of birth? You pitiful son-of-a-bitch. I knew you were weak. I just didn't know you were stupid."

His taunt struck home as Duncan stood and glared furiously at the man he should have been. "Shut up," he warned, and took steadier aim at the third button on King's shirt.

"Back off, mister," the police said to King, but he ignored them as well as their order.

"Go ahead," King shouted, losing what was left of his control. "Shoot an unarmed man. I know you're capable. Anyone who'd use an innocent woman just to get back at me would do anything."

Duncan's face crumpled. For the first time, King saw genuine regret.

"She wasn't supposed to get hurt," he muttered. "He wasn't supposed to touch her."

"No?" King drawled sarcastically. "You were just going to kidnap her, scare her to death, cause her mental anguish for the rest of her life, but you weren't going to hurt her? What the hell kind of a twisted plot is that?"

"Well," Duncan sneered, "it wasn't smart. I'll admit that. But after all, what did you expect? I'm not the 'King.' So," he continued, "where does that leave us? I have no intention of going to jail and watching you walk away with everything, including Jesse."

King started forward, taking each step with controlled deliberation.

"Now's your chance," he snarled back in Duncan's face. "Pull the damn trigger, and get your misery over with."

"No!" a policeman shouted at King.

"Drop your weapon," the other ordered Duncan.

But the big man didn't stop advancing, and his mirror image remained, gun aimed, poised at the edge of making the last big mistake of his life.

Duncan blinked, startled that King was no longer under his control. He felt a sick, sinking feeling start at the bottom of his boots and crawl steadily upwards toward the huge knot of horror stuck in his throat. Now he had to make a choice, and he knew he had none left.

Duncan took unsteady aim, cocked the pistol, and called aloud in a jeering fashion, "The King is dead, long live the King."

A shot rang out. King stopped, his next step forgotten as the wide, spreading pain tightened around his chest. A denial of rage erupted from his mouth, but it was too late. He watched, horrified, as Duncan dropped limply to the floor, the life in his eyes disappearing as a pool of blood appeared beneath him.

Duncan McCandless, as usual, had taken the easy way out of a bad situation. He'd taken his own life.

"Aw, hell," one of the policemen muttered as they pushed past King's frozen figure. "Get an ambulance," he ordered, and his partner quickly responded.

Neither man had time to spend assuring King there was nothing that could have prevented this. When a crazy man has a loaded gun, someone's bound to get hurt. He could have just as easily turned it on them.

King turned and walked blindly toward the open door into the hall as the pain in his chest expanded into his mind. He felt helpless, uncertain, and betrayed in a way he'd never imagined.

The arrival of paramedics and OSBI officers clogged

the narrow hallway as King wandered aimlessly toward the elevator. He had to get away from this nightmare. The only thing that was keeping him from coming apart was the thought of Jesse. She was out there… somewhere. And he knew he had to find her.

"What's happening?" Jesse asked nervously, as Captain Shockey maneuvered his way through Tulsa traffic, a red light on the dash of his car flashing a warning to allow him easier access. Jesse could hear the traffic on the police radio, but nearly everything was in code. She couldn't decipher their messages, yet the look on Shockey's face told Jesse something was wrong. She was afraid of his answer.

"Police and paramedics are on the scene," he replied gruffly.

"Paramedics?" Jesse felt sick to her stomach. It was almost more than she could ask. "Someone is hurt?"

Shockey hitched his position in the car seat, trying to find a cooler, more comfortable spot. But the sun coming through the windows beat out the faltering air conditioner's weak airflow, and the seats in these cars weren't ever going to be comfortable. One way or another, a policeman was always on a hot seat. Finally, he cleared his throat and blurted out, "Someone's not hurt," he replied. "Someone is dead."

"Not King," she moaned, and buried her face in her hands. It wasn't King. She couldn't face it if it was. "Hurry, please!" She choked back a sob, and gripped the armrest on the car door until her fingers turned white.

There were so many official vehicles in the apartment parking lot that Shockey had trouble turning into the entryway. Jesse looked frantically from man to man in the milling crowd around the cars and in the doorway. She saw nothing but uniforms.

Shockey hit the brakes, flashing his badge as an officer momentarily halted their progress. Jesse took the opportunity to bolt from the car. She was out and pushing her way through the policeman before Shockey had unbuckled his seat belt. Her heart was pounding so viciously against her ribcage that it hurt to breathe. Fear weakened her legs so that each step she took was a test of endurance. Yet she continued blindly toward the darkened doorway, shaded by a wide, striped awning over the walkway. More than one officer noted the pretty, dark-haired woman in the green dress darting through the crowd, but each time a hand stretched out to restrain her, she would elude the order to stop.

King saw a flash of green coming through the crowd, and felt all the anxiety of the last few minutes pour from him in a rush. It was Jesse. He fixed on that sundress with desperation, and came out of the shadowed doorway into the sun.

Jesse saw him pause, saw the stunned, blank expression and the almost aimless stride. Then she saw him focus and start toward her with unwavering determination. She was in his arms!

King clutched desperately, tangling his fingers in her hair as he drew strength and sanity just from holding her against his heart. He couldn't talk. It was beyond him to tell her, at least…not yet. He couldn't admit to himself the festering guilt that was beginning to spread inside him. How had he been so blind? How could he have been so unaware of such vicious, demented hate?

Maybe if he'd noticed sooner? There had to have been signals over the years. Maybe...just maybe he could have prevented this. But it was too late to speculate. Jesse had nearly died...and Duncan *was* dead. And in some way, King had decided, it was all his fault.

Jesse felt him begin to shake, felt the desperation in his grasp, and tightened her hold on him, breathing a prayer of thanksgiving that he was alive and in her arms.

Minutes passed. They were surrounded by OSBI and Captain Shockey, all wanting answers to their questions. They wanted to know what had tipped him off. How had he realized who was the mastermind behind Jesse's failed kidnapping? Finally King had enough.

"We're going home," he said tersely, daring anyone to argue. "If you have any other questions, come to the ranch, or call. You have our number."

No one disagreed as King ushered Jesse toward the car.

"King," Jesse said. "Let me drive."

He looked down at the concern on her face, and the way she kept holding back tears. His mind was blanking out. Whenever there was a lull in the conversation, King saw that last look on Duncan's face over and over. He knew if he got behind the wheel of the car, he wouldn't see traffic. He wouldn't hear anything but Duncan's last accusations flung into his face.

He nodded, opened the door on the driver's side for Jesse, then hurried around to get in. A KTUL camera crew had just arrived. He had no desire to be on the six o'clock news.

"We're home," Jesse said quietly. She pulled into the

long driveway and looked at King with a worried expression in her eyes. He'd ridden the entire trip without speaking a word.

He blinked, looked up with a startled expression, and then wearily wiped his hands across his burning eyes.

"How am I going to tell everyone?" he muttered. "What do I say? Oh, by the way, Duncan is dead now? He hated me so much that when his plan to get even failed, he shot himself?"

"King," Jesse rebuked softly. "It's not your fault. Nor is it mine. I could be sitting here telling myself that if I'd loved him, instead of you, you'd both be alive. The world does not run on 'what ifs.'"

King glanced sideways at Jesse, grimaced, and then opened the door.

"I'll tell Maggie, I'll find the words...somehow."

"We'll tell her together, King," she replied, as she walked beside him toward the house. She slipped her hand in his and squeezed gently. "We'll tell them *all* together."

Somehow the deed had been accomplished. Uttering the words aloud had, in some way, increased the horror. But the telling was over. Now all they had to do was bury Duncan and get on with their lives. It was easier said than done.

It was late as Maggie bid good night and finally departed to her bedroom for a much needed rest. Jesse walked through the house, moving quietly on bare feet as she checked the locks on the doors. This was usually something King did, but not tonight. Jesse knew a nightly routine would be the last thing on his mind.

The memorial service had been disastrous. How could one mourn the loss of a stranger? That's what Duncan had become. All Jesse had been able to do was say a prayer, hoping he'd find a peace that had escaped him in life elsewhere. She hadn't known what King was thinking during the services. He'd remained too silent, watching it all from a distance, not allowing himself to grieve in any manner. As soon as they'd come home, King shut himself in the den...away from phone calls... away from sympathy or pity.

But it was late, and Jesse had worried herself into tomorrow. King had had enough time alone. She was going in, and she wasn't taking no for an answer.

She opened the door and stood silently in the doorway, allowing her eyes to adjust to the darkness inside.

"Close the door."

King's voice came out of the shadows and Jesse stepped inside, complying with his gruff order.

"Where are you?" Jesse asked softly, and started to turn on the lamp beside the door when another order in the form of a plea stopped her hand.

"Don't turn on the light, please."

Jesse followed the sound of his voice to the long, overstuffed leather sofa in the middle of the room. She stopped as her foot touched the corner, walked around behind the sofa, and traced her hand along the cushions and down the side until she felt the uneven rise and fall of King's bare chest.

"Sweetheart," Jesse said, and then felt King clutch at her hands in desperation.

"Come here," he coaxed, as he reached upward, pulling Jesse gently off her feet and over the back of the sofa until she lay stretched full length on top of him.

He clasped her face in his hands and ran the tips of his thumbs carefully along the line of her cheeks down to the corners of her mouth, before he pulled her into his kiss with a low, hungry groan.

He drank from the comfort of Jesse's touch, seeking solace from her taste just as he'd sought solace from the empty glass and half-empty bottle on the floor beside the sofa. Neither took away the slow burn inside his belly.

Finally he released Jesse's mouth and buried his face in her hair.

"I can't make it go away," King whispered hoarsely. "I can't even get drunk. Help me, Jesse Rose. Just help me get through tonight."

King felt her tears fall in sparse sprinkles on his face and neck, as her mouth captured the sun-tanned skin on his body in sharp, hungry bites. She moved silently over him, feeling with every caress of her fingers the growing urgency and need in his body.

King yearned for Jesse in a way he'd never imagined possible. Tonight, they both needed to be reminded of life—death had been too near.

King lay still, a willing victim of Jesse's tender mercies. When he heard her removing her clothing in the thick darkness, he quickly followed suit.

Suddenly there was no time for pretense, no time left to wait for the passion to build. Urgency took away what was left of will power as King took Jesse into his arms in one powerful motion, and drove his hard, aching body into her sweet warmth with a desperate thrust.

The sensation was devastating. Every muscle in Jesse's body tensed and then pulsed around and on King. She felt him begin to shudder, heard the harsh gasps for breath as he thrust into her again and again.

Tiny moans slipped between their mouths as Jesse took King's breath and traded it for her own. Her hands clasped tightly behind his neck as her legs wrapped around his waist, pulling him deeper and deeper into the only solace she could provide.

Release came suddenly in the form of a white-hot flash of pleasure that sent them both falling backward onto the sofa in weak relief.

Jesse sat straddling his lap, as King buried his face in the gentle swell of her breasts beneath his searching hands. She felt the tension flowing from his shoulders and his heartbeat kick into a lower rhythm as all sense of desperation and urgency passed in the quiet darkness.

"I love you, King McCandless," Jesse whispered as she gently brushed the damp locks of his hair from his forehead.

King sighed softly and pulled her into a fierce hug of thanksgiving. He just wished he could love himself. Maybe then this awful, growing guilt would disappear and he could love Jesse back the way she deserved to be loved.

The following week was a nightmare Jesse feared would never end. It began with continuous phone calls, most from old friends, some from journalists, looking for a new angle to an old story.

The more confusion that erupted, the further King withdrew. He didn't communicate with anyone unless he had to. Even Jesse suffered from his long bouts of moody silence. She knew he'd eventually come to realize none of this had been his fault, but it would take time. Nothing she nor anyone said now was getting through to him. He needed time. She was going to give it to him.

She had to go back to St. Louis and tie up the loose ends of her old life. She was ready for a new one.

"Maggie," Jesse called down the hallway, "is Turner outside yet?"

"No, honey. But he should be here soon. Need any help?"

"No," she answered, and dashed breathlessly into the living room where Maggie stood watching for her ride to the airport. "I'm just taking an overnight bag. I don't plan on being gone more than a day…two at the most. I'll spend the night with my friend Sheila, and use the day to finalize my errands. I'll be home before you know I'm gone."

"I already miss you, honey," Maggie said, hugging Jesse quickly, then returning to her vigilant post as lookout for Turner and his pickup truck.

Jesse had tried several times over the last few days to talk to King. She wanted to tell him about her need to go back to St. Louis for a short time. She had a buyer for her house, and needed to see her principal at the school and get an official release from her teaching contract.

But each time she broached the subject, King would plead an urgent duty or totally ignore her efforts to get close. He wouldn't touch her except in the most casual of manners. It was as if their time together had never existed. Jesse was staying in her own room again, alone and frustrated at King's refusal to share his sorrow with anyone. He wouldn't even admit he felt sorrow, when in fact he was utterly miserable.

"He's here!" Maggie called. And, before she knew it, Jesse was gone. She had a feeling that when King came home tonight, he wasn't going to like this one bit.

A long, hungry rumble accompanied the clouds darkening the sky over Tulsa. Maggie looked anxiously out the window and muttered, "Lord, if you're just teasing, stop it right now. We've needed rain too long to be disappointed again."

But the thunder continued, and the sky got darker and darker. Maybe this time it was finally going to rain.

King hammered the last nail in place in the big gate separating the house and cattle pastures. His muscles ached, his blue chambray work shirt had a three-cornered tear Maggie was going to fuss about, and the perspiration had plastered his Levi's to his long legs with stubborn stickiness. He was tired, dirty, and hadn't felt this good in weeks. Maybe when he got home this evening, he could talk Jesse into going out for dinner, that is, if she was still talking to him.

He knew he'd been uncommunicative. He knew he should have been able to talk to Jesse, but somehow he just couldn't. He felt so responsible for what had happened to her, and he kept remembering how he'd wanted to kill the man who'd hurt her. No matter what his brain kept telling him, his heart told him differently. Duncan was dead, and he'd watched it happen.

But over the past few days, being back at the ranch

and working long, hot hours either with the men or alone, he'd begun to heal.

Thunder rumbled across the sky. He looked up in surprise. He hadn't noticed the air cooling, or the sky darkening. He whistled for Tariq, who was grazing aimlessly along the fence line, and watched with admiration as the beautiful animal jerked his head up and answered his call on the run.

"Come on, boy," King murmured, as he slipped his tool belt into the saddle bag. "We better get off this hill before we fry."

He wasn't anxious to be a target for the lightning he saw in the gathering clouds. "Let's go home."

King made it to the house just ahead of the first deluge. The clouds opened and literally poured water onto the arid land. The drought was over.

"Where's Jesse?" King asked, as he wandered back to the kitchen where a very stern Maggie was preparing the evening meal.

"Gone," she announced shortly. She, too, was irked at King's continuing silences. If he'd listened, he would have known where Jesse had gone.

King felt the floor tilt beneath him. A dull, aching throb began behind his eyelids. He could barely speak.

"Where?" he asked softly.

"St. Louis," Maggie replied. "She tried to tell you for three days, but you were too busy to listen. It couldn't wait any longer."

"She left me?" King whispered, and sank down to the bar stool behind him.

Maggie relented at the look of utter desolation on

King's face. He'd suffered enough the last few days to last a lifetime.

"She'll be back," Maggie said, and walked over to King. "Come here, boy," she said softly. "I need a hug."

King felt her arms go around his neck as she pulled his head down on her ample shoulder.

"I'm sorry," he said, past the ache in his throat. He relished the familiar comfort, yet the empty spot in his heart continued to grow wider. He fiercely returned her hug.

"I'm not the one you need to be saying that to, mister," Maggie said. She planted a swift kiss on his cheek, then turned and busied herself back at the sink. She didn't want him to see her cry.

Maggie needn't have worried. King couldn't have seen her tears for the ones blinding him. He walked slowly out of the house and stood beneath the shelter of the porch as the rain continued to fall, washing the trees and the land clean from the long months of stifling dust and heat, as it washed the last remnants of guilt from King's soul. He watched the day end with a promise in his heart of a better tomorrow.

"I need a one-way ticket to St. Louis," King growled. He couldn't believe he was actually getting back on a damn airplane. But it was the fastest way to get to Jesse.

"Yes, sir," the lady behind the ticket counter replied. "Moving, are you?"

"No!" King answered, ignoring the curious look on the woman's face.

"Have you checked your baggage?" she asked,

stamping his ticket, then handing it back across the counter.

"Don't have any," King said shortly, then glared, daring her to continue her nosy harangue. "I'm coming back today."

"Then you'll want a round-trip ticket," she announced, and started to pull the ticket away.

"No, I don't," he argued, and stuffed the ticket in his pocket. "This is the last time I willingly get on an airplane. I'm coming home today. If I have to, I'll buy a car, but I won't get back on another damn tin bird."

He walked away, already dreading the sick sensation of lifting off the ground and the feeling of being out-of-control. Jesse better know how much he loved her, because he wouldn't be able to do much more than shake when he arrived.

Jesse folded the last of the clothes she intended to take back to Tulsa, and piled the rest in a stack headed for Goodwill.

The painters had done a good job of cleaning up her bedroom, yet she could hardly bring herself to stay long enough in it to get her belongings. Too many bad memories hung heavily in the air. Her principal was more than happy to release her from her contract. The certified substitute he hired had proven to be a good teacher. It was going to work out nicely all around.

Jesse said goodbye to her friend Sheila, made promises to visit, and breathed a sigh of relief. Now all she had to do was load her car and she would be on her way home…to King. When she got back, if she had to, she'd kidnap *him* until he stopped this foolish silence. King was just going to have to learn how to share more than his body with her. She smiled a slow, secretive smile, and thought to herself, *But, his body was a good place to start the sharing process. We'll take it from there.*

She worked in comfortable silence until the ringing doorbell interrupted her progress. Assuming that it was probably Goodwill coming to pick up her clothing donation, she got the shock of her life when a man's large shadow loomed in the doorway.

"King!" Jesse cried. "Honey, are you all right?"

The look of desolation in his eyes scared her silly. Had something else happened? She was almost afraid to ask as she pulled him by the arm into her house.

"You left me," he accused in a husky voice.

Jesse breathed a relieved sigh, threw her arms around him in a boisterous welcome, then began kissing his shirt front. It was as far as she could reach.

"Didn't Maggie tell you?" Jesse asked, as she cupped his face in her hands. "I tried to, but you wouldn't listen…and this couldn't wait."

King closed his eyes, turning his face into the palm of her hand, tracing her lifeline with the tip of his tongue, then grabbed her roughly and pulled her off the floor.

"Jesse," he whispered against her lips. "I'm so sorry, baby, I know I should have been able to talk…especially to you. But somehow it got all twisted up in my head. I felt like it was my fault. It took days for that feeling to lessen. I need you to make it go away."

"Sweetheart," she murmured, and brushed her mouth softly across his lips. "You already have me. You didn't need to follow me here. You should have known I'd be back."

King watched the love in her eyes grow, and felt a healing warmth flow between them.

"I love you so much, Jesse Rose."

"I love you, too, King. But you should have trusted me. I wouldn't leave you...not again."

"I know that, baby," he said gruffly.

"Then why are you here?" Jesse asked, as King lifted her into his arms.

"I'm just doing what I should have done three years ago, Jesse Rose. I've come to take you home."

* * * * *

Delores Fossen, a *USA TODAY* bestselling author, has written over one hundred novels, with millions of copies of her books in print worldwide. She's received a Booksellers' Best Award and an RT Reviewers' Choice Best Book Award. She was also a finalist for a prestigious RITA® Award. You can contact the author through her website at deloresfossen.com.

Books by Delores Fossen

Harlequin Intrigue

The Lawmen of McCall Canyon

Cowboy Above the Law
Finger on the Trigger
Lawman with a Cause
Under the Cowboy's Protection

HQN

Lone Star Ridge

Tangled Up in Texas
That Night in Texas (ebook novella)
Chasing Trouble in Texas

A Coldwater Texas Novel

Lone Star Christmas
Hot Texas Sunrise
Sweet Summer Sunset
A Coldwater Christmas

Visit the Author Profile page at Harlequin.com for more titles.

NATE

Delores Fossen

Chapter 1

Lieutenant Nate Ryland took one look at the preschool building and knew something was wrong.

He eased his hand over his Glock. After ten years of being a San Antonio cop, it was an automatic response. But there was nothing rote or automatic about the iron-hard knot that tightened in his stomach.

"Kimmie," he said under his breath. His fifteen-month-old daughter, Kimberly Ellen, was inside.

The side door to the Silver Creek Preschool and Day Care was wide open. But not *just* open. It was dangling in place, the warm April breeze battering it against the sunshine-yellow frame. It looked as if it'd been partially torn off the hinges.

Nate elbowed his car door shut and walked closer. He kept his hand positioned over his gun and tried to rein in the fear that had started to crawl through him.

He recognized the feeling. The sickening dread. The last time he'd felt like this he'd found his wife bleeding and dying in an alleyway.

Cursing under his breath, he hurried now, racing across the manicured lawn that was dotted with kiddie cars and other riding toys.

"What's wrong?" someone called out.

He snapped toward the voice and the petite brunette whom he recognized immediately. It wasn't a good recognition, either.

Darcy Burkhart.

A defense attorney who had recently moved to Silver Creek. But Nate had known Darcy before her move. Simply put, she had been and continued to be a thorn in his side. He'd already butted heads with her once today and didn't have time for round two.

Nate automatically scowled. So did she. She was apparently there to pick up her child. A son about Kimmie's age if Nate recalled correctly. He remembered Kimmie's nanny, Grace Borden, mentioning something about Darcy having enrolled the little boy in the two-hour-long Tuesday-Thursday play sessions held at the day-care center.

"I asked, what's wrong?" Darcy repeated. It was the same tone she used in court when representing the scum she favored defending.

Nate ignored both her scowl and her question, and continued toward the single-story building. The preschool was at the end of Main Street, nestled in a sleepy, parklike section with little noise or traffic. He reminded himself that it was a safe place for children.

Usually.

He had no idea what was wrong, but Nate knew that

something was—the door was proof of that. He prayed there was a simple explanation for the damage. Like an ill-timed gust of wind. Or a preschool employee who'd given it too hard a push.

But it didn't feel like anything *simple*.

Without stopping, he glanced at the side parking lot. No activity there, though there were three cars, all belonging to the employees, no doubt. He also glanced behind him at the sidewalk and street where he and Darcy had left their own vehicles. If someone with criminal intentions had damaged the door, then the person wasn't outside.

That left the inside.

"Why is your hand on your gun?" Darcy asked, catching up with him. Not easily. She was literally running across the grassy lawn in high heels and a crisp ice-blue business suit, and the slim skirt made it nearly impossible for her to keep up with him.

"Shhhh," he growled.

Nate reached the front porch, which stretched across the entire front of the building. There were four windows, spaced far apart, and the nearest was still a few feet away from the door. He tested the doorknob.

It was locked.

Another sign that something was wrong. It was never locked this time of day because, like he had, other parents would arrive soon to pick up their children from the play session.

He drew his gun.

Behind him, Darcy gasped, and he shot her a get-quiet glare that he hoped she would obey. While he was hoping, he added that maybe she would stay out of the way.

She didn't.

Continuing to be a thorn in his side, she trailed along right behind him with those blasted heels battering like bullets on the wooden planks. Of course, he couldn't blame her. Her son was inside, and if she had any intuition whatsoever, she knew something wasn't right.

Nate moved to the window and peered around the edge of the frame. He tried to brace himself for anything and everything but instead saw nothing. The room was empty.

Another bad sign.

It should literally be crawling with toddlers, the teacher and other staff members. This should be the last fifteen minutes of the play session, and the staff was expecting him. Nate had called an hour earlier to let them know that he would be arriving a little early so he could watch Kimmie play with the other kids. Maybe Darcy had had the same idea.

He lifted his head, listening, and it didn't take him long to hear the faint sound. Someone was crying. A baby. And it sounded like Kimmie.

Nothing could have held him back at that point. Nate raced across the porch and jumped over the waist-high railing so he could get to that door with the broken hinge. He landed on the ground, soggy from the morning's hard rain, and the mud squeezed over the toes of his cowboy boots. It seemed to take hours to go those few yards, but he finally made it. Unfortunately, the sound of the crying got louder and louder.

Nate threw open the broken door and faced yet another empty playroom. His heart went to his knees. Because the room wasn't just empty.

There were signs of a struggle.

Toys and furniture had been knocked over. There was a diaper bag discarded in the middle of the floor, and it looked as if someone had rifled through it. The phone, once mounted onto the wall, had been ripped off and now lay crushed and broken on the counter.

He didn't call out for his daughter, though he had to fight the nearly overwhelming urge to do just that and therefore alert a possible intruder. Kimmie had to be all right. She just had to be. Because the alternative was unthinkable. He'd already lost her mother, and he couldn't lose her.

Trying to keep his footsteps light so he would hopefully have the element of surprise, Nate made his way across the room and looked around the corner. No one was in the kitchen, but the crying was coming from the other side. It was one of the nap rooms, filled with beds and cribs, and normally it wasn't in use on Tuesday afternoons for the play group.

He heard the movement behind him, and with his Glock aimed and ready, he reeled around. It was Darcy, again. She gasped, and her cocoa-brown eyes widened at the gun pointed directly at her.

"Stay put," Nate whispered, using the hardest cop's expression he could manage. "Call nine-one-one and tell my brother to get out here."

Even though Darcy was new in town, she no doubt knew Sheriff Grayson Ryland was his brother. If she hadn't realized before there was something wrong, then she certainly knew it now.

"My son!" she said on a gasp.

She would have torn right past him if Nate hadn't snagged her arm. "Make the call," he ordered.

Her breath was gusting now, but she stopped struggling and gave a shaky nod. She rammed her hand into her purse and pulled out her cell phone.

Nate didn't wait for her to call the sheriff's office. She would do it, and soon Grayson and probably one of his other brothers would arrive. Two were deputies. And a nine-one-one call to respond to the preschool would get everyone in the sheriff's office moving fast.

Nate took aim again and hurried across the kitchen toward the nap room. The baby was still crying. Maybe it was Kimmie. But he heard something else, too. An adult's voice.

He stopped at the side of the door and glanced inside. At first, Nate didn't see the children. They weren't on the beds or in the cribs. But he looked down and spotted them.

Six toddlers.

They were huddled together in the corner with the teacher, Tara Hillman, and another woman Nate didn't recognize, but she no doubt worked there since both women wore name tags decorated with crayons. The babies were clinging to the adults, who were using hushed voices to try to comfort them.

"Lieutenant Ryland," Tara blurted out. Her eyes, like the other woman's, were red with tears, and they looked terrified.

With a baby clutched in each arm, Tara struggled to get to her feet. "Did you see them?"

"See who? What happened here?" Nate threaded his way through the maze of beds to make it to the other side of the room. He frantically looked through the huddle so he could find Kimmie.

"Two men," the other woman said. "They were wearing ski masks, and they had guns."

"They barged in before we could do anything to stop them," Tara explained.

"What happened here?" Nate repeated. He moved one of the babies aside. The one who was crying.

But it wasn't Kimmie.

"They took her," Tara said, though her voice hardly had any sound.

The words landed like fists against Nate and robbed him of his breath, maybe his sanity, too. "Took who?" He knew he was frantic now, but he couldn't stop himself.

"Kimmie." She made a hoarse sound. "They took Kimmie. Marlene, the other helper who works here, was holding her, and they made Marlene go with them. I couldn't stop them. I tried. I swear, I tried."

Everything inside Nate was on the verge of spinning out of control. That knot in his stomach moved to his throat and was choking him.

"What did they want? Where did they go?" he somehow managed to ask.

Tara swallowed hard and shook her head. "They drove away in a black van about ten minutes ago."

"Which direction?" Nate couldn't get out the question fast enough.

But Tara shook her head again. "They made us get on the floor, and I can't see the windows from there. They said if we went after them or if we called the sheriff that they'd come back and kill us all."

Nate turned to run. He had to get to his car *now*. He had to go in pursuit. He also had to get at least one of the deputies out to protect Tara and the babies just in case the gunmen followed through on their threat and returned. But he only made it a few steps before he smacked right into Darcy.

"They took Kimmie," he heard himself say.

But Darcy didn't seem to hear him. She was searching through the cluster of children. "Noah?" she called out. She repeated her son's name, louder this time.

Nate couldn't take the time to help her look. He had to find that van. He snatched his phone from his pocket and pressed the number for his brother. Grayson answered on the first ring.

"We're on the way," Grayson assured him without waiting for Nate to say a word. His brother had obviously gotten Darcy's call.

"According to the teacher, two armed men took Kimmie," Nate got out. "They kidnapped her and one of the workers, and they left in a black van. Close off the streets. Shut down the whole damn town before they have a chance to get out with her."

Nate didn't hear his brother's response because of the bloodcurdling scream that came from the preschool. That stopped him, and it wasn't more than a second or two before Darcy came tearing out of the building.

"They took Noah!" she yelled to Nate.

Hell. Not just one kidnapped child but two. "Did you hear?" Nate asked Grayson. He ran toward his car.

"I heard. So did Dade. He's listening in and already working to get someone out to look for that van. He'll get there in just a few minutes."

Dade, his twin brother and a Silver Creek deputy. Nate had no doubts that Dade would do everything he could to find Kimmie, but Nate wasn't going to just stand there and wait. He had to locate that van. He had to get Kimmie back.

"I'm going east," Nate let his brother know, and he ended the call so he could drive out of there fast.

Nate grappled to get the keys from his pocket, but his hands wouldn't cooperate. He tried to push the panic aside. He tried to think like a cop. But he wasn't just a cop. He was a father, and those armed SOBs had taken his baby girl.

He finally managed to extract his keys, somehow, and he jerked open his car door. Nate jumped inside. But so did Darcy. She threw herself onto the passenger seat.

"I'm going with you," she insisted. "I have to get Noah."

"We don't even know who has them," Nate said. He dropped his cell phone onto the console between the seats so he could easily reach it. He needed it to stay in touch with Grayson.

"No, we don't know who has them, but they left this." She thrust a wrinkled piece of notebook paper at him. "It was taped to the side of the fridge."

Nate looked at her, trying to read her expression, but he only saw the fear and worry that was no doubt on his own face. He took the paper and read the scrawled writing.

This was his worst nightmare come true.

Nate Ryland and Darcy Burkhart, we have them.
Cooperate or you'll never see your babies again.

Chapter 2

Cooperate or you'll never see your babies again.

The words raced through Darcy's head. She wanted to believe this wasn't really happening, that any second now she would wake up and see her son's smiling face. But the crumpled letter in Nate Ryland's hand seemed very real. And so was the fear that bubbled up in her throat.

"Cooperate?" she repeated. "How?"

There were a dozen more questions she could have added to those, but Nate didn't seem to have any more answers than she did. The only thing that appeared certain right now was that two gunmen had taken Nate's daughter, her son and a preschool employee, and they had driven off in a black van.

Nate's breath was gusting as much as hers, and he had a wild look in his metal-gray eyes. Even though his hands were shaking and he had a death grip on his gun, he managed to start his car, and he sped off, heading east, away from the center of town.

"This is the way the kidnappers went?" Darcy asked, praying that he knew something she didn't.

He dropped the letter next to his cell phone. "We have a fifty-fifty chance they did."

Oh, God. That wasn't nearly good enough odds when it came to rescuing Noah. "I should get in my car and go in the opposite direction. That way we can cover both ends of town."

"Grayson will do that," Nate snarled. He aimed a glare at her. "Besides, what good would you do going up against two armed men?"

"What good could I do?" Darcy practically yelled. "They have my son, and I'll get him back." Even though she didn't have a gun or any training in how to fight off bad guys. Still, she had a mother's love for her child, and that could overcome anything.

She hoped.

"You'll get yourself killed and maybe the children hurt," Nate fired back. "I'm not going to let you do that." And it wasn't exactly a suggestion.

He was right, of course. She hated that, but it was true. Even if she managed to find the van, she stood little chance of getting past two armed men, especially since she didn't want to give them any reason to fire shots. Not with her baby in that vehicle.

Nate flew past the last of the buildings but then slammed on the brakes. For a moment she thought he'd spotted the van. But no such luck. He was stopping for the dark blue truck that was coming from the opposition direction.

"My brother Dade," Nate told her. "He might have some news that'll help us narrow the search."

Good. She was aware that Nate had a slew of brothers, all in law enforcement. And she was also aware that Dade was a deputy sheriff since only two months earlier he'd been involved in the investigation of one of her former clients. A client killed in a shoot-out with Nate.

The two vehicles screeched to a stop side by side, and both men put down the windows. Darcy ducked down a little so she could see the man in the driver's seat of the truck.

Yes, definitely Nate's brother.

He had the same midnight-black hair. The same icy eyes. But Dade looked like a rougher version of his brother, who had obviously just come from his job in SAPD. Nate wore jeans but with a crisp gray shirt and black jacket. Dade looked as if he'd just climbed out of the saddle, with his denim shirt and battered Stetson.

The brothers exchanged glances. Brief ones. But it felt as if a thousand things passed silently between them. "Anything?" Nate asked.

Dade's troubled eyes conveyed his answer before he even spoke. "Not yet."

"There was a note," Nate said, handing it through the window to his brother. He immediately started to slap the fingers of his left hand on the steering wheel. He was obviously eager to leave and so was Darcy. "Later I need it bagged and checked for prints."

Later. After they'd rescued the children. Darcy didn't want to think beyond that.

"Once one of the other deputies arrives at the pre-school, I'll be out to help you look," Dade offered. "Was anyone in the building hurt?"

Nate shook his head. "It looked like a smash and grab. Entry through the side door. No signs of...blood."

Dade returned the nod. "Good. Hang in there. We'll find these goons, and we'll find Kimmie."

Nate gave Dade one last brief look, maybe to thank him, and he hit the accelerator again. He sped off in the opposite direction of his brother while he fired glances all around. He wasn't just checking Main Street but all of the side roads and parking lots.

Silver Creek wasn't a large town, but there was a solid quarter mile of shops and houses on Main Street. And there were no assurances that the kidnappers would stay on the main road. Most of the side streets wound their way back to the highway, and that terrified her. Because if the kidnappers made it to the highway, it was just a few miles to the interstate.

"I have to do something," she mumbled. Darcy couldn't stop the panic. Nor the fear. It was building like a pressure cooker inside her as Nate sped past each building.

"You can do something." Nate's voice was strained, like the muscles in his face. "You can keep watch for that van and try to figure out why those men did this."

That didn't settle the panic, but it did cause her to freeze. Why had those men done this? Why had they specifically taken Nate's daughter and her son?

"You're a cop," she blurted out. "This could be connected to something you've done. Maybe someone has a grudge because you arrested him." It was a possible motive. And that caused anger to replace some of the panic. "This could be your fault."

It wasn't reasonable, but by God she wasn't in a reasonable kind of mood. She wanted her son back.

Nate kept his attention nailed to the road, but he also scowled. He clearly wasn't pleased with her accusation. Or with her. But then he always scowled when she was around.

"If this is my fault, then why did they take your son?" Nate asked.

She opened her mouth to explain that away, but she couldn't. Darcy could only sit there and let that sink in. It didn't sink in well.

"If I counted right, there were eight toddlers in that play group today. Eight," he spat out with his teeth semi-clenched. "And they only took ours. They said cooperate or we'd never see our babies again. *Our babies,*" he emphasized. "So what the devil did you do to bring this down on us? You're the one who likes to muck around with slime."

She shook her head, trying to get out the denial. Yes, she was a defense attorney. She'd even successfully defended the man who'd originally been arrested for masterminding the murder of Nate's wife. But that was resolved. His wife's killer was now dead, and so was her former client Charles Brennan.

But he hadn't been her only client.

In the past she had indeed defended people with shady reputations, and in some cases she hadn't been successful. Maybe one of those less-than-stellar clients was holding a grudge.

Oh, mercy. Nate was right. This could all be her fault.

The tears came. She'd been fighting them from the moment she realized something was wrong in the preschool, but she lost that fight now.

"I need you to keep watch," Nate growled. "You can't

do that if you're crying, so dry your eyes and help me look for that van."

"But this is my fault." She tried to choke back a sob but failed at that, too.

"Stop thinking like a mother for just a second. They took both children so it's connected to both of us. Not just me. Not just you. *Both*."

Her gaze flew to his, and she met his frosty-metal eyes. The raw emotions of the moment were still there, deep in those shades of gray, but she could also see the cop now. Here was the formidable opponent she'd come up against in the past.

"The man who killed your wife is dead," she reminded him. "And so is the person who hired him."

"Wesley Dent isn't in jail," Nate provided. He took his attention off her and put it back on the road.

Yes. Wesley Dent was her client. A San Antonio man under investigation for poisoning his wife. Dent had retained her a few days after his wife's death because he was concerned about the accusatory tone the police were taking with him. She'd accompanied him to several interviews and had successfully argued to put limits on the search warrant that was being issued for his house and vehicles.

And the lead investigator in the case was none other than Nate.

Darcy gave that some thought and shook her head. "I don't think Wesley Dent would do this. I'm not even sure he's capable of poisoning anyone."

"He's guilty," Nate said with the complete confidence that only a cop could have.

Darcy was far from convinced of that, but to the best of her knowledge, Dent was the only thing that connected Nate and her. Still, it didn't matter at this point if Dent was the one responsible. They needed to find the van.

Nate's cell phone rang, and without picking it up, he jabbed the button to answer the call on speaker.

"It's Grayson," the caller said.

The sheriff, and from what she'd heard, a very capable lawman. Darcy held her breath, praying that he had good news.

"Anything?" Nate immediately asked.

"No. But we're putting everything in place." He paused just a second. "Dade said you have Ms. Burkhart in the vehicle with you."

"Yeah. She jumped in as I was driving away."

The sheriff mumbled something she didn't catch, but it sounded like profanity. "I shouldn't have to remind you that if you find this van, you should wait for backup. You two shouldn't try to do this alone."

Nate paused, too. "No, we shouldn't. But if I see that van, nothing is going to stop me. Just make sure you have a noose around the area. I don't want them getting away."

"They won't. Now, tell me about this note you gave Dade."

"It said, 'Nate Ryland and Darcy Burkhart, we have them. Cooperate or you'll never see your babies again.' And yes, I know what that means." Nate tightened his grip on the steering wheel. "They won't harm the children because they want them for leverage. I think this is connected to a man named Wesley Dent. Call my captain and have Dent brought in for questioning. Beat the truth out of him if necessary."

Darcy knew she should object to that. She believed

in the law with her whole heart. But her son's safety suddenly seemed above the law.

"I don't suppose it'd do any good to ask you to come back to the station," Grayson said. "We have plenty of people out looking for the van."

"I'm not coming back. Not until—" Nate's eyes widened, and she followed his gaze to what had grabbed his attention.

Oh, mercy. There was a black van on the side street. It was moving but not at a high speed.

Noah could be in there.

"I just spotted the possible escape vehicle on Elmore Road," Nate relayed to his brother. "It's on the move, and I'm in pursuit."

Nate turned his car on what had to be two wheels at most, and with the tires squealing, he maneuvered onto the narrow road. There were houses here, spaced far apart, but thankfully there didn't seem to be any other traffic. Good thing, too, because Nate floored the accelerator and tore through the normally quiet neighborhood.

So did the driver of the van.

He sped up, which meant he had no doubt seen them. Not that she'd expected them to be able to sneak up on the vehicle, but Darcy had hoped they would be able to get closer so she could look inside the windows.

Nate read off the license-plate number to his brother, who was still on the line, though she could hear the sheriff making other calls. Grayson was assembling backup for Nate. She only prayed they wouldn't need it, that they could resolve this here and now.

"Can you try to shoot out the tires or something?" she asked.

"Not with the kids inside. Too risky."

Of course, it was. She obviously wasn't thinking clearly and wouldn't until she had her baby safely in her arms. "How will we get it to stop?"

"Grayson will have someone at the other end of this road. Once the guy realizes he can't escape, he'll stop."

Maybe. And maybe that shoot-out would happen, after all. Darcy tried not to give in to the fear, but she got a double dose of it when the van sped over a hill and disappeared out of sight.

"Are there side roads?" she asked. She'd never been on Elmore or in this particular part of Silver Creek.

"Yeah. Side roads and old ranch trails."

That didn't help with the fear, and she held her breath until Nate's car barreled over the hill. There, about a quarter of a mile in front of them, she could see the van. But not for long. The driver went around a deep curve and disappeared again.

It seemed to take hours for Nate to reach that same curve, and he was going so fast that he had to grapple with the steering wheel to remain in control. The tires on her side scraped against the gravel shoulder and sent a spray of rocks pelting into the car's undercarriage. It sounded like gunshots, and that made her terror worse.

They came out of the curve, only to go right into another one. Nate seemed to realize it was coming because he was already steering in that direction.

Darcy prayed that it wouldn't be much longer before Grayson or someone else approached from the other side of the road so they could stop this chase. She didn't want to risk the van crashing into one of the trees that dotted the sides of the road.

She could hear the chatter on Nate's cell, which was

still on speaker. People were responding. Everything was in motion, but the truth was Nate and she were the ones who were closest to the van. They were their children's best bet for rescue.

"Hold on," Nate warned as he took another turn. "And put on your seat belt."

Her hands were shaking, but she managed to get the belt pulled across her. She was still fumbling with the latch when their car came out of yet another curve followed by a hill.

The moment they reached the top of the hill, she saw the van.

And Darcy's heart went to her knees.

"Stop!" she yelled.

Nate was already trying to do just that. He slammed on the brakes. But they were going too fast. And the van was sideways, right in the middle of the road. The vehicle wasn't moving, and there was no way for Nate to avoid it.

Darcy screamed.

Just as they crashed head-on into the black van.

Chapter 3

Nate heard the screech of his brakes as the asphalt ripped away at the tires. There was nothing he could do.

Nothing.

Except pray and try to brace himself for the impact.

He didn't have to wait long.

The car slammed into the van, tossing Darcy and him around like rag dolls. The air bags deployed, slapping into them and sending a cloud of the powdery dust all through the car's interior.

It was all over in a split second. The whiplashing impact. The sounds of metal colliding with metal.

Nate was aware of the pain in his body from having his muscles wrenched around. The mix of talc and cornstarch powder from the air bag robbed him of what little breath he had. But now that he realized he had survived the crash, he had one goal.

To get to the children.

Nate prayed they hadn't been hurt.

He lifted his head, trying to listen. He didn't hear anyone crying or anyone moaning in pain. That could be good.

Or very bad.

Next to him, Darcy began to punch at the air bag that had pinned her to the seat. He glanced at her, just to make sure she wasn't seriously injured. She had a few nicks on her face from the air bag, and her shoulder-length dark brown hair was now frosted with the talc mixture, but she was fighting as hard as he was to get out of the vehicle. No doubt to check on her son.

"When we get out, stay behind me and let me do the talking," Nate warned her.

Though he doubted his warning would do any good. If the kidnappers hadn't been injured or, better yet, incapacitated, then this was going to get ugly fast.

Nate got a better grip on his gun and opened his door. Or rather, that's what he tried to do. The door was jammed, and he had to throw his weight against it to force it open. He got out, his boots sinking into the soggy shoulder of the road, and got a good look at the damage. The front end of his car was a mangled heap, and it had crumpled the side of the van, creating a deep V in the exterior.

Still no sounds of crying. In fact, there were no sounds at all coming from the van.

"I'm Lieutenant Nate Ryland," he called out. "Release the hostages *now!*"

He waited, praying that his demand wouldn't be answered with a hail of bullets. Anything he did right now was a risk and could make it more dangerous for the children, but he couldn't just stand there. He had to try something to get Kimmie and Noah away from their kidnappers.

In the distance he could hear a siren from one of the sheriff department's cruisers. The sound was coming from the opposite direction so that meant Grayson or one of the other deputies would soon be there. But Nate didn't intend to wait for backup to arrive. His daughter could be hurt inside that van, and he had to check on her.

Darcy finally managed to fight her way out of the wrecked car, and she hit the ground running. Or rather, limping. However, the limping didn't stop her. She went straight for the van. Nate would have preferred for her to wait until he'd had time to assess things, but he knew there was no stopping her, not with her son inside.

"Noah?" she shouted.

Still no answer.

That didn't stop Darcy, either, and she would have thrown open the back doors of the van if Nate hadn't stepped in front of her and muscled her aside. This could be an ambush with the kidnappers waiting inside to gun them down, but these SOBs obviously wanted Darcy and him for something. Maybe that *something* meant they would keep them alive.

"Kimmie?" Nate called out, and he cautiously opened the van doors while he kept his gun aimed and ready.

It took him a moment to pick through the debris and the caved-in side, but what he saw had him cursing.

No one was there. Not in the seats, not in the back cargo area. Not even behind the wheel.

A sob tore from Darcy's mouth, and if Nate hadn't

caught her, she likely would have collapsed onto the ground.

"Where are they?" she begged. And she just kept repeating it.

Nate glanced all around them. There were thick woods on one side of the road and an open meadow on the other. The grass didn't look beaten down on the meadow side so that left the woods. He shoved his hand over Darcy's mouth so he could hear any sounds. After all, two gunmen and three hostages should be making lots of sounds.

But he heard nothing other than Darcy's frantic mumbles and the approaching siren.

"They were here," Nate said more to himself than Darcy, but she stopped and listened. He took the hand from her mouth. "That's Kimmie's diaper bag." It was lying right against the point of impact.

"And that's Noah's bear," Darcy said, reaching for the toy.

Nate pulled her back. Yes, the children had likely been here, but so had the kidnappers. The diaper bag and the toy bear might have to be analyzed. Unless Nate found the children and kidnappers first.

And that's exactly what he intended to do.

"Wait here," he told Darcy. "I need to figure out where they went." He tried not to think of his terrified baby being hauled through the woods by armed kidnappers, but he knew it was possible.

By God when he caught up to these men, they were going to pay, and pay hard.

"Look!" Darcy shouted.

Nate followed the direction of her pointing index finger and spotted the name tag. It was identical to the ones he'd seen Tara and the other woman wearing in the preschool. This one had the name Marlene Lambert, a woman he'd known his whole life. Her father's ranch was just one property over from his family's.

"The name tag looks as if it was ripped off her," Darcy mumbled.

Maybe. It wasn't just damaged—one of the four crayons had been removed. He glanced around the name tag and spotted the missing yellow crayon. It was right at the base of the rear doors.

"She wrote something." Darcy pointed to the left door at the same moment Nate's attention landed on it.

There was a single word, three letters, scrawled on the metal, but Nate couldn't make out what it said. Later, he would try to figure it out, but for now he raced away from the van and to the edge of the road that fronted the woods.

Nate didn't see any footprints or any signs of activity so he began to run, looking for anything that would give them a clue where the children had been taken. Darcy soon began to do the same and went in the opposite direction.

He glanced up when Dade's truck squealed to a stop. His brother had put the portable siren on top of his truck, but thankfully now he turned it off. Unlike Darcy and Nate, Dade was coming from a straight part of the road and had no doubt seen the collision in time. That was why Nate hadn't bothered to go back to his car and try to retrieve his cell phone so he could alert whoever would be coming from that direction.

"They're not inside," Nate relayed to his brother, and he kept looking.

Dade cursed. "There's a helicopter on the way," he let

Nate know. "And I'll call the Rangers and get a tracker out here. Mason, too," Dade added the same moment that Nate said their brother's name.

Mason was an expert horseman, and he was their best bet at finding the children in these thick woods. First, though, Nate needed to find the point at which they'd left the road. That would get him started in the right direction.

And he finally found it.

Footprints in the soft shoulder of the road.

"Here!" he called out to his brother. But Nate didn't wait for Dade to reach him. Nor did he follow directly in the footsteps. He hurried to the side in case the prints were needed for evidence, and there were certainly a lot of them if castings were needed.

But something was wrong.

Hell.

"There's only one set of footprints," Nate relayed to Dade.

Dade cursed too and fanned out to Nate's left, probably looking for more prints. There should be at least three sets since the adults would be carrying the babies.

"The person who made this set of prints could be a diversion," Nate concluded, and he hurried to the other side of the road, hoping to find the real trail there.

Darcy quickly joined him. She was still limping, and blood was trickling down the side of her head. He hoped like the devil she wasn't in need of immediate medical attention or on the verge of a panic attack. He needed her help, her eyes, because these first few minutes were critical.

"Go that way," Nate instructed, pointing in the opposite direction where he intended to look.

He ran, checking each section of the pasture for any sign that anyone had been there. He knew the kidnappers weren't on the road itself because Darcy and he had come from one end and Dade the other. If two kidnappers and three hostages had been anywhere near the road, they would have seen them.

Nate made it about a hundred yards from the collision site when he heard Dade's cell ring. He didn't stop looking, but he tried to listen, hoping that his brother was about to get good news. Judging from the profanity Dade used, he hadn't.

"This van's a decoy," Dade shouted.

Nate stopped and whirled around. Darcy did the same and began to run back toward Dade. "What do you mean?"

"I mean two other eyewitnesses spotted black vans identical to this one."

Darcy made it to Dade, and she latched on to his arm. "But there's proof the children were inside. Noah's bear and Kimmie's diaper bag. Marlene's name tag is there, too."

Dade looked at Nate when he answered. "This was probably the van initially used in the kidnapping, but the children and Marlene were transferred to another vehicle. Maybe they were even split up since at least two other vans were seen around town."

Nate had already come to that conclusion, and it made him sick to his stomach. He couldn't choke back the groan. Nor could he fight back the overwhelming sense of fear.

"If they split up, then there are probably more than two of them," Nate mumbled.

That meant things had gone from bad to worse. The

kidnappers could have an entire team of people helping them, and heaven knows what kind of vehicle they had used to transfer the children.

Nate was betting it wasn't a black van.

It could have been any kind of vehicle. Darcy and he could have driven right past the damn thing and wouldn't have even noticed it.

"We have people out on the roads," Dade reminded them. "More are coming in. And there's an Amber Alert and an APB out on the van. SAPD and all other law-enforcement officers in the area will stop any van matching the description. We'll find them, Nate. I swear, we'll find them."

Nate checked his watch. About twenty minutes had passed. That was a lifetime in a situation like this. The kidnappers could already have reached the interstate.

"I'll take you back to the sheriff's office," Dade insisted. He glanced down at Darcy. In addition to the nicks on her face, her jacket was torn, and there were signs of a bruise on her knee. "You need to see a medic."

"No!" she practically shouted. "I need to find my baby."

But the emotional outburst apparently drained her because the tears came, and Nate hooked his arm around her waist. He didn't feel much like comforting her, or anyone else, for that matter, but the sad truth was there was only one person who knew exactly how he felt.

And that was Darcy.

She sagged against him and dropped her head on his shoulder. "We have to keep looking," she begged.

"We will." Nate looked at his brother. "We need another vehicle. And I need to call the San Antonio crime lab so they can come out and collect this van." Silver

Creek didn't have the CSI capabilities that SAPD did, and Nate wanted as many people on this as possible.

Nate adjusted Darcy's position so he could get her moving to Dade's truck, but he stopped when he took another look at the scrawled letters written in yellow crayon. He eased away from Darcy and walked closer.

"You think Marlene wrote that?" Dade asked.

Nate nodded. "She might have tried to leave us a message." He studied those three letters. *"L-A-R,"* he read aloud.

"Lar?" Dade shook his head, obviously trying to figure it out, too.

"Maybe it's someone's initials," Darcy suggested. She moved between Dade and Nate, and leaned in. "Maybe she's trying to tell us the identity of the person who took her."

It was possible. Of course, that would mean it wasn't Wesley Dent, and it would also mean Marlene had known her kidnapper. That possibility tightened the knot in Nate's stomach. But there was something more here.

Something familiar.

Dade rattled off names of people who might fit those initials. He only managed two—an elderly couple with the last name of Reeves. Nate figured neither was capable of this. But his own surname began with an *R*.

Did that mean anything?

"A street name, then," Darcy pressed.

Dade lifted his phone and snapped a picture. "Come on. Let's go. We'll try to work it out on the drive back to the sheriff's office."

It was a good plan, but Nate couldn't take his attention off those three letters. They were familiar, something right on the tip of his tongue.

"Let's go," Darcy urged. She tugged on Nate's arm to get him moving.

They only made it a few steps before Nate heard a phone ring. Not Dade's. The sound was coming from his wrecked car, and it was his phone. He hurried toward it, but it stopped ringing just as he got there. He located his cell in the rubble and saw the missed call.

The number and caller's identity had been blocked.

Hell. It had probably been the kidnappers. "It could have been the ransom call."

"Try to call them back," Darcy insisted. But the words had hardly left her mouth when another phone rang. "That's my cell." She frantically tore through the debris to locate her purse. She jerked out the phone and jabbed the button to answer it.

She pressed the phone to her ear, obviously listening, but she didn't say a word. When the color drained from her face, Nate moved closer.

"But—" That was all she managed to say.

Nate wanted the call on speaker so he could hear, but he couldn't risk trying to press any buttons on her phone. He darn sure didn't want to disconnect the call. All he could do was wait.

"I want my son. Give me back my son!" she shouted. The tears welled up in her eyes and quickly began to spill down her cheeks. Several seconds later, Darcy's hand went limp, the phone dropping away from her ear.

Nate snatched the phone from her, but the call had already ended.

"Who was it and what did they say?" Nate demanded.

He caught her by the shoulders and positioned her so that it forced eye contact.

She groaned and shook her head. "The person had a mechanical voice, like he was speaking through some kind of machine, but I think it was a man. He said he had the children and Marlene and that if we wanted them back, he would soon be in touch. Then he hung up."

"That's it? That's all he said?" Nate tried to calm down but couldn't. "He didn't say if the kids were safe?"

"No," she insisted.

Nate took her phone. He tried the return-call function on his cell first. It didn't go through. Instead he got a recording about the number no longer being in service. The same thing happened when he tried to retrieve the call from Darcy's phone.

A dead end.

But maybe it was just a temporary one.

Dade gathered both cells. "I'll see if we can get anything about the caller from these. Darcy, you need to write down everything you can remember from that conversation because each word could be important."

She nodded and smeared the tears from her cheeks. "Let's get that other vehicle so we can look for them."

Nate agreed, but he stopped and stared at the three letters written on the door of the van.

LAR.

"I already have a picture of it," Dade reminded him. "You can study it later."

Nate cursed. "I don't need to study it." He started to run toward Dade's truck. "I know what Marlene is trying to tell us. I know where we can find the children."

Chapter 4

"LAR," Darcy said under her breath.

Lost Appaloosa Ranch.

Well, maybe that's what the initials meant. Of course, Nate could be wrong, and it could turn out to be a wild-goose chase. A chase that could cost them critical time because it tied up manpower that could be directed somewhere other than the remote abandoned ranch. According to Nate, the owner had died nearly a year ago, and his mortgage lender was still trying to contact his next of kin.

"Hurry," Darcy told the medic again. And yes, she glared at him. She'd spent nearly fifteen minutes in the Silver Creek sheriff's office, and that was fifteen minutes too long.

Darcy didn't want to be here. She wanted to be out looking for Noah, but instead here she was, sitting at the sheriff's desk while a medic stitched her up. God knows how she'd gotten the cut right on her hairline, and she didn't care.

She didn't care about anything but her son.

"I'm trying to hurry," the medic assured her.

She knew from his name tag that he was Tommy Watters, and while she hated being rude to him, she couldn't stop herself. She had to do something. *Anything.*

Like Nate and his four brothers were doing.

Just a few yards away from her, Nate was on the phone, his tone and motions frantic, while he talked with the helicopter pilot, who was trying to narrow down the search zone.

"No," Nate instructed. "Don't do a direct fly over the Lost Appaloosa. I already have someone en route, and if the kidnappers are there, I don't want to alert them. I want you to focus on the roads that lead to the interstate."

Nate had a map spread out on the desk, and every line on the desk phone was blinking. Next door, Deputy Melissa Garza was barking out orders to a citizens' patrol group that was apparently being formed to assist in the hunt for the kidnappers and the babies. The dispatcher was helping her.

Grayson, Dade and Mason were all out searching various parts of Silver Creek, interviewing witnesses and running down leads on the other black vans that had been spotted. The other deputy, Luis Lopez, was at the day care in case the kidnappers returned.

Darcy was the only one not doing anything to save Noah and Kimmie.

"I can't just sit here." The panic was starting to whirl

around inside her, and despite the AC spilling over her, sweat popped out on her face. She would scream if she couldn't get out of there and find Noah.

Darcy pushed aside the medic and would have run out of the room if Nate hadn't caught her shoulder.

He got right in her face, and his glare told her this wasn't going to be a pep talk. "You have to keep yourself together. Because I don't have time to babysit you. Got that?"

She flinched. That stung worse than the fresh stitches. But Darcy still shook her head. "Noah is my life." Which, of course, went without saying. Kimmie was no doubt Nate's life, too.

Nate nodded, and eased up on the bruising grip he had on her shoulder. The breath he blew out was long and weary. He looked up at the medic as he put Darcy back in the chair. "Finish the stitches *now*," he ordered.

Actual fear went through the medic's eyes, and he clipped off the thread. "It'll hold for now, but she should see a doctor because she might have a concussion."

Before the last word left the medic's mouth, Darcy was out of the chair. "Let's go," she insisted.

Thank God, Nate didn't argue with her. "We're headed to the Lost Appaloosa, Mel," he shouted to Deputy Garza, and in the same motion Nate grabbed a set of keys from a hook on the wall.

Finally! They were getting out there and doing something. She hoped it was the *right* something.

"You have to keep yourself together," Nate repeated. But this time, there was no razor edge to his tone. No glare. Just speed. He practically ran down the hall. "My brother Kade should arrive at the Lost Appaloosa in about ten minutes, and then we'll have answers."

"Answers *if* the babies are really there," Darcy corrected.

Nate spared her a glance, threw open the back door and hurried into the parking lot. "Marlene probably risked her life to write those initials. They mean something, and if it turns out to be the Lost Appaloosa, then Kade will know how to approach the situation."

"Because he's FBI," she said more to herself than Nate.

Darcy prayed Nate's FBI brother truly knew what he was doing. It gave her some comfort to know that Kade would likely be willing to risk his life to save his niece. And maybe Noah, too.

Nate jumped into a dark blue SUV, started the engine and barely waited long enough for Darcy to get inside before he tore out of the parking lot.

"I need to know if you're okay," he said, tipping his head to her new stitches.

"Don't worry about me," Darcy said. "Focus on the kids."

"I can't have you keeling over or anything." The muscles in his jaw stirred. Maybe because he didn't like that he had to be concerned about her in any way.

"I'm fine," she assured him, and even though it was a lie, it was the end of the discussion as far as Darcy was concerned. "How far is the Lost Appaloosa?"

"Thirty miles. It's within the San Antonio city limits, but there's not much else out there." His phone buzzed, and he shoved it between his shoulder and ear when he answered it.

She listened but couldn't tell anything from Nate's monosyllabic responses. He certainly wasn't whooping for joy because the babies had possibly been found.

Darcy leaned over to check the odometer so she would know when they were close to that thirty miles, and her hair accidently brushed against Nate's arm. He glanced at it, at her, and Darcy quickly pulled away.

"Thirty miles," she repeated, focusing on the drive and not on the driver. Nate put his attention back on the call.

That was too many miles between her and her baby, and the panic surged through her again. Nate was already going as fast as he could, but at this speed and because of the narrow country roads, it would take them at least twenty, maybe twenty-five, minutes to get there.

An eternity.

Nate cursed, causing her attention to snap back to him. She waited, breath held, until he slapped the phone shut. "Grayson just found another empty black van on a dirt road near the creek. Only one set of footprints was around the vehicle."

So, not a call from Kade. Just news of another decoy van. Or else the team of kidnappers had split up. Did that mean they'd split up the children and Marlene, as well? Darcy hoped not.

"Shouldn't you have heard from Kade by now?" she asked.

He scrubbed his hand over his face. "My brother will call when he can."

Nate looked at her again, and his eyes were now a dangerous stormy-gray. "The person behind this has a big motive and a lot of money," he tossed out there. He was all cop again. Here was the lieutenant she'd butted heads with in the past. And the present.

"You mean Wesley Dent," she supplied.

Darcy didn't even try to put on her lawyer face. Her

head was pounding. Her breath, ragged. And her heart was beating so hard, she was afraid her ribs might crack. She didn't have the energy for her usual power-attorney facade.

"Wesley Dent," Nate verified, making her client's name sound like profanity. "He's a gold digger, and I believe he murdered his wife."

Darcy shook her head and continued to keep watch in case she spotted another black van. She also glanced at the odometer, remembering to keep her hair away from Nate's arm. Twenty-five miles to go.

"I won't deny the gold-digging part," she admitted, "but I'm not sure he killed his wife."

Though it did look bad for Dent.

A starving artist, Dent had married Sandra Frasier, who wasn't just a multimillionaire heiress but was twenty-five years his senior. And apparently she often resorted to public humiliation when it came to her boy-toy husband, who was still two years shy of his thirtieth birthday. Just days before what would have been their first wedding anniversary, Sandra had humiliated Dent in public at Dent's art show.

A day after that, she had received a lethal dose of insulin.

"Sandra was diabetic," Darcy continued, though she really didn't want to have this conversation. Twenty-four miles to go. "So, it's possible this was a suicide. Her husband even said she wrote about suicide in her diary." But her death certainly hadn't been accidental because the amount of insulin was quadruple what she would have normally taken.

"There was no suicide note," Nate challenged. "No sign of this so-called diary, either."

But that didn't mean the diary didn't exist. Dent had told her that his wife kept it under lock and key, so maybe she'd moved it so that no one would be able to read her intimate thoughts.

"The husband is often guilty in situations like this," Nate went on. He had such a hard grip on the steering wheel that his knuckles were white. "And I think Dent could have orchestrated this kidnapping to force me to stop the investigation. I'm within days of arresting his sorry butt for murder."

Darcy wished the pain in her head would ease up a little so she could think straighter. "There are other suspects," she reminded him.

"Yeah, the dead woman's ex-husband and her son, but neither has as strong a motive as Dent."

"Maybe," Darcy conceded. Another glance at the odometer. Twenty-three miles between the ranch and them. "But if Dent masterminded this kidnapping to stop the investigation, then why take Noah? I'm his lawyer, the one person who could possibly prevent him from being arrested."

Nate shook his head, cursed again. "Maybe he thinks if he has your son that you'll put pressure on me to co-operate."

She opened her mouth to argue, but that kind of fight just wasn't in her. Besides, there was a chance that Nate could be right.

In some ways it would be better if he was.

After all, if Dent took the children, then he would keep them safe because he would use them to make a deal. Darcy was good at deals. And she would bargain with the devil himself if it meant getting her son back.

Nate didn't tack anything else on to his speculations

about Dent, and the silence closed in around them. Except it wasn't just an ordinary silence. It was the calm before the storm because Darcy knew what was coming next.

"Charles Brennan," she tossed out there since she knew Nate had already thought of the man. Over a year ago Brennan had hired the triggerman who'd murdered Nate's wife.

"Yeah," Nate mumbled. "Any chance he's behind this?"

Well, Brennan was dead, but she didn't have to remind Nate of that. Because Nate had been the one to kill Brennan in a shoot-out after the man had taken a deputy hostage.

"Brennan made me executor of his estate," Darcy volunteered. "I've gone through his files and financials, and there is no proof he left any postmortem instructions that had anything to do with you. Or me, for that matter."

"You're sure?" Nate pressed.

"Yes." As sure as she could be, anyway, when it came to a monster like Brennan.

Nate made a sharp sound that clipped from his throat. It was the sound of pure disapproval. "Brennan was a cold-blooded killer, and you defended him."

She had. And two months ago she would have argued that it was her duty to provide representation, but that was before her client had nearly killed a deputy sheriff, Nate and heaven knows how many others.

Darcy kept watch out the window. She didn't want to look at Nate because she didn't want him to see the hurt that was in her eyes. "There's nothing you can say that will make me feel worse than I already do," she let him know.

Silence again from Nate, and Darcy risked touching him so she could lean in and see the mileage. Just under twenty miles to go. Still an eternity.

Nate's cell buzzed. "It's Kade," he said and flipped open the phone.

Just like that, both the dread and the hope grabbed her by the throat. She moved closer, until she was shoulder to shoulder with Nate. Darcy no longer cared about the touching risk. She had to know what Kade was saying.

"I'm on the side of the hill with a good binocular view of the Lost Appaloosa," Kade explained. "And I have good news and bad."

Oh, mercy. She wasn't sure she could handle it if something had happened to the children. Nate's deep breath let her know he felt the same.

"The good news—there's a black van parked on the side of the main house," Kade continued. "Something tells me this one isn't a decoy."

"How do you know?" Darcy asked before Nate could. She wanted to believe that was good news, but she wasn't sure. "Do you see the children?"

"No sign of the children," Kade told them. His voice was practically a whisper, but even the low volume couldn't conceal his concern.

Kade paused. "Nate, call Grayson and the others and tell them to get out here right away. Because the bad news is—there are at least a half-dozen armed guards surrounding the place."

Chapter 5

Nate parked the SUV near Kade's truck—a good quarter mile from the Lost Appaloosa ranch house.

This had to work.

He'd already set his phone to vibrate and had Darcy do the same. Now, he slid his gun from his shoulder holster, eased his SUV door shut and started down the exact path his brother had instructed him to take. A path that would hopefully keep them out of sight from those guards patrolling the place.

Nate glanced back at Darcy and put his index finger to his mouth, even though he had already made it clear that they had to make a silent approach. Not easy to do considering Darcy was wearing those blasted high heels. Still, she'd have to adjust. The last thing he wanted was to give anyone a reason to fire in case the babies were nearby.

Part of him prayed this wasn't another decoy—even though, according to Kade, the half dozen or more guards were armed to the hilt. At least if Noah and Kimmie were here, then Nate would finally know where the children were. Of course, that was just the first step.

He had to get them out—safe, sound and unharmed.

Even though it was late afternoon, it was still hot, and sweat began to trickle down his back. So did the fear. He'd never had this much at stake. Yes, he'd lost Ellie, but that had been different. His wife had been a cop, capable of defending herself in most situations.

Kimmie was his little girl.

Nate choked back the fear and followed the beaten-down path until he spotted Kade on the side of a grassy hill. His brother was on his stomach, head lifted so he could peer over the top. Kade also had his gun drawn.

Kade glanced at him, but his brother's eyes narrowed when he looked at Darcy.

Yeah.

Nate wasn't pleased about her being there, either, but he hadn't had a choice. If he'd left her at the sheriff's office, she would have just tried to follow them. And he couldn't have blamed her. If their situations had been reversed, he would have done the same.

"The others are on their way," Nate whispered. He dropped down next to Kade.

Darcy did the same, her left arm landing against Nate's right one. Close contact yet again. Contact Nate decided to ignore. Instead, he took Kade's binoculars and looked at their situation.

It wasn't good.

Nate didn't need but a glimpse to determine that.

All the windows had newspaper taped to the glass. No way to see inside.

Outside was a different set of problems.

There were armed gunmen milling around the ranch house. All carried assault rifles and were dressed in black. Nate counted three, including the one standing guard at the front door, but then he saw one more when the man peered out from around the back of the house. There was yet another on the roof and one on the road near the cattle gate that closed off the property.

The gunmen had an ideal position because they controlled the only road that led to the ranch, and they obviously had good visibility with their comrade perched on the roof. Plus, there was a lot of open space around the ranch house itself. There were barns and a few other outbuildings that could be used for cover, but it wouldn't be easy to get to the house without being spotted by one of those armed goons.

"Are the children there?" Darcy whispered.

"Can't tell." Nate handed her the binoculars so Darcy could see for herself.

"Grayson and the others should be here soon," Nate relayed to Kade. "I called him just a few minutes before we got here, and he's bringing an infrared device so we can get an idea of who's inside."

And how many. That was critical information so they would know the full scope of what they were up against.

"How many will be with Grayson?" Kade asked.

Nate mentally made a count. Grayson, Dade, Mason and Mel. "Six total with you and me."

Even odds. Well, even odds for the gunmen outside the house, but Nate was betting there was some firepower inside, as well.

"The FBI should have a choke hold on the surrounding area in place in about an hour," Kade let him know.

A choke hold. In other words, the agents would be coming from the outside and moving in to make sure no one got away if the gunmen scattered. Nate was thankful for the extra help, but an hour was a lifetime. Besides, he didn't want the gunmen spotting the agents and opening fire.

"This is San Antonio P.D.'s jurisdiction," Nate reminded his brother.

Kade nodded. "I want family calling the shots on this."

Yeah. Because for Nate and the rest of the Rylands, this was as personal as it got. Nate trusted the FBI, had worked well with them on many occasions, but he didn't want anyone thinking with their trigger fingers or their federal rules. But he also didn't want emotions to create a deadly scenario.

That included Darcy.

Beside him, her breath was still racing, and she had the binoculars pressed to her eyes. "How do we get in there?" she asked.

"*We* don't," Nate quickly corrected her. He took the binoculars from her and had another look. "You'll stay here."

"And what will you be doing?" she challenged.

That would be a complicated answer so he turned to Kade. "I need a closer look at the house. A different angle so I can try to see in one of the windows."

Kade gave him a flat look. "Grayson is bringing infrared," he reminded Nate.

Yes, but Nate didn't think he could just lie there waiting for his brother and the equipment to arrive. "I have to know if Kimmie is all right," he mouthed, hoping that Darcy wouldn't hear him and echo the same about Noah.

Kade huffed, glanced around and then grabbed the binoculars. "You stay here with Ms. Burkhart."

Nate caught his arm. "It's my daughter. I should take the risk."

No flat look this time. This one was cocky. "Won't be a risk if I do it," Kade assured him. "Stay put, big brother. My head is a lot more level than yours right now."

Nate couldn't argue with that, but man, he wanted to. He wanted just a glimpse of his baby to make sure she was okay.

Kade hooked the binoculars around his neck, shot a stay-put glance at them and began to crawl to the left side of the hill. He went about twenty feet, ducking behind some underbrush and then behind an oak.

Nate kept his eyes on Kade until he disappeared from sight, and he turned his attention back to the gunmen. He wouldn't be able to see as well without the binoculars, but at least he could detect any movement that might indicate if one of them had spotted Kade.

"They have to be all right," Darcy mumbled. She, too, had her attention nailed to the patrolling gunmen.

Nate heard the sniffle that she was trying to suppress. This was obviously ripping her apart, and he wanted to comfort her.

Okay, he didn't.

He didn't want to be pulled into this strange bond that was developing between them. He couldn't. But then Darcy sniffed again, and Nate saw the tear slide down her cheek.

Hell.

So much for cooling down this bond.

He couldn't slip his arm around her because he wanted to keep his gun ready, but he did give her a nudge, causing her to look at him.

"I'm a good cop," he reminded her. "So are my brothers. We *will* get the children out of there."

Darcy blinked back fresh tears. Nodded. And squeezed her eyes shut a moment. She also eased her head against his shoulder. It wasn't a hug, but it might as well have been. Nate felt it go through him. A warmth that was both familiar and unfamiliar at the same time. He recognized the emotions, the comfort, that only a parent in Darcy's position could give.

But there was also some heat mixed with that warmth.

Even though she was still the enemy on some levels, she was also a woman. An attractive one. And his body wasn't going to let him forget that.

She opened her eyes, met his gaze. Until Nate turned his attention back where it belonged—on the gunmen.

"I could go out there," Darcy whispered. "I could offer myself in exchange for the children. Hear me out," she added when he opened his mouth to object. "If they kill me, then you'd still be here to save Kimmie and Noah."

"Admirable," Nate mumbled. "But stupid. We don't need a sacrificial lamb. We just need some equipment and a plan."

And apparently both had arrived.

He heard movement—footsteps—and Nate took aim in that direction just in case. But it wasn't necessary because he spotted Grayson, Dade, Mason and Mel inching their way through the grass toward them.

Nate eased away from Darcy, putting a little space

between them, but it was too late. He knew from Grayson's slightly raised eyebrow that he'd taken note of the contact and was wondering what the devil was going on.

"Kade's trying to get a look inside the windows," Nate said, ignoring Grayson's raised eyebrow. He tipped his head in the direction where he'd last seen Kade.

"This should help." Grayson handed Nate the hand-held infrared scanner, and all four crouched down on the hill next to Darcy and him.

Nate didn't waste any time. He put his gun aside, turned on the device and aimed it at the house. The human images formed as red blobs on the screen, and the first thing he saw was an adult figure.

And then two smaller ones.

"The babies," Darcy said on a rise of breath. She probably would have bolted off the hill if Nate hadn't latched on to her and pulled her back to the ground.

Yes, the smaller figures were almost certainly the children, and the person who appeared to be holding them was probably Marlene. Judging from the position of the blobs, Marlene was sitting with the babies on her lap. They were in a room at the back of the ranch.

Mason mumbled some profanity, and Nate didn't have to guess why. Marlene and the babies were alone in the room, but they weren't *alone*. There were two larger figures at the front part of the house. Men. And judging from the placement of their arms, they were holding weapons.

"At least eight of them," Nate supplied. That meant whoever was behind this had some big bucks and a very deep motive.

Dade took the infrared and aimed it at other out-buildings, no doubt to see if there were guards inside.

The movement to their left sent them all aiming their weapons in that direction, but it was only Kade.

"The windows of the house are all covered," he relayed to them. "But I do have some good news. No cameras or surveillance equipment that I can see mounted on the house or anywhere near it. Plus, four FBI agents are in place on the outside perimeter of the property, and more are on the way. The ones here are waiting for orders."

Grayson pulled in a long breath and looked at Nate. "We should wait here for another call from the kidnappers. It's clear they want something, and eventually they'll have to say what so we can negotiate release of the hostages."

It was standard procedure. The most logical option. And Grayson had spelled it out like the true cop he was.

"Wait?" Darcy challenged. Nate kept her anchored to the ground by grabbing her arm.

Grayson nodded. "I've already alerted the bank in case we need a large sum of cash, and every road leading away from the area is being watched."

"But our babies are in there," Darcy sobbed. She was close to hysterical now, and Nate knew he had to do something to keep both her and himself calm.

"I vote for having a closer look," Mason said. With just those few words, he had everyone's attention.

"We don't need a warrant because we've seen proof that the children are inside with armed kidnappers. That makes it an immediate-threat situation."

Nate couldn't argue with that.

"I brought a tranquilizer gun rigged with a silencer, and I can get on the roof and take out the guard there. That would give us some breathing room. Plus, I'm wearing all black, just like them, so I can blend in."

Nate took that all in and saw an immediate problem. "The guy on the road—"

"Would have to be taken out, too," Kade supplied, finishing what Nate had started to say. "I can do that hand-to-hand. I can sneak up on him using those trees to the right. I'll knock him unconscious before he can take a shot and neutralize the threat." He looked back at Mason. "And how the devil do you plan on getting up on the roof?"

"Black van," Mason growled. "It's parked right by the side of the house."

It was, and if Mason could make it that far undetected, he might be able to crawl on top of the van and tranquilize the guard on the roof. The key to this kind of approach was to go in as quietly as possible.

"And then what?" Grayson pressed, staring at Mason.

Mason shrugged. "I'll see if I can quietly take out some of the others with the tranquilizer gun."

Grayson stayed silent a moment and then tapped the infrared screen. "Someone would have to be positioned to go in through the back to get to Marlene and the children while someone else is occupying the two in the front of the house—especially the one on the porch."

"I'll take the front," Dade volunteered. "Once Kade's finished playing hand-to-hand with the guy on the road, he'll be close enough to move in so he can help me out if I need it."

"That leaves the back of the house for me," Grayson spelled out.

"Or me," Nate piped up.

"Bad idea," Grayson let him know.

Kade echoed the same, and it was Kade who continued. "If you're down there and the kidnappers call, then you could get us all killed just trying to answer your phone."

"Best if Darcy and you wait here," Grayson finished.

Darcy looked at Nate and shook her head. "I have to do something to help."

Oh, this was going to be hard. Nate understood Darcy's need because it was his need, too, but Grayson was right. A call from the kidnappers could be deadly if Darcy and he were near the ranch house.

"We have to stay here," Nate told her. And like before, he got at face level with her so he could force eye contact. He kept his voice as calm and gentle as he could manage. "We'll be able to help. We can keep watch and alert them if anything changes or goes wrong."

There was no debate in her eyes. Just the inevitable surrender. "I'll watch the infrared," she finally said. Darcy took the device and focused on it.

Nate looked up at Grayson. "You'll need backup."

"Yeah. I'll have Mel positioned with a rifle somewhere down there." Grayson pointed to a heavily treed area that was still on high ground but much closer to the ranch than they were now.

"And then there's you," Grayson added. He handed Nate another rifle, which he'd taken from the equipment bag that Mel had with her.

His brother didn't mention that if Nate had to fire, it would be dire circumstances. But it would be.

"Kade, call your agents and tell them the plan. I want them positioned and ready as backup." Grayson paused a moment. "And if anything goes wrong, then we all pull out. No shots are to be fired into the house." He glanced at each of them. "Questions?"

No one said a thing. Grayson gave Nate one last

glance, and his brothers and Mel started to move. They were already out of sight before Nate admitted to himself that the plan could be a really bad idea. But staying put could, too. Without a working crystal ball, he had no idea what approach was best, but he did know he had to do everything to get the babies out of there.

The sooner, the better.

"It'll be okay, right?" Darcy asked without taking her attention from the infrared.

"It will be." Nate tried to sound as convinced as he wanted to be, and he put his handgun in his holster so he could get the rifle into position.

"I think they're sleeping," she added, staring at the screen. "And it looks as if Marlene is rocking them."

It did. The babies certainly weren't squirming around, but that made him wonder—had they been drugged?

That tore right at Nate, and he had to take a deep breath just to loosen the knot that put in his throat.

"Noah will want his dinner soon," Darcy whispered.

Nate knew where she was going with this, and he figured it had to stop. They would drive themselves mad considering all the things that could go wrong. He glanced at her. But stopped when he heard a sound.

A snap, as if someone had stepped on a twig.

Not to the side, where the others had walked. This sound came from behind them.

Nate turned, trying to get the rifle into position. But it was already too late.

The man stepped through the wall of thick shrubs, and aimed the gun right at Nate.

Chapter 6

From the corner of her eye, Darcy saw the alarm register on Nate's face.

She whirled around, praying it was one of Nate's siblings but no such luck. Dressed head to toe in black, the man also had black-and-dark-green camouflage paint smeared on his face. He had on some kind of headset with a marble-size transmitter positioned in front of his mouth.

But it was the gun that grabbed her attention.

It was big and equipped with a silencer similar to Mason's weapon.

Oh, mercy.

This was *not* part of the plan.

"Don't," the man warned when Nate tried to shift his rifle toward him. "If you want to live long enough to see your kids, then put the gun down. Slowly. No sudden moves."

Darcy hung on every word. She didn't want to do anything to cause him to fire. But she also studied what she could see of his face.

Did she know him?

It certainly wasn't Wesley Dent or anyone associated with his case. In fact, she was reasonably sure she'd never seen this man before.

"Boss," the gunman said into the transmitter of his headset, "we got visitors. The kids' parents are up here in the woods. They got guns and infrared. They're looking at you right now."

Darcy glanced at the infrared screen and saw one of the men move from the front of the house to the back, where Marlene and the children were.

"Will do," the man said to his boss. He kept his cold, hard stare and his gun on Nate. "Stand up," he demanded. "We're going for a little walk."

That nearly took the rest of Darcy's breath away, but then it occurred to her, if he'd wanted them dead, he could have just shot them while he was in the bushes.

Nate started to move, but the man growled, "Wait!" in a rough whisper. His eyes narrowed, and he adjusted the transmitter portion of his headset. "Boss, there's a uniform with a rifle at your eight o'clock. About three hundred yards from where I'm standing. She's in firing range of the house."

Oh, no. He'd spotted Mel, and the deputy wasn't looking back at them. Mel had no idea she'd been detected.

Darcy couldn't hear what the person on the other end of the line was saying, but she figured it wasn't good.

"How many are here with you?" the gunman demanded, his attention still fixed on Nate.

"Just the three of us," Nate lied.

The gunman didn't respond to that, but his eyes narrowed. "Boss, I'll take out the uniform and then bring these two down for a chat."

Darcy watched in horror as the gunman took aim at Mel. She reacted completely out of instinct. She drew back her foot and rammed the thin heel of her right shoe into his shin. Nate reacted, too. He dived at the man, slamming right into him, and they both went to the ground. So did the man's headset.

"Run!" Nate told her.

Darcy turned to do just that, but she stopped. Nate was literally in a life-and-death struggle with a much larger, hulking man, and she had to do something to help.

But what?

She glanced over her shoulder to see if Mel had noticed what was going on. The deputy hadn't. Darcy started to yell out a warning to her, but again she stopped. If she yelled, heaven knew how many gunmen she'd alert, and the men inside the house might try to get away with the children.

Or they might do something worse.

Besides, Mason and the others were probably close to approaching the house now, and if she sounded the alarm, it could get one of them killed.

Darcy looked around and spotted the rifle. She couldn't risk firing a shot, but maybe she could use it. She grabbed the barrel and tried to use the rifle butt to hit the gunman.

She failed.

Nate and the man were rolling around, their bodies locked in the struggle, and if she were to hit Nate accidentally, then it could cost them the fight. And this was a fight they couldn't lose.

"What's going on?" she heard someone ask over the headset.

Her heart dropped again. It wouldn't take long before the person on the other end of that transmitter realized something was wrong, and that might cause the boss to take some drastic measures.

Nate must have realized that, as well, because she heard him curse, and he revved up his attempt to control the man's gun. Both had fierce grips on the weapon, and the gunman was trying to aim it at Nate.

Darcy kicked the guy again when she could reach his leg. And again. While Nate head-butted the man.

The sound somehow tore through the noise of the struggle.

It was a loud swish. As if someone had blown out a candle. But Darcy instinctively knew what it was. The gun had been fired, the sound of the bullet muffled through the silencer.

"Nate!" she managed to say.

Oh, mercy. Had he been hit?

She dropped to her knees and latched on to Nate's shoulder, to pull him away. There was blood. Lots of it. And a hoarse sob tore from her throat.

"I'm okay," Nate assured her. But he didn't say it aloud. He mouthed it so that no one on the other end of that transmitter could hear him.

But Darcy shook her head. He couldn't be okay, not with that much blood on the front of his shirt.

He repeated, "I'm okay." Again, it was mouthed, not spoken. And he scrambled off the gunman, who was now lying limp and lifeless on the ground.

Nate wrenched the gun from the man's hands and put his mouth right against Darcy's ear. "He pulled the trigger," he let her know. "And missed me. He hit himself instead."

Her sob was replaced by relief, and she threw her arms around him. Nate was alive and unharmed. She couldn't say a prayer of thanks fast enough.

"We can't stay here," Nate insisted, his mouth still against her ear. He glanced at the headset next to the dead man.

Darcy nodded. He was right. They couldn't stay there because it wouldn't be long before someone came to check on him. Nate and she had to be long gone by then.

Nate kept the gun with the silencer in his right hand, and caught her arm with his left. He started to run, hauling her right along with him, and he headed in the direction that his brothers had taken.

Darcy's heart was already pounding from the fight, and her heels didn't make it easy to race over the uneven terrain. But she couldn't stop or give up. Not with her baby's life at stake.

She wanted to know where Nate was taking her, but she didn't dare ask. The woods were thick, without much sunlight here, and she didn't know if there were other armed guards hiding in the shadows, waiting to strike.

They ran, zigzagging their way through the trees and underbrush. No sign of his brother or Mel, even though Darcy thought they were heading in the deputy's direction.

Nate glanced down at his hip, and for one horrifying moment, she thought maybe he'd been hurt, after all.

But she realized his phone was vibrating. He mumbled some profanity and ducked behind a tree.

"It's Grayson," he whispered. Nate didn't answer it. Instead, he fired off a text: Position compromised. Am on the run.

Nate shoved his phone back in his pocket and took her by the arm again. He jerked her forward as if ready to run but then stopped.

"Hell," he mumbled. His grip melted off her arm.

Nate lifted his hands in the air. Darcy did, too, though it took her a moment to realize what was going on. She finally saw the gun. Not a handgun, either, but some kind of assault rifle.

And, just like earlier, it was aimed right at them.

"Drop your gun," the man ordered Nate. "Take the other one from your holster and drop it, too."

Nate couldn't believe this. He still had blood on his hands from the last attack, and here he was looking down another gun barrel.

"Now!" the man snarled.

Nate glanced at Darcy, to let her know he regretted what he had to do, and he dropped the guns. First, the one he'd taken from the dead guard and then his own Glock.

"Start walking," the gunman demanded the moment the weapons were on the ground. He used the assault rifle to point the way.

This guy was even bigger than the other, and he kept several yards between them so it would be next to impossible for Nate to attack him.

"What do we do?" Darcy whispered. She stumbled, and Nate caught her arm to stop her from falling.

"We look for an opportunity to escape," he whispered back. But he knew that wouldn't be easy.

The guard was leading them straight to the ranch.

Darcy's suddenly rapid breathing let him know that she realized that, as well.

Nate kept walking and glanced around, hoping he'd see one of his brothers or Mel. But he saw no one, other than the guard who was patrolling the road. Once Darcy and he were out of the trees and into the open, the guard on the porch would spot them, as well.

But where were Mason and Kade?

They should have made it to this point now. Nate prayed nothing had gone wrong.

And then there was Mel to consider.

If she was still perched on the side of that hill, she might try to take out one or two of the guards when she saw that Darcy and he had been taken captive. That would mean bullets being fired much too close to the house. Nate knew Mel was a good cop with good aim, but he was uneasy enough with Mason's plan. Nate didn't want bullets added to this already dangerous mix.

Darcy stumbled again right as they reached the dirt road that separated the woods from the ranch. Again, Nate caught her.

"Should I pretend to faint or something?" she whispered.

"Keep moving!" the guard demanded, and this time he didn't whisper.

"Do as he says," Nate instructed. It appeared the guy had plans to take them inside the house.

When they stepped out onto the road, the guard moved closer to them. Probably to protect himself. Did he know Grayson and the others were out there? Maybe. Or maybe he was just being cautious.

The guard by the cattle gate came closer, as well, and he kept his rifle aimed at Darcy and Nate. The man fired glances all around, and his message was clear—if anyone took a shot at him, he would shoot back, and at this range, he wasn't likely to miss.

"They're taking us to the children," Darcy mumbled. She quickened her pace, hurrying across the yard and to the porch.

The door swung open, and the two guards forced them inside, following right behind them. They shut the door and immediately started watching out the gaps in the newspapers that covered the two front windows.

Other than a tattered sofa and some boxes, the room was empty, and Nate couldn't hear the babies or Marlene.

"Welcome," a bulky man said from the doorway of the kitchen. Like the others, he was dressed all in black and had camo paint on his face. And he was armed.

"Are you the boss?" Nate asked.

"Yeah," he readily admitted.

Nate tried to commit every detail of this man's appearance and demeanor because when this was over, the boss was going down.

"Where are the children?" Darcy demanded. Her voice was shaking. So was she. But she managed to sound as if she was ready to tear them limb from limb.

"I'll let you see for yourself." The boss stepped to the side and motioned for them to go toward the back of the house.

Was this some kind of trick?

Maybe.

Nate certainly didn't trust them, but several of the guards had had more than ample opportunity to kill them.

"This way," the boss instructed. He led them through a dining room and then to a hall.

That's when Nate saw the open door. And the room.

"Noah!" Darcy practically shoved the boss aside and hurried toward Marlene and the babies. They'd been right about the rocking chair. Marlene was seated in it with Kimmie in the crook of one arm and Noah in the other.

Marlene's eyes widened, but that was her only reaction. Maybe because she was in shock. No telling what these goons had put her through.

"Noah," Darcy repeated.

She scooped up her sleeping son into her arms. Nate did the same to Kimmie, but neither baby stayed asleep for long. Noah immediately started to fuss, and Kimmie slowly opened her eyes.

Nate felt the rush of panic as he tried to check his daughter to make sure she hadn't been hurt. She was still wearing her pink overalls, and there were no signs of bruises or trauma.

"Da Da," Kimmie babbled, and she smiled at him.

That nearly broke his heart and filled it in the same beat. His baby had been through so much—too much—and yet here she managed a smile. Nate didn't even attempt one. He just pulled Kimmie deep into his arms and held her as close as he could while he kept an eye on the goon standing behind them.

Beside him, Darcy was doing the same to Noah, and there were tears streaming down her face.

"I tried to stop them," Marlene said, shaking her

head. She backed away from them as if she might try
to bolt through the window.

"She did," the boss verified. "And she might have a
few bruises because of it."

Nate had to stop his hands from clenching into fists.
He wanted to break this guy's neck for hurting Marlene
and putting them through this nightmare. But he had
to hold on to his composure. He would do battle with
him, but it wouldn't happen now. First, he had to figure out how to get Kimmie, Noah, Marlene and Darcy
out of there.

"Why did you do this?" Nate demanded. He tried to
keep the rage out of his voice for Kimmie's sake.

The boss met Nate's glare. "I've been instructed to
offer you and Ms. Burkhart a deal."

"What kind of deal?" Darcy snapped. Noah was still
fussing so she began patting his back.

Nate waited for what seemed an eternity for the boss
to respond, and the dangerous thoughts kept going
through his head. All the things that could go wrong.
His brothers might not know Darcy and he were inside, and if they didn't, they could be about to put their
plan in motion.

A plan that might cause these SOBs to fire shots.

Nate brushed a kiss on Kimmie's forehead and
prayed nothing would go wrong.

"It's a simple request." The boss didn't continue until
he leaned against the doorjamb. What he didn't do was
lower his gun. "You're to transfer two million into an
offshore account."

This was about money?

Of course, Nate had considered it, but then why had

they taken Noah? Darcy was doing okay financially, but he was pretty sure she wasn't rich.

"Two million?" Nate verified. He could transfer that amount with a phone call.

"Yeah," the boss said. "For starters. Part two of the deal is slightly more…complicated. You're to make sure Wesley Dent is not only arrested for his wife's murder. He's also to be convicted."

Nate heard Darcy pull in her breath. He had a similar reaction, including disgust. Yeah, he thought that Dent might be guilty, but he wasn't a dirty cop, and he didn't fix investigations.

So, why did this bozo want him to fix this one?

His first guess was that these gunmen worked for either Sandra Dent's son, Adam, or her ex-husband, Edwin. Both had motives for wanting Dent behind bars.

Which meant Dent might be innocent, after all.

"Wesley Dent is my client," Darcy clarified. "I'm supposed to defend him to the best of my abilities."

"Admirable," the man snarled. "But being admirable won't get your son back."

"What do you mean by that?" Nate demanded.

"I mean we're holding your children until we have the results we want for Dent. If you want to speed things up, I suggest you get Dent to confess. Or create a confession for him."

"That can't happen." Nate turned, adjusting his position so that Kimmie wouldn't see the anger on his face. "And you can't keep our children for what could turn out to be months."

Another shrug. "Well, we can't keep them here, of course. We have to move them as soon as you leave."

He checked his watch. "And your time is up. You have to go now."

"No!" Darcy tightened her grip on Noah.

"This could all be over by tomorrow," the boss calmly explained. "Talk Dent into confessing and then arrange for his suicide because he feels so guilty for killing his wife."

"No," Darcy repeated, and she looked at Nate and shook her head. "I can't leave Noah here."

Nate was about to assure her that they weren't leaving, but the sound stopped him cold. Not a shot.

But a thud.

The boss's expression changed immediately. He was no longer calm. "See what's wrong," he barked to the young gunman behind him. The boss reached out, latched on to Marlene's hair and pulled her in front of him.

And he put the gun to her head.

Hell.

They didn't need that. Nate had figured he could give Kimmie to Marlene so his hands would be free, but that option was out now. Instead, he handed her to Darcy, and he was thankful that his baby seemed to enjoy being in the arms of this stranger, who cuddled her as protectively as she was cuddling her own son.

"Don't do anything stupid," the boss warned Nate.

There was another sound. Not a thud. But the noise of a tranquilizer gun.

Mason.

His brother was out there. The Ryland plan was in motion.

Nate moved closer to Darcy and the babies, positioning himself between them and the gunman. It wasn't much, but it was the best he could do for now. He braced himself in case he had to lunge for the guy. What he didn't brace himself for was the crash that came through the window behind him.

Darcy tried to move away from the breaking glass. And the boss let go of Marlene. The man took aim at the window and probably would have fired, but Nate dived at him, knocking both the man and his weapon to the floor. His body was still stinging from the fight with the last guard, but he had adrenaline and need on his side. His baby's life was at stake.

"Mason?" Darcy called out. There was relief in her voice, which hopefully meant his brother hadn't been hurt.

Nate continued the struggle, trying to pin the boss to the ground. But the guy just wasn't giving up, and he was fighting hard.

"Stay back," he heard Mason say, and a moment later, his brother was there. The tranquilizer gun was in the waist of his pants, and he'd drawn his sidearm.

Mason reached into the scuffle, and he grabbed the boss by the throat. He dragged him away from Nate and put his gun directly under the man's chin.

"Move and I'll kill you now," Mason warned. "Less paperwork for me to do."

Nate thought that was a bluff. But then, maybe not.

"Get Darcy and the babies out of here," Mason told Nate. He hauled the boss to his feet and muscled him toward the front. "Marlene, too. And hurry."

Nate took Kimmie from Darcy. "Is the outside secured?" Because he didn't want to bring the children out of the house if the gunmen were still out there.

"Kade's people found some explosives," Mason informed him. "They disarmed the ones they found, but they might not have gotten them all."

"Explosives?" Darcy asked. There was no relief in her voice now.

"Yeah," Mason verified. "We must have tripped a master wire or something because they're all set to detonate in about five minutes. Get out of here *now*."

Chapter 7

Run!

The word kept racing through Darcy's head as she, Nate and Marlene rushed out of the house with the babies cradled in their arms.

Mason was behind them, dragging the boss along, but Darcy concentrated only on her own steps. Running in high heels put her at a huge disadvantage, but she couldn't fall. Couldn't stop. Even though her lungs were already burning.

She had to get her baby away from a possible explosion.

"This way!" someone shouted.

It was Dade, and he was motioning for them to follow him onto the road. Beside him, on the ground, was one of the gunmen, and he was either unconscious or dead because he wasn't moving. There was no sign of Grayson or Kade.

Nate dropped behind her and used his free hand to latch on to her arm. Good thing, too. Because she stumbled, and if it hadn't been for Nate she would have fallen.

"I'm taking genius, here, this way," Mason let them know.

And he started in another direction through the woods where Darcy had last seen Mel. Maybe because Mason didn't want the boss anywhere near the children. Darcy was thankful for that, but she also hoped the gunmen wouldn't attack again and help their boss escape.

The sound that came from behind them was deafening, a thick blast. Darcy just held her son closer and didn't look back, but it was clear that something had blown up. She prayed Nate's brothers, Mel and the FBI agent hadn't been hurt or killed.

Both Noah and Kimmie were crying now, and their sobs tore at her heart the way nothing else could.

Mercy, what they'd been put through.

And for what?

To rig the investigation so that her client would be arrested and convicted of his wife's murder. Once they were safely away from this place, Darcy wanted answers about who had orchestrated everything. No one was going to get away with endangering these children.

Dade led them back toward the start of the path, where they'd left the vehicles. It seemed to take forever, and each step was a challenge.

"Get in the SUV," Nate ordered, and he jerked open the door and shoved Darcy into the backseat. He pushed Kimmie into her arms and looked behind him.

"Where's Marlene?" Nate asked.

Dade, who was breathing hard, looked behind them, as well. He only shook his head and cursed.

Marlene was nowhere in sight. God, no. Had she fallen? Darcy certainly hadn't heard her, but then she hadn't been able to hear much over the roaring in her ears.

"Go ahead," Dade insisted. "Get them away from here. I'll look for her."

Nate didn't argue. He ripped the keys from his pocket, jumped into the driver's seat and started the engine. He gave Dade one last glance before he hit the accelerator and sped away.

Darcy held a crying baby in each arm, and she pulled them to her and tried to soothe them. "Shhh," she whispered, brushing kisses on each of their heads. "It's okay. Mommy and Daddy are here."

Kimmie looked up at her, the tears spilling down her cheeks, and she glanced at Nate, whose attention was fastened to the road. For a moment Darcy thought the little girl might sob again, but Kimmie rubbed her eyes, smearing the tears on her little hands, and she settled her head against Darcy's shoulder.

All right.

That required a deep breath. Darcy hadn't expected to feel this, well, attachment to Nate's daughter. But Kimmie felt as right in her arms as Noah did. Strange. It had to be a reaction to the fear.

Darcy didn't have time to think about it because there was another blast. It was so loud, so strong, that it shook the SUV.

"Hell," Nate mumbled.

Terrified of what she might see, she looked back and

saw more of the nightmare that had started when she'd first learned someone had kidnapped her son.

The house was a fireball. The barn, too.

And so were the woods where she'd last seen Mason.

"Call me the minute you know anything," Nate said to Grayson.

Nate pushed the end-call button on his cell and released the breath he'd been holding. Finally, he had some good news to go with the not so good. Of course, the best news was in his arms.

Kimmie was asleep, her head resting right against his heart, and they were safely back at the Ryland ranch.

Nate had already said prayers of thanks, but he intended to add a lot more. Having Kimmie safe was the most important thing in his life, but his brothers were a close second.

He looked across the foyer and saw Kimmie's nanny, Grace Borden. The petite woman with graying red hair was studying his face. "Well?" she asked in a whisper.

"My brothers are okay," he relayed. Grayson had just let him know that. "And they found Marlene hiding in some bushes. She's shaken up but all right."

Grace nodded and walked to him. "Why don't you let me take Kimmie and put her in her crib for the night?"

Nate wanted to hold her. Heck, he didn't want to let go, but his baby would sleep much better in her own bed than in his arms. Besides, he had to check on Darcy and Noah. He didn't want to wake Kimmie doing that.

Grace eased Kimmie from his arms. "I'll take good care of her," she assured him. It wasn't necessary. Nate trusted her completely, but it still tugged at him to see his daughter being whisked away. It might be a lifetime or two before he started to forget that she'd been stolen from him.

Someone would pay for that.

He felt the anger boil inside him. A lethal mix, but he pushed that powder keg of emotion deep inside him. Soon, he would get the men responsible for what had happened.

Nate went to the bar in the living room and poured himself a shot of whiskey. He took it in one gulp, even though he preferred beer to the fireball of heat that slid down his throat. Still, he needed something to settle his nerves.

He made his way to the family room, where he'd left Darcy as soon as they'd gotten back from the Lost Appaloosa. He had to tell her that Bessie, the housekeeper, had fixed a room for Noah and her.

Before he even got there, he heard the voices coming from the family room. Not Darcy's voice. But Kayla Brennan's, Dade's fiancée, who had already moved into the ranch. Good. Maybe talking with Kayla had managed to calm Darcy down because Nate didn't want to tackle that job.

"Yes, that was an obstacle," Kayla said. "Dade's family hated me."

Nate groaned silently and stopped. This didn't sound like a calming-down kind of conversation. He peered around the corner and saw both women seated on the leather sofa. Darcy held a sleeping Noah in her lap. Kayla had her sleeping son in her arms.

"I was Charles Brennan's daughter-in-law," Kayla continued. "The man who ordered Nate's wife to be killed."

"But Dade and his brothers obviously got past that," Darcy pointed out.

Yeah. But it hadn't been easy. Just a short time ago, Kayla had been the enemy.

Much as Darcy was now.

And that gave Nate a jolt. A nasty feeling in the pit of his stomach.

"That's true." Kayla shrugged. "I fell in love with Dade, and everything else fell into place. The Rylands and my son are my family now." Her gaze flew to the doorway, where he was standing. "Nate," she greeted. She stood, slowly. "You have news?"

"They're all okay," Nate said as quickly as he could. "Dade doesn't have a scratch on him, and he'll be home soon."

Kayla made a sound of relief and blinked back tears. "Thank you."

Darcy mumbled a thank-you under her breath, and she closed her eyes for a moment.

Kayla glanced down at her son. Then, at Darcy, before her gaze went back to Nate. "It's time I put Robbie to bed." There was an inflection in her voice, an implied *so you two can talk*.

Yeah, they needed to do that. And Darcy probably wasn't going to like what he had to say. Nate waited until Kayla was out of the room before he started what was essentially a briefing.

One with a bad twist.

"Are your brothers really okay?" she asked.

"They are. Kade has a few cuts and scratches because he was close to one of the blasts, but his injuries are minor." He took a deep breath and rested his hands on his hips. "And they found Marlene. She said she got separated from us when we were running, and she hid in some bushes."

"That's good." Darcy stared at him, waiting.

"Come on." Nate motioned for her to stand. It might be better to finish this if he didn't have to see her face. There was concern, and fear, written all over it. "Bessie made up a bed for you. Noah, too."

She stood, not easily. Her legs were wobbly, but Nate didn't move to help her. He'd been doing too much of that lately. Instead, he led her out of the family room, across the foyer and into the hall that fed into the west wing of the house.

"Okay, what's wrong?" Darcy asked.

Well, the woman was perceptive. "Only one of the kidnappers survived. The boss, aka Willis Ramirez. And he's not talking. Plus, I'm not sure how long we can even hold him."

"What?" It wasn't a whisper, either. Noah jolted, and Darcy frantically started rocking him. She also stared at Nate. "The man kidnapped our children."

"Yes, but Mexico has an extradition order for him. He worked for one of the drug lords and gunned down six people, including a high-ranking police officer."

The color blanched from her face, and he got her moving again so she could put Noah down. She looked too shaky to be holding anything right now, especially a baby.

"How much time do we have to interrogate him?" Darcy wanted to know.

"Not much. A day or two at most. Grayson is with him now and will keep pressing until the federal marshals arrive and take custody."

Darcy shook her head, mumbled something. "Grayson has to get a confession. We have to find out who hired him to kidnap the children."

"We will," Nate promised.

He opened the door to the guest suite and took her through the sitting area and into the bedroom where Bessie had prepared the crib. Bessie had also left Darcy a loaner gown, a robe and some toiletries.

Darcy laid the baby down, kissed one cheek and then the other. She lingered for several moments, and Nate didn't rush her. He understood her reluctance to leave her baby.

Finally, she stepped away, keeping her eyes on Noah until she was in the sitting room. She groaned softly and leaned against the wall. "I don't know how I made it through this day," she whispered.

Nate was right there with her on that. He'd faced down armed criminals before, had even been wounded in the line of duty. But only Ellie's death came close to this.

"Tomorrow I'll have someone drop by your house and get some things," he told her. "If you need anything specific, make a list."

The weariness didn't fade from her eyes, but they did widen a bit. "I'm not going home?"

"No." Nate thought about how to say it and decided to just toss the truth out there. "The danger isn't over. If Ramirez doesn't give up the person who hired him, then one way or another I'll have to find out who he is. That might take some time."

She didn't argue. Didn't look as if she had the strength to put up even a token resistance. "And in the meantime?"

"Noah and you will stay here." That was the logical solution. The ranch had a security system. Plus, there were at least a dozen ranch hands on the grounds at any given moment. It also didn't hurt that five lawmen lived there.

And four of those lawmen might be a problem.

"Your brothers?" she said, getting right to the heart of the matter.

"There'll be tension," he admitted. "But no one here will turn you out. The kidnappers went after our children. They might try again."

She shivered, and closed her eyes. Did she see the same nightmarish images that he did? The gunmen, the children huddled on the floor of the preschool? The explosions that tore apart the Lost Appaloosa only minutes after they'd rescued Noah and Kimmie?

Her eyelids fluttered open, and she met his gaze. "If Ramirez doesn't talk, I think we know where your investigation starts. Sandra Dent's son, Adam, or her ex-husband, Edwin Frasier."

Yeah. That ball was already rolling. Mason was arranging for both men to be brought to Silver Creek for questioning. Too bad they couldn't find the dead woman's missing diary. Then maybe they would know who was behind this. Nate knew from accounts from Sandra's friends that the diary existed, but it hadn't turned up in any of the searches of her estate. Of course, her killer could have destroyed it, and with it any possible evidence.

"I can't rule out Dent himself," Nate added. "He could have orchestrated this to make himself look innocent." He braced himself for the lawyer to kick in.

But she only nodded. "About how much would it have cost to put this kidnapping together?"

"Three vans, seven men, weapons, explosives. We're probably looking at a minimum of a hundred thousand." He hesitated. "Unless Ramirez's drug-lord connections are behind this. Then the men could have been coerced into helping with the kidnapping."

A heavy sigh left her mouth, and she plowed her hands through her hair to push it away from her face. But then she winced when her fingers raked over her stitches.

Nate moved her hand so he could have a look, which required him to push aside a few strands. Her hair was as soft as silk. And despite their ordeal in the woods, she didn't smell of sweat and blood but rather the faint aroma of the fragrant cedars. Her own scent was there, too. Something warm and musky.

Something that stirred feelings best left alone.

"Well?" she prompted.

"The stitches held." But there was an angry bruise around the edges. He made a mental note to call the doctor and ask him to come out to the ranch to examine Darcy. He also made a mental note not to let her scent get to him.

"How does it look?" she asked. But she waved him off. "Never mind. I know I look bad."

That was the problem. She didn't. Even with the fatigue, the stitches and the bruise, Darcy managed to look amazing.

Beautiful.

And that was not a good thing for him to notice.

Nor was her body. It was pretty amazing, too. She was a good eight inches shorter than he was. On the petite side. But she still had interesting curves. Curves that reminded him it'd been too long since he'd held a woman.

Or had one in his bed.

His own body responded to that reminder. His blood started to race. His heart, too. And his jeans were no longer comfortable.

Nate stepped back, or rather, tried, but she caught his arm. "I'm sorry."

Of all the things he'd expected her to say, that wasn't one of them.

He studied her eyes. Also beautiful. And he shook his head, not understanding her apology. He was the one with the bad reaction here.

"I'm sorry for everything," Darcy clarified. Her voice was mostly breath now. "Especially for defending the man whose hired gun killed your wife. I'm sorry I managed to keep him out of jail so that he could go after Dade and Kayla."

Oh, hell, no. Nate didn't want to go there. He didn't want to talk about Ellie. So he shook off her grip and turned to leave.

"For what it's worth," Darcy continued, "I've applied to be the assistant district attorney here in Silver Creek."

That froze him in his tracks, and Nate eased back around to stare at her. As the A.D.A, she'd have to work with Grayson, Dade and Mason. Work *closely* with them, on the same side of the law.

"I'm not a bad person." Her voice trembled again. So did her bottom lip, and her eyes began to water. "I just got wrapped up in doing…what I thought I needed to do. Old baggage," she added in a mumble. "Something you might know a little about."

Oh, yeah. His old baggage had baggage.

"When did yours start?" she asked.

Nate didn't have to think about that. He also didn't have to think about it to know this was a conversation he didn't want to have. But he answered her, anyway. "Twenty years ago when I was fifteen, my grandfather was murdered, and it was never solved."

"Yes. Sheriff Chet McLaurin. Kayla asked me about him."

Nate was sure he blinked. "Why would she ask you that?"

"She called me a few weeks ago and wanted to know if I'd come across a photo of your grandfather in any of Charles Brennan's things. She faxed me a copy of the picture and said it was taken on the day the new sheriff's office opened."

Now, he understood. Kayla had asked because Darcy was the executor for Brennan's will, and the picture was definitely in question. Kayla had seen a copy, and now the family wanted to know why a man like Brennan had held on to a photo seemingly unrelated to him.

"Did you find the picture in Brennan's things?" Nate asked.

Darcy shook her head. "I looked but didn't find anything. It might turn up, though, because I'm still going through his estate." She paused. "Is it important?"

"Could be. Maybe there's something in Brennan's files that will tell us who killed our grandfather."

"I see." And a moment later, she repeated it. "When this is over, I'll look again." Another pause. "His death is the reason you became a cop?"

"Yeah." And this was another wound Nate didn't want reopened tonight so he turned the tables on her. "What baggage made you become a defense attorney?"

A pained look flashed across her face, and Darcy opened her mouth. Closed it. And that pained look got significantly worse.

"It's okay," he quickly assured. "The conversation's over." And he was probably as thankful for that as she was.

They didn't need to be delving into baggage or what had brought them to this point. Didn't need to be discussing anything personal.

He especially didn't need to be thinking of her as an attractive, troubled woman he should haul off to his bed.

Besides, he had a mountain of stuff to do—stuff that didn't require getting Darcy naked and in his bed. Phone calls to make. An investigation to start. He also needed to see if Grayson had made any progress with Ramirez.

"If you need anything, my room is just across the hall," he let her know. "The security system is on, and all the ranch hands are on watch to make sure no one suspicious enters the property."

There. He'd doled out all the info she needed for the night, and he could go. Good thing, too, because he was exhausted.

But he didn't move.

His feet seemed glued to the floor.

Her eyes widened, as if she knew a fierce storm was already upon them. And it was. The storm inside him. Nate cursed. Because he saw the alarm on Darcy's face.

Followed by the heat.

Oh, man.

One-sided lust was bad enough, but two-sided was a disaster in the making.

His feet finally moved. In the wrong direction. Nate went to her, catching her hands and pinning them against the wall. Hell, he pinned her, too. Pressing his body against hers as he lowered his head.

And kissed her.

He captured her breath and the sound of her surprise all at once. Nate might as well have had sex with her because the slam of pleasure was that intense. The instant awareness that he was about to lose it. And that taste.

Yeah.

Like something forbidden.

"Nate," she managed to say, the heat burning her voice.

He didn't attempt to say anything for fear that the sound of his voice would bring him back to his senses. For just this moment he wanted to be pulled deep into the fire.

He wanted to feel.

And he did. For those scalding-hot moments, Nate felt it all. The desire for a woman. The need to take her. The ache that he'd suppressed for way too long.

But he forced himself to remember that even with all those aches and burning needs, he shouldn't be kissing Darcy. Nate pushed himself away from her. Not easily. He had to force his body to move, and then he had to force it not to go right back after her again.

Their gazes collided.

In her eyes, he saw all that fire still raging. Heard it in her thin breath. Felt it pulsing in her wrist.

He let go of her, and her hands dropped to her sides. Nate watched her recover, hoping that he could do the same.

"What was that?" she asked, breathless.

"A mistake." He was breathless, too.

She stared at him, the pulse hammering in her throat.

Since looking at her throat made him want to kiss her there, Nate took another step back. And another for good measure.

Her gaze slid over his face, his chest, which was pumping as though starved for air. In a way, it was. Then, her eyes lowered to the front of his jeans.

Where she no doubt—*no doubt*—saw the proof of just how much that kiss had aroused him.

"We can blame it on the adrenaline," she whispered.

For some reason, a stupid one, probably, that made him smile. For a split second, anyway. And then reality crashed down on his head. He shouldn't be kissing her and he shouldn't be smiling.

"Good night, Darcy," Nate told her.

"Wait. There's something bothering you. Something other than *that*," she clarified, her attention dropping to the front of his jeans again.

Oh, man. This brain connection they had was almost as bad as the fire she'd started in his body. Darcy was right—something was bothering him. He'd intended to keep it to himself. Because it could alarm her. But heck, he'd already opened a big box of alarm just by kissing her.

"Did you think there was anything strange about Ramirez when the gunman took us into the ranch house?" he asked.

She stayed quiet for a moment. "You mean stranger than the fact he had kidnapped our children?"

"Yeah. He didn't ask us how we'd found them."

"You're right." Darcy pulled in her breath. "Neither did the gunmen in the woods."

Nate made a sound of agreement. "They seemed ready for us. As if they'd been expecting us all along.

But why would that be? The only reason we went to the Lost Appaloosa was because Marlene wrote the initials on the van door."

She pressed her fingers to her forehead. "And from what we know, Marlene might not have even been in that particular van. It could have been just a decoy."

"So who wrote the initials?" Nate finished for her. "And why did Ramirez want us to find him?"

"I don't know." She shook her head. "Do you?"

"No. But first thing in the morning, I intend to find out."

Chapter 8

"I'm fine, really," Darcy told the Stetson-wearing doctor again, but Dr. Doug Mickelson continued to slide his penlight in front of her eyes. He'd already examined her stitches and a small cut she'd gotten on her elbow.

She wanted this exam to end so she could go back to her son. Darcy could feel the anxiety creeping through her, again, and she wondered how long it would take before she could get past the ordeal of the kidnapping.

Never was a distinct possibility.

"You're sure the children are okay?" Darcy asked when the doctor plugged the stethoscope into his ears so he could listen to her heart.

"They're right as rain," he assured her. "They were lucky."

Yes, and she hated that something as fragile as luck had played into keeping Noah and Kimmie safe.

"All done," the doctor finally said. He hooked the stethoscope around the collar of his cowboy-style light blue shirt. "No concussion, but I'll need to see you early next week so I can take out those stitches."

She nodded but couldn't think beyond the next hour, much less next week. Darcy hurried off the foot of the bed, then out of the guest room and into the hall, leaving the doctor as he was putting his gear back into his medical bag. She got to the nursery, where she'd left Noah with Kimmie and the nanny, Grace Borden.

But the nursery was empty.

Just like that, the panic grabbed her by the throat. *No!* Had her son been taken again? She knew that wasn't a logical conclusion, but her mind wasn't logical right now. The pain was still too fresh.

"Noah?" she called out. She didn't even wait for an answer before she shouted out his name again.

"In here," Nate answered.

Darcy practically rammed into the doctor coming out of the guest suite, but she followed the sound of Nate's voice. And the sound of laughter. She found him in the last room at the end of the hall. A massive sun-washed playroom. Bright. With lots of windows and shelves loaded to the brim with books and stuffed animals.

It took her a moment to pick through the toys and the brightly colored furniture, but she finally spotted Nate. Not in danger. Not trying to stop another kidnapping. He was on his hands and knees on the floor.

Both Kimmie and Noah were on his back.

And Nate was giving them a pseudo horsey ride. He was even making the neighing sounds while holding on to them.

Kimmie's auburn curls were bouncing all around

her face. Noah was doing some bouncing, too. Clearly her brain had overreacted because the children were in no kind of danger.

"Grace is in the kitchen having some breakfast, and Bessie brought you some of that cinnamon tea you said you liked," Nate let her know, tipping his head toward the tray on a corner table. But he must have noticed her expression. "What's wrong?"

"Nothing," she managed to say. "I panicked when I couldn't find Noah."

"Sorry. I thought it would be okay to bring him down here while you were with Doc Mickelson." He reached behind him and gently moved the children off his back and to the thick play mat.

"It's okay." Her son had obviously been having fun, and her panic had ended that fun.

Well, sort of.

Even though Noah was no longer on Nate's back, her son giggled and crawled into Nate's lap the moment he sat up. Noah babbled something and threw his arms around Nate's neck for a hug.

"He's not usually this comfortable with strangers," Darcy remarked. To give her hands something to do, and to settle her nerves, she went to the table and poured herself a cup of tea.

Nate shrugged. Or rather, he tried to, but Kimmie toddled right into him and he had to catch her to keep her from falling. Noah giggled again. Kimmie did, too.

"I guess Noah knows I like kids," Nate remarked.

And he did. There was no mistaking that. Nate started a gentle wrestling game that ended up with both babies landing on him in a tumbled heap.

Now, Nate was the one to laugh.

The sound was rich, thick and totally male. It went through her much as his kiss had the night before, and suddenly the panic was gone. In its place was that spark. Okay, it was more of a jolt that touched every part of her body.

Every part.

His looks didn't help ease that jolt. Nate was drop-dead hot—that was a given—but this morning he was rumpled hot with his dark stubble, jeans and charcoal gray shirt. It was only partially buttoned, and she got a great look at the perfectly toned chest that he'd used to pin her against the wall for that kiss.

Suddenly, Darcy wanted to be pinned and kissed again.

"What?" Nate asked, snapping her attention back to him. "You're smiling. I've never seen you smile before." His gaze slid down her body. "And I've never seen you wear jeans."

She glanced down at her jeans and rose-colored top because for a moment she forgot she was wearing anything at all.

Get ahold of yourself.

"Someone picked up clothes from my house for Noah and me," she told him, but he obviously already knew that.

"Kade," he supplied. "He also brought your cosmetics and meds that he found in your bathroom."

Oh.

Meds, as in birth-control pills.

She almost blurted out that the pills were to control her periods and not because she was having sex, but that seemed way too personal to tell Nate.

"I'll make sure to thank Kade. And all your brothers.

Bessie and Grace, too." She added some milk to the tea so she could cool it down for a quick drink. "Your family really pitched in when we needed them."

"They always do," Nate mumbled, and it sounded like a personal confession that he hadn't intended to reveal to her.

Darcy understood. Other than Noah, she hadn't had any family for a very long time, and she missed the closeness. The blind acceptance.

The love.

And that was a personal confession she wasn't ready to make, either.

Since it seemed the wrestling play might go on for a while, Darcy finished her tea, put the cup aside and sank down on the floor next to them. Nate didn't look at her. He kept his attention on the children.

"Do I need to apologize?" he asked.

For a moment Darcy had no idea what he meant, but then Nate glanced at her. And she knew. This was about that scalding-hot kiss. "No apology needed. We just got caught up in the moment."

And that moment was still causing some heat to flow through her body.

"Yeah." He sounded as if he wanted to believe that. Did that mean he was still thinking about the effects of that kiss, too?

Darcy decided it was a good time to change the subject, especially since they had plenty of non-kissing things to discuss. "Any news about Ramirez?"

Nate shook his head. "He's still not talking, and the extradition is moving at lightning speed."

So, time was ticking away. Darcy hoped the man

would spill something before he was flown back to Mexico.

"Grayson's bringing in both Adam and Edwin for questioning." He glanced at the cartoon clock on the wall. "He'll let us know when they arrive."

Good. Sandra Dent's son and ex-husband were keys to unraveling all of this. Darcy just hoped she could hang on to her temper and composure if one of them confessed to taking the children.

"The rangers have their CSIs at the Lost Appaloosa. Or rather, what's left of it. The explosions destroyed a lot of potential evidence." Nate paused. Definitely no smile or laughter now, though he continued to play with the children. "Two of the gunmen have been identified, and they both belonged to a drug cartel linked to Ramirez. One of them is Ramirez's kid brother."

"His brother?" she questioned.

"Yeah, his name was David Ramirez. He was just nineteen, and he was the one I got in a wrestling match in the woods. The one I shot." Another pause. "We believe the brother and all the gunmen belonged to the cartel because they each had a coiled rattlesnake tattoo on their left shoulders. That's the cartel's symbol."

That erased the warm, jolting memories of the kiss and chilled her to the bone. Drug dealers had kidnapped her son. The doctor had been right—they were lucky. Things could have gotten a lot worse than they had.

"It's okay," she heard Nate say. And she felt his hand on her arm. Touching her. Rubbing gently with his fingertips. Darcy figured she must have looked on the verge of fainting or something for him to do that.

"I've run financial reports on Adam and Edwin Frasier," he explained. His voice wasn't exactly all cop now. Or maybe that was her interpretation because he was still touching her. "Both father and son have the ready cash to set up an operation like the kidnapping."

"But why would they have risked something like this?" she asked.

"More money, maybe. Sandra Dent died without a will. That means her husband will inherit everything."

"Unless he's convicted of her murder," Darcy supplied. "Then Adam would inherit everything. And that makes him the top suspect."

"Yes, it does. But it's possible Adam and his father worked out this deal together. Or if Edwin is working alone, he could have figured it'd be easier to continue to get an allowance from his son than Dent. As it stands now, Edwin is paid an allowance for managing Sandra's charity foundations. You can bet if Dent inherits everything, he'll cut off Edwin without a penny."

Yes. But Darcy was having a hard time wrapping her mind around anyone risking children's lives for money. Even the fifty million dollars that was in Sandra Dent's estate.

She jumped when she heard a sudden sound in the doorway. It was Mason. With his shoulder propped against the frame, he was holding a cup of coffee and had his attention fastened to Nate's hand, which was still touching her.

Darcy quickly got to her feet.

She didn't want to cause trouble between Nate and his brothers, and judging from Mason's semi-glare, he didn't approve of her or little arm rubs.

"Ma Ma Ma," Kimmie babbled, and with her wispy curls haloing around her face, she toddled toward her dark, brooding uncle.

Mason put his cup on a shelf and scooped her up. "We gotta work on that vocabulary, curly locks. It's Uncle Mason, not Ma Ma."

Kimmie smiled a big toothy smile, dropped a kiss on his cheek and babbled some more. "Ma Ma Ma."

"Don't give her any candy," Nate warned when both Kimmie and Mason started to reach in his denim shirt pocket.

"Later," Mason whispered to the little girl. He placed his hand over hers. "When Daddy's not watching. I'll leave one for your pint-size boyfriend, too."

Darcy was more than a little surprised that this particular Ryland also had a way with children. Mason always made her want to take a step back, and until now she'd never suspected there was a fatherly bone in his body. Noah, however, didn't move. He stayed right by Nate.

"A problem?" Nate asked his brother. He stayed on the floor and accepted some plastic blocks that Noah began to dump in his lap.

"Not with the investigation. A ranching situation. Another cutter quit this morning."

"Again?" Nate mumbled something indistinguishable under his breath. He was clearly upset, and this conversation was a reminder that the Rylands had more going on in their lives than law enforcement.

"Yeah," Mason snarled. "What can I say? I'm not into arm touching to keep folks happy."

Mason had noticed, after all. She felt herself blush.

"What's a cutter?" Darcy asked to fill in the very uncomfortable silence that followed. "I was born and raised a city girl," she clarified when Mason gave her a flat look.

"A person who trains cutting horses. They're used to cull out or cut individual livestock from a herd," Mason finally explained. "But folks use them for competitions and shows."

"People pay a lot of money for a well-trained cutting horse," Nate went on. "And despite going through a trainer every six months, Mason produces some of the best cutting horses in the state."

If Mason was flattered by that, he didn't show it. Instead, he gave Kimmie one of those flat looks. "You impressed, curly locks? Didn't think so."

Mason kissed Kimmie on top of her head and set her back on the floor. "Cause some trouble today, okay?" He eased two foil-wrapped pieces of candy on the shelf, grabbed his coffee cup and strolled away.

"Bye-bye." Kimmie added a backward wave and then reached up toward the shelf where she'd no doubt seen her uncle leave the candy.

"Later, baby," Nate insisted.

But Kimmie didn't give up. The little girl went to Darcy, caught her hand and babbled something.

"Maybe I can distract her," Darcy said, smiling, and she lifted Kimmie into her arms.

Kimmie waggled her fingers in the direction of the shelf with the candy, but Darcy took her in the opposite direction. To another shelf.

One Darcy hadn't noticed when she walked into the room.

There were more pictures here. Dozens of them, all in gleaming silver frames. Some were candid shots of Nate and his brothers, including one Ryland she'd never seen. That had to be his late brother, Gage, who resembled Mason except he had a cocky grin. There was also a copy of the picture of Nate's grandfather, the one that Kayla had faxed her.

"I called my assistant this morning," Darcy told Nate, "and asked her to look into the matter of your grandfather's photo. If Charles Brennan had something to do with Chet McLaurin, then we might find it in his files."

Files that she and her assistant had total access to. If she could give Nate and his family this information, then she would. Of course, Darcy hoped it wouldn't be another round of bad news because her former client, Brennan, was now dead, but when alive he'd no doubt committed murder and a litany of other crimes.

"There's Daddy." Darcy pointed to one of Nate holding Kimmie. Behind them were several horses.

"Da Da Da," Kimmie babbled, and then she switched to "Ma Ma."

Darcy expected to see a photo of Mason, but it wasn't. She recognized the beautiful smiling woman from articles in the newspaper. This was Nate's late wife, Ellie, and she was wearing a wedding dress.

"Ma Ma," Kimmie repeated, and she clapped her hands.

"Ellie died when Kimmie was six weeks old," Nate said softly. "I thought the picture might help her know who her mother is."

Well, it was obviously working because Kimmie was reaching for the photo now and had forgotten all about the candy. Darcy carefully lifted the picture from the shelf and brought it closer to Kimmie.

"Ma Ma." And the little girl kissed it. Darcy saw then that there were dozens of smudges on the glass. No doubt from Kimmie's kisses.

It put a lump in Darcy's throat, and she eased the

picture back onto the shelf. She saw it then. The little silver disk. When Kimmie reached for it, Darcy picked it up so the little girl couldn't get to it. She didn't want to risk Kimmie choking on it.

"A concho," Nate provided.

Darcy turned it over and saw the double *R*s on the back. "For your ranch?"

"Yeah." And that was all he said for several seconds. His mood darkened a bit. "My father gave me and each of my five brothers a concho. A family keepsake, he said. And then a few weeks later, he walked out and never came back."

She turned, stared at him. "What happened?"

But judging from the pain that went through his eyes, she was sorry she'd asked. "I'm not sure why he left. My mother wasn't sure, either, and his leaving destroyed her. She killed herself, and in her suicide note she begged Grayson to keep the family together." Nate lifted his shoulder. "And he did. End of story."

No. Not the end. The pain was still too raw for that. It didn't help with that lump in her throat, and it gave her added respect for the Ryland brothers. They'd raised themselves, kept their family together, and they'd done that under the worst of circumstances.

"Do you hate your father for abandoning you?" Darcy asked, holding her breath.

"Yeah. All of us do. Well, except for Kade. He was only ten when our father walked out." Nate tipped his head to the concho. "Mason put a bullet through his. Dade threw his away."

"But you kept yours," she pointed out. And he'd polished it. Or someone had. Because it had a gleaming shine.

"Only so I could remember how much it hurts when people do irresponsible, selfish things." He shook his head. "I don't want to be anything like my father because I would never put Kimmie through that. *Never.*"

It was the answer she'd feared. "Noah's father, Jake Denton, abandoned him. Jake's never seen Noah and swore he never would." And Darcy could see firsthand the pain that abandonment could cause.

Would Noah have the same bitterness that Nate had?

Darcy hated Jake for that. Hated that Noah would have this wound.

"It's my fault, of course," she added. "I should have chosen a better partner." Even though her pregnancy had been an accident. One she certainly didn't regret.

"Sometimes, even when you choose the right partner, it's not enough," Nate said. She followed his gaze, and he was staring at Ellie's picture.

Kimmie looked at her dad. Then, at Darcy, and even though she was just a baby, she seemed to realize something wasn't right. Kimmie hooked her arms around Darcy's neck and kissed her cheek.

Darcy smiled in spite of the sad moment.

Children were indeed magical, and Nate's daughter was no exception. Noah, however, disagreed. He must have objected to Darcy giving this little girl so much attention because he toddled toward them and tugged on her jeans. Darcy treated herself to holding both of them, even though they were a double armful.

She glanced at Nate, who was smiling again. After the hellish day they'd had, this seemed like a moment to savor.

What would it be like to have moments like this all the time?

Darcy hadn't let herself consider a relationship, not after Jake had burned her so badly. But what would it be like to be with Nate? Thinking about that caused the heat to trickle through her body again.

Nate made a *hmm* sound.

Did he know what she was thinking? Probably not. But that didn't erase the little fantasy in her head.

Then Nate's phone buzzed, and the moment vanished. Darcy snapped back to reality. Especially when she heard Nate greet the caller.

"Grayson," he answered. "You have news?"

She stepped closer, watching Nate's face.

"What?" Nate asked several second later, and he paused. Darcy couldn't hear anything his brother was saying, but Nate finally snapped his phone shut.

"Edwin and Adam Frasier just arrived at the sheriff's office," Nate relayed to her after dragging in a long breath. He was the cop again. All business. And he got to his feet.

"What's wrong?" she asked, afraid to hear the answer.

Nate looked her straight in the eyes. "Edwin and Adam both claim Dent and *you* were behind the kidnapping plot, and they say they can prove it."

Chapter 9

Darcy wasn't denying anything that Edwin and Adam Frasier had claimed. In fact, she hadn't said more than two words on the drive from the ranch to the sheriff's office. She just sat in the passenger's side of his SUV and stared out the window.

That caused Nate to do some mental cursing.

He didn't need this now. He needed clear answers that would lead him to the person responsible for kidnapping Kimmie and Noah, and with this latest allegation, Nate was afraid these interviews wouldn't give him anything useful.

The moment Nate parked the SUV, Darcy got out, and she didn't wait for him. She stormed toward the back entrance, threw open the door and hurried inside.

"Where are they?" Darcy asked Mel, and the deputy hitched her thumb toward the interview room at the front of the building.

"Grayson's in there with them now," Mel let her know. "How are the kiddos?"

"Fine," Darcy mumbled. "Kade and Mason are staying with them while I straighten out this mess."

Okay. She clearly wasn't pleased, and Nate couldn't blame her since they'd accused her of being involved with the kidnapping. Still, he hoped she wouldn't try to attack one of them. He'd faced Darcy in court and legal hearings and had never once seen her lose her composure. But now her fuse seemed short and already lit. Just in case her temper was about to explode, Nate hurried to catch up with her.

She marched into the room and shot past Grayson, who was standing. Edwin and Adam were seated, and Darcy planted her fists on the metal table that separated them. She leaned in and got right in their faces.

"Explain to me what *proof* you think you have that would implicate me in this crime," she demanded.

The men exchanged glances but didn't exactly seem unnerved. Nate decided to do something about that. He, too, moved closer.

"Ms. Burkhart asked you a question," Nate clarified. He shut the door, locked it, pretended to turn off the interview camera and then slid his hand over his gun in his shoulder holster.

That got their eyes widening.

Nate knew both men. Had interviewed them extensively about Sandra's death. Edwin was fifty-three and looked pampered and polished in his blue suit. To the best of Nate's knowledge, the man had never had a job in his life, even though he did get an allowance for managing his late wife's charity foundations.

Adam was a younger version of his father. There were no threads of gray in his brown hair. No tiny lines around his blue eyes. But there was no mistaking he was his father's son. Like his father, he also lived off an allowance from his mother's estate.

"You're going to shoot us?" Edwin challenged, eyeing the stance Nate had taken with his gun.

"Depends," Nate tossed back. Normally, he didn't play cop games, but he was almost as pissed off as Darcy was. "Right now, I consider you two my top suspects. I think one or both of you is responsible for endangering my daughter and Ms. Burkhart's son."

Nate adjusted his position and leaned in so that Darcy and he were shoulder to shoulder. "And I'm also thinking you're both dangerous enough to try to run out of here now that you know you're suspects. If you do that, I'll stop you."

Adam practically snapped to attention, but the threat didn't seem to faze Edwin. Except for the slight stirring in his jaw muscles. Because Nate had interviewed him and because he'd cataloged the man's responses, Nate was guessing that Edwin was also riled to the core. The man was just better at hiding his emotions than his son.

"Why would you say I had a part in this?" Darcy demanded again.

Edwin lifted his shoulder, but it was Adam who answered. "Because you stole seventy-five thousand dollars from my mother."

Darcy looked at Nate and shook her head. "When, where and how did this supposedly happen?" Nate asked.

"A week ago at my mother's estate," Adam continued. "The money was taken from a safe while Darcy was in the house."

Darcy huffed. "I was there," she admitted. "With two San Antonio police officers who work for Nate. I wanted to see where Sandra had died in case it came up at the trial. But I didn't go anywhere near a safe, and I didn't take any money."

"Well, it was there before you arrived, and it wasn't there after you left." Adam folded his arms over his chest. "We think you used the money to orchestrate this kidnapping."

"And why would I do that?" Darcy spaced out each word and glared at Adam.

"Simple. This makes your client look innocent. He's not. But the truth doesn't matter to you. The only thing that matters to you is winning and letting a killer like Dent go free."

Since that seemed to eat away at what little fuse Darcy had left, Nate took over. "You have any proof she took it? Security surveillance tapes? Eyewitnesses?"

"No." Edwin didn't glare. He just looked smug. "But who else would have done it? Adam did an inventory of that safe just minutes before she arrived, and when he checked the safe again later that afternoon, the cash was gone. Are you saying your own officers are thieves?"

"No." Nate could play the smug game, too. "I'm saying you two are troublemakers or liars. Maybe both. You honestly think Darcy would have done anything to endanger her son or my daughter?"

Darcy made a slight sound. Relief, maybe? Nate glanced at her and realized that's exactly what it was.

Oh, man. Had she really thought he might believe she'd put her child in danger to clear a client?

But Nate took a mental step back.

Yesterday, he might have indeed believed it. Before he'd seen her reaction to Noah's kidnapping. Before he'd witnessed firsthand how terrified she was.

Before he'd kissed her.

Yeah, that was playing into this, as well.

The sweltering attraction. But Nate knew in this situation that the kiss wasn't clouding his judgment. Darcy hadn't taken that money, and she hadn't had anything to do with kidnapping the babies.

Grayson moved to the end of the table and sat down. He studied Edwin and Adam for a moment. "So, you're suggesting a lawyer with no criminal record would do something like this?" He didn't wait for them to respond. "Because she's not a suspect, and you two are."

"I did nothing wrong!" Adam shouted.

"Nor did I." Edwin's voice was almost calm. *Almost.*

"That remains to be seen," Nate let them know.

Edwin got to his feet. "Are you arresting us? Because this was just supposed to be an opportunity for us to tell you about her stealing that money and trying to clear her client. And I don't appreciate your intimidation tactics. If I'd known we would be grilled like this, I would have brought my attorney."

"Come on," Grayson fired back. "Did you really think you could walk in here and put this kind of spin on what happened? If Darcy had wanted to clear her client, she would have gone about it differently. Not using reverse psychology."

"And if she had criminal intent, she could have created and paid for a witness," Nate explained. "One that would have given Dent an airtight alibi. It would have been far cheaper. Far safer. And it wouldn't have put her baby's life on the line."

Nate leaned in so he could look them in the eyes. "But you two have a lot to gain if you put Dent behind bars. Or better yet, get him the death penalty."

"Dent made his own bed," Edwin insisted. "He's running scared because he's guilty. And he knows you can prove it. You've said so yourself that you believe he's guilty."

Nate had said that. He couldn't deny it. And maybe Dent was behind the kidnapping, but Darcy certainly wasn't. So, that meant either these two had been duped into thinking Darcy was guilty, or they were the ones trying to do the duping.

Edwin gave his suit an adjustment that it in no way needed. "We're done here. We've given you the information, and now we'll go to your captain at SAPD. We'll press him to file charges against..." He cut his eyes toward Darcy. And smiled an oily smile. "Well, whatever she is to you."

Nate didn't consider himself someone who had a bad temper, but Edwin's suggestion sent anger boiling through him.

"Who said we're done?" Nate fired back.

Surprise showed in Edwin's eyes. Adam seemed alarmed.

Grayson stood, gave Nate a nod. "I'll take things from here." He looked at the two men. "You have the right to remain silent—"

"You're arresting us?" Edwin howled.

"Detaining you for questioning and possible arrest

for multiple felonies," Grayson clarified. "When you're done hearing your rights, I suggest you call a lawyer."

The two men started to protest, but Grayson glanced at Nate, and he knew what that glance meant. This was now an official interrogation. Not an interview. And that meant Darcy and he shouldn't be there.

"We can wait in Grayson's office," Nate said to her.

She looked ready to argue, and her gaze flew to Grayson as if he might allow her to stay. But Grayson only shook his head.

"Come on." Nate caught her arm and led her out of the room.

"Thank you," she whispered. "For sticking up for me in there."

He maneuvered her inside Grayson's office but didn't shut the door. Privacy and Darcy weren't a good idea, especially since her nerves were raw and right at the surface.

"It was a no-brainer. As I said, you love Noah too much to put him in danger."

Darcy looked at him and shook her head as if she didn't know how to respond to that. But she did respond. Man, did she. She stepped forward until she was pressed against him, and slipped her arms around him.

"I'm wired to handle stress," she whispered. "But not this kind."

Was she talking about Noah now, or this suddenly close contact between them? Nate wasn't sure, but that didn't stop him from pulling her into a hug.

Unfortunately, a hug he needed as much as she did.

He, too, was wired to handle stress, but it was different when his entire world was tipping on its axis. For so long he'd been living in a dark cloud of grief and pain over losing Ellie that he had nearly forgotten what it was like to feel something, well, good.

His body was burning for Darcy. There was no denying that. But that didn't make things easy. Or even acceptable. Wanting Darcy could put a wedge between him and his family.

Without breaking the armlock they had on each other, she eased back a little and looked up at him. A soft breath left her mouth. Like a flutter. And her face flushed with what he thought might be heated attraction.

Nate tested that theory by brushing his mouth over hers.

Yeah, attraction.

"We shouldn't act on this," Darcy whispered.

But she didn't back away. She kept her mouth hovering just beneath his. Her breath smelled like the cinnamon tea she'd had earlier, and he wanted to see if she tasted as good as she smelled.

But Nate didn't get the chance. The sound of the footsteps stopped him.

He braced himself for a face-to-face with one of his brothers, who would almost certainly notice all the heavy breaths and lust-filled eyes that Darcy and he had for each other. But it wasn't his brother.

It was Wesley Dent.

Nate stepped into the hall, directly in front of the man.

They knew each other, of course. Nate had interviewed and interrogated him at least a half-dozen times. Times that Dent apparently hadn't liked because his green eyes narrowed when he looked at Nate.

Unlike Edwin and Adam, there wasn't much polish

here. Dent wore his usual jeans and untucked white button-down shirt that was fashionably rumpled. It was the same for his shoulder-length, highlighted, brown hair. As a rule, Nate didn't trust a man who got highlights and manicures. He especially didn't trust Dent.

Was he looking at the person behind the kidnapping?

Just the thought of it caused the anger to boil up inside him again.

"I heard about your daughter. And your son," Dent said, glancing at Darcy before he brought his attention back to Nate. "You've arrested Edwin and Adam?"

"Not at the moment," Nate informed him. "They're here for questioning."

Dent's eyes narrowed again. "Why not just arrest them? They're behind this."

"Where's the proof?" Nate challenged.

"The motive is proof." Dent looked up, huffed, as if he couldn't believe Nate hadn't done the obvious— arrest his dead wife's ex and son. "Those two morons wanted you to set me up. To fix the investigation. If that isn't proof, I don't know what is."

"Maybe," Nate mumbled and he left it at that.

"How did you know about the kidnapping being tied to you?" Darcy asked. She stepped out into the hall with them.

Dent wearily shook his head. "It's all over the news. I tried to call your office, to make sure you and your son were okay, but your secretary said you were out indefinitely."

All over the news.

Though he hadn't turned on the TV or opened a newspaper, Nate didn't doubt that word had gotten out. Heck, this was probably a national story by now, especially with so many deaths and the kidnapping from a small-town preschool. But he did have to wonder how many of the details had been leaked. Details like the possible identity of the person who'd hired Ramirez to force Darcy and Nate into throwing the investigation.

"So, when will you be back at work?" Dent asked Darcy. "We need to discuss what's happened. *Alone,*" he added, sparing Nate a glance.

That was reasonable. After all, Darcy was his attorney, but Dent's remark stirred up other feelings inside Nate. Old wounds about Darcy and he being on opposite sides. And new wounds about his confused feelings for her.

"I'm not sure when I'll be back," Darcy let him know. She looked over her shoulder when the bell on the front door jangled.

Nate looked, too. After what had happened, he didn't feel completely safe even in the sheriff's office. He couldn't see who had arrived because Tina Fox, the dispatcher, stood to greet the person and blocked Nate's view. He did relax a little, though, because it was obvious Tina wasn't alarmed.

"Look, I know you've been through a lot," Dent complained to Darcy, "but my life is at stake. If the cops arrest me—"

"Mr. Dent, effective immediately I'm resigning as your lawyer," Darcy interrupted.

Both Nate and Dent stared at her, and Nate didn't know which of them was more surprised.

"I wouldn't be able to give my full attention to your defense," she continued. Her voice wavered a little but not her composure. "My secretary or assistant can give you other recommendations."

"I don't want another lawyer," Dent howled. "Good grief, the police are trying to pin my wife's murder on me. I need you to make sure that doesn't happen."

"I'm sorry." She shook her head. "But I simply can't represent you." She turned to go back into Grayson's office, but Dent stepped in front of her.

"You can't do this," Dent insisted. "I won't let you do it." He flung his hand toward Nate. "Is it because of him? Because he's turned you against me? Well, you're stupid to believe Nate Ryland. He's had it in for me since the moment Sandra drew her last breath."

Enough was enough. Nate stepped between Darcy and the man. "Dent, my advice is to make some calls. Find another attorney. Because you're probably going to want one with you when Sheriff Ryland questions you."

"Sheriff Ryland?" he said like profanity. "If any of you badge-wearing cowboys want to question me, then you get a warrant for my arrest because I'm done playing games." He aimed a glare at Darcy. "I'll settle things with you later."

Nate latched on to Dent's shirt and snapped the man toward him. "Is that a threat?"

Dent opened his mouth as if he might verify that, but he must have decided it would be a bad idea. He tore away from Nate's grip, cursed and turned, heading for the door.

Nate followed him, to make sure he did leave. Grayson would indeed want to question him, but that probably wasn't a good idea with Edwin, Adam and Darcy there. Besides, Dent needed a new attorney. Later, Nate would talk to Darcy about that, to make sure she was doing this for all the right reasons—whatever those reasons were.

For now, he watched.

Dent was moving at lightning speed. Until he reached the dispatcher's desk. And then he stopped and stared at the person on the other side of Tina.

That got Nate moving. Darcy, too. Nate wasn't sure who had captured Dent's attention, and he was more than a little surprised that it was Marlene. She had a bandage on her cheek, another on her arm, but she looked as if she'd physically weathered the kidnapping ordeal. Not mentally, though. The woman was practically cowering.

"Grayson said I needed to sign some papers," Marlene said, her head lowered, her bottom lip trembling.

"Papers?" Dent challenged, and his booming voice caused Marlene to look even more rattled. "Please don't tell me this woman had something to do with the kidnapping."

Nate put his hands on his hips and tried to figure out what the heck was going on.

"The gunmen took me hostage," Marlene explained. "I work at the Silver Creek Preschool and Day Care."

Dent stared at her. And then he laughed. "Oh, this is *good*."

That got Marlene's gaze off the floor. "I didn't do anything wrong," she insisted. And then she turned the pleading gaze on Nate and Darcy. "I swear."

"What do you mean?" Nate demanded. When Marlene didn't answer, Nate looked at Dent.

But the man just smiled and headed for the door. "Why don't you ask her? Or better yet, ask Edwin. I'm sure he'd like to tell you all about it."

Chapter 10

Darcy kept watch out the SUV window while Nate drove back to the ranch.

Even though she didn't think anyone was following them, she wanted to make sure. With the eerie turn in the investigation, Darcy didn't want to take any chances with their safety. Or the babies'. She certainly didn't want a second wave of kidnappers trying to follow them to the ranch.

Nate was keeping watch, too, but he also had his cell phone clipped to the dash. Ready. And waiting for a call from Grayson that would hopefully explain why her former client had suggested Marlene was associated with Edwin. Grayson hadn't quite dismissed the semi-accusation, but he'd insisted that Nate and she head back to the ranch and leave him to handle the questions, not just for Edwin but for Marlene.

That was probably a good idea because the anger was already starting to roar through Darcy. Not just for Marlene's possible involvement but because she'd seen firsthand the venom inside Dent. She'd thought he was innocent, but she wasn't so sure of that now. Plus, there was the money taken from Sandra's safe. Dent could have stolen it and used it to fund the kidnapping.

Of course, the same could be said for Edwin or Adam.

"In all the interviews I did regarding Sandra Dent, Marlene's name never came up," Nate commented.

"Same here." But what had come up was the tyrannical way that Sandra had treated others—especially her husband, her ex and her son. It was that behavior, and her net worth, that had provided the possible motive for her murder.

Nate took the final turn to the ranch, and finally his cell rang. And Darcy saw that it was Grayson's name on the caller ID. Nate jabbed the button to answer and pressed the speaker function.

"Well?" Nate immediately asked.

Grayson huffed. "Edwin and Marlene know each other."

That kicked Darcy's pulse up a notch. "How?" Nate and she asked in unison.

"In the worst way possible for our investigation." Grayson sounded tired, frustrated and riled. "They had an affair."

"An affair?" Darcy challenged. "Those two don't exactly run in the same social circles."

"No," Grayson agreed. "But they apparently met at a bar in San Antonio. He bought her a drink, and things went from there."

Nate cursed, and it mirrored exactly how Darcy felt. "Any idea if Marlene had something to do with the kidnapping?" Nate pressed.

"She says no. So does Edwin. He puts the blame directly on Dent."

Of course, he would. Dent was putting the blame on Edwin and Adam, and the finger-pointing was just going in circles.

"Edwin says the affair was short, just a few weeks, and that it ended months ago," Grayson continued. "Marlene echoed the same, but I got to tell you, I'm not sure I believe her. After all, she had an entire day to give me a heads-up about her relationship with Edwin, and she didn't even mention it. I have to ask myself why."

Darcy's pulse went up more than a notch. "Are you holding her?"

"No. I told her not to leave town, that I would have more questions for her once I did some checking. I'll get her phone records and go from there. Edwin's, too. If they put this kidnapping together, I'll find a way to prove it."

"Thanks," Nate told him.

"There's more," Grayson said before Nate could hang up. "The two deputy marshals are here to extradite Ramirez."

"Already?" Nate cursed. And Darcy didn't blame him. They'd hoped to have more time to get Ramirez to talk.

"Yeah. And the marshals want to leave immediately. I can't stop them from taking him," Grayson explained. "But I'll try."

Nate thanked his brother again, hit the end-call button and stopped the SUV in front of the ranch house.

But he didn't get out. Neither did Darcy. They sat there trying to absorb what they'd just learned. A woman they had thought they could trust, a woman they had believed had helped them by writing those initials, could be the very person who had helped put their children in grave danger.

Darcy stared up at the iron-gray sky for a moment. Everything suddenly felt heavy. Dreary, even. Probably because a storm was moving in. Literally. But that storm was inside her, too.

They got out of the SUV, and Darcy glanced around at the lack of other vehicles in the driveway. Good. Fewer brothers to face. When they went inside, she could smell Bessie's lunch preparations, but none of the others were around. However, there were several notes on the table, which Nate stopped to read.

"Where is everyone?" she asked, automatically making her way to Nate's wing of the house. Maybe it was the news about Marlene, but she had to see her son and make sure everything was okay, and she headed in that direction.

Nate was right behind her. "According to the notes, Mason is in his office in the ranch hands' quarters. Kayla and Grayson's wife, Eve, are in San Antonio. Eve had a doctor's appointment."

Alarmed, Darcy stopped and whirled around to face him. "Is that safe? I mean, the person behind the kidnapping might go after members of your family."

He shook his head and ran his hand down her arm. "It's okay. Kade's with them. Grayson considered having Eve reschedule the appointment, but because of her age, her doctor here wanted her to see a specialist in the city. It's just a routine checkup."

"Routine," Darcy repeated under her breath. An impending birth that the family should be celebrating, but instead they were under this cloud of fear. Well, she was, anyway. Darcy didn't think she could forgive herself if something happened to another member of Nate's family.

"Come on." His gentle touch morphed into a grip and he led her in the direction of Kimmie's nursery.

There were no sounds. That was a cause for more alarm until Darcy realized both children were in the nursery. Sharing Kimmie's crib. And they were both asleep. Grace, the nanny, was seated in a rocking chair, a paperback in her hand, and she put her finger to her lips in a *shhh* gesture and joined them in the hall.

"They were both tuckered out," Grace whispered. "Fell asleep after their snacks so I decided to let them have a little nap."

Noah didn't normally take a morning nap, but Darcy figured he'd earned one because of the ordeal and the disruption in his routine.

"We'll be in my office," Nate whispered to the nanny. "Buzz me when they wake up."

Nate took Darcy toward the end of the wing until they reached his office. Like the rest of the rooms, it was large. There was a sitting area with a massive stone fireplace, several windows, but the remaining walls were filled with floor-to-ceiling bookshelves.

"I like to read," he commented when she stood in the doorway with her gaze shifting from one section of the shelves to the other.

Judging from the sheer number of books, that was an understatement, and it made her wonder when he found time to do that. Or exercise. But his toned body certainly indicated that he worked out, and the tread-mill in the corner looked well used. It was the same for the desk, which was topped with all kinds of office equipment.

Including a red phone.

"Are you a secret agent or something?" she joked.

The corner of his mouth lifted. "It's a secure line. I need it sometimes if I'm here in Silver Creek and some sensitive SAPD business pops up."

She figured that was often. Nate was a lieutenant, an important man in SAPD. "It must be hard to live this far away from your headquarters."

"Sometimes. But it'd be harder if I didn't have my family around to help." Nate took two bottles of water from the fridge behind his desk and handed her one. His fingers brushed hers.

A totally innocent touch.

But like all of Nate's touches, it had a scalding effect on her.

And Nate noticed. "Sorry," he mumbled.

She tried to shrug it off and get her mind onto other subjects. It wasn't easy, but thankfully there were many things in the room—not just Nate—to distract her.

There were the monitors, for instance. A trio of flat screens had been built into the wall. They were all on, and she recognized the playroom and the nursery where the babies were sleeping. The third, however, was an exterior shot of a lush green pasture dotted with horses.

"A way for me to keep watch on the ranch," he explained.

Nate typed something on his computer keyboard, and the pasture scene switched to one of the outbuildings. She saw Mason talking with one of the ranch hands.

"We all pitch in to do what we can to run the ranch, but Mason has the bulk of the workload on his shoulders." There was regret in his voice. And fatigue.

Darcy strolled to the fireplace to study the photos on the mantel. As in the playroom, there was a picture of his murdered grandfather.

Nate's old baggage.

Funny that his old baggage was intertwined with some of her unfinished business. She took a sip of water, turned to him. "As the executor of Charles Brennan's estate, I can give you keys and access codes for all of his properties, including his safety-deposit boxes. If my assistant doesn't come up with anything, you might be able to find something that connects him to your late grandfather."

Nate blinked. "You'd do that?"

"Of course," Darcy said without hesitation.

But she was aware that just two days ago she would have done more than hesitate. She would have refused, citing her client's right to privacy, but her views weren't so black-and-white now. Being around Nate and having her life turned upside down had given her some shades of gray to consider. And since Charles Brennan had been a cold-blooded killer, she felt no obligation to hide his sins from the world.

Or from Nate and his family.

"Thank you," Nate said, his voice just above a whisper.

She shrugged and stared at the family pictures. "I know something about family love. And pain," she added. "About how complex relationships can be."

He studied her. "Are you talking about yourself now?"

Darcy smiled before she could stop herself. "Maybe. A little." But the smiled faded. "I'm responsible for my father's murder."

It was the first time she'd said that aloud, but mercy, it was always there. In her thoughts, dreams. Nightmares.

Always.

Nate put his water bottle on his desk, shoved his hands in his jeans pockets and walked closer. "You think you're responsible?" he challenged. "From what I remember, your father went after the eighteen-year-old thug who attacked you when you were sixteen."

She whirled around, her eyes already narrowing. "How do you know that?"

He slowly blew out his breath. "I always do background checks on the lawyers I come up against in court."

It felt like a huge violation of her privacy. And it was. But then she remembered she'd done the same thing to Nate and any other cop she might be grilling on the witness stand.

"Know your enemy," she mumbled. She lowered her head. "I hate that you learned that about me. I keep professing I'm a good person—"

"You are." And that was all he said for several seconds. "Why would you think you're responsible for his death?"

The pain from the memories was instant. Fresh and raw. It always would be. "Because I shouldn't have been out with Matt Sanders to begin with. My dad had forbidden me from dating him because he believed Matt was a rich bully. He was," Darcy admitted. "But I didn't learn that until it was too late." Her gaze flew back to his. "Please tell me you didn't see the pictures."

But his silence and suddenly sympathetic eyes let her know that he had. Pictures of the assault. Black eyes. A broken nose. Busted lip. Along with assorted cuts and bruises. All delivered to her face by Matt after Darcy had gotten cold feet about having sex with him.

"If someone had done that to Kimmie, I would have gone after him, too," Nate confessed.

"Maybe."

He took his hands from his pockets, touched her chin with his fingertips, lifting it so that it forced eye contact. "Your father made a mistake by carrying a gun to confront your attacker, but you did nothing wrong."

That was debatable. A debate she'd had often and lost. "My mother blamed me. Even on her deathbed." Dying from breast cancer hadn't stopped her from giving Darcy one last jab of guilt.

"Your mother was wrong, too." He sounded so sincere. So right. But Darcy couldn't feel that rightness inside her.

Her father had shot and killed Matt Sanders. And because they hadn't had the money for a good lawyer, the public defender had done a lousy job, and her father had been given a life sentence. Which hadn't turned out to be that long since less than a year later, he'd been killed while trying to break up a fight in prison.

"Your father is the reason you became a lawyer," Nate stated, as if he'd read her mind—again. His voice soothed her. A surprise. Nothing had ever been able to soothe her when it came to the subject of her father. "One day, maybe we'll both be able to remember the good without the bad mixed in."

Darcy wished that for both of them. Especially Nate. And that hit her almost as hard as learning that he knew all about her past. She'd known that her feelings for Nate were changing. She blamed the danger and the attraction for that change of heart. But she was more than surprised to realize that she cared about his healing.

About him.

And that went beyond the danger and the attraction.

Oh, mercy.

She was in huge trouble here.

The corner of Nate's mouth hitched. As if once more he knew what she was thinking. Maybe he did.

"I'm about to make a big mistake," he warned her. "Stop me?"

Right. She had less willpower than he did.

"Not a chance."

Nate frowned now. Cursed himself. Then cursed her.

Clearly he was not pleased that neither of them was going to do anything about this. He leaned in. Closer. Until she felt his warm breath brush against her lips. She also felt the pulse in his fingers that were still touching her chin.

And she felt his body.

Because he closed the distance between them by easing against her.

It flashed through her mind that while they shouldn't be playing with fire, it felt right. As if they should be doing this. And more. Then, he put his mouth on hers, and Darcy had no more thoughts. No more mind flashes.

The fiery heat took over.

It was as if they were starved for each other because Darcy wound her arms around him when he yanked her to him. They fought for position, both trying to get closer, but that was almost impossible.

Darcy's burning body offered her a quick solution for that.

Get naked and land in bed. Or in this case, the sofa, since it was only a few feet away.

But Nate didn't take her to the sofa. He turned her, anchoring her against his desk while he kissed the breath right out of her. His mouth was so clever, just the right pressure to make her beg for more. And then he gave her more by deepening the kiss.

The taste of him made those flames soar.

But it wasn't just the kiss. He touched her, too. First her face. Then her neck. Using just his fingertips, he traced the line to her heart. To her left breast. And to her nipple. It was puckered from arousal, and he used those agile fingers to work some heated magic there.

Darcy would have gasped with pleasure if her mouth hadn't otherwise been occupied by his.

She hoisted herself onto the desk so she was sitting. Behind her, things tumbled over, and she heard the sound of paper rattling. But that didn't matter. The only thing that mattered now was feeding this fire that Nate had started. So, she wrapped her legs around him and urged him closer.

Until his sex was against hers.

Yes, she thought to herself. This was what she needed, and judging from the deep growl that rumbled from Nate's throat, he needed it, too.

The kiss got even more frantic. It was the same for the touching. Each of them was searching for more, and Nate did something about that. He eased her down, so that her back was on his desk, and he followed on top of her. The contact was perfect. Well, except for their clothes, and Darcy reached to unbutton his shirt.

But Nate stopped her by snagging her wrist.

He looked her straight in the eyes. "This is just stirring up trouble," he mumbled. "I'm sorry for that."

For a moment, a really bad moment, Darcy thought he was about to call the whole thing off. But Nate shoved up her top and pulled down her bra. He put his mouth to her breasts and kissed her.

Okay, this was the opposite of stopping. She reached for his shirt again. However, Nate let her know that he was calling the shots because he got on the desk with her, pinning her in place with his body.

They were going to have sex, she decided. Right here, right now. And while she tried to think of the problems that would cause—and it would cause problems— she couldn't wrap her mind around anything logical.

Especially when Nate unzipped her jeans.

And slid his hand into her panties.

His first touch was like a jolt, and Darcy might have jolted right off the desk if he hadn't continued to pin her down. He kept up those maddening kisses to her breast and neck while he touched her in the most intimate way. It was making her crazy. Making it impossible to speak. Or move. Or do anything except lie there and take what his hand and mouth were dishing out.

Darcy felt herself racing toward a climax and tried to pull back so that Nate and she could finish this together. She wanted more. She wanted sex. But she was powerless to stop what Nate had already set in motion.

His fingers slid through the slick heat that his touch had created, and he didn't stop. Not with the touching.

Not with the kissing. But what sent her over the edge was what he whispered in her ear.

"Let go for me, Darcy."

And she did. Darcy shattered, her body closing around his fingers as his mouth claimed hers. He kissed her through the shattering and deep into the aftermath.

Until reality hit her squarely between the eyes.

Mercy.

What the heck had she just done?

"Yeah," Nate mumbled. It was that "I'm right there with you" tone. "Trust me, though, it would have been, um, harder if we'd had sex."

Because Nate was indeed hard—she knew because of the way they were still pressed together. Darcy couldn't help herself. She laughed.

Nate's eyebrow rose, and he smiled. "I thought there'd be regret."

Oh, there was some of that. Nate was probably regretting it'd happened at all, and Darcy was regretting they hadn't just taken it to the next level.

"Hand sex crossed just as many lines as the real thing," she let him know. "Plus, it was only pleasurable for me."

He leaned in. Kissed her hard. "Don't think for one minute that you were the only one who enjoyed that."

And it seemed like an invitation for more. Darcy's body was still humming, but one look at Nate and she was ready for him all over again.

"It'll have to wait," he insisted.

For a moment Darcy thought the buzzing sound was all in her head, but then Nate let go of her. That's when she realized the sound was coming from his desk.

He pulled in several hard breaths as he made his

way to the phone. Not the red one but the other land-line. Nate snatched it up.

While she got off the desk and fixed her clothes, she looked up at the monitors. The babies were still asleep, thank goodness. But her sense of relief faded when she saw the look on Nate's face.

"Where?" he demanded of the caller.

Nate cursed and punched some buttons beneath the monitor of the pasture and zoomed in on the high chain-link fence. Darcy saw nothing at first, but then the movement caught her eye.

There.

Someone was scaling the fence. Dressed in dark clothes with a baseball cap shadowing the face, the person dropped to the ground.

And that someone was armed.

"Stay put and lock down the house. I'm going out there to confront this SOB," Mason insisted.

"Be careful." Nate knew it was an unnecessary warning. Mason was always careful, and his brother would no doubt take a ranch hand or two with him. But the sight of a gunman meant plenty of things could go wrong.

Or maybe they already had.

Had Ramirez's boss hired someone else to come after them? Was this the start of another kidnapping attempt?

Nate hung up, and while he kept his attention on the monitors, he pressed in the code that would set the alarm for every door and window of the main house. He also took the gun from his desk drawer.

Beside him, Darcy was trembling now. She had her fingers pressed to her mouth. Her eyes were wide with concern and fixed on the screen with the intruder. An opposite reaction from what she'd had just minutes earlier.

Later, Nate would figure out why he'd had such a bad lapse in judgment by taking her that way on his desk. But for now, they had a possible kidnapper on the grounds.

"Please, not again," Darcy whispered.

Nate knew exactly how she felt. He didn't want the children, Darcy or anyone else to be in danger again. And in this case the danger didn't make sense. The person behind this had already failed to get Darcy and him to throw the investigation. Heck, Darcy was no longer even Dent's attorney.

But maybe this guy didn't know that.

"I need to go to the children," she insisted and headed for the door.

"No. Stay here. For now we just need to keep watch, to make sure Mason can handle this. There are no viewing monitors in the nursery, and it'll only upset the kids if you wake them from their naps."

Nate tapped the screen where the nursery and the babies were displayed on the monitor and hoped she would keep her focus there.

She didn't.

Darcy volleyed glances between the babies and the menacing figure making his way across the back pasture. Nate zoomed in on the intruder, trying to get a better look, but the baseball cap obstructed the man's face. Still, Nate had a sense of his size—about six-two and around one-eighty.

"How far is he from the house?" Darcy's voice was trembling, too.

"A good three miles. That part of the property is near the county road." And that was probably why he was there. It wouldn't have been difficult to drive off the road and onto one of the old trails. Then hide a vehicle in the thick woods that surrounded the ranch. And maybe the intruder hadn't realized that any movement on the fence would trigger the security system.

"He's moving fast," Darcy observed.

Yes. He was practically jogging. While he kept a firm grip on his gun. A Glock, from the looks of it. There was something familiar about the way the man was holding it.

And that created an uneasy feeling inside Nate.

He flipped open his phone and called Grayson. "Tell me Ramirez is still behind bars."

Grayson didn't answer for a second or two, and that was an answer in itself. "Dade and Mel are on their way out there right now. It's possible Ramirez escaped."

Nate cursed. "He did. And he just scaled the west fence and is headed toward the ranch. How the hell did that happen?"

"Still trying to work that out, but neither of the marshals is responding."

Probably because they were dead. Nate didn't want to believe the marshals were in on this, that they'd let Ramirez escape, but later he'd have to consider it. If so, Ramirez's boss not only had deep pockets, he had connections.

"Dade is calling Mason now to tell him," Grayson explained.

Good. At least then Mason would know what he was up against. "How soon before Dade and Mel arrive?"

"Ten minutes."

That wouldn't be soon enough because once they arrived, they would still have to make it out to the pasture. There was no way Mel and Dade would get there in time to give Mason immediate backup.

"I've tapped into the security feed," Grayson went on. "I can see everything that's happening, and I'll alert Mason if the gunman changes directions." With that, he hung up.

Nate could only curse again and watch the monitor. Yeah. It was Ramirez all right. But why come after them here? Why continue a plan that had already failed?

Those questions created an unsettling possibility.

"Ramirez will spend the rest of his life in jail if he's extradited," Darcy pointed out. "And his life might not be worth much since he killed a police officer. He must know he could die a violent death in prison." She paused. "This could be a suicide mission."

Oh, yeah. Death by cop. But Nate kept that agreement to himself.

He gave the security cameras another adjustment and located Mason. His brother was armed, of course, and was on horseback. One of the ranch hands was indeed with him, and they were both riding hard. It wouldn't take them long to close the distance between Ramirez and them.

When Nate went back to Ramirez, he saw that the man was now talking on a phone. Unless it was a pre-paid cell, maybe they could trace the person he was calling. Nate opened his phone to request that trace, but he stopped cold.

"What's Ramirez doing?" Darcy asked. She moved closer to the screen.

Nate wasn't sure. Well, not sure of anything but the

obvious, and that was Ramirez had quit jogging. He rammed the cell into his pocket, turned and broke into a run—heading back toward the fence.

"He's leaving." There wasn't just fear in Darcy's voice. There was alarm.

Nate was right there with her. Even though it would put Mason in some danger, he wanted this situation to end now. He wanted Ramirez captured. Or dead. He didn't want him melting back into those woods so he could regroup and come after Darcy and the children again.

He turned to Darcy, knowing she wasn't going to like this, but also knowing there was no other choice.

"Go to the children," Nate ordered. "Lock the nursery door and don't come out until I give you the all clear."

She snapped toward him and grabbed his arm. "What are you doing?"

"I'm stopping Ramirez." Nate brushed a kiss on her cheek, shook off her grip and ran as fast as he could.

Chapter 11

Things were moving so fast that Darcy had trouble catching her breath.

She raced to the nursery as Nate had insisted and locked the door. She braced herself to explain everything to Grace, the nanny, but the woman was on the phone. Judging from her pale face and frantic tone, she was already aware of the danger. Thankfully, though, the children weren't.

Both Kimmie and Noah were still sound asleep.

"We're leaving," Grace said the moment she got off the phone. "When Dade and Mel get here, they're taking us to the sheriff's office. We're supposed to meet them at the front door." The woman hurried to the crib to scoop up Kimmie.

Darcy shook her head. "But what about Nate and

Mason?" She didn't want to leave until she was certain they were safe.

"Grayson's orders," Grace explained. "He's worried that Ramirez could double back and get close enough to the house to shoot through the windows."

Darcy's heart nearly stopped.

She hadn't even considered the attack could escalate like that. Yes, she was still terrified for Nate and Mason, but she had to put the babies first.

Darcy grabbed a diaper bag, picked up Noah, who immediately started to fuss, and followed Grace out of the room, through the hall and foyer, and to the door. The timing was perfect because Dade and Mel pulled to a screeching stop directly in front of the steps.

"Hurry!" Dade insisted.

It was starting to drizzle, and Darcy tried to shield Noah with the diaper bag.

With his phone sandwiched between his shoulder and his ear, Dade continued to talk with someone. Grayson, she quickly realized. Dade rushed them into the backseat of the SUV, and Mel sped away. There were no infant seats so Darcy and Grace kept the babies in their laps.

Darcy wiped the rain from Noah's face, then Kimmie's, and looked out at the endless pasture, but she couldn't see Nate anywhere. That only caused her heart to pound harder. Not good. She felt on the verge of a panic attack, even though she knew it couldn't happen. Dade didn't have time to coddle her now, not while two of his brothers were in immediate danger.

"What if Nate and Mason need backup?" Darcy asked.

"They're cops," Dade reminded her. "Plus, the ranch

hands are there." He sounded confident about that, but she noticed the hard grip he had on his gun, and his attention was glued on the pasture.

Soon, though, the pasture and the ranch were out of sight, and Mel sped down the country road toward town. Grace had her hands full trying to comfort a crying Kimmie. Noah was still crying, too. But Darcy tried to hear the phone conversation Dade was having with Grayson. She did. And heard something she didn't want to hear.

"The marshals are dead?" Dade asked. "Both of them?"

Oh, mercy.

She knew which marshals he meant—the ones who'd been escorting Ramirez. And now Nate was out there with a monster who'd killed before and wouldn't hesitate to kill again.

"Are you okay?" Grace whispered to her. Probably because the nanny had noticed that Darcy was trembling from head to toe.

"Everything will be all right," Darcy answered, and she repeated it, praying it was true.

Mel didn't waste any time getting them to the sheriff's office, and she pulled into the parking lot, angling the SUV so they were at the back entrance. Both Dade and Mel helped them into the building, and Dade locked the door before he rushed ahead of them to Grayson's office.

Grace stayed back a little, maybe so she could try to calm Kimmie, but since Noah's cries were now just whimpers, Darcy went with Dade in the hopes that she'd be able to hear news about Nate and Mason.

But Grayson stepped into the hall first. One look at

his face, and Darcy knew something was wrong. "Is it Nate?" she asked, holding her breath.

"He's okay." Grayson's attention went to Dade. "But Ramirez got away."

That robbed her of her breath. This couldn't happen. This nightmare had to end. "Nate's out there. Ramirez could come after him."

Grayson shook his head. "Nate's already on his way back here."

Darcy was thankful for that, but she knew until he stepped inside the sheriff's building that he was essentially out there with a killer.

Dade started to curse, but he bit off the profanity when he glanced at Noah. "How did Ramirez escape?" Dade demanded, taking the question right out of her mouth.

Grayson shook his head again. "He made it back to the fence before Mason could get to him, and he disappeared. We'll keep looking," Grayson said first to Dade and then to her.

Darcy didn't doubt they would look, and look hard, but as long as Ramirez was a free man, then Nate, the children and she were all in danger.

"We're bringing in the rangers to assist in the search," Grayson explained. "The FBI, too."

"What do we do with them?" Dade hitched his thumb to Noah and her.

Grayson scrubbed his hand over his face and leaned closer to his brother so he could whisper. "Take them upstairs to the apartment. For now." He looked past Darcy and into the room behind her. "While we're waiting for news, I'll start this interview."

Darcy turned and saw Adam seated at the gray metal

table. She turned to Grayson for an explanation as to why Adam was still there, but the young man got up and went to the door. However, he didn't focus on Grayson but rather Darcy.

"I didn't know," Adam said. "I swear."

"Didn't know what?" Darcy asked. And her mind began to whirl with all sorts of bad answers. She wasn't sure she could stop herself from going after Adam if he was about to confess to having some part in Ramirez's escape and the murder of those federal officers.

"About my father's affair with Marlene." Adam's forehead was bunched up. "He never said a word to me about it, and now I have to wonder—what else is he keeping secret?"

Darcy wasn't sure she had the focus or energy to deal with this, but as an attorney she knew it could be critical to the investigation.

"Do you think Marlene helped your father plan the kidnapping?" she asked, shifting Noah in her arms so she could face Adam head-on.

Adam didn't answer right away. He squeezed his eyes shut and groaned. "It's possible. It's also possible my father stole the money from the safe. He was there. I let him in myself, and I know he was in my mother's office."

"Did you see him take it?" Darcy pressed.

"No. But he had my mother's briefcase with him when he left the house." Adam opened his eyes and met her stare. "He could have used that seventy-five thousand to fund the kidnapping."

Grayson and Dade exchanged glances, and it was Grayson who stepped forward, right next to Darcy. "Why do you think that?" he asked Adam.

Again, Adam took several seconds to answer. "I heard him on the phone speaking to someone in Spanish. I don't speak the language myself, but I heard him say *pistolero*. I looked it up on the internet, and it means—"

"Gunman," Darcy and Grayson said in unison.

That admission changed everything. Father and son were no longer in the camp of accusing Dent, and now Adam had just pinned both means and opportunity on his father. Edwin already had motive—revenge against his ex for divorcing him and marrying a much younger man. Plus, he had to be worried that Dent would cut off his allowance the moment he inherited Sandra's estate.

"I'll go upstairs with Grace and Kimmie," Mel volunteered. She took Noah from Darcy.

"I'll be up soon," Darcy let her know. But first she wanted to ask Adam a few more questions. "Why didn't you tell us this before now?"

"I didn't know about Marlene until today." He dodged her gaze. "And I didn't want to…believe my father could do something like this to my mother. Even though they were divorced, my parents were still in love, in their own way. It would have crushed my mother to know he was carrying on with a woman like Marlene."

Adam sounded sincere enough. There was even a slight quiver in his voice, especially when he said *my mother*. And maybe he did love her, even though after interviewing Sandra's so-called friends and family, Darcy was having a hard time believing that anyone actually loved the woman. But plenty of people loved her money. Of course, Adam would only benefit financially if his stepfather was convicted of the murder. Not his father.

But Darcy rethought that. Could Edwin benefit somehow?

It certainly wasn't an angle she'd researched, but she made a mental note to do just that. Maybe it was the kidnapping or Ramirez's escape, but she wasn't in a trusting mood.

"My father said Marlene is crazy in love with him," Adam went on. "Emphasis on the *crazy*. I think she'd do anything for him, with or without his consent. She might have believed this was a way to get him back in her life."

Darcy looked back at Grayson to see if he shared the same opinion, but the sheriff only lifted his shoulder. *Mercy.* That meant this investigation was about to head out on a new tangent. She didn't mind that in itself, but the more tangents, the longer it might take to figure out who was creating the danger and make an arrest.

"Put all of this in writing," Grayson told Adam. The sheriff pointed toward the paper and pen that were already on the table.

When Adam went back inside the interview room, Grayson shut the door. "Adam will have to wait. I've already asked for a check on Marlene's financials, but I doubt the woman had the money to hire gunmen."

True. After all, she worked at a day care and preschool. "Can you run Edwin's financials, too?" Darcy asked.

"Yeah." And Grayson didn't ask why, which meant he'd already considered that money might be playing into Adam's bombshell about his father's possible guilt. He tipped his head to the back stairs. "There's an apartment on the second floor where Mel and Grace took the children. Why don't you wait up there with them?"

Darcy wasn't about to argue with that, but before she could head in that direction, the back door flew open and someone walked in.

Nate.

She felt herself moving. Running toward him. Yes, it was stupid with his brother and heaven knows who else around. But she went to him. And was more than surprised when Nate closed the distance between them and pulled her into his arms.

"I'm okay," he whispered.

It was the same thing Grayson had told her, but this time she believed it. Still, the panic already had hold of her. Her breath broke, and Darcy disgraced herself by crying. Nate came to the rescue again and wiped the tears from her cheeks.

His hands were already damp. His hair, too. And the rain had soaked his shirt.

"How are the children?" Nate asked. He leaned down, cupped her face and looked her straight in the eyes.

It was the one subject that could get her to focus. "They're fine."

"Good." He pushed her hair from her face and brushed a kiss on her mouth. His lips were also wet from the rain. "Don't worry. We'll find Ramirez."

Again, she believed him and wished she could stay longer in his arms. But the sound of footsteps had them pulling apart. It was Grayson, and even though Darcy felt better, it was clear that Nate's brother didn't share her relief. No doubt because of the kiss he'd just witnessed.

"Where's Mason?" Grayson practically growled.

Nate kept his arm around her waist, causing Gray-

son's gaze to drop in that direction. "At the ranch, waiting for the rangers and the FBI," Nate told him. "After
they arrive, he's driving Bessie to her sister's house."

Darcy hated that she was causing this tension between Nate and his brother, but she would hate even
more having to distance herself from Nate. This attraction probably couldn't lead anywhere, but she wasn't
ready to let go of it just yet.

Grayson continued to stare at the embrace for several moments. Then he mumbled something and headed
back down the hall, saying what he had to say over his
shoulder. "I have Adam Frasier in an interview room
writing a statement. Darcy can fill you in on what's
happening."

Well, at least Grayson hadn't said her name as if it
were profanity.

"Adam says now that his father could be behind the
kidnapping. Or Marlene," she explained. "Grayson is
already digging to see if it's true. Or if Adam is just
trying to cover up his own guilt."

Nate wearily shook his head. "Maybe when we catch
Ramirez, we can get him to talk."

Darcy was about to remind him that at best Ramirez
was a long shot, but then she heard the voices. One familiar voice in particular.

Wesley Dent.

She turned and spotted him making his way down
the hall toward them. Tina, the dispatcher, was right
behind him, telling him that he would have to wait in
reception.

"It's okay, Tina," Nate assured the woman, and he
stepped in front of Darcy. Probably because Dent looked
riled enough to explode.

"You'd better not be here to threaten Darcy again," Nate warned.

"No threat. I'm here because I found something." Dent started to reach into his jacket pocket, and before he could get his hand inside, Nate had his gun drawn and pointed it right at the man.

Dent glanced at the gun. Then Nate. Dent looked as if he tried to smirk, but he failed. "I'm not the killer, Lieutenant Ryland." Now, he managed some smugness. "But I have something that could blow your investigation wide open."

That got her attention. Nate's, too. And Dent waited until Nate eased his gun back down before he reached into his pocket and extracted a small black leather-bound book. One look and Darcy immediately knew what it was.

Sandra Dent's missing diary.

"Read it," Dent said, thrusting it toward Nate. "And then you'll know who killed my wife."

Chapter 12

Nate didn't touch the diary, but he figured if this was the real deal, then any fiber or print evidence on it had already been compromised.

Still, they might get lucky.

With Grayson and Darcy right behind them, Nate led Dent into Grayson's office, took a sterile plastic evidence bag from the supply cabinet and placed it on the center of the desk. Nate motioned for Dent to place the diary there.

"Where did you find it?" Nate asked Dent. But he didn't look at the man. He grabbed a plastic glove, as well, and lifted the diary's cover.

"In the back of Sandra's closet. It'd been shoved into a coat pocket."

Nate was certain the cops had gone through Sandra's closet, but it was possible they'd missed it.

"Go to the last entry," Dent instructed.

Nate did, and Darcy and Grayson moved closer so they could look, as well. The handwritten words practically jumped off the page.

Adam and I argued tonight again. Money, always money. He's too much like his father. Let's see how sorry he is when his allowance is gone.

"Sandra was about to cut off Adam's allowance," Dent emphasized.

Nate mentally went back through his notes. Adam's allowance was a hundred thousand a year and was paid out through a trust fund, but it was a trust fund with strings. Adam could only get the hundred grand per year and that was it. He couldn't touch the principal amount itself for any reason.

A hundred thousand wasn't a huge sum by Sandra's standards, but maybe this was motive for Adam to kill her—especially since the allowance would have continued for the rest of his life. Well, it would continue unless Sandra managed to disown him and rewrite the conditions of the trust.

"Adam didn't say anything about this during his interview," Grayson mumbled, the disgust and frustration in his voice.

Nate understood that frustration. This case just kept getting more complicated, and they had to find the culprit soon so they could end the danger for the children.

"Adam's still here," Grayson added. "I need to talk to him again."

When Grayson walked out, Nate stayed and continued with the diary, but he quickly realized the page was the last thing Sandra had written. He checked the date at the top.

The night before she died.

Well, the timing was suspect. But then Nate noticed something else. The ragged edge, barely visible, indicating a subsequent page had been ripped out.

Nate looked up at Dent. "Know anything about this missing page?"

Dent seemed surprised by the question and had a look for himself. "No. I didn't see that until now. Maybe Adam tore it out?"

"You'd like them to think that, wouldn't you?" Adam snarled from the hall.

With Grayson right behind him, Adam marched into the room and looked at the diary. When he reached for it, Nate blocked his hand.

"It's evidence now," Nate informed him. "I'll have it couriered to the SAPD crime lab for immediate analysis." He pointed to the blank page beneath the one that had been torn out. "I think we might have impressions so we can figure out what your mother wrote."

Both Dent and Adam went deadly silent. For a few seconds, anyway.

"We don't even know if that is my mother's diary," Adam concluded.

"True," Nate acknowledged. "But we have her handwriting on file. It shouldn't take long for the lab to do a comparison."

The muscles in Adam's jaw turned to iron, and he snapped toward Dent. "You're setting me up." He whirled back to Nate. "Yes, my mother and I argued, but we worked out everything before someone murdered her."

"I didn't kill her," Dent calmly replied. He seemed to be enjoying Adam's fit of temper.

"Well, someone did. Either you or my father." Adam poked him in the chest with his index finger. "And if it was you, then I'm going to prove it."

That washed away Dent's calm facade, and Nate was concerned the two men might come to blows. He was too tired to break up a fight. "Are you done with Adam?" he asked Grayson.

His brother nodded.

"Both of you can leave," Nate told Dent and Adam.

"But what about the diary?" Adam demanded.

"We'll let you know what the lab says."

"And then they can arrest you," Dent concluded. He smiled and walked out.

Adam cursed him, but he didn't rush after his step-father. "Don't let him get away with murder," Adam demanded.

Nate huffed and motioned for him to leave. For a moment, he thought Adam might argue, but the man finally stormed out.

Grayson put on a pair of gloves and picked up the diary. "I'll have Tina fax the pages to the crime lab so they can do a quick comparison of the handwriting to make sure it's Sandra Dent's. Then, I'll have a courier pick it up."

Nate thanked him, and once Grayson was out of the room, he turned his attention to Darcy. She looked several steps beyond exhaustion. And worried. Because he thought they could both use it, he brushed a kiss on her mouth.

Yeah, he needed it, all right, and wasn't surprised that the kiss worked its magic and soothed him.

Man, he was toast.

"Why don't you go check on the kids?" he suggested. "I need to make some calls."

She didn't question that. Darcy only nodded, turned but then turned back. She kissed him. Like his, it was brief, barely a touch, but she pulled back with her forehead bunched up and a frown on that otherwise tempting mouth.

"We'll deal with this later," he promised, figuring she knew exactly what he meant. The only question was how they would deal with it.

Except that wasn't in question, either.

They'd deal with it in bed. With some good oldfashioned sex. And yeah, it would mess things up with his family. It might even become the final straw of stress that would break his proverbial back. But Nate was certain that sex would happen no matter how it messed up things.

She ran her hand down the length of his arm. "Just yell if you want me," Darcy whispered.

Despite the fatigue, he smiled. So did she—after she blushed.

Nate watched her walk away. He felt the loss, or something. And wondered when the heck Darcy had become such an important part of his life. Cursing himself and cursing her, he pushed that question aside and got to work. He called Sergeant Garrett O'Malley at SAPD headquarters, the cop working on the Dent case. And now the kidnapping, as well.

"Garrett," Nate greeted. "What do you have on Marlene Lambert's financials?"

"There's nothing much in her checking account, but something else popped up," he explained, and in the background was the sound of the sergeant typing on a computer keyboard. "Two months ago she sold some land she'd inherited from her grandparents. The buyer gave her a check for nearly fifty thousand, which she cashed, but that fifty grand hasn't shown up in her financial accounts."

Nate felt the knot twist in his stomach. This was a woman he'd known for a long time. A woman he'd trusted with the safety and care of his baby girl.

"Of course, Ms. Lambert might have a good explanation," Garrett went on, "but I'm not seeing it right now."

So, Nate knew what had to be done. Grayson would have to bring her back in for questioning and grill her until she told them everything. Fifty thousand probably wasn't enough to have pulled off the entire kidnapping plot, but it would have been enough to get it started.

"What about the financials on Edwin and Adam Frasier?" Nate asked. "I wanted someone to take a harder look at those."

"I did," Garrett assured him. "And if either of them spent an unexplained chunk of money from any of their accounts, I can't find it."

Those financials had been a long shot since neither man would have been stupid enough to have the money trail lead straight back to them. Especially when Adam or Edwin could have just stolen that money from the safe. But Nate had still hoped he could pin this on one of them. On anyone. He just needed this to end.

"I did see something that might be important," Garrett said a moment later. "Adam is the sole heir to his father's estate, and while Edwin doesn't have a lot of cash, he does own a house that he got from the divorce settlement. It's worth close to two million. If something happened to Edwin—jail, death, whatever—Adam would be executor of his father's estate."

Interesting. Nate was betting Edwin would do something about that now that his son had implicated him in the kidnapping. It was also interesting that if either Dent or Edwin went down for Sandra's murder, then Adam would benefit.

Yeah. That was motive, all right.

Of course, Dent had just as big a motive. And Nate couldn't discount Edwin's jealousy of his ex-wife's new boy toy. Or Marlene's possible misguided love.

In other words, he was still at square one. All four of his suspects had motives, and worse, they could have had the means and opportunity, as well.

Nate thanked the sergeant, hung up and was about to check on Darcy and the children, but Grayson was right outside the door. Waiting. And judging from his brother's expression, something bad had happened.

"The children?" Nate automatically asked.

"Are fine," Grayson assured him. He stretched his hand across his forehead and ground his thumb and finger into his temples. "But I'm thinking we need to get them to a safe house."

That nearly knocked the breath out of Nate. "What happened?"

Grayson tipped his head in a follow-me gesture and started toward the front of the building to the dispatcher's desk, where Tina was packaging the diary for the courier.

"Did you find something in the diary?" Nate demanded.

"No. But Tina did fax copies, so we might know something soon." Grayson went toward the computer on Tina's desk. "While you were on the phone, I got a call from Kade. About twenty minutes ago, Ramirez was spotted on a security camera at a gas station off the highway. Less than five miles from town."

Oh, mercy. That was way too close for comfort. "Is Kade going out there to try to arrest him?"

Grayson shook his head. "Ramirez is already gone." He turned the computer monitor so Nate could see the feed from the security camera.

Yeah. It was Ramirez, all right, standing under the sliver of the overhanging roof of the gas station. And he wasn't alone. There was another broad-shouldered man with him. Both were wearing baseball caps and raincoats, but the bulkiness in their pockets indicated they were carrying weapons.

"We have this image and a description of the vehicle," Grayson pointed out, tapping the black four-door sedan stopped in front of the gas station.

But not just parked. It was directly in the line of sight of the security camera. Nate watched as Ramirez looked up at the camera.

Ramirez smiled.

The anger slammed through him, and Nate wished he could reach through the screen and teach this moron a hard lesson about endangering babies.

"What's he doing there, anyway?" Nate asked. Because it was clear Ramirez wasn't filling up the car or buying something.

"He's leaving a message," Grayson mumbled.

Yeah. That was obvious. "And that message is he's begging for me to go after him."

"Not quite."

Since Nate hadn't expected to hear Grayson say that, he snapped toward him. "What do you mean?"

"Just watch," Grayson instructed.

Nate did, and his heart started to ram against his chest. Within seconds, Ramirez pulled a folded piece of paper from his raincoat pocket, lifted it toward the camera and then tucked it into the glass door. He gave the camera one last smile, and the men got into the vehicle and sped away.

Not quietly.

The tires howled against the wet concrete and created enough noise to get the clerk's attention. The young man hurried to the door, opened it and caught the note before it dropped to the ground. He read it, his eyes widening with each passing second, and then he raced back into the station and grabbed the phone.

"The clerk called nine-one-one," Grayson supplied. "And in turn the dispatcher called here. He read me the note." Grayson took the notepad from the desk and handed it to Nate.

He knew this wouldn't be good, and Nate tried to brace himself for the worst.

But the message turned Nate's blood to ice.

Nate Ryland and Darcy Burkhart, you killed my brother and my men. This is no longer a job. It's personal, and I'm coming after both of you. Get ready to die.

"Uh, guys," Tina said, "I think we have a problem."

At first Nate thought she was talking about the note. Yeah, it was a problem, all right. A big one. But Tina was looking out the window.

"There." Tina tipped her head to the building just up the street.

The rain was spitting on the glass, but Nate could still see the shadowy figure using the emergency ladder on the side of the hardware store. The guy was climbing onto the roof.

And Nate reached for his gun.

"Wait," Grayson warned. "The windows here are tinted. He can't see us to shoot inside."

Grayson was right. Besides, the guy wasn't in a shooting stance. Once he reached the roof, he dropped onto his belly and pressed binoculars to his eyes.

"Recognize him?" Grayson asked.

Yeah. Nate did. It was the man who'd been with Ramirez on the surveillance footage. Nate automatically glanced around, looking for the man who'd just threatened to kill Darcy and him.

But Ramirez was nowhere in sight.

"You going out there?" Tina asked them.

"No," Grayson and Nate said in unison.

"Not right now," Nate finished.

Good. Grayson and he were on the same page, and Nate knew what he had to do. Darcy wasn't going to like it. Heck, *he* didn't like it. But it was necessary if he had any chance of keeping all of them out of the path of a killer.

Chapter 13

Darcy read the note again. And again.

Each time it felt as if the words were razor-sharp knives slicing through her. A monster, a cold-blooded killer, was coming after Nate and her.

"I won't let him get to you," she heard Nate say.

Darcy believed that Nate would try. But Ramirez wasn't just after her. He was after Nate, as well.

She tore her attention from the note and looked at Nate, who was seated next to her. He'd made her sit on the sofa in the second-floor apartment at the sheriff's office before he'd handed her the note, and that was probably a good thing. After reading it, her legs were too wobbly to stand.

"We have a plan," Grayson explained. He was standing, his hands on his hips. Grace was behind him, seated on the floor and playing with the babies, trying to keep them occupied.

"Please tell me that plan includes making sure the children are safe." Darcy's voice cracked, and she hated feeling scared out of her mind for Noah and Kimmie. Nate, too.

"It does," Nate assured her. "We're going to set a trap for Ramirez." He caught her shoulders and waited until they'd made eye contact. "And I'll be the bait."

Oh, mercy. That required her to take a deep breath. Thankfully, Grayson continued so she didn't have to ask about the details of this plan, which she already knew she didn't like. She wouldn't approve of anything where Nate made himself bait.

"First, we've made arrangements to move Grace, you and the children. We'll secretly take all of you to a safe house in a neighboring town, where both Mel and I will be with them. So will the town's sheriff and the deputy."

Okay. The security was a good start, but it wasn't enough. Maybe nothing would be with Nate's life at stake. And that required another deep breath.

"Secretly," Nate repeated. "Someone is watching the building."

"Who?" she immediately wanted to know. "Not Ramirez?" Darcy would have jumped off the sofa if Nate hadn't kept hold of her.

"No. It's a man who was on the surveillance video with him. Right now, he's on the roof of the hardware store just up the street. The dispatcher spotted him there about an hour ago. Once we knew he was there, Grayson and I sat down and came up with this plan."

Darcy shook her head. "Why don't you just arrest him? Make him tell you where Ramirez is?"

"We considered it," Grayson explained. "But we figured the guy would die before giving up his boss. And we don't want a gunfight with the children here. So we decided to make it work for us."

"How?" she wanted to know.

"Soon, it'll be dark, and Nate will pretend to leave. It's raining so we'll give him a big umbrella and bundles of something to carry. It'll look as if he has the children with him, but actually we'll sneak them and you out through the back and into my SUV. Kade will be here as additional protection just in case this guy comes off the roof. But we don't think he will."

Darcy tried to think that through. She wished her thoughts would settle down so she could figure out why this sounded so wrong. "You think he'll report to Ramirez that Nate's left and then he'll follow him?"

Nate nodded. "He'll follow me to the ranch. Ramirez will, too, and that's where we'll set the trap for them."

"The ranch?" she challenged. Now, she came off the sofa. "Your family is there."

Nate stood, slowly, and stuffed his hands into his pockets. "We've already moved them. Eve, Kayla and Kayla's son, Robbie, are already on their way to SAPD headquarters, where they'll stay until this situation with Ramirez is resolved."

Yes. And it wouldn't be resolved until Ramirez was dead. Darcy got that part, and she got other things, too. "There's a big flaw in your plan," she told them, even though they already knew it. "If Ramirez wants us both dead, then he won't be satisfied just trying to kill you. He'll want to come after me, as well."

Nate attempted a shrug but didn't quite pull it off. "He might."

"He *will*," Darcy corrected. "And if Ramirez gets lucky and finds me, he'll find the children, too."

Neither Grayson nor Nate could deny that. "We won't let Ramirez get near them."

Darcy took a deep breath and braced herself for the argument they were about to have. An argument she would win because there was no way she was going to give Ramirez a reason to go after Kimmie and Noah again.

"There's only one thing that makes sense—for both of us to lead Ramirez away from the children. Anything less than that puts them in danger."

Nate's jaw muscles stirred. "But coming with me puts you in danger."

"Yes." And she didn't hesitate. "We know what has to be done here. You don't have to like it. Heck, I don't like it. But I won't be tucked away at a safe house knowing that I could be putting our children in jeopardy."

He opened his mouth, probably to continue the argument, but Darcy nipped it in the bud. "You can't change my mind. I'm going with you."

Nate looked at Grayson, who only huffed and mumbled something. Nate looked as if he wanted to mumble some profanity, but he didn't. He sat down, his jaw muscles battling, and then he finally nodded.

Darcy tried not to look too relieved. It was easy to do, since she knew full well she was putting herself in the line of fire. Still, better her than the babies.

Nate simply nodded again. "If Ramirez knows we're at the ranch, he'll come after us so he can try to avenge his kid brother's death. But we'll be ready for him."

"How?" she asked.

Nate eased her down onto the sofa, but they both glanced back when the children giggled. Grace was reading them a story and making funny voices. The laughter certainly helped Darcy's nerves and reminded her of why this plan had to work.

"We think the man on the roof is the person who helped Ramirez escape. We also believe he's the one who called Ramirez when he climbed over the fence. He probably told his boss to get out of there because he'd seen Dade and Mel driving out to the ranch. In other words, he's Ramirez's eyes and ears, and we want to feed this guy some info."

"Bad info," Grayson explained. "We want Ramirez to believe this storm has knocked out both the power and the security system for the ranch. We want him to come across that fence again. And when he does, we'll have Kade and a half-dozen federal agents waiting."

Darcy nodded but then thought of something. "What if Ramirez doesn't use the fence? What if he uses the road and comes directly to the house?"

"Mason and I will be waiting for him," Nate assured her. "And if he's managed to hire more goons to come with him, then we'll know because Kade will have someone watching the road." He paused again. "It's the fastest way to put an end to this."

She couldn't argue with that. Darcy couldn't argue with the plan, either. Nate was a good cop, and she trusted him with her life. But she couldn't discount that Ramirez was as driven to kill them as they were to stay alive and keep their children safe.

"How much time before you and the children leave for the safe house?" she asked Grayson.

He glanced out the window. "Not long."

So, she needed to say her goodbyes. Darcy got up, forcing her legs to move, and she got down on the floor next to the children. Both Noah and Kimmie were still involved with the story, but Noah climbed into her lap. Kimmie babbled some happy sounds and did the same.

Everything was suddenly better.

And worse.

They had so much at stake. Darcy hugged the babies close to her. Kimmie might have sensed something was wrong because she kissed Darcy on the cheek and put her head on Darcy's shoulder. The moment was pure magic, and Darcy realized she'd come to love this child as her own.

"I'll just freshen up and get ready for the drive to the safe house," Grace offered, and she disappeared into the bathroom, no doubt to give them some time alone.

Grayson mumbled something about having to make some calls and walked out, as well.

Nate sat down beside her, and Darcy expected Kimmie to switch to his lap, but she stayed put. It was Noah who made the shift when he spotted Nate's shoulder holster. But Nate distracted her son by unclipping his badge from his belt and handing it to Noah.

"Oooo," Noah babbled, obviously approving of the shiny object. He looked up at Nate and offered him a big grin.

The moment hit Darcy hard, partly because her son had never had a male figure in his life, and partly because everything seemed to fit. Kimmie in her arms. Noah in Nate's. Her heart and body, burning for this man.

A man she couldn't have.

Nate was just now healing from his wife's death, and he needed his family to help him and Kimmie through the rest of that process. She couldn't put that wedge between them.

She kissed the top of Kimmie's head and ran her fingers through those fiery curls. The little girl had her mother's looks, but that smile and those silver-gray eyes were genetic contributions from her daddy.

"Me," her son said, and he handed the badge to Kimmie. "Me," he repeated.

"I think he's trying to say her name." Nate smiled.

But the smile and the moment ended when Nate's cell phone buzzed. He took the phone from his pocket and glanced at the screen.

"It's the SAPD crime lab." Nate put the call on speaker. "Lieutenant Ryland," he answered.

"Sir, we got that handwriting comparison you requested on the faxed pages," the tech said. "It's a match to the sample of handwriting we have for the deceased, Sandra Dent."

So, the diary was real. Of course, that created more questions than answers. Had Dent really just found it, or had he known all along where it was?

"The handwriting is consistent through all the pages," the tech added.

And that meant Sandra had written the entry about quarreling with her son and planning to cut him out of her life. Maybe Adam knew that. Maybe not. But Dent might have just given them a motive for Adam to kill his mother.

"What about the pages that were torn out?" Nate asked.

"We can't get anything from the paper itself. There's not even any partial letter there, but there could be some DNA or trace fibers. The lab has it now and has started the testing. They're also looking at the indentations on the pages following the ones that'd been torn out."

"And?" Nate prompted.

"It doesn't look good, Lieutenant. It appears some-one has actually rubbed or applied pressure to flatten out the indentations, but the lab will do what it can."

Nate wearily dragged his hand over his face, but then smiled when Noah attempted to do the same. "Call me if you find out anything else," Nate instructed the tech, and he ended the call.

The phone grabbed Kimmie's attention, and she dropped Nate's badge so she could go after it. Just like that, Nate had both kids in his lap, and he adjusted, giving them both room, as if it were second nature for him. However, even the half smile he gave the children didn't mask his frustration.

"It would have been nice to know what Sandra wrote on that last page," Darcy said. "She might have named her killer, or at least given us some hint of who that per-son might be. I mean, why else would the pages have been torn out?"

Nate didn't answer her, but something flashed through his eyes. He took out his phone again and put it on speaker.

"Grayson," he said when his brother answered. "Is our guest still on the roof of the hardware store?"

"Still there. He's getting soaked, but he hasn't moved."

Darcy hoped he'd stay put. And catch pneumonia.

"I just finished talking with the lab," Nate explained to his brother. "The handwriting matches Sandra's, but the indentations probably won't give us anything. What I want is for all four of our suspects to believe other-wise. I want them to think the lab uncovered what Sandra had written and that SAPD is making arrangements for an arrest."

Grayson made a sound to indicate he was contemplating the idea. Darcy thought about it, too. If it worked, they could have Sandra Dent's killer in custody within hours.

"You think this'll flush out her killer and cause him or her to go on the run?" Grayson asked Nate.

"Yeah, I do. But I don't think it'll cause the killer to come after Darcy, me or the children again. He or she must have figured out by now that they can't use us to fix the murder investigation."

Grayson made a sound of agreement. "I'll make some calls and have the roads and airports watched. And then we'll have to make the suspects believe that one of them is about to be outed. That'll be easy to do for Marlene since she's already here."

"Why?" Darcy and Nate asked in unison.

"Your guess is as good as mine, but she's insisting that she talk to Darcy and you, too."

Nate groaned and looked at her. "You up for this?"

Darcy nodded. She didn't want to waste any more time with Marlene, but the woman might actually be there to confess to orchestrating the kidnapping. If she was, then Darcy very much wanted to hear what she had to say.

Darcy gave both babies a kiss, and Nate did the same. Then she knocked on the bathroom door to signal Grace should come out. Once Grace was back on the floor with the kids, Nate and Darcy headed downstairs to confront Marlene.

They didn't have to go far.

Marlene was in the hall, just outside of Grayson's

office, and the moment she spotted them, she walked toward them. Grayson stepped out of his office and joined them, too.

"I didn't help anyone kidnap your children," Marlene volunteered. "When I heard the kidnappers say they were taking us to the Lost Appaloosa, I wrote the initials so you'd find us."

"But the van where you wrote them was a decoy," Nate pointed out.

"I didn't know that, either. That's the van they put us in when they first took us, and then they moved us to another one. I wouldn't have done anything to help them take Noah and Kimmie, and you have to believe me."

"Maybe I will believe you," Nate told her, "if you'll explain what you did with the fifty thousand you got for selling the land you inherited."

Marlene flinched as if he'd slapped her. "That has nothing to do with the kidnapping."

Darcy folded her arms over her chest and stared at Marlene. "Then where's the money?"

Marlene looked around as if she wanted to be anywhere but there, and for a moment Darcy thought she might bolt. Would that mean Marlene was guilty?

"You're wasting our time," Nate accused.

Marlene shook her head, but it still took her several moments to say anything. "Someone's trying to kill me."

And she didn't add more. Just that little bombshell.

"Who's trying to kill you?" Darcy asked. "Ramirez?"

"No." But then Marlene paused. "Well, maybe it's him, but I don't think so. If he'd wanted me dead he could have killed me when I was his hostage."

"Were you?" Nate demanded, and then he clarified, "His hostage?"

"Yes. Those gunmen took me when they took the children, and it doesn't have anything to do with the money I got from selling the land."

Nate huffed. So did Grayson. "Look," Grayson warned, "either you explain about the money now, or I arrest you for obstruction of justice."

Marlene's eyes widened, and it seemed to hit her that she was in big trouble. "I gave the money to my sister in San Antonio." She paused again. "She was in debt to a man who was threatening to kill her. I had to pay him off."

Nate rolled his eyes. "Let me get this straight—someone's trying to kill both you and your sister, and not once did you consider telling Grayson about this?"

"I couldn't." Again, she shouted, but then she blinked back tears. "The loan shark would have killed my sister if she'd gone to the cops. And as for me, I don't think this man has anything to do with the threats on my life."

Darcy could practically feel the frustration coming off Grayson and Nate. She felt it, too, and only wanted this woman to spill it and get out of there. Soon, very soon, the children would be leaving for the safe house, and she wanted to spend a little more time with them.

"Explain why you think someone's trying to kill you," Grayson insisted, and it wasn't a gentle request.

Marlene hiked up her chin and clearly wasn't pleased that Grayson and Nate seemed to doubt her. If she was innocent, Darcy would apologize to the woman, but for now she wanted the same thing Nate and Grayson did—the truth.

"Someone's been following me," Marlene started. "And before the kidnapping, I was getting hang-ups."

Grayson, Nate and Darcy all looked toward the front of the building when the bell jangled, indicating someone had opened the front door. Nate stepped in front of Darcy. Grayson, too. And they both slid their hands over their guns.

Darcy held her breath, praying the man from the roof hadn't decided to come in and try to kill them. But the person who walked through the door was a familiar face, although not a welcome one.

It was Edwin.

He used his hand to swipe the rain from his face, and he stormed toward them. He didn't make it far. Tina, the dispatcher, stepped in front of him to block his path. Edwin did stop, but he aimed his index finger and a scowl at Marlene.

"Whatever she says, it's a lie," Edwin growled.

Marlene frantically shook her head. "It's true. Someone is trying to kill me. Or scare me at least. And I think it's *you*."

"Please." Edwin stretched out the syllables. "You were a cheap fling, nothing more, and I never gave you a minute's thought until that damn kidnapping."

Edwin's anger seemed genuine enough, and it seemed genuinely directed at Marlene. However, Darcy wasn't about to cross either of them off her list of suspects. Judging from Nate's expression, neither was he.

"Are you trying to kill her?" Nate asked him.

Edwin cursed. "She's not worth killing." He pointed at Marlene again. "I plan to do everything in my power to find proof that you set up the kidnapping so that Dent would be tossed in jail. Trust me, I want him in jail, but

I don't need or want your help for that. You're a stalking, obsessive wacko, and I want you out of my life."

Marlene opened her mouth, no doubt to return verbal fire, but Nate put up his hand in a *stop* motion. "In a few hours we'll know who killed Sandra."

Edwin and Marlene both seemed to freeze, and each stared at Nate. "What do you mean?" Marlene asked Nate.

"Dent found Sandra's diary—"

"It's a fake," Edwin interrupted.

Nate shook his head. "It's not. The lab just confirmed that the handwriting is hers."

His voice was so calm. He was all cop now, and Darcy watched as he took one menacing step closer to Marlene. But the woman wasn't the only one to earn some of his attention. Nate turned those suddenly cold gray eyes on Edwin, too.

"The next step is for the lab to lift the indentations Sandra made when she wrote the page that was torn out," Nate continued. "The page that sealed her fate and named her killer."

"Someone could have planted information to make me look guilty," Edwin snarled.

"Or me," Marlene piped up.

Nate lifted his shoulder again. "Then maybe you two should call your attorneys. Because I'm betting one or both of you will need a good lawyer before the night is over."

Edwin stood there, glaring, as if he would launch himself at Nate or Marlene, but then he cursed again, turned and walked back out into the rain.

"Excuse me," Grayson mumbled when his desk phone rang.

Marlene, however, didn't storm out with Edwin. In fact, she didn't budge an inch. "I believe Edwin is trying to scare me. Or worse." She groaned. "He's trying to make me look guilty because he's the one who put all of this together. He killed his ex-wife, and he wants Wesley Dent to go to jail because he hates him that much."

All of that could be true.

Or none of it.

"You got proof?" Nate asked.

Marlene groaned again, more softly this time, and she stared at Nate. "You really believe Sandra wrote her killer's name in her diary?"

"I do," Nate said, sounding totally confident.

"Good," Marlene whispered. Then she mumbled a goodbye and hurried down the hall.

Darcy didn't release the breath she'd been holding until Marlene was out the door.

"Lock it," Nate instructed Tina. "We've had enough surprise visitors today. Besides, I don't want anyone walking in when we're transferring the children into the van that will take them to the safe house."

Darcy shook her head. She'd thought it was too early for the children to leave, but she was wrong. It was still an hour or so before actual nightfall, but the rain and the iron-gray clouds made it seem like night.

The darkness was closing in.

And so was her fear.

Nate must have sensed what she was feeling because he gave her arm a gentle squeeze. He was still doing that when Grayson threw open his office door.

"Everything is ready for the children," Grayson told them. There was both sympathy and concern in his voice. "It's time."

"Come on," Nate whispered to her. "We need to tell Kimmie and Noah goodbye."

Darcy swallowed hard. *Goodbye.* It hit her then that while their children would be safe, Nate wouldn't be. They would have to face the devil himself and somehow come out of it alive.

Or this was the last time they would ever see their children.

Chapter 14

The plan was in place. Nate knew he'd done everything possible to make this work.

Well, *logically* he knew that.

But in the back of his mind, he hated that he couldn't guarantee all of them would come out of this unscathed.

He ended the call with Kade. One of many calls Nate had made over the past hour since Darcy and he had arrived at the ranch. More would no doubt have to be made.

"Well?" Darcy asked the moment he hung up.

She was in the doorway of his office, her hands bracketed on the door frame. All the lights in the house were off—that was part of their plan, to lure Ramirez with a fake power outage—but Nate didn't need to see her face to know she was worried and on edge. He could hear it in her voice. In that one word. In the air zinging around them. The storm brewing outside only added to the menacing feel.

"The children are fine," he assured her. "They're all tucked in for the night at the safe house."

Her breathing was way too fast, and he thought he could even hear her heartbeat. "Thank God," she whispered.

Nate echoed that. "So far none of our suspects has shown up at the airport or the border. None has withdrawn any money from their bank accounts. No suspicious activity of any kind even though Adam is out driving around. Dade is watching him, and we have surveillance on the others' houses."

Darcy shook her head. "But they could sneak out."

"They could," he admitted. "But if that happens, and the killer heads in this direction, we'll know. Kade and his men are scattering out all over the ranch to set up surveillance equipment."

"What about the man who was on the roof of the hardware store?" she asked.

"He left right after we did. On foot. He disappeared into the alley behind the stores."

That didn't help her breathing.

"We figure he's already joined up with his boss, Ramirez." He walked closer to her. "When all the equipment is set up and everything is in place, the ranch hands will pretend there's an emergency. A fence down from the storm. And they'll appear to leave the area. If Ramirez is watching the ranch, and we're almost positive he is, then he'll believe that's his opportunity to strike."

Her breath shivered, and Nate pulled her into his

arms. It wasn't much of a hug, but it helped to relax her. Him, too. But it didn't help the attraction.

Not a good time for it.

But then, there'd never been a good time.

"Why don't you try to get some rest?" he said softly. Trying to stay calm. Trying not to let her hear the concern in his own voice.

A burst of air left her mouth. Not exactly a laugh. "Rest? Right." And then she did something that shouldn't have surprised him. But it did.

Darcy put her arms around him and kissed him. Not a peck of reassurance. Not this. The kiss was long, hard and filled with way too much need. And urgency.

"Rest," he repeated. Not easily. That kiss had made him crazy in a bad way. He was starting to think that kissing and maybe adrenaline sex might be the way to get through the waiting.

Darcy pulled back and hesitated. The moments crawled by while he waited for her response.

"Rest with me," she insisted.

An *okay* nearly flew right out of his mouth before he remembered he had to set up the surveillance on his laptop. Not that he would actually be able to see anything in the dark and rain, but the motion detectors were on, and he would get the alert over the laptop if Ramirez did come across any part of the fence. His brothers and the ranch hands already had equipment to detect movement, but Nate wanted it as a backup for himself. And in case something went wrong with the exterior detection equipment.

"I'll be in my room," Darcy added, and she walked away.

Nate stared at the empty doorway for a second. And

he cursed himself for what he knew would happen before the night was over. He should have one thing on his mind: Ramirez. But Ramirez wouldn't get anywhere near the place without Nate and the others knowing.

There was time to kill.

Or so he rationalized.

He could kill that time in his office, waiting and watching. He could stay away from Darcy and give her the possibility of getting some rest.

But that didn't happen.

Nate turned on his laptop and tapped into the security feed. It didn't take long for the images to appear on the screen. And just as he'd figured, nothing was going on. He couldn't see a thing in the rainy darkness so he tucked the laptop under his arm, took a deep breath and launched into what would no doubt be a very pleasurable but stupid mistake.

He walked straight to Darcy's room.

The door was open, and he stepped inside so he could put his laptop on the table just a few feet away. He took off his shoulder holster, as well, and dropped it next to the laptop.

Bright white lightning flashed through the rain-streaked window. For a second Nate saw Darcy sitting on the edge of the bed. Her ivory-colored top, her dark hair, her pale skin all made her look a little otherworldly. A siren, maybe. Or a rain goddess.

But then the darkness took over the room again.

He stood there, letting his eyes adjust, waiting for another jolt of lightning. He didn't have to wait long. It came. Stabbing across the sky and giving him another look at her. He felt starved for the sight of her.

And he groaned at that somewhat sappy realization.

"That bad, huh?" she asked.

He waited for the lightning again to see if she was smiling. She was. Well, sort of. "I'm thinking thoughts I don't usually think," he confessed. "Sappy ones."

He heard the mattress creak softly as she stood. Then heard her footsteps on the bare wood floor. "Good," she whispered.

Oh, man. Did she know how hot she sounded all breathy like that? Apparently, he was starved for the sound of her voice, too.

"Good?" he challenged when he remembered how to form words with his mouth. His body didn't want to contribute any energy to something that didn't involve getting Darcy naked. "You want me to think sap?"

She stepped closer so he could see the half smile, and her face. "You've done a number on my mind. My body. I figure it's only fair that you're sappily confused."

Nate sighed and slipped his arm around her waist. "Oh, I'm not confused, Darcy. I know exactly what I want—and that's *you*."

The slam of thunder gave his confession a little more punch than he'd intended, and Darcy laughed. It was smoky and rich, and Nate kissed her so he could feel that laughter on his lips.

"Good," she repeated. "Because I want *you*."

Yeah. He knew that.

And that was the problem. Neither was going to stop this getting-naked part. Ditto for some raunchy, memorable sex. The door was locked. They had some privacy for the first time in, well, forever. And even though there would be hell to pay, Nate eased her to him and deepened the kiss.

Later, he would pay hell.

Now, he just wanted to kiss her blind. For starters, anyway.

There was something about her, about that taste, that made him crazier than he already was, and he felt his body rev up to take her hard and fast.

Especially hard.

He considered something mindless, maybe even sex against the wall. Sex where he didn't have to think of the consequences. But a rain goddess who tasted like sin deserved something better than that. And Nate wasn't surprised that he wanted to make love to her.

He leaned back, to make sure there wasn't any doubt in her eyes or expression. He could see her face, the rain shadows sliding down her body. She was beautiful. But he hadn't needed to see her face to remember that.

Nate scooped her up and headed for the bed. Even in this position, she fit, as if she belonged there in his arms. In his bed. Heck, maybe his life. He pushed that aside. It was too deep and too complicated to deal with now.

The lightning came again. And the thunder. As he eased her onto the bed, the mattress creaked softly and creaked some more when he followed on top of her. This fit, as well, and so did the way their mouths came together for the kiss.

It didn't take long, barely seconds, for the kisses to give way to touches. Darcy started it by sliding her hand down his chest. That did it all right. The simple, easy pressure of her hands on his body. And just like that, he was hard and aching to take her.

"You're like a fantasy," she whispered.

Despite his rock-hard body, Nate lifted his head to see what she meant by that.

"You are," she insisted. She didn't stop touching him or kissing his neck, and because she was apparently going for torture, she lifted her hips, brushed against the front of his jeans and caused his eyes to cross. "As in you're really hot. The kind of guy I always fantasized about…well, you know, in bed."

He couldn't imagine that he looked hot with crossed eyes and the hard ache behind the zipper of his jeans, but at the moment he was just pleased that she wanted him as much as he wanted her. Especially since she was fulfilling a few of his own fantasies.

Her top had to go—more of his fantasy fulfillment—and Nate stripped it off. Her bra, too. And he kissed her breasts the way he wanted to kiss her, his tongue circling her nipple.

That brought her hips off the bed again, and she made a sweet sound of pleasure. A sound that slid right over him like the warm rain on the cool glass.

"You, too," Darcy insisted. And she went after his shirt.

While she fumbled with the buttons, Nate did some more sampling. He moved his mouth to her stomach and smiled when she made more of those pleasure sounds.

"I'm on fire," she let him know and gave his shirt a fierce tug.

Nate was pleased about that fire he'd helped build. Until her lips went to his chest. Oh, man. She wasn't a rain goddess. She was a witch, casting a spell with that mouth and setting him on fire.

When he could take no more of the scalding pleasure, he dropped to his side, pulling her on top of him so he could rid her of her jeans. Darcy didn't help much, mainly because she went after his zipper. He was hard and very aware of her touch.

Again, when he could take no more, he put her back on the mattress and shimmied her jeans and panties off.

The lightning cooperated.

Oh, yeah. She was beautiful all right, and Nate kissed her right in the center of all that heat.

She made another sound. This one had an urgency to it, but she didn't stop him. Darcy wound her fingers deep into his hair and took everything he was giving her.

Nate considered finishing her off like this, but he wanted more. He wanted to be inside her so he could watch and feel her shatter all around him.

"Your jeans," Darcy reminded him.

He was painfully aware that his remaining clothes were in the way of sex, and Nate helped her get off his boots and jeans.

But Darcy didn't play fair.

She was the one who removed his boxers, and she did it by sliding her hands down his lower back and his butt. And she didn't just use her hands. She used her knees and legs, and when she was done, when his boxers were dangling on her foot, she wrapped her legs around him.

Nate moved down as she moved up, and he slid into that tight, wet heat of her body. Stars. Yeah, he saw them. Hell, maybe fireworks, too. There was something exploding in his head, and the pleasure, well, it was something he was glad he didn't have to put into words.

He moved deep and hard inside her. But he didn't stop kissing her. Couldn't. After being so long without, he wanted it all. The taste of her in his mouth. Her scent on his skin. The feel of the hot, intimate contact of their sex.

"A fantasy," she repeated. Her eyes were wide, and she was staring at him.

Yes, it felt good enough to be her fantasy, and in the back of his mind he wondered if anything would ever feel this good again. But then the need took over, and his mind cleared of any thoughts except one.

Finishing this.

Turned out that was Darcy's goal, as well, because she met his thrusts, using her legs to pull him right back in. Over and over. Robbing him of his breath. Maybe his mind. Everything. Until all he could see and feel was Darcy.

She dug her fingers into his back when she climaxed, bucked beneath him, and her breath was mixed with hoarse sobs of pleasure.

Nate listened and watched her as long as he could. Cataloging every sound. Every move. Every expression. Until he could take no more. Until the ripples of her climax forced him into letting go.

The lightning came again. The thunder. And even over the thick rumble, Nate heard the single word he whispered.

"Darcy."

Chapter 15

Darcy didn't want to move. Nor did she want to break the intimate contact with Nate.

But Nate apparently did.

He rolled off her and landed in a flop on his back. He didn't say anything, but Darcy could still hear the way he'd spoken her name in the last climactic moment.

Somehow, that had sounded more intimate than the sex itself.

In the back of her mind, she'd considered that Nate had been thinking about his late wife. That would have been, well, natural even though it was painful for her to consider. But it'd been Darcy's name on his lips. And he'd certainly made love to her as if she was the woman he wanted.

But did he?

Had this been a primal reaction to the danger?

She couldn't dismiss it, but she so wanted it to be

real. She wanted Nate and not just his body—though Darcy wanted that, too.

And speaking of his body, she looked over at him. He was still naked, of course, and thanks to a jagged flash of lightning, she got a good look at him.

Oh, mercy.

Yes, she wanted to feel more of those toned muscles on his chest and stomach. More of his clever mouth and the kisses that could make her burn to ash. She wanted to be wrapped in his strong arms again. She wanted it all.

Darcy groaned and hoped the rumbling thunder concealed the sound that had escaped.

It didn't.

Nate tilted his head and looked at her. "Well?" he asked.

Sheesh. Where should she go with a question like that? Anything she said could make him regret what had just happened and might send him running for cover.

"Well," she repeated, giving herself some time to think, "the sex was amazing."

He stared at her. "Then why did you groan?"

That required another pause—and a deep breath. "Because this might have been easier for both of us if it hadn't been amazing."

Nate stayed quiet a moment and then made a sound of agreement. He brushed a kiss on her cheek, got up and started to dress.

Darcy wanted to smack herself for that stupid groan. It had reminded Nate of the trouble a possible relationship could stir up. That groan had broken the spell and caused him to move away from her.

Nate's phone buzzed, and he rifled through his

clothes on the floor to find it. He glanced at the caller ID before he answered it.

"Kade," Nate answered.

Darcy prayed this was good news, but since Nate didn't put the call on speaker, she couldn't tell.

She got up, as well, and began to gather her clothes. Suddenly, Darcy felt awkward and uncomfortable about being stark naked in front of Nate. She dressed as quickly as she could. Not easy to do since her clothes were scattered everywhere.

"Did he have a suitcase or anything with him?" Nate asked his brother.

Again, she couldn't hear Kade's answer.

"A lot of people are watching the place," Nate responded. "If he shows up, we'll see him." And he hung up.

Darcy waited, her breath stalled in her lungs.

"It's Dent," Nate told her. "He left his house about a half hour ago, and he had a suitcase with him. He managed to lose the tail we had on him."

Darcy leaned against the wall and let it support her. She also put her hand over her breasts since she was still braless. Where was the darn thing?

"This doesn't mean Dent is a killer," Nate pointed out. He looked at her but then just as quickly turned away. "He could just be running scared."

True. But Darcy wasn't ready to trust Dent or any of the other suspects.

Nate finished dressing before her and went straight for his laptop, which he'd left on the table near the door. When he lifted the screen, it created a nightlight of sorts, and she was able to find her bra. It was dangling on the bedpost.

"No sign of Ramirez," he relayed to her, and he slipped his shoulder holster back on.

Ramirez. Just the thought of him chilled the remaining heat she felt after making love with Nate. How could she have forgotten, even for a few minutes, that a killer wanted them dead?

Sex with Nate wasn't just amazing.

It apparently caused temporary amnesia.

And stupidity.

Darcy finished dressing and saw that Nate was still staring at his laptop screen. "Is there a problem?" she said, praying there wasn't.

"No. I'm just reading an email from Grayson."

"Grayson?" She hurried across the room to see what the message said. "It's about the children?"

Of course, she immediately thought the worst, but what she saw on the screen wasn't the worst at all. There was a picture of both Kimmie and Noah. They were asleep side by side in a crib.

"Grayson snapped it with his cell phone and emailed it," Nate explained. "He thought it would make us feel better."

It did.

Darcy couldn't help herself. She touched the screen, running her fingers over those precious little faces. "I miss them so much."

"Them," Nate mumbled.

It hit her then that he might think she was trying to push her way into his life by using his daughter. Darcy frantically shook her head. "What I feel for Kimmie doesn't have anything to do with you."

He lifted his eyebrow and paused for what seemed

an eternity, then nodded. "I know. You love kids." Nate added a shrug. "I love kids."

Darcy waited, but he offered nothing else. Especially nothing else about what he might be feeling for her. Or feelings about what had happened in that bed just minutes earlier. But because she was watching him so closely, she saw his expression change from that of a loving father to that of a very sad widower. He, too, touched the image on the screen, and Darcy suspected he was wishing that Ellie were alive.

"You miss your wife," Darcy said before she could stop herself.

"Yeah." No hesitation. Nate kept his gaze fixed on the screen for several seconds before he pulled back his hand and switched to the feed from the security system. He split the screen so that it showed six different camera angles at once.

She considered pushing a little and asking Nate to talk about his feelings. He'd no doubt rather eat razor blades than do that, so Darcy decided to give him the time and space to work out whatever was going on in his head. Heck, she needed that space, too.

But one look at the screen, and she realized her attention was going to be otherwise occupied. She saw movement in the top-left screen.

"Ramirez?" she managed to ask.

Unlike before, Nate didn't give her an immediate answer, but he did draw his gun from his shoulder holster. "I don't think so."

Whoever it was, the person wasn't on foot. Nor was he coming across the fence. This was a car, and the headlights were on, slicing through the thick rain. The vehicle was traveling on the ranch road.

Toward the house.

Oh, mercy. Darcy had thought she was ready for this. Well, as ready as anyone could be. But just the sight of that car made her heart spin out of control.

"I doubt Ramirez would drive right up to the front door," Nate added.

And that's exactly what the driver appeared to be doing. Darcy clung to that hope, that it wasn't Ramirez, but then she had to wonder, if it wasn't the killer, who was it? It was hardly the hour for guests, and all of Nate's brothers were occupied with either the children or setting the trap for Ramirez.

Nate's phone buzzed, and he answered it without taking his focus off the car. He clicked the speaker function.

"Nate," she heard Dade say. "Adam should be arriving at the ranch any minute now. I was tailing him, but I got…distracted. I spotted someone in the woods on the back side of the ranch, and I stopped. I think it might be our watcher from the roof. Can you deal with Adam on your own?"

"Sure," Nate answered. "What does Adam want?"

"Who knows. He checked into a hotel in Silver Creek, but about forty-five minutes ago, he came barreling out of the driveway like a man on fire. I guess he must have gone out to the parking lot through the emergency exit at the back of the hotel."

"Is he armed?" Nate wanted to know.

"Couldn't tell. I barely got a glimpse of him before he sped away from the hotel. I stayed back so he wouldn't spot me, but he didn't make it easy. He stopped on the side of the road twice, changed directions a couple of times, but then he finally headed out to the ranch."

"Any sign of Edwin, Dent or Marlene?" Nate asked.

"No. And I've been keeping my eye out for all of them in case they head out this way." In the background, Darcy could hear the storm winds howling. "You're positive you can handle Adam?"

"Don't worry about us. Just watch your back." Nate ended the call, picked up the laptop and started out of the room.

Darcy caught his arm. "You're not planning to let Adam in?"

"No. But I do want to talk to him. And I want to be closer to the door in case he decides to break in."

Darcy's grip melted off his arm. "Break in?" But she knew what Nate meant. Adam could have killed his mother, and the lie they'd planted about the diary could have sent him spinning out of control. With everything going on with Ramirez, she'd forgotten that someone had originally hired that monster to kidnap the children.

Was it Adam who'd done that?

And was he there to finish what he'd paid Ramirez to start?

Darcy followed Nate down the hall and toward the foyer, but he didn't go into the open area. Instead, he placed the laptop on the floor, and they crouched down where they could both still see it.

On the screen Darcy saw the car and then heard it come to a screeching halt. Adam certainly wasn't trying to conceal his arrival. Nate and she waited, watching, but Adam didn't get out. However, Nate's phone buzzed again, and when he flipped it open, it was Adam's name on the screen.

"What are you doing here?" Nate demanded when

he answered the call. Darcy whispered for him to put it on speaker, and he did.

"I'm trying to stay alive, and you have to let me in. I need to be in protective custody." Adam sounded scared out of his mind. Of course, Darcy knew it could all be an act.

"And you thought the way to stay alive was to come here?" Nate tossed right back.

Adam mumbled something she didn't catch. "Dent is trying to kill me. He murdered my mother, and now he's trying to kill me so he can inherit her entire estate and my trust fund. I want him arrested *now.*"

"There's still no proof to arrest him. Or you, for that matter," Nate added. "But we might soon have proof with the diary."

"Yes," Adam mumbled. "The diary." He said it in the same tone as he would profanity. "Dent doctored that diary, and I'm betting he did that to make either me or my father look guilty of murder. When your lab people check those so-called indentations, they'll be fake, added by the real killer. And that real killer is Dent."

Darcy certainly couldn't discard that theory. But Dent had been the one to find the diary, and if her former client thought for one minute that it could have implicated him in his wife's murder, then he wouldn't have brought it to Grayson and Nate.

So, Dent was either innocent or stupid.

"If you really believe someone is trying to kill you," Nate said to Adam, "then go the sheriff's office or SAPD headquarters. Dent won't come after you there."

"No. But his hired gun would, and I'd rather have you protecting me than the deputy at the sheriff's office." Adam cursed. "I know Dent hired that psycho,

Ramirez. He took the money from my mother's safe to pay him. And now he's hired Ramirez to come after me. And Darcy and you, too."

Nate glanced at her, and Darcy saw some doubt, but Nate wasn't totally dismissing what Adam had accused Dent of doing.

"What makes you think Ramirez is after you?" Nate demanded.

"I *know* he's after me. He came to my hotel room." Adam's voice cracked on the last word. "I'm sorry. He gave me no choice."

Darcy felt the icy chill go through her. "What do you mean?"

Adam took his time answering. "I mean Ramirez came here in the trunk of my car, and he got out just a few minutes ago—before we got to the security camera at the end of the road.

"I'm sorry," Adam repeated. "But Ramirez is on the grounds."

Chapter 16

Nate prayed that Adam was lying. Or playing some kind of sick joke.

Yes, Nate was fully aware that Ramirez was after Darcy and him, but if Adam had hand-delivered a killer to their doorstep, then there would be a bad price to pay.

"I don't see Ramirez," Darcy said, her voice filled with nerves, her breath racing. She dropped to the floor, grabbed the laptop screen and moved closer, frantically studying it.

Nate looked, as well, and saw the same six screens he had earlier. All showed different parts of the ranch, including the front of the house, where Adam was parked. He didn't see Ramirez, either, but the thought had no sooner crossed his mind when white static filled the screen.

Hell.

"Ramirez," Darcy mumbled. "He did this?"

"Maybe." Nate sandwiched his cell between his shoulder and ear and sat next to Darcy. He took the laptop and typed in the security codes again to adjust the cameras.

Nothing.

"Ramirez jammed your security system, didn't he?" Adam asked. The man didn't sound smug. He sounded as concerned as Nate felt. "He said he would. Said he had the equipment to do it. Now he can come after you, and you can't even see where he is."

"How do I know you didn't do this?" Nate fired back. "After all, you're the one who claims to have brought Ramirez here to the ranch." Nate mentally cursed when he tried the codes again. And they failed, again.

"It's not a claim. It's the truth," Adam insisted. "I had to bring him here or he would have killed me on the spot. He broke into my hotel room, put a gun to my head and forced me to drive him here. I couldn't just let him shoot me."

"He'll kill you, anyway," Nate pointed out.

He gave up on reactivating the exterior cameras and checked to make sure the intruder alarms for the doors and windows were still armed.

Thank God. They were.

"I'm not sitting out here in the open any longer," Adam said. "Ramirez could decide to come after me before he finishes you two off." At least that's what Nate thought the man said, but he couldn't be sure because Adam gunned the engine.

Darcy's gaze flew to his, and she started to get up from the floor, but Nate caught her shoulder to keep her where she was. Right now, the floor was the best place for her, especially since it meant she was away from the windows. The security system would trigger the alarms if anyone tried to break in, but Ramirez could still shoot through the glass.

"Adam's getting away," she reminded him.

"For now. And that's not a bad thing. I don't want to have to deal with him right now. Only Ramirez." Besides, if Ramirez attempted to kill Adam, Nate would have to do something to stop it. He only wanted to concentrate on keeping Darcy and his brothers alive.

"We need another weapon," he said. He handed her his cell phone. "Stay put and call Mason to let him know what's going on. Tell him that Ramirez is probably headed straight for the house."

She gave a shaky nod, but her eyes widened when he handed her his gun. "It's just a precaution," he added. And maybe it would stay that way—a precaution—but Nate doubted it. Ramirez was a crazy man on a mission of murder.

He ran back down the hall while Darcy made the call to Mason. Nate tried to listen to the conversation, but thanks to the relentless storm, Darcy's voice soon faded from hearing range when he hurried into his office.

Where there were windows.

The windows were the reason he'd wanted Darcy to stay put.

Nate tried to make sure Ramirez wasn't lurking outside one of them, but the rain streaks on the glass and the darkness made it impossible. So, he stayed low and went to his desk. To the bottom drawer. It had a combination safety lock, and once again the darkness wasn't in his favor, but he finally entered the correct code and jerked open the drawer.

Two guns.

He slid one in his holster, held on to the other one and crammed some extra magazines of ammo into his pockets. It was more than enough to fight off one man, but Nate had no way of knowing if Ramirez had brought backup.

The moment Nate stepped back into the hall, his attention went to Darcy. She wasn't talking on the phone, but she was staring at the laptop screen.

"Did you get Mason?" he whispered. Also a precaution. Even though it was a long shot, he didn't want Ramirez to hear them and know where to shoot.

She nodded, still not taking her wide eyes from the screen. "Look," she insisted.

Nate cursed. He didn't have to guess that something was wrong. Darcy's expression said it all. And Nate soon knew what had caused her reaction.

Five of the security screens were still filled with static, but the sixth was working. Working, in a bad way.

Ramirez's face was on the screen.

He was clearly soaked, but he was giving them that slick grin that made Nate want to come through the computer and rid the man of his last breath.

"Can he see us?" Darcy asked.

"No." The security cameras didn't have a two-way feed. But Nate could certainly see Ramirez.

"Where is he? Can you tell?" she wanted to know.

Nate really hated to say this aloud. "I can't tell from the screen." Mainly, because Ramirez was blocking the entire camera. "It's camera five, and it's on this wing of the house."

"Oh, mercy," she mumbled.

And Nate had to agree. Ramirez had gone directly to the spot where they were, and Nate didn't think that was a coincidence. He studied the screen, looking for any sign that the man had an infrared device with him, but Nate could only see that face. That grin. And the evil in his eyes.

As a cop, Nate had faced cold-blooded killers before, but Ramirez was the worst of the worst.

"What's he saying?" Darcy asked when Ramirez's lips began to move.

There was no audio, but it didn't take Nate long to figure out that Ramirez was repeating the same three words.

Ready to die?

Judging from the gasp Darcy made, she had figured it out, as well.

"Mason said he'd let everyone know that Ramirez is on the grounds," Darcy relayed. "They're moving closer to the house so they can try to spot him."

Good. That meant in ten minutes or so, Darcy and he would have plenty of backup. Of course, Ramirez might have plenty, as well, and he needed to warn his brother that they might be walking into an ambush. Mason would already be prepared for that, but Nate wanted to make it crystal clear.

He took his phone back from Darcy. Just as Ramirez moved. Ramirez stepped to the side, and Nate then saw the other person behind Ramirez.

A man several yards away from the camera.

And this man wasn't a stranger. Far from it.

"What the heck is he doing here?" Darcy asked.

Nate cursed. He wanted to know the same damn thing.

Wesley Dent's face stared back at Darcy.

But not for long. The screen went fuzzy again. A Ramirez mind game, no doubt. The man was trying to keep Nate and her off-kilter.

It was working.

Instead of focusing on the impending attack, Darcy was wondering what her former client was doing outside the ranch house with Ramirez. Was Dent there to try to kill them, too? And if so, why?

She tightened her grip on the gun and hoped she would have answers soon. So much for believing in Dent's innocence. He looked pretty darn guilty to her.

Crouched next to her, Nate flipped open his phone.

"You're calling Mason?" Darcy asked.

But Nate didn't have time to answer. Darcy heard the cracking sound and prayed it was a violent slash of lightning. But no. This was violence of a different kind.

A bullet slammed through a window.

Nate automatically shoved her lower to the floor, even though they weren't directly in front of the window. *Any* window. But it was certainly nearby because she could hear the broken glass clatter to the floor.

"The guest room," Nate supplied.

Her pulse kicked up a notch, and the blood rushed to her head. The guest room was where they'd made love less than a half hour earlier.

Nate made the call to Mason and warned him what was happening. The moment he ended the call, he moved her, positioning her behind him so that he was facing the side of house where that shot had been fired.

"Please tell me Mason is nearby," Darcy whispered.

"He's on his way."

On his way didn't seem nearly close enough, and yet she didn't want Mason or anyone else walking into gunfire.

The jolt of lightning lit up the hall, but the crashing noise from the following thunder was minor compared to the next shot that slammed into the house.

More broken glass fell to the floor.

"That was also in the guest room," Nate explained. He took out an extra clip of ammo and handed it to her. "Just in case," he added.

That gave her another slam of adrenaline.

So did the next bullet.

No broken glass. Just a loud, deadly-sounding thud.

"It went through the wall," Nate whispered. She could hear the adrenaline in his voice, too, but his hand seemed steady.

Unlike hers.

Darcy was afraid she was shaking too hard to aim straight. The one good thing in all of this was that the children were safe. As bad as it was having Ramirez shoot at them, it would have been a million times worse if Kimmie and Noah had been anywhere nearby.

"Watch the foyer," Nate instructed, and he angled his body so that his aim was fastened to the guest-room door.

Darcy turned, as well, and watched, though it was hard to see anything in the pitch-black foyer. However, she was certain if Ramirez managed to come through the front door, then she would hear him. And the alarms would go off.

Another shot slammed through the wall.

Beside her, Nate's phone buzzed, and he answered it without taking his aim off the doorway. Since Darcy was so close, she could actually hear the person on the other end of the line.

Adam, again.

"You have to let me inside," Adam demanded. "I tried to leave, but someone fired a shot at me."

Darcy hadn't heard such a shot, but it could have happened far enough away that the storm could have drowned it out.

"Not a chance," Nate informed him. "We're under attack and going to the door to let you in would be suicide for all of us."

"Then what the hell am I supposed to do out here?" Adam yelled.

"My advice? Keep your voice down so Ramirez doesn't hear you. Then, find a place to take cover." Nate didn't wait for Adam to respond. He snapped his phone shut and crammed it back into his pocket.

Darcy wanted to ask if Nate thought Adam was in on this. Or Dent. But the next shot stopped her cold. Again, no broken glass. This was a heavy thudding sound, but in the murky darkness, she saw the drywall dust fly through the air.

Oh, no.

The shot hadn't gone through just the exterior of the wing, it had actually made it through the interior wall.

Just a few yards away from them.

She heard Nate's suddenly rough breath, and he

glanced around as if trying to decide where to move. Any direction could be dangerous.

And the next bullet proved that.

The blast was louder, much louder than the others, and she saw the large hole it made in the hall wall.

Closer this time.

"Ramirez is using heavier artillery," Nate whispered. "Get all the way down on the floor."

But he didn't wait for her to do that. He put his hand on her back and pushed her, hard, until her face was right against the hardwood.

Just as another bullet tore through the wall.

Sweet heaven. This one was even closer.

Maybe Ramirez was using infrared to find them, but if so, why hadn't he just aimed at them right from the beginning?

"Shhh," she heard Nate say, and he brushed the back of his hand over her cheek.

It took her a moment to realize he was doing that because her breathing was way too fast and shallow. She was on the verge of hyperventilating, and that couldn't happen. She couldn't fall apart because Nate needed her for backup in case Mason didn't get there in time.

Darcy concentrated on leveling her breath. And her heartbeat. She fixed her mind on Noah's smiling face. Kimmie's and Nate's, too, and just like that, her body started to settle down. She fought to hang on to her newly regained composure even when the next bullet slammed through the wall.

This one was just inches away.

"We have to move," Nate whispered, and he caught her arm.

Darcy wasn't even off the floor yet when there was another sound. Not a bullet this time.

Something much worse.

The security alarm blared, the noise seemingly shaking the walls. And she gasped. Because she knew what that sound meant.

Ramirez was inside the house.

Chapter 17

Nate knew the nightmare had just gotten worse.

The clanging of the security alarms was deafening, but that wasn't his biggest concern. With that noise, he couldn't hear Ramirez or anyone else. And he needed to hear because in addition to Ramirez, he had both Adam and Dent on the grounds. For that matter, Marlene and Edwin could be at the ranch, as well.

Anything was possible.

Plus, he had to watch out for his brothers and everyone else trying to stop Ramirez.

Nate tried to keep watch all around them, but he had no idea where the intruder had entered. It could be any window or door in the house.

"I have to turn off the alarms," Nate shouted, though Darcy only shook her head and touched her fingers to her ear.

Nate grabbed her, lifted her from the floor and turned her to the side so she could keep watch at the back of the foyer. He would take the front door and the hall, the most likely point of entry since the shots had come from that direction.

Trying to make sure they weren't about to be ambushed, Nate led her into the foyer. Darcy kept her gun ready and aimed. Nate did the same. And they made their way across the open space.

Too open.

The sidelight windows around the door were especially worrisome because a gunman could fire right through those.

He held his breath, prayed and moved as fast as he could to the keypad panel on the wall between the foyer and the family room. His mind was racing. His heart, pounding. And it took several precious seconds to recall the code. The moment he punched in the numbers, the alarms went silent.

Nate lifted his head. Listened. The rain was battering against the door and windows, but he heard the wind, too. Not from the storm. This wind was whistling through the broken windows. He tried to pick through all those sounds so he could hear what he was listening for.

Footsteps.

They barely had time to register in his mind when a bullet slammed into the wall next to them. Darcy gasped and dived toward the family room. Nate was right behind her, and he fired in the direction of the shooter.

"You missed!" someone yelled out.

Ramirez.

It was true. The killer was inside.

As quietly as he could, Nate positioned Darcy behind the sofa. It wouldn't be much protection against bullets, but it was better than nothing. He cursed himself for this stupid bait plan and wondered how the devil he could get Darcy out of this alive. And how soon.

Where were Mason and the others?

Maybe someone had managed to nab Dent, Adam or anyone else outside waiting to help Ramirez.

Ramirez fired another shot at them. "You killed my brother," he shouted. "Did you really think I wouldn't make you pay for that?"

Nate didn't answer him. He didn't want Ramirez to use Nate's voice to pinpoint their position. However, Nate let his aim follow Ramirez's voice.

He sent another bullet toward the man.

Nate couldn't see him, but he was pretty sure he missed. Ramirez's laughter confirmed it. He'd moved. Maybe to the rear of the foyer?

If so, he was getting closer.

"Before I kill you," Ramirez shouted, "I think it's only fair I should tell you who hired me to kidnap your little brats."

Darcy's breath rattled, and she tried to come up from behind the sofa, but Nate pushed her right back down. He put his finger to his mouth in a stay-quiet warning. He hoped she realized that this was a trick that could get them killed, but he knew the firestorm Ramirez's offer had created inside her. She was afraid, yes, but like Nate, she wanted justice.

"Maybe you'd like me to take care of my boss before I punish you?" Ramirez asked.

The only thing Nate wanted was a name because when this was over, he would deal with that SOB, too.

For now, though, he waited and listened for Ramirez to come into view. All Nate needed was one clean shot.

"Well?" Ramirez prompted.

There. In the deep shadows of the foyer, Nate saw what he'd been watching for. The silhouette of a man. He took aim. But before he could squeeze the trigger, there was god-awful sound of wood splintering, and the man ducked out of sight.

The door.

Someone had kicked it down.

Nate didn't fire because it could be one of his brothers, and because of that, he had to break his silence. "Ramirez is in the house!" Nate warned.

"What the hell?" Ramirez snarled.

And a shot tore through the foyer.

Everything seemed to freeze, and Darcy felt the sickening dread slice through her.

The bullet wasn't the same as the others. There had been no sound of the metal ripping through drywall or glass.

No.

This was a deadly thud. Followed by a gasp. And Darcy knew. The bullet had been shot into *someone*.

She shoved her hand over her mouth so she couldn't cry out. This couldn't be happening. Ramirez couldn't have shot Mason or Kade. She couldn't be responsible for Nate losing anyone else in his life.

Darcy tried to get up, again, but once again Nate kept her pinned behind the sofa. "Stay put," he warned.

Nate, however, didn't heed his own warning. Neither did the person in the foyer because she heard footsteps. Someone was running, probably trying to escape.

With his gun aimed and his attention pinned to the foyer, Nate started walking. Slow, inch-by-inch steps. Darcy wanted to tell him to stop, but she couldn't. If one of his brothers was hurt or worse, then Nate would need to go to him. He would have to help. Or at least try.

It might be too late for help of any kind.

And then there was the flip side. Someone had already been shot, but Ramirez was still alive. Still armed. He would shoot Nate or anyone else if he got the chance, and that's when Darcy knew she couldn't obey Nate.

She had to help him.

Darcy eased up from behind the sofa and took aim in the same direction as Nate.

Nate mumbled some profanity, and that's when Darcy spotted the body on the foyer floor. She couldn't see the man's face because he was sprawled out on his stomach, but he was dressed all in black.

No. God, no.

Was it Mason?

Nate obviously thought it was his brother because she heard the shift in his breathing. Heard him whisper a prayer.

Darcy followed Nate to the edge of the foyer, but she waited, watching in case someone came through the now-open front door. Ramirez had perhaps gone out that way, but it didn't mean he wouldn't be back.

Nate inched closer, his gaze firing all around, and when he reached the body, he leaned down and touched his fingers to the man's neck. No cursing this time, but he groaned, a painful sound that tore right through her heart.

And he flipped the body over.

Nate froze for just a second, and Darcy started to go

to him, to try to comfort him. But there wasn't time. He stood, and in the same motion, Nate whirled back around to face her.

Darcy shook her head, not understanding why he'd done that. She didn't get a chance to ask because someone karate chopped her arm, causing her weapon to go flying through the air. But she felt another gun, cold and hard, when it was shoved against her back.

"Move and your boyfriend dies," the person behind her growled in a hoarse whisper.

Her breathing went crazy, started racing. As did her heart. And she looked past Nate's suddenly startled face and stared at the body on the foyer floor.

Not Mason.

It was Ramirez.

Darcy's stomach went to her knees. Because if Ramirez was there, lifeless and unmoving, then who had a gun jammed in her back?

"Sorry about this," the person whispered. It was a man, but she couldn't tell who. "You have to be my hostage for a little while."

Darcy had no intentions of being anyone's hostage.

She moved purely on instinct. She jerked away from her captor and dived to the side. But so did he, and he hooked his arm around her and held her in place. Still, she didn't give up. She didn't stop struggling.

Until the blast from a gun roared through her head.

Everything inside her went numb, and it took her a moment to realize she hadn't been shot. That it was the deafening noise from the bullet that had caused the pain to shoot through her. In fact, the gun hadn't even been aimed at her. The shot had been fired over her head.

"Darcy?" Nate called out.

She tried to answer him but couldn't get her throat unclamped. Darcy cursed her reaction and forced herself to move. She didn't intend to die without a fight so she rammed her elbow into her captor's stomach. It wasn't much, but it was enough for her to break the hold he had on her and scramble away.

She got just a glimpse of her attacker's face.

But a glimpse was all she needed to recognize him. It was Adam.

He fired another shot, again over her head, and it slammed into the wall just a fraction of a second before he hooked his arm around her throat and put her in a choke hold.

Oh, mercy. She couldn't breathe. That caused panic to crawl through her. And worse, Nate was coming closer. Putting himself out in the open so that Adam could kill him, instead.

"Stop fighting me," Adam warned her. "Or Nate dies. Your choice."

That was no choice at all. She stopped fighting and prayed it would save Nate.

"Good girl," Adam whispered in a mock-sweet tone. But he did loosen the grip on her throat. Darcy frantically pulled in some much-needed air and hoped it was enough to stop her from passing out.

"Adam, give this up," Nate ordered. "You can't get out of here alive."

"No?" Adam answered. He kept his arm around her neck but aimed his gun at Nate. "So far, so good. Ramirez is dead."

"Yeah." With his own gun aimed at Adam, Nate inched closer, but he stayed in the foyer, out of Adam's direct line of fire. "You killed him before he could tell us that you were the one who hired him to set up the kidnapping."

Adam didn't deny it, and Darcy realized it was true. Adam was the one who'd put the children in danger. Her fear was replaced by a jolt of anger.

How dare this moron do that!

"All this for money," Nate continued. He moved again. Just a fraction. And Darcy realized he was trying to get into a position so he could take Adam out.

Good. She wanted Adam to pay for what he'd done.

"Hey, it's always about money," Adam joked. He started inching toward the foyer. "If you'd just arrested Dent and tossed his sorry butt in jail, then my mother's estate would have been mine, and we wouldn't be here right now."

"But Dent isn't guilty," Nate concluded.

"No. But Dent is dead," Adam confessed. "I killed him about ten minutes ago."

Dead? Darcy tried hard to hang on to her composure. She was already losing that battle before Adam fired a shot into the foyer. She heard herself scream for Nate to get down, and somehow he managed to duck out of the way.

Adam cursed. "Move again, Lieutenant, and I'll shoot Darcy in the shoulder. It won't kill her, but it won't be fun, either." He shoved her forward, keeping his choke hold and his gun in place.

"Don't you have enough blood on your hands?" Nate asked. "First your mother with a lethal dose of insulin. Then, you kill Dent. Now, Ramirez. All of this to cover up what you've done. My theory? You knew what your mother had written in her diary so you tore out the page that would have incriminated you. But something happened, something that prevented you from destroying it."

"Yeah," Adam readily agreed, "and that was my mother's fault. She saw me rip out the page, and she grabbed the diary and ran. She hid it before I found her and then wouldn't tell me where she'd put it. That's when I killed her."

Darcy could almost see it playing out. Sandra, terrified of her own son as he shoved a needle into her arm. She understood that terror because she was feeling it now.

"Unless you do something to ruin my plan," Adam went on, "the diary is what will keep you both alive."

"What do you mean?" Darcy asked.

But Adam didn't answer her. He nailed his attention to Nate. "I want you to give me the diary so I can destroy it."

"Impossible," Nate fired back.

"No. It's doable for a man in your position. I'll take Darcy someplace safe while you go to the crime lab. When you bring me the diary, then I'll let Darcy go. Well, after I've cashed in my mother's estate and escaped, of course."

The adrenaline and the anger were making it hard for her to think, but Darcy could still see the faulty logic. Adam wouldn't let them go. If he got his hands on the diary and Sandra's money, he would kill them so he could cover up his crimes.

Or rather, he'd try to kill them.

"There's no need to take Darcy," Nate bargained. "I can call and have the diary brought to us."

She latched on to that, hoping Adam would agree. If

they could somehow prevent him from leaving the ranch with her, then she would have a better chance of escape.

But Adam shook his head.

"Not a chance. As long as I have Darcy, you'll do whatever it takes to cooperate." Adam tightened his grip on her and muscled her into the foyer and toward the front door. "Lieutenant, tell your brothers and anybody else out there to back off." He shoved Darcy forward again, toward the door.

Nate's gaze slashed from Adam's gun to her own eyes, and she saw the raw, painful emotions there. Nate was blaming himself for this. She wanted to tell him that it wasn't his fault. But there was no time to tell him anything. Because Adam dragged her out onto the porch, down the steps and toward his car, which was parked behind Nate's SUV. Adam had obviously pretended to drive away from the ranch.

The storm came right at her, assaulting her. The rain stung her eyes, but that didn't stop her from seeing the shadowy figure on the side of the house.

Mason.

He had his gun drawn, like Nate, who was now in the doorway, but neither could fire. The way Adam was holding her would make it next to impossible for either of them to get a clean shot.

"Lieutenant, tell your brother to back off," Adam warned, forcing Darcy into the yard.

But Mason stepped out. "She makes a lousy hostage," Mason snarled. "She's a good six inches shorter than you, and that means somebody out here has a good chance at a head shot. *Your* head."

She felt Adam's arm tense, and he crouched farther down behind her. Maybe Kade or one of the others was behind them, but that still didn't mean there'd be a clean shot. After all, the bullet could go through Adam and into her.

"I'd make a better human shield," Mason offered. He shrugged as if he didn't have a care in the world. "I'll take her place."

Part of her was touched that Mason would even make the offer, but she didn't want to place Nate's brother in even more danger. Apparently neither did Nate because he inched down the steps.

"What a dilemma, Lieutenant," Adam mocked. He clucked his tongue. "Your brother or your lover. So, which one will it be?"

Oh, mercy. Darcy hadn't thought this could get any worse, but she'd been wrong. It was sick to force Nate into making a choice like this.

"It's okay," Darcy insisted. "I'll go with him." Well, she would, but she would also try to escape. She wasn't about to give up.

"No, you won't go with him," Nate said. "If Adam won't take me, then Mason will go."

Adam made a sound of amusement. "You're choosing her over your own blood?"

Nate gave him a look that could have frozen Hades. "Mason's a cop. Darcy's a civilian."

Mason just shrugged again and then nodded.

Adam didn't respond right away, and she couldn't see his expression. However, she could feel his muscles tense again. "No deal," Adam finally said. "She'll be a lot easier to control than either of you. Besides, Darcy knows if she doesn't cooperate, I'll just go after her son again."

It took a few seconds for those words to sink in, and

they didn't sink in well. How dare this SOB threaten Noah again.

Her hands tightened to fists.

And that was for starters.

The slam of anger created a new jolt of adrenaline, and it wasn't just her hands that tightened. The rest of her body did, too. Suddenly, she was primed and ready for a fight and needed someplace to aim all this dangerous energy boiling inside her.

She saw the anger—no, make that *rage*—go through Nate's eyes, and she knew he was within seconds of launching himself at Adam. That couldn't happen because Adam would shoot him. But maybe there was something she could do to improve Nate's odds.

Darcy frantically looked around her. There was nothing nearby that she could grab. No shrubs, rocks or weapons. But the car was directly behind them, and Darcy watched. And waited.

Until Adam reached to open the door.

She used every bit of her anger and adrenaline when she drew back her elbow and rammed it into Adam's ribs. He sputtered out a cough and eased up on his grip just enough to give her some room to maneuver. Darcy lifted her foot, put her weight behind it and punched her heel into his shin.

"Get down!" Nate yelled to her.

Darcy had already started to do just that, but Adam latched on to her hair. The pain shot through her, but she kicked him again. And again. Fighting to get loose from him.

She succeeded.

Darcy fell facedown onto the slick driveway, the rough, wet concrete grating across her knees and forearms. She immediately tried to scramble for cover behind the car.

But it was too late for that.

From the corner of her eye, she saw Adam lift his gun. Take aim.

And he fired.

Chapter 18

Nate felt the searing pain slice through him.

Just like that, his legs gave way, and he had no choice but to drop to the ground.

Hell.

Adam had shot him.

That, and the pain, registered in his mind, and he maneuvered his gun so he could try to protect Darcy. He had to stop Adam from taking her.

Or worse.

The sound of another gunshot let him know that worse could have already happened.

"Darcy?" Nate managed to call out.

She didn't answer, and he couldn't see her, but there was the sound of chaos all around him.

Another shot.

Mason shouted something that was drowned out by

the thunder, and suddenly there was movement. Footsteps. Some kind of scuffle. A sea of people—FBI agents and the ranch hands. All of them converged on Adam and took him to the ground.

"Darcy?" Nate yelled.

He had to make sure she was safe. He had to see for himself. If Adam had managed to shoot her... But he couldn't go there. Couldn't even think it. Because he was responsible for this.

No.

It was more than that.

Nate couldn't lose her. It was as simple as that. He couldn't lose her because he loved her.

He would have laughed if it hadn't been for the godawful pain searing his left shoulder. It was a really bad time to realize just how he felt about Darcy.

"Nate?" he heard someone say.

He lifted his head and amid that swarm of people, he saw her. Darcy. She had mud on her face and clothes, and he couldn't tell if she'd been shot. But she was moving.

Or rather, running.

She hurried to him and pulled him into her arms. He saw the blood then and had a moment of rage where he wanted to tear Adam limb from limb.

But then he noticed that the blood was his.

Thank God. Darcy was all right.

"You're hurt," she said, her voice shaking almost violently.

Yeah, he was, but that didn't matter now. "Are you okay?"

"No." She made a sobbing sound, and her tears slid

through the mud on her cheeks. "I'm not okay because you've been shot."

Oh. That. The relief didn't help with his pain, but it helped with everything else.

Darcy was okay.

Adam hadn't managed to shoot her, after all.

"Can you stand?" she asked. "I don't want to wait for an ambulance. I'll drive you to the hospital."

Nate hated the worry in her eyes. Hated those tears. But he couldn't refuse her offer. Even he wasn't too stubborn to refuse a trip to the hospital—though he did want to first make sure that Adam had been neutralized. Nate glanced around, but he couldn't tell. Because he couldn't actually see the man who'd just tried to kill him.

However, he did see Mason.

His brother broke from the group and made a bee-line for him. "Hurt much?" Mason asked. But he didn't wait for an answer. With Darcy on one side of him and Mason on the other, they got Nate to his feet and headed toward his SUV.

"What about Adam?" Nate wanted to know.

"Kade is on him." Mason glanced back at the huddle of activity. "Literally. He's not going anywhere except to jail."

Good. One less thing to worry about right now. Later, he would deal with his hatred for this SOB who'd nearly cost Nate everything.

Darcy pressed her hand to his shoulder, right where it was burning like fire, but he guessed she was doing that to stop the blood flow and not to make him wince in pain.

"Are you okay?" Darcy whispered as they hauled

Nate onto the backseat of the SUV. Darcy followed right in beside him and crouched on the floor. Mason peeled out of the driveway, the tires of the SUV kicking up gravel and rain.

"I'm okay," Nate tried.

"Are you really?" she questioned.

Since she sounded very close to losing it, Nate decided to give her some reassurance. He slid his hand around the back of her neck, pulled her to him and kissed her. He wasn't surprised when it gave him some reassurance, too.

"Can't be hurt that bad if you can do that to her," Mason growled.

"I'm not hurt that bad," Nate verified. And he was almost certain that was true. It was hard to tell through the blistering pain.

"You were shot," Darcy pointed out. The frantic tone was back in her voice. "Adam could have killed you."

"He could have killed you, too," Nate reminded her.

But it was a reminder that cut him right across the heart. He would see Adam in his nightmares. Darcy would, too. And Nate would never forgive Adam for that and for placing Noah and Kimmie in grave danger.

"Adam got some blood on his hands tonight," Mason said, his attention glued to the wet road. The wipers slashed across the windshield. "I'm the one who found Dent just a few seconds before he died from a gunshot wound to the chest. He told me Adam had called him to come to the ranch and said that he had proof it was Edwin who'd killed Sandra."

Dent had been stupid to fall for that, but then Adam had probably convinced him that he'd be safe at the ranch with a cop, an FBI agent and a deputy sheriff.

"What about Ramirez's partner?" Nate asked. "Someone needs to make sure he doesn't try to help Adam."

"He can't help anybody," Mason assured him. "Right before Adam grabbed Darcy, Kade found Ramirez's partner—dead."

Adam, no doubt. With Ramirez and Sandra Dent, that meant Adam had killed at least three, maybe four people. A lot of murder and mayhem all for the sake of money. But the high body count along with the kidnapping charges meant there was no way Adam could escape the death penalty.

"How much longer before we get to the hospital?" Darcy asked.

"Not long," Mason assured her. "One of the ranch hands is calling ahead so the E.R. will be expecting us."

She kept her hand pressed over his wound and kept mumbling something. A prayer, he realized.

"The pain's not that bad," he lied.

But more of her tears came, anyway, and they were followed by a heart-wrenching sob. "I should have held on to Adam's arm. I should have kicked him harder." Darcy shook her head. "I should have done something to stop him from firing that gun."

"Hey, don't do this." Nate touched her chin and lifted it. "I'm the one who planned for us to be bait."

"The plan worked," Darcy reminded him, though she had to draw in a deep breath before saying it. "What didn't work was that I allowed Adam to take me at gunpoint. That's when things went wrong."

He could have told her that things went wrong when Adam killed his mother, but Nate didn't think Darcy would hear the logic. No, she was hurting and worried, and he was the cause of that.

Nate hoped he could also be the cure.

He pulled her back to him for another kiss. And another. And he kept it up until oxygen became a big concern for both of them. But he figured he might need her a little breathless for what he was about to say.

"I don't want to lose you," he let her know.

She shook her head, smeared the tears from her cheeks. "Adam isn't a threat anymore. Nor Ramirez. We'll be safe."

Yeah. But that wasn't where Nate was going with this. "I don't want to lose you," he repeated.

Darcy blinked. Shook her head again.

"Part of me will always love Ellie," he explained. "But I can't live in the past, and she was my past...."

"We're here," Mason announced, and he braked to a screeching halt directly in front of the E.R. door.

Nate choked back the pain that was blurring his vision and gathered his breath. He wanted to finish this now.

"Darcy, will you marry me?"

She opened her mouth, but nothing came out. *Nothing.* And then the moment was gone.

Everything started to move way too fast. Two medics threw open the SUV's door and hauled him onto a gurney. Nate got one last glimpse of Darcy's startled, bleached face before the medics whisked him away.

Darcy was afraid if she sat down, she'd collapse. So, she kept pacing and waiting. Something she'd been doing for nearly an hour. It felt more like an eternity.

"SAPD is booking Adam right now," Mason relayed

to her from the chair in the corner of the waiting room. He had his feet stretched out in front of him as if he were lounging, and he'd been on and off the phone— mainly on—since they'd arrived at the E.R.

Mason certainly didn't seem crazy scared, like she did. But then, neither did Dade, who had his shoulder propped against the wall. He, too, was on the phone, with his fiancée, and from the sound of it, both Kayla and Grayson's wife, Eve, were on their way to the hospital to see Nate. Kade was the only Ryland who showed signs of stress. He was seated, elbows on knees, his face buried in his hands.

"What about Marlene and Edwin?" Darcy asked. Because it occurred to her if Adam had killed Dent, his mother and Ramirez, he might have killed others.

"They're safe and sound," Mason answered. "Neither appears to have had anything to do with this. According to Mel, Edwin's pretty torn up."

Of course. His son would be facing the death penalty.

"Adam was chatty when he arrived at the sheriff's office," Mason went on. "He admitted to trying to make his father look guilty. He wanted the blame placed on anyone but him. Edwin might not be so torn up when he learns that sonny boy was willing to let him take the fall for murder." Mason's phone buzzed again.

Darcy continued to pace until she heard Mason mention Grayson's name, and that stopped her. She certainly hadn't forgotten about the children, but with Nate's injury, she'd put him at the top of her worry list.

Until now.

She hoped Grayson wasn't phoning because there was a problem. She moved closer to him so she could try to hear, but the call ended quickly.

"Grayson and the kids are on their way here," Mason relayed. "Everybody's okay."

The blood rushed to her head. A mix of relief and happiness overcame her when she realized she would soon get to see Noah and Kimmie. But Darcy knew there wouldn't be total relief until she saw Nate. Until she talked to him.

Until she asked him about that *question*.

Heaven knows how long that would be. Besides, he might not even know what he'd said. Nate had been in so much pain, and mixed with the blood loss and the shock, he might have been talking out of his head.

Everything suddenly felt still and silent. None of the Rylands were on their phones. Like her, they were fully in the wait mode. Except for Mason. He was studying her with those intense, steely eyes.

"Well?" he asked.

Darcy froze. Because even though that one word hardly qualified as a question, she was positive what Mason meant. After all, Mason had been in that SUV, and he'd almost certainly heard Nate's question.

Kade lifted his head. Looked at Mason. Then at her. "Well what?"

Oh, no. She hadn't wanted to do this tonight and especially not before she'd had a chance to speak with Nate.

But apparently Mason did. "Right before the medics took him into the E.R., Nate asked Darcy to marry him."

The room was suddenly so quiet that Darcy could hear her own heartbeat. It was racing.

All three Rylands stared at her. And stared. But it was Dade who walked toward her. He stopped just a few inches away, and she braced herself for a good tongue-lashing about how she'd played on Nate's vulnerability.

"What was your answer?" Dade asked.

She managed to shrug, somehow, though her muscles seemed frozen in place. "There wasn't time for an answer."

Dade waited, still staring, and it became clear that he expected her to reveal what that answer would be.

"I want to tell Nate first," she explained. And she braced herself for Dade to demand to know.

But he reached out, put his arm around her and eased her to him. He brushed a kiss on her forehead. "I hope you'll say yes."

Darcy couldn't have been any more stunned. "You do?"

The corner of his mouth lifted, probably because all that shock had made it into her voice. "You're good for Nate."

Kade stood, crammed his hands in his pockets and walked closer, as well. "You are good for him," he verified. "It's nice to see Nate happy for a change."

Again, she got another dose of being stunned. "I'm in love with him," she blurted out. *Oh, mercy.* She hadn't expected to say that. Not to them, anyway.

"Does he know that?" Dade asked.

Darcy shook her head, causing Kade and Dade to grumble under their breaths. "You need to tell him," Dade insisted.

She would. Once she could speak. And once she got past the whole "maybe Nate was talking out of his head" thing. Maybe he wouldn't remember proposing to her.

"I hope like the devil that you two get married the

same time as Kayla and Dade," Mason mumbled. "No way do I want to wear a monkey suit twice."

Kade huffed. "Ignore Mr. Congeniality over there. You name the date for him to be in a monkey suit, and he'll be in one. There are four of us and one of him."

Mason matched that huff. "Yeah, and it'll take all four of you weenies to try." He sounded serious enough, but Darcy suspected he was joking.

She was about to ask for clarification, but the door behind them swung open.

And there was Nate.

His shirt was open, exposing the bandage on his shoulder, and his left arm was in a pristine-white sling. He looked exhausted. And really confused when his gaze landed on all of them.

Darcy hurried to him, slipped her arms around his waist and tried to give him a gentle hug. "You're okay?" she asked. And she cursed the tears that came automatically.

"I am," Nate verified. "The bullet went straight through. No real damage. The doctor says I'll be fine in about a week or so."

Now, here was the flood of relief that she'd waited for. Nate was all right.

He brushed a kiss on her cheek and ducked down to make eye contact. "Is something, uh, wrong?"

"No," Darcy jumped to answer. Unfortunately, Dade and Kade jumped to answer with their own noes.

Mason just made a snorting sound. "I told them about your marriage proposal. And Darcy told us that she's in love with you." He looked at Nate. "Yeah, we were surprised, too. We didn't consider you, well, all that lovable."

That brought on some snickers from Kade and Dade, but Nate just kept looking at her. "Did you tell them the answer to my proposal?"

Suddenly all eyes were on her again. "No. I said I needed to talk to you first."

Nate's face dropped, and around her she heard the murmurings of the Ryland brothers as they started to leave, giving them some time alone to absorb what she was about to say. Of course, judging from the sudden mood in the room, they thought she was about to say no.

So, Darcy tried one of Nate's ploys.

She kissed him. She didn't keep it exactly gentle, either. It was best if he knew just how deep, and how hot, her feelings were for him. She didn't break the mouth-to-mouth contact until Mason cleared his throat, a reminder that Nate and she weren't alone, after all.

Darcy eased back and looked Nate in the eyes. "I'm in love with you."

Nate smiled that little smile that made her want to kiss him again. And haul him off to bed.

But bed could wait.

"Yes," she added. "I want to marry you."

Nate's smile suddenly wasn't so little. "Good. Because I'm in love with you, and I definitely want to marry you." He hooked his uninjured arm around her and hauled her closer to him for a perfect kiss.

One that caused Dade and Kade to whoop.

Nate and she broke away laughing. And then kissed again.

Darcy hadn't thought this moment could get any better, but then she heard the familiar voices. Grayson was making his way toward them, and he was carrying both babies. Amazingly, both were wide-awake and were squirming to get down. Grayson eased them both onto the floor, and the two toddled into the waiting area.

"Here," Kade said, peeling off his jacket and slipping it on Darcy.

That's when Darcy realized she had blood on her top. Nate's blood. And she didn't want the children to see that. "Thank you," she whispered to Kade.

"Anything for my new sister-in-law." He brushed a kiss on her cheek and moved away so she could kneel down and give both babies a big hug.

Kimmie started babbling as though trying to tell Darcy all about their adventure at the safe house, and Darcy scooped up both of them so that Nate wouldn't have to bend down for all-around kisses.

"Boo-boo," Noah announced when he spotted the bandage on Nate's shoulder, and when he kissed it, Kimmie repeated the syllables and kissed it, as well.

"Your mom and I are getting married," Nate told Noah. "How do you feel about that?"

Noah looked pensive for a moment, then grinned and babbled some happy sounds.

Her son was obviously okay with this. "And what do you think?" Darcy asked Kimmie.

Kimmie looked at her uncle Mason. "Your call, curly locks," he told her.

Even though there was no way Kimmie knew what that meant, she giggled and clapped her hands.

Darcy had never thought she could feel this much happiness, but then she saw Grayson, the only person in the room who hadn't given some kind of thumbs-up. She wouldn't take back her yes. She loved Nate too much to walk away because his brother disapproved, but she wanted it just the same.

"I'm in love with Nate," Darcy told Grayson, just in case he'd missed that part.

Grayson nodded. "Then I guess that leaves me with just one thing to say." He leaned in and brushed a kiss on her cheek. "Welcome to the family."

A breath of relief swooshed out of her, causing Kimmie to laugh and try to make the same sound. Darcy looked at Nate and saw the love he had for all of them.

Nate kissed her despite the fact he had to maneuver through both kids to do that. "Ready to go home?" he whispered against her mouth.

Darcy didn't even have to consider this answer. "Yes."

And with Nate's arm around her, they took their first step toward their new life together.

* * * * *

**IF YOU ENJOYED THIS BOOK
WE THINK YOU WILL ALSO LOVE**

INTRIGUE

Seek thrills. Solve crimes. Justice served.

Dive into action-packed stories that will keep you
on the edge of your seat. Solve the crime
and deliver justice at all costs.

6 NEW BOOKS AVAILABLE EVERY MONTH!

Still haunted by the serial killer she couldn't catch, police detective Bree Clark doesn't hesitate to accept PI Ryland Beck's offer of redemption. The Smoky Mountain Slayer cold case has gone hot again and working together could bring the murderer to justice. But is the culprit the original slayer—or a dangerous copycat?

Read on for a sneak preview of
Serial Slayer Cold Case,
part of A Tennessee Cold Case Story series,
from Lena Diaz.

Chapter One

Maintaining a white-knuckle grip on the steering wheel while negotiating the treacherous curves up Prescott Mountain on his daily commute was typical for Ryland Beck. *Smiling* while he resolutely refused to look toward the steep drop on the other side of the road *wasn't* typical. Nothing, not even his phobia of heights, could dampen his enthusiasm this chilly October morning. Today he'd begin his investigation into a serial killer case that had gone cold over four years ago.

Bringing down the Smoky Mountain Slayer was the challenge of a lifetime. No suspects. No DNA. No viable behavioral profile. In spite of the lack of evidence, Ryland was determined to put the killer behind bars. He wanted to give the families of the five victims the answers and justice they deserved.

Unfortunately, what he couldn't give them was closure. Closure, as he well knew, was a fictional construct. The death of a loved one would always leave a gaping hole in the hearts and lives of those left behind. But knowing the victim's murderer had been caught and punished would go a long way toward making the excruciating grief more bearable.

He continued winding his way up the mountain toward UB headquarters as he considered the limited information he'd found on the internet about the killings. The Slayer's modus operandi was consistent: all of his victims were strangled, their bodies dumped in the woods in Monroe County. But aside from them being young women, the victimology was all over the place. Their educational and economic backgrounds varied, as did their ethnicity. Some were married, some weren't. Some had children, some didn't. All of that made it nearly impossible to build a useful profile to help figure out who'd murdered them.

The detectives from the Monroe County Sheriff's Office had deemed the case unsolvable. But here in Gatlinburg, Ryland had a unique advantage: an über-wealthy boss who knew firsthand the suffering a victim's family endured when a murder case went cold.

Seven years after his wife was killed and his infant daughter went missing, Grayson Prescott had given up on the stagnant police investigation. He decided to create a cold case company called Unfinished Business. Just a few months later, UB had solved the case. Now, the thirty-three counties of the East Tennessee region had formed a partnership with UB and were clamoring for them to work their cold cases.

Don't miss
Serial Slayer Cold Case *by Lena Diaz,*
available March 2022 wherever
Harlequin books and ebooks are sold.

Harlequin.com

Love Harlequin romance?

DISCOVER.

Be the first to find out about promotions,
news and exclusive content!

Facebook.com/HarlequinBooks

Twitter.com/HarlequinBooks

Instagram.com/HarlequinBooks

Pinterest.com/HarlequinBooks

YouTube.com/HarlequinBooks

ReaderService.com

EXPLORE.

Sign up for the Harlequin e-newsletter and
download a free book from any series at
TryHarlequin.com

CONNECT.

Join our Harlequin community to
share your thoughts and connect
with other romance readers!
Facebook.com/groups/HarlequinConnection

Get 4 FREE REWARDS!

We'll send you 2 FREE Books <u>plus</u> 2 FREE Mystery Gifts.

Harlequin Intrigue books are action-packed stories that will keep you on the edge of your seat. Solve the crime and deliver justice at all costs.

FREE Value Over **$20**

YES! Please send me 2 FREE Harlequin Intrigue novels and my 2 FREE gifts (gifts are worth about $10 retail). After receiving them, if I don't wish to receive any more books, I can return the shipping statement marked "cancel." If I don't cancel, I will receive 6 brand-new novels every month and be billed just $4.99 each for the regular-print edition or $5.99 each for the larger-print edition in the U.S., or $5.74 each for the regular-print edition or $6.49 each for the larger-print edition in Canada. That's a savings of at least 12% off the cover price! It's quite a bargain! Shipping and handling is just 50¢ per book in the U.S. and $1.25 per book in Canada.* I understand that accepting the 2 free books and gifts places me under no obligation to buy anything. I can always return a shipment and cancel at any time. The free books and gifts are mine to keep no matter what I decide.

Choose one: ☐ **Harlequin Intrigue** ☐ **Harlequin Intrigue**
  Regular-Print **Larger-Print**
  (182/382 HDN GNXC) (199/399 HDN GNXC)

Name (please print)

Address   Apt. #

City   State/Province   Zip/Postal Code

Email: Please check this box ☐ if you would like to receive newsletters and promotional emails from Harlequin Enterprises ULC and its affiliates. You can unsubscribe anytime.

Mail to the **Harlequin Reader Service:**
IN U.S.A.: P.O. Box 1341, Buffalo, NY 14240-8531
IN CANADA: P.O. Box 603, Fort Erie, Ontario L2A 5X3

Want to try 2 free books from another series? Call 1-800-873-8635 or visit www.ReaderService.com.